No!
JOCKS DON'T
DATE GUYS

Wade Kelly

Published by
DREAMSPINNER PRESS

5032 Capital Circle SW, Suite 2, PMB# 279, Tallahassee, FL 32305-7886 USA
www.dreamspinnerpress.com

No! Jocks Don't Date Guys
© 2015 Wade Kelly.

Cover Art
© 2015 Anne Cain.
annecain.art@gmail.com
Cover content is for illustrative purposes only and any person depicted on the cover is a model.

ISBN: 978-1-61372-909-0
Digital ISBN: 978-1-61372-929-8
Library of Congress Control Number: 2015952910
First Edition December 2015

Printed in the United States of America
(∞)
This paper meets the requirements of
ANSI/NISO Z39.48-1992 (Permanence of Paper).

I would like to dedicate this novel to my readers, who continue to support me with encouragement, love, and praise: I need you, I thank you, and I could not go on without you. Thank you for waiting so long after Jock 1.

To my beta readers, who keep me on my toes and push me to reinvent myself in order to deliver the best story possible. Thank you Beth, Jeff, Will, and Taryn for believing in me… one more time! And to Mandy, thank you for joining my pack.

To my newest friend Lance. I'm so glad I met you. There are very few people in the world who carry about them an aura as warm and peaceful as yours. I hope you never lose your "Lanceness" because you are truly one of a kind.

And randomly, I dedicate this book to Rick R. Reed, who mentioned getting up at 4:30 a.m. in order to get his writing done early. You inspired me, and 2015 has been the most productive, and consistent, I've ever been as a writer. Thank you.

Readers love
My Roommate's a Jock? Well, Crap!
by WADE KELLY

MY ROOMMATE'S A JOCK?
Well, Crap!
Wade Kelly

By WADE KELLY

Names Can Never Hurt Me

THE JOCK SERIES
My Roommate's a Jock? Well, Crap!
No! Jocks Don't Date Guys

UNCONDITIONAL LOVE
When Love Is Not Enough
The Cost of Loving

Published by DREAMSPINNER PRESS
www.dreamspinnerpress.com

Chapter 1
New Coach

SOCCER PRACTICE was about to start when I noticed a guy all dressed in black walk around the corner of the stadium fence and climb the steps, two at a time. I watched this lone spectator out of the corner of my eye as I squirted water into my mouth, and then all over my face, from my favorite water bottle with the pull-top spout. My best bud, Doug, had given it to me for my birthday last May, and I swear it was the best gift ever because not only did it not leak in my car, but when the top was screwed off, the opening was wide enough to get my hand in to wash it. I took it with me everywhere.

I snapped the spout closed and tossed it in my bag. A casual glance around told me that guy was still there—watching.

As I assessed his ocular trajectory from the way his head was positioned, I realized he wasn't watching me. He was taking in the whole field. Although the same thing could be said of me as I surreptitiously noted his characteristics while turning my head as if scanning the bleachers and the nearby sandpit. I was the sly, stealthy kind, if I did say so myself. Practice makes perfect, after all. The rest of the team didn't need to know how easily I could get distracted from the actual reason we were all here at 8:00 a.m. Soccer was life, but in the other three hours of the day—when soccer, food, and sleep were not on my brain—I liked observing people. Guys in particular because I was always on the prowl for that one guy who would grab my soul and melt my heart.

Okay, enough sentimentality.

I mainly noticed *this* guy because one solitary dude, sitting at the top of the football stadium bleachers, dressed in a black trench coat and combat boots, in August, two weeks before classes started, wasn't normal. Maryland was freaking hot in August! I picked up on details like that all the time. Things out of the ordinary, juxtaposed against the backdrop of college soccer, were fascinating. His presence was idiosyncratic in this setting and the very definition of my weakness. The oddities of life, the strange and weird, always drew me in.

Why was he here?

Sometimes I hated the way I spotted details, because people often wanted to go undetected when their individual oddity wasn't popular or pleasant. Scars, for instance, rarely escaped my attention no matter how hard I tried to overlook them.

Case in point: the left wing on the team, Marshall, had a scar on his lip. I'd surmised it was from cleft-lip surgery, though I knew no one else would have given it a second thought. He had a mustache to cover up the tiny scar, which had to have been there since he was a child, yet I'd still noticed it enough to speculate about its origin. There was something in the way he smiled. Normal and bright, yet off-center enough not to slip by my keen observation.

I also had a thing for tattoos, piercings, and Mohawks because I always wanted to know the motivation behind them. Was the hairstyle for attention, or did the person simply get pleasure from the dramatic flair? Did a tattoo have special meaning or was it a random decision? Things like that went through my mind all the time. I had one tattoo on my ribs, which held particular meaning to me. It was a quote from *Hamlet*, but since I'd had it inked in Latin, most people didn't know what it said, and oddly, no one ever asked.

The trench-coat guy met the criteria for my fascination.

During the sixty seconds I spent on the sidelines, taking a drink of water and scoping out our unexpected spectator, the rest of the team came stumbling in behind me.

"Chris! Why you always gotta show off and beat the team back?" Preet asked, doubling over and grabbing his sides.

He was a fun guy with a Pakistani father and a Turkish mother who'd both been in the United States since way before Preet was born. He had dark skin and feathery hair that I often thought about touching, except that he was straight. I answered him with a chuckle. "Preet, the captain always needs to lead the team, even if it means running the first three laps the fastest." I clapped him on the back as my buddy Doug winked at me. "Don't tell me you're tired already. Practice hasn't even started."

Preet groaned. I suspected he'd spent way too much of his summer in front of the television. *Sucks to be him!*

Doug knew about me and my ever-so-slight crush on the handsome defensive player. He knew everything there was to know and probably some things I didn't even know myself. We'd been best buds since elementary school, when I'd dropped my chocolate milk in the cafeteria and he offered me his. Chocolate milk had solidified our friendship and it still worked to this day. If we ever had an argument, all Doug needed to do was buy me a little carton of chocolate milk and I'd forgive him. So far, he's only had to do that twice in ten years.

"Don't try to understand him. Preet, just go with it," Doug instructed.

The other players flopped on the grass all around me, some heaving as if I'd taken them on a five-mile sprint, others sipping on their water bottles as they waited for the next drill. I'd hoped the coach would have shown up by now, but he was late. I grabbed my phone from my bag and checked for any texts.

Coach Marks had been the school's soccer coach for years and our soccer coach for the past two seasons. I use the term "our" loosely because some of the guys who'd turned up for this first practice were obviously freshmen. The coach had been at tryouts, and these guys were obviously good enough for him, but I was skeptical. But coach… where was he? I was a junior, looking to have another awesome season playing with many of the same guys as the year before, and also with my buddies Doug and Cullen. It was unusual for the coach to be this late. No texts. This was disconcerting. I'd just seen him on Saturday, and he hadn't said anything.

I glanced up from my phone in time to see the athletic director riding his golf cart around the track and through the gate that encircled the football field. Normally we didn't play on the stadium field, nor did we practice there on a daily basis. The soccer team had a practice field for sprints, drills, and tryouts, as well as its own official fields to play on, but the coach had made it a tradition to start on this field the first day to give the players a visual of professionalism and grandeur. He had told us in previous years that the team needed to be just that—a team. Without teamwork, the parents and fans who came to fill the stadium seats gathered only to witness a bunch of little boys running around kicking a ball with no purpose.

"Is that why you're here?" Coach had asked.

In unison we'd answered, "No, sir!"

"Then look around you, boys," he'd charge us, "and take it in. You must earn your spot with skill, sportsmanship, and teamwork. We come together as a team out there"—he would point toward the practice field beyond the fence and visitor side bleachers—"so we come in here. We dominate our home field as one fluid unit." He'd also commented about the costs involved in building a brick stadium. If we ever wanted a more prominent place to play, we needed to impress investors.

His words meant a lot to me. They had settled over us as a team, and we'd done fairly well last year even if our record showed eight wins, eight losses, and a tie. Coach had been proud because we played our hearts out. He'd gotten us to think as one, and I was looking forward to pulling the new guys into our flow.

But where was the coach?

I met the athletic director as he stepped out of the golf cart. "Hey, Mr. Mathews," I greeted him. "Where's Coach Marks?"

He shook my hand and nodded to the team as they closed in around us. "Hello, Chris. I hate to inform you like this because I know how much Tom Marks means to you boys, but he won't be coaching you this season."

"What?" I asked as the others groaned, not wanting to believe him yet seeing his sincerity.

He nodded some more. "I'm sorry."

"What happened?" I asked. "He's okay, isn't he? He was just here for tryouts. What happened?"

"He's fine. It's his wife's family. There was a death, and as far as I understand, they left Westminster for Portland last night. He tendered his resignation and apparently plans on moving the whole family to Oregon. That's all I know until he e-mails me back."

I looked at a few of the other players. Their eyes hopped from one to another and back again. It was as if no one really knew what to say to that. I admit, the reason was an odd one. I'd never known anyone to up and move so spontaneously, but then I hadn't had a family member die that I could remember, other than my grandmother and she was old. But this was plain weird. What would we do? Who would coach us? How would the school find someone before our first scrimmage next Thursday?

I spoke up and voiced what the team had to be thinking. "Um, what about a new coach? Is it going to be you?" I asked, but I was hoping the answer *wasn't* yes.

"No, Chris. Not me." He grinned. "I don't know enough about soccer to do you boys any good. Golf is my game. No, the school board has been searching for a new coach all day. Don't worry, that's why I'm out here. I was going over my e-mails from yesterday before deleting them when I came across one the administrator sent to the new coach, which I was copied on. Good thing, too, because the date was incorrect. He was originally told to start coaching August twentieth."

Cullen piped in, "But today is the tenth. Our first scrimmage is on August twentieth. What do we do until then?"

"Exactly my point," Mr. Mathews concurred. "I jumped on the horn right away and told him about the mistake. Ironically, he'd second-guessed the date himself because he had the soccer schedule already programmed into his calendar. He was on campus, setting up his office, and planned to contact me tomorrow. I simply beat him to it."

"Office?" I asked. Somewhere the details were getting muddled, and I personally liked filling in those gaps.

"Yes. He's the new English teacher on staff. His office is on the third floor of the English building. Anyway, he was already here and hoping to meet with me this afternoon. When I called, he said he'd drop what he was doing so he could head over to meet everyone. He's a very exuberant young lad."

I raised my eyebrow. "Young lad? How young are we talking?" I wondered because most of us were between eighteen and twenty-two. It would be weird to take orders from a guy our age. In fact, if the guy was my age, I think I'd push to coach the team myself. Who was this "young lad" anyway?

"He's twenty-three." The murmurs started, and Mr. Mathews held up his hands. "And before you all get up in arms over his age, let me tell you I was a bit skeptical myself. But as it was explained to me, he wasn't hired to coach soccer. He was hired to take Mrs. Blakely's position when she retires. His background in soccer was coincidental and convenient. They offered him the position tentatively because Coach Marks left the school in a tight spot. If he isn't working out within a few weeks, I'll take over until a permanent coach can be found. He can't officially start coaching until Thursday because of other obligations, so that leaves you all on your own for a couple days, which I think you can handle. What I want from you all is patience and cooperation. Can you do that?"

I turned and looked at my guys. I met their eyes one by one. I could read their minds even if only by the strength of their expressions. I knew them. My teammates, even the younger newbies, all had one goal on their minds—winning. If winning came at Coach Young Lad's hand, or at Mr. Mathews's, or from my leadership through example, we'd all be happy. So yeah, the "young lad" would get his chance in the sun.

I turned back around and held out my hand, and Mr. Mathews shook it. "Yes, sir," I answered. "You've got our promise to do our best. And this new coach, no matter his age, will find he has the best group of guys if ever there was a team to coach."

"Thank you, Chris. I kind of figured I could count on you. Tom told me you were an outstanding leader."

"So when's he getting here?"

"Um, hopefully before practice ends. I caught him fresh out of the shower when I called."

I turned around and slapped my hands together. "Okay, you heard him, guys. What we want to do is show this new coach what we're made of. When he gets here, whenever he gets here, we're going to be full out doing drills and working it hard. No slackers on my field. Coach Marks might be gone, but his motto still stands. We play as a team! We learn teamwork off the field so that when we walk onto the turf of the Green Terror Soccer Complex on game day, everyone watching will know we play as one." Then I shouted, "Are you with me?"

They all shouted back, "Yes, sir!"

I chuckled to myself. No one called me sir normally, and it was funny to hear it now, but I knew they meant it figuratively. I wasn't going to gloat or bask in it.

"All right," Mr. Mathews said. "I'll leave you to it. He should be along anytime."

"First things first. We're going to do another mile around the track. Tomorrow we're going to do two miles. Wednesday we're going to do timed laps, and anyone under the coach's tryout time gets fifty pushups and then has to run again. Got it?"

Then it occurred to me I hadn't asked the new coach's name. I turned and shouted at Mr. Mathews as he pulled away in his little golf cart. "You didn't tell me his name." But he must have been too far away to hear.

Doug clapped me on the shoulder. "Maybe it slipped his mind. Remember last year when he kept calling me Derek? Sometimes he's not all in there."

"True."

"So you're on board with all this?" Doug asked.

I shrugged and encouraged him into a private huddle with my arm around his shoulders. I told him quietly, "I guess I have to be. You know our team needs to be a *team*. If I lead them into mutiny because I don't like the terms of Young Lad's leadership, then I'm not the leader Coach told Mr. Mathews about. I'd be a mutineer, a traitor, and in danger of being thrown overboard."

"You're gonna call him Young Lad to his face, aren't you?" Doug asked with a smirk.

I grinned back and chuckled. "Oh God, I hope not. He wouldn't get it, and then I'd be that doofus who didn't know his name."

"But you don't know his name."

I pulled back and gave him a nonthreatening glare. "Of course, you go there. Great. Now you've jinxed it. He'll get here and I'll be all like 'Hey, Coach Young Lad. How's it going?' Great. Thanks, Doug. You're a real pal."

He laughed and we turned around to look at the rest of the guys, who were sitting or standing but all wondering what the heck we were talking about. That was my cue. I knew playtime was over.

I rubbed my hands together vigorously and got down to business. "Okay, team. Let's hit that track!"

They groaned, and I kind of thought it was from their disapproval of my satisfaction with temporary leadership. I, on the other hand, enjoyed it immensely. Maybe I was born to be a drill instructor. I laughed all the way to the track, and all the way around it, and while I waited for all of my teammates to catch up. Yes, it was good to be king.

TWO HOURS later, my guys were drenched in sweat and ready to hit the showers. I told them to meet at the practice field the rest of the week at 8:00 a.m. every morning for two hours and again at 6:00 p.m. for an hour of shooting drills and goal kicks. The guys groaned, but everyone agreed to it. Besides, practices twice a day were only until classes started. I wasn't a sadist.

I grabbed my bag and looked toward the bleachers. Trench-coat dude was still there. He had sat in the same spot for two hours in the morning sun, watching. Who was he watching? Or was it just the solitude that thrilled him?

As the guys drifted away, climbing the hill toward the athletic building or their dorm rooms, respectively, leaving only a few of us on the field, trench-coat guy stood up and started descending the steps. *Interesting.* Maybe I could follow him and find out his deal.

Or, maybe I could get arrested for being a perverted stalker. Yeah, my ideas weren't the best.

Before I took a step, another peculiar guy hove into sight. This one was jogging right up to me with a bright smile on his face, and I could not say when I'd ever seen a whiter set of teeth.

He held out his hand to me and said, "Hi! My name's Ellis Montgomery. I'm your new coach."

Wow. I have to admit that I probably would have addressed him as Young Lad if I'd been on my game, and made a joke or something to distract myself from his incredibly gorgeous blue eyes and the hot soccer-player bod under his tight red tank, but my mind was zeroed in on the other guy, all dressed in black, who'd sat for two hours in the sun watching us practice soccer and who'd just hit the last step and was about to exit through the gate and ascend the steps toward the wellness center before I could catch his attention.

I desperately needed to know who trench-coat guy was and why he was so interested in our team. Coach Blue Eyes would just have to wait.

Chapter 2
Small Talk

I DIDN'T get a chance to follow after the darkly clad spectator because the new coach was rattling on about how excited he was coaching for the first time. He told me how he hoped he'd make a good impression on the team because soccer had been ultraimportant to him for most of his life. He said coaching seemed like the next best thing if he couldn't play for Real Madrid.

I held up my hand and halted the conversation right there. "Real Madrid? Are you kidding me? You're just picking them because they're currently ranked in the top five."

"No, I'm not. They *are* my favorite team," he explained. Then he relented, "I admit... I used to like Milan about three years ago, but I've been a fan of Real Madrid for a while now."

I dropped my bag back onto the grass. This was about to get serious, and I didn't need my gear in the way of what could turn out to be wild gesticulations. "No way! Manchester United is the best team in the history of soccer."

"Not according to the club's world ranking. They may have been in the number three slot a couple years, but they've been struggling to maintain their pace. This summer is the lowest I've ever seen them in the standings, even if the number is climbing now. They hit fifty in July, which is terrible."

I threw my hands out to the side. "Statistics! That's all they are," I argued. "Any given website has their own specifications for placing teams in certain rankings. My team's been around for a hundred and thirty-seven years. Real Madrid can't boast the same."

Coach Young Lad smirked.

"What?" I questioned gruffly. I didn't see humor in my logic.

"You used the word specifications. Makes me think there's a whole lot more to you than being a jock."

His comment threw me. "Of course there's more to me than that!" I got a little angry with him because I'd been dealing with crap like that my whole life. "I pride myself on being a walking conundrum, thank you very much. I'm not squeamish about blood, but I detest horror movies. I like cherries, but not cherry-flavored *anything* because it always reminds me of cough medicine. And I'm a closeted theater fanatic who sings show tunes in the shower." I stopped myself abruptly and leaned closer to him. "Although I'd appreciate it if singing show tunes never got out. It might knock my manliness factor down a few pegs."

The new coach chuckled. "Fair enough. I think I can keep it a secret."

I decided right then I liked this guy. He had a winning smile and a kind expression that spoke to me. I couldn't explain it, but I felt connected somehow. Not attracted, even though he was extremely good-looking, but connected. I held out my hand and introduced myself. "My name's Chris Jackson. I'm the team's captain."

He shook my hand firmly. It was a good strong handshake. "Ellis Montgomery."

He'd said that once, but I was glad for the reiteration since Young Lad kept circling around with the intention of being spoken. With any luck, his real name would stick. "Nice to meet you, Mr. Montgomery."

He made a face. "Ouch! Please use my first name, if you don't mind. Mr. Montgomery's my dad. Besides, I graduated last year. It's weird to be coaching guys who are practically my age, so if you start calling me mister, then it adds to the surrealism."

"Yeah, I admit it was a shocker. How'd you get a job here anyway? Aren't teaching jobs difficult right after graduation, let alone at a college?"

"I don't know how I got it. I know it's not common for grad students. I applied for the position and I guess they liked what I wrote in my cover letter. Plus, I'm not sure how many people could afford to take it. I teach *one* class. Most teachers couldn't survive on that."

"Oh."

"I heard that the college was trying something new. By hiring me to train for a position in the future, they don't have to pay me very much. So… if you don't mind my asking, do you always use words like 'specifications,' or was that for my benefit knowing I'm an English teacher?"

I shrugged, feeling slightly embarrassed. "It's normal," I sighed. "You don't know many people think I'm pretentious, but it's really not my fault. I blame my parents."

"Word nerds?" he asked, truly interested.

"Sort of. My dad was a football player, but his mom was a medical technician at a hospital who loved to read. He told me she'd ride him about learning proper articulation so if he ever made the pro teams he wouldn't sound like an idiot. My grandmother thinks jocks need to be schooled on proper speech, which wouldn't be a bad thing. Anyway, my dad told me stories of how he'd ask her the meaning of a word when he was doing his homework, and she would tell him the definition using another word he didn't understand. She forced him to look everything up. After a while, he started collecting words in a little box. Each new word had its own index card. I think he still has that box in his toolroom."

Ellis nodded. "Interesting. How did *you* become a fellow logophile and sesquipedalian enthusiast? Did your father use the same tactics on you as his mother did on him?"

"Not really. Well, sort of. He listens to talk radio a lot, and his favorite show is called 'A Way with Words.' I was intrigued that my dad could scream at the television one day because the Ravens dropped the ball, but on the next listen to the history of colloquial expressions and why we eat *beef* and not *cow*. When I was a kid, these radically different sides of his personality became my obsession. In fact, I'm still drawn to things that don't quite fit, and my favorite word is juxtaposition."

"That's a good word." He chuckled. "Sounds like your dad is an interesting guy."

"Yeah, my parents are fun. When I was nine years old, my dad asked me if I was feeling lugubrious at the dinner table. I responded by asking him what a lugoober was?"

Ellis laughed heartily.

I liked his laugh. "Interactions like that over the years really gave me a boost. By high school, I was in mostly AP classes. I think my IQ was higher than the English teacher's, which meant she didn't like me too much."

He laughed. "I think I can relate."

I sort of wanted to know more about him, but I was getting tired of standing in the middle of the field. We had all season to chitchat. "Well, I hate to shake your hand and run, but I'm hungry. I don't eat before I play, and all this talking has me hankering for a ham and cheese omelet with hash browns and buttermilk biscuits."

"Sounds good."

"I'm sure we can talk another day." I shouldered my bag of gear and started off.

Ellis called after me, "Did the athletic director tell you I'm starting on Thursday?"

I turned around, walking backward toward the gate. "Yup. No problem. We'll see you then and I'll introduce you to the team."

"I look forward to it."

"I do too," I yelled, nearing the gate and leaving him on the field. "Even if you're a Real Madrid fan!"

Ellis smiled and I left with a feeling deep in my gut that he would become a really good friend in the months to come.

PRACTICE WENT well the next couple of days. Even the newer players easily attained the flow of what Coach Marks had called our "fluid unit." In fact, I thought our team looked more together now than it had in the past two seasons we'd played together. I wasn't sure what had done the trick, but if we remained this gelled, then I could imagine a state championship in our hands by the end of the season.

My main disappointment as I ran around the field was not seeing the trench-coat dude watching us from the bleachers. To be fair, the bleachers next to the field didn't lend much privacy. They were right on the other side of the metal fence, shaded by some trees but close enough for the players to talk to the spectators if they wanted to. Unlike the football stadium, where the stands were vast and the track ran between them and the field.

The couple of sets of metal bleachers next to our field were better than those back in high school at least. We'd had weathered wooden bleachers the cheerleaders often absconded with so they could congregate near the girl's field hockey area and gossip with their friends. I didn't have proof of this; I only surmised that was their intent since the cheerleaders always seemed giggly and mischievous whenever jocks were around. Probably talking about our muscles. Back then, the soccer practice field was lucky to retain the netting on the goals, so I didn't care if the cheerleaders stole the rickety bleachers.

Our college cheerleaders would be hanging around the soccer field soon enough. Whatever. I was friends with most of them even if I'd never been interested in dating them.

"You okay?" Ellis asked, jogging up to my side and keeping stride with me as we walked off the field. I couldn't explain my comfort with him, but I definitely felt it. He seemed like a very congenial guy, besides the fact that he was very knowledgeable when it came to soccer.

"Yeah. Fine. Just distracted."

"You seemed like it. Was there someone you expected to show up?"

"What do you mean?" I eyed him curiously. We might be comfortable with each other, but I sincerely hoped he could not read my mind.

"I don't know. You kept looking around the field as if someone was missing, that's all."

Trench-coat guy. I wasn't going to admit it out loud since I had no logical explanation for my fixation on him. "No." I kept my answer short. Ellis hadn't known me long enough to know short answers only came when I was uncomfortable or angry. I was wordy by nature—a rambler at heart. Ellis was a great guy, but I had only come out to one guy so far—Doug—and I didn't need to tell Coach Montgomery my deepest secrets… yet.

"Okay," he said. I guess my lack of response prompted his departure because then he said, "I guess I'll see you tomorrow."

"Yup." I waved and he took a left at the next sidewalk juncture.

I couldn't explain my mood, so after I showered, I took a walk around town to try and clear my head.

FRIDAY MORNING after practice, I headed over to the dining hall to see if anyone was there. Not too many people were on campus yet, mostly the jocks and cheerleaders readying for the coming sports season. The regular students normally arrived a week before classes to get situated in the dorms and familiar with the campus, but jocks had to try out and then get several practices in before the first game.

The drawback was perpetual boredom if no one was around. Another reason I liked practicing twice a day.

As soon as I entered the building, Katherine Stewart rushed over to give me a hug. "Hey, Kat," I said, hugging her back lightly. I'd known her for several years. She'd gone to a different high school, but had grown up in the same town as me. Last semester we'd had one class together, which made studying more fun initially. But after a few weeks, I'd gotten tired of her giggling and the smell of her nail polish. I'd wanted to study! That was the whole point of us getting together. But because I couldn't say no, we'd studied together way more often than necessary.

My dad liked her. She was blonde and perky and fit all the basic stereotypes associated with cheerleaders. He'd always had a crazy obsession with cheerleaders, probably because my mom was one. They'd been high school sweethearts, and I think he expected me to fall for someone like that too, but I hadn't. I knew he'd been disappointed when I chose soccer instead of football, but since I'm really good, he came around and cheered me on at my games.

When I took Kat home a couple of times, he'd thought we were dating, and I kinda, sorta, forgot to mention we weren't. This was the only part of my life I couldn't grab ahold of—coming out to my dad. In the back of my mind, I thought it would be easier if I had a boyfriend to lend moral support. Since I lacked one, coming out to my parents had gotten delayed longer than I'd intended.

I followed Kat over to a table full of her friends. Cheerleaders. "Hey," I said and sat. "What's going on?"

"Nothing. I can't wait for classes to start," said Jill, another blonde, with boobs bigger than my head. It amazed me she could do cartwheels without losing her balance.

"Don't say that," I replied. "I have hard classes this semester, and I don't look forward to all the reading."

"*Pft!*" Kat made a noise.

"What?" I asked.

"You get straight A's. I don't know what you're worried about."

I shrugged. I didn't have an answer. I did get A's, and normally it didn't take much effort. I guess I didn't *want* it to take effort. I liked my leisure time and soccer; I didn't want classes to get in the way.

"So how many practices do you have each day?" Katherine asked me. This was the fourth time she'd brought it up in three days. It wasn't that I thought she was vapid because she was a cheerleader, but I swear she didn't retain information with the same level of absorption as everyone else. Her brain must have been a sponge at some point because she had a high GPA, but maybe it had been coated with Scotchgard recently.

"Kat, I told you yesterday, we practice twice a day. Eight to ten in the morning and again at six for another hour. It's intense, but part of it is our choice. Other teams only practice once a day, but Coach Marks suggested a heavy practice in the morning and a lighter, shooting-oriented one in the evening. I'm following his lead."

"But didn't he quit?" Jill piped in. "I thought the hot English teacher replaced him." She was at least right about one thing: Ellis *was* hot. He just wasn't my type, not that I had a clear definition of what my type was.

"Yeah, Coach Montgomery replaced him, but he's taking cues from me since I've been around the last two seasons. He's being really cool about it."

Mindy sat down next to Katherine and leaned in. "Do you know if he's single?" she asked expectantly.

"He's so much older than you," Jill said.

"So? I'm legal. And I heard he's only twenty-three, which is five years diff. No big deal."

"I don't think he's right for you, Mindy," I told her. I spied a package of something yummy next to her purse and I pointed. "Are those gummy bears?"

She grabbed the bag and held it protectively. "Yes, and you may not have them."

"Why?"

"Because you're a pig, Chris. Last time you ate the whole bag!"

"No, I didn't. I shared with Candice." I pointed to my accomplice, but she was texting and not paying attention.

"How? I don't remember that. Candice was sitting on the other side of the class when I looked over and the bag was empty." Mindy was annoyed, and I thought it was funny. "You had to have eaten them all."

"I threw them to her," I explained.

"I don't believe you."

"Yes, I did. Watch." I looked at Kat and pointed behind her. "Go over there and sit at the other table."

She complained. "No. You go sit at a different table. I like this one."

I exhaled loudly. She was so annoying sometimes. "Fine." I got up and moved to the other table. I opened the bag of gummy bears and took one out. As I opened my mouth to give Kat instructions, I noticed a guy watching us from a booth about ten feet away from our table, over by the window. He had black hair, a black shirt, and a black coat folded over the back of the seat next to him.

I'd bet dollars to doughnuts it was a *trench* coat!

Oh my God. How do I concentrate now?

I blinked and refocused before I drew attention to my distracted state. No, I had to do this. All the cheerleaders were watching me, and if I told them about that guy, then they would all want to know who he was and why I cared.

"Kat, sit up straight and open your mouth wide."

"Why?" She always had to argue with me.

"So I can prove my point."

She rolled her eyes but opened her mouth. I held up the bear and aimed. Toss. Score!

Mindy jumped out of her seat. "How did you do that? You're four feet away from her?"

I grinned. "I can shoot farther if you like. That one was easy." I flicked my gaze over to the guy, and his eyes caught mine. I thought he almost smirked before he turned back to the book that lay open on the table in front of him.

I moved to another table, making the gap about fifteen feet. Toss. Score. I could do this all day.

Kat chewed and then complimented me. "I don't believe it, but I'm amazed. You have amazing aim. You should be on *America's Got Talent* or something amazing like that."

"For my amazingness?" I mocked her, but she missed it. However, black-shirt guy didn't. I saw his cheek move, like for a smile, maybe. Was he listening in and internally laughing at us?

"Here, Mindy, you're next." She was on the other side of the table. Adding another two feet to the challenge. No problem. "He shoots, he scores!" I leapt to my feet and did a victory stride around the table, arms stretched high overhead.

As I triumphantly circumnavigated the table and retook my seat, I kept an eye on that guy who was trying hard *not* to look at me. That piqued my interest with a capital pique.

"So ladies, what other *amazing* feats can I perform for you?" I *had* to emphasize Kat's adjective one more time.

"None," Jill said, standing up. "I need to get my nails done for tomorrow. I have a date."

"Can I go with?" Kat said. "I'm looking for a new place. I haven't been happy with my nail salon the past few times."

"Sure." Jill looked at Mindy. "Are you coming? You can pump Chris for information about the hot coach another day."

Mindy huffed. "Fine. I'll come." She patted my shoulder. "Later, Chris. You owe me a new bag of gummy bears. Come on Candice."

Candice, who had been playing on her phone the whole time, stood and walked out without making a sound. Thankfully, she didn't run into the door frame.

"And then there were two," I mumbled, noting that me and black-shirt guy were the only people left in this part of the dining hall.

Now what am I supposed to do?

I drummed my fingers on the tabletop and glanced casually around the room.

Typical college eatery. Big signs explaining what food type was offered at which station. Burgers. Pizza. Soup. Whatever. Even an area for vegan delights, which I would never partake of but Jill would love. Most of them weren't operational since attendance was still light, but I knew those food stations would be primed and ready with caloric comestibles once campus was packed with students. I couldn't wait.

I stole a glance at the goth guy. No, probably more emo than goth, not that I really knew the difference. Since I'd been in college, I hadn't seen too many underclassmen continue the emo, dark-and-brooding look after high school.

Most other students I knew realized that social groups dispersed in college. Kids were seen as young adults by then, and grades were the focus instead of which clique you fell into. Sure, there were jocks and geeks and beauty queens, but somehow they blended together more in college.

Seeing this guy took me back to sophomore year in high school when the artists and the dreamers used to gather together to wax poetic about the woes of misunderstood youth. Was this guy like that? I took a deep breath and walked over to him.

"Hey," I said, trying to draw his attention out of the book.

The guy's eyes shifted from the page to me. "Heeey," he replied tentatively, as if wondering why I was standing there.

I felt stupid. "Um, yeah, I know this is going to sound weird, but are you the same guy who was watching the soccer team practice on Monday?"

He looked down immediately, and I knew I'd been right. It was him!

He replied, "It's a college campus. There's no law that says other students can't watch."

But when he spoke toward the table and didn't make eye contact, his answer only inspired more of my curiosity. However, I couldn't stand there like a creeper, I needed a reason to stay. I had to think of something to ask. "Are you a soccer fan?" Seemed like a good place to start.

He closed his book and stared at me, possibly thinking of an answer. "Maybe."

Why did he sound as though he thought I'd get angry if he said yes? What did he think I was going to do? Like he said, this was college, and students were allowed to watch practices.

"Hey, it's cool. I was just wondering. I saw you sitting in the stands, and I found it coincidental to run into you again. Are you stalking me?" I jested.

He pulled his shoulders back and said defensively, "No. I moved across country to go here, and I came a week before the other students because I don't like people all that much. I didn't think there would be a congregation of cheerleaders in this room when I came here to read. Again, there's no law that says I can't."

From the tone of his voice, I'd offended him with my implication, which I regretted even if I didn't understand why. I normally don't offend people with my jokes, and I didn't like that I'd done it with this guy before I even knew his name. I held one hand up and apologized. "I'm sorry. I was joking. I didn't mean to upset you. I'm fairly observant, and I don't catch too many emo guys watching soccer. It surprised me. Seriously, I was joking when I called you a stalker."

He narrowed his dark brown eyes at me. "Just because I wear black doesn't mean I'm emo."

"No," I agreed. "But the nail polish and eyeliner might." I grinned. I had to point it out. It was in my nature to be right, and this guy was all agitated. He might not think he was emo, but I wasn't going to concede his point without listing my reasons for jumping to the conclusion. He was fitting a stereotype whether he intended to be or not.

He opened his mouth, but didn't reply. Instead he dropped his gaze to his hands. Perhaps he was considering my points. When he glanced back up, his expression was softer. "I guess you're right. I do look emo. So why does it matter to you?"

I shrugged. "It doesn't. I wasn't saying I minded. I was saying I'd noticed. It's August and you're wearing a black trench coat. I guess I wondered why."

He furrowed his brow and asked, "Who are you?"

"My name's Chris. May I sit?"

"No."

Normally I would take that as a sign to back away and never engage again, but something about him had grabbed my interest. He was unique and perplexing, besides being cute as all get out. What was an emo guy doing watching soccer practice, laughing at my gummy bear antics, and reading *Lord of the Flies*? He was seriously unusual, and I liked it. Plus, *brown* eyes.

Oh God, did he have nice eyes, a rich dark brown with long black lashes.

"Okay," I said lightly, hiding my disappointment. I backed away and playfully added, "We practice tomorrow at nine instead of eight because it's Saturday, in case you planned on watching." I winked as I turned to walk out of the building. Right before I left, I stuck my head back in the door. "We're on the soccer complex field. It's directly behind the fitness center, down the hill and in front of the baseball field. The bleachers are three feet from the field, under the trees, but if you don't want to be seen, then sit on the inside of the baseball field fence. It's lined with privacy mesh so you can watch without being noticed."

Then I left.

Twenty feet from the entrance it hit me. "I winked at him," I said out loud. "Oh shit." Suddenly my heart was racing. Had I really winked at the guy? *I did!* I sat on the nearest bench, trying to catch my breath. I hoped no one I knew walked by and felt the need to chat with me. I suddenly needed a drink. I couldn't explain what had come over me. Sure, I'm a friendly guy, but I'm not flirtatious, especially with boys— *men*. I don't flirt with men.

But I had.

His brown eyes flashed in my memory. Dark, mysterious, and outlined with long dark lashes that curled on the ends. I really had a thing for brown eyes.

"Oh my God," I acknowledged to myself. "I'm attracted to him. I have to be. There's no other reason for all the details I picked up in two minutes." I spoke out loud, but only because I didn't believe myself. This wasn't happening. Yes, I had a photographic memory at times, but it was never this intent on remembering details like these.

He wore nail polish; I had already pointed that out. Black. But his right pinkie finger was half-red. He had a long-sleeved shirt under a black Green Day T-shirt, and a leather wrist cuff. His eyebrow piercing caught my attention because there were holes yet no jewelry. They weren't healed over, so why not wear a silver hoop or a bar?

And the black hair was definitely natural because his eyebrows and chin scruff were the same color.

"I gotta get out of here," I told myself, standing up from the bench. I needed to work out in the gym and shake the image of that guy from my head. I only hoped he hadn't seen me wink because I wasn't about to explain I'd never flirted with a guy before.

This guy, the nameless emo, wasn't going to be my first. No! Jocks date cheerleaders. Jocks don't date college guys who paint their fingernails and wear makeup. My dad would kill me. My dad expected me to marry someone like Kat. It was better for me to forget emo-guy's brown eyes and suppress my natural urges as long as I possibly could. When I was out of school, and successfully transplanted across country far away from my folks, I could give in to my silly crushes on the same gender. Until then, I had to remember I was here on my father's hard-earned dime, four different scholarships, and one tiny government grant, all so I could earn a degree in history and play soccer. I didn't actually have a clue what I wanted to do after I graduated, but I couldn't risk my future by falling for a guy—*now*.

I sprinted for my dorm room and took a cold shower.

NEXT PRACTICE I spent all my time watching the baseball field fence, wondering if he was there or sitting behind the pine trees so I couldn't see him. It drove me crazy. I even fell during a throw-in, and Doug laughed at me. I felt so stupid. I got up, took a few deep breaths, and decided I would not allow myself to like a guy solely based on his alluring brown eyes. That was infantile and something Candice would do. No, I was a man. I needed irrefutable evidence that he was 1) gay, 2) interested, and 3) smart enough to hold a conversation. These were valid arguments, especially number three. I'd had too many disappointments over the years making friends with people who got offended when I used words they didn't understand. I wasn't wasting my time, or my hormones, thinking about a guy who very well might be straight or petty.

"Hey, Jackson," Cullen yelled across the field. "Are you playing soccer or daydreaming?"

Shit. I'm spacing out now in the middle of practice. I'm such a loser.

"I'm playing!" I ran in and stole the ball from Marshall, who had dribbled it around Doug.

ON MONDAY morning, I thought I caught a glimpse of a silhouette behind the meshing, but I refused to confirm. If he was there, fine. If he wasn't, then my mind was playing tricks on me, and I was an idiot for spending the weekend walking the campus hoping to randomly run into him again.

WEDNESDAY NIGHT'S practice was more for calculating our shooting percentage, so while I waited for my turn, I had more time to glance around for the cute emo guy. Our first scrimmage was tomorrow, Thursday night, against Howard Community College, and the guys lacked aim. We needed to shoot goals. After I made my fourth goal against our goalkeeper, Steve, I circled around to head to the back of the line and spotted movement by the gigantic pine trees behind our tiny metal bleachers.

Trench-coat guy was watching, and my stomach flipped.

My next shot, I hit the upper nineties, and Steve didn't stand a chance at blocking it. Perfect corner shot. I threw my hands up in celebration and did a backflip on the field.

"Hey, stop showing off, Jackson. This isn't conference finals. It's practice!" Steve griped.

I felt somewhat regretful, but I waved it off, as I was not doing it to show off in front of the team. I'd done it for the guy watching us from behind the bleachers, hoping that next time I saw him, he'd comment. Not too many guys I knew could do a standing backflip. I had skills.

I strutted to the back of the line and caught it from Doug too.

"Dude, what's up with you? You've been dragging around like soccer was a chore these last few practices, and now, all of a sudden, you're doing backflips over a goal that you knew you could make. I don't get you."

I shrugged. "Sorry. Too much pent-up energy, I guess."

"Well, quit it. We all know how good you are. You don't need to act like an asshole."

I'd never heard him talk to me like that, but the sting of his words was lessened by the knowledge of a certain guy lurking around the bleachers behind me who *wasn't* aware of my talents.

AFTER WE lost our first scrimmage by one, practice on Friday morning was subdued. I lumbered to the dining hall afterward, needing a strong cup of coffee. I hadn't seen the trench-coat guy since Wednesday night, but I refused to admit it affected my mood. No, I was bummed over losing and only contributing one goal myself. Last night's game sucked.

I walked through the door and saw Kat and her gang to the left. I wasn't in the mood for their ridicule. I hadn't played well at all, and I knew Kat would comment. Or Jill. They could be a vicious bunch. I turned right hoping to find a quiet spot to sulk even though there were four times as many people in here than there had been last week. Classes started on Monday, and I guessed most students had moved into the dorms by now. Finding a secluded spot in this place seemed almost impossible. As soon as I rounded the corner, away from Kat's view and the deli station, I stopped short at the sight of a guy dressed in black.

His back was to me, and I couldn't tell if he was wearing a trench coat. He might even turn out to be another guy entirely, but I needed to find out. I took a step. Was I really going to approach him? What if he didn't want my company? He was in a booth facing the wall, which suggested privacy, and he *did* mention an aversion to people.

He shifted in his seat and his boot came into view as he bent his leg back. A rugged combat boot with two large silver buckles and straps over the laces, and silver chains looped around the back. It had to be him. He wasn't emo; this was definitely more goth or maybe steampunk. Sexy.

I steeled my nerves and strode over. Without asking, I slipped into the seat opposite. He looked up.

"Second Friday I find you here at eleven. Coincidence or routine? For me it's a routine. I don't eat before practice, so after I shower I like to catch a big meal to energize me for the rest of the day."

"I doubt you need energizing," he commented.

I think I expected him to yell at me for sitting without permission, but he seemed closed, unemotional, and that bothered me more than if he'd yelled. Still, I had to see the positive. He was a blank canvas I could poke to get a rise out of. But which emotion would surface? Annoyance or amusement? He was reading another book, so I started there.

"*The Call of the Wild*. Cool. Jack London is a brilliant author."

"You read?" He seemed shocked.

I could have gotten belligerent, and I would have if Kat had made what I considered a snide remark, but from him I ignored it. I answered with a half grin, "Yes. I read a lot, thank you." I was trying to be coy, wondering if he'd like it.

He blankly stared. Was he assessing me or readying a sarcastic comeback?

I continued before he could scoff. "In fact, I finished reading *Alive* by Piers Paul Read a couple of weeks ago." I had also watched the movie, but that was more for the eye candy. I thought the young Ethan Hawke was a hottie. His crooked teeth always made me fixate on his mouth and daydream about which movie star I'd most like to kiss.

He snorted. "I bet you watched the movie because you didn't understand the book." He closed his book and stacked it on top of a notebook with hand-drawn sketches on the cover. Then he shoved them into his bag and grabbed his black coat.

"Hey! I read it," I countered. "I admit to watching the movie, but it wasn't because I didn't understand the book."

He stood up. "Fine. You read it. Many people have. But it's just another survival story that doesn't hold a candle to *Mawson's Will*."

"By Lennard Bickel?" I asked as he took a step away.

He stopped and turned back, regarding me. "You've heard of it?" he asked.

His question wasn't "you've read it," but "you've heard of it," which indicated he was perplexed how a jock like me could have such knowledge. I smirked and paused, toying with him. I could not get enough of those brown eyes staring at me. "Yes. It's the greatest survival story ever written. Douglas Mawson was an incredible explorer and he mapped more of the Antarctic territory than anyone else of his time. I've read it twice."

He sat back down, still clutching his bag. "So you do read?"

I smiled. His befuddlement amused me. "Yes."

"You didn't have practice last night." Implied as a question though lacking the inflection—he was asking without asking where we'd been.

"Scrimmage at Howard Community College."

He nodded slowly, thinking it over. "You're really good," he said.

I smiled again, wider than before. "Thanks. We have another scrimmage tomorrow against Frederick. It's at the soccer complex if you care to watch."

"Thanks, but no thanks." He abruptly stood and walked away. He was out the side entrance, which led to the bookstore and the history building beyond, before my good sense pushed me to run after him.

"Hey," I called, jogging up to his side. He kept walking and didn't look at me. "Can I at least get your name?"

"No."

I pivoted around so I was facing him and walking backward. "Come on. Please?" I lifted my eyebrows and pleaded. His eyes flicked to mine and then back at the ground. He picked up his pace, and I had to turn back around or worry about tripping.

"Why?" he asked.

"So if I see you on campus I don't have to yell out 'Hey, trench-coat dude! Save me a seat in the cafeteria so we can discuss Tolstoy over coffee.'"

I was positive he tried ducking his face away so I wouldn't see him smirk, but I caught it. I also noticed one adorable dimple appear briefly on the side of his face and then vanish as he sped up. I gave up, defeated, allowing him to rush away. I threw my hands out to the sides with one more pathetic plea, "Oh, come on."

Just when I thought he'd keep me guessing for another week, he whirled around in a melodramatic flourish of black leather, calling, "If you really want to know, my name's Alonzo." For the first time his eyes weren't hard as he regarded me. He gave me a slight smile before turning away and hurrying off.

Alonzo, I repeated in my head. I smiled and heaved a sigh. "Oh yeah, he's interested."

Chapter 3
Family Traditions

I COULDN'T explain this odd feeling that suddenly appeared in my stomach. Okay, not suddenly, but specifically—specifically when Alonzo smiled and told me his name. I went to sleep that night picturing his eyes and mouth and the sound of his voice. I'd never felt such a rush, and I guess I would have been able to ignore it if not for the same feeling rematerializing after our scrimmage on Saturday.

We'd won, and after I finished congratulating the other team on a game well played, I turned to head back to the bench and spotted Alonzo. He wasn't looking my way as he descended the bleachers, head down, but he'd been there, watching. My stomach did that little flippy thing again, and I knew it wasn't simply a thrill from my initial intrigue. True, he was different, and I'd always had a thing for "different," but Alonzo's unusual attire for August wasn't enough to make my insides quiver. This was way more than fascination.

I was physically attracted on a level I'd never experienced before. I'd had crushes in the past, but nothing that felt this strong, this hypnotizing. Years ago, I'd had a thing for Cullen's green eyes. I felt the lust burning for a time, but it went away on its own. I'd always known Cullen was straight, the same as I'd always known I was gay. I liked his eyes and his smile, but knowing nothing would ever happen made the feelings fizzle. It was never a battle.

With Alonzo, my body was entering unknown territory. Sure, I felt lust building, making my groin ache because he had remarkable eyes, but I also felt a strong captivation over his mind, and an inquisitive pull to unravel his introversion. Alonzo was a puzzle, and it thrilled me. He read books—good books—and gave me the impression it was for pleasure and not for college classes.

"HERE'S YOUR lunch, sweetheart," my mother said, setting a plate before me where I sat on the back porch, staring out at the yard.

I blinked.

"Honey, are you all right?" she asked, sitting across from me. "Why are you staring at the grass? Do you think it needs to be mowed? I thought your brother took care of that for your father before he left." She turned to look at it and then addressed me again. "I think it looks fine. What's wrong with you?"

I shook my daydreams of Alonzo's bashful eyes and adorable dimple out of my head. "I'm fine, Mom. I was just thinking."

"Oh, okay. You looked catatonic there for a second, and I wondered if you were worried about school starting tomorrow. You're not, are you? I thought you said your class load was going to be harder this semester. Your father said you'd be fine, but I always worry you'll take on too much and crack under the pressure. You don't need to take so many classes, and you don't need to live on campus."

I reached across the table and patted her hand. She'd never wanted me to live in the dorms, but luckily my grant had been enough to cover it. "Mom, I'm fine. Really. I was just thinking about some things, some new friends I've made and stuff. Our coach is really cool. I'll have to introduce you at the game on Friday. He's an English teacher, so I think you guys will like him."

"Sounds wonderful. How did he stumble into coaching? You never told us what happened to Coach Marks." I loved how interested in my life she'd always been. Some moms were overbearing, and some aloof; mine was a healthy dose of both, knowing when to prod and when to leave me be. She was a great mom.

"I'll tell you when I have all the details. I don't really know. Something personal with his family."

"That's a shame. I know you liked him a great deal."

"I did, but this new coach is great. He used to play soccer too. He seems very knowledgeable and has high hopes for the team."

"Oh good. Your father will be pleased to hear that."

I took a bite of my sandwich and thanked her for it.

"You're welcome, dear. Now that you're back on campus, I don't get to see you as often. I'm glad you don't mind stopping by the house when you have time."

I washed my food down with a large gulp of water. "Of course I don't mind, Mom. But I told you, don't be surprised if I don't come by every week. Once classes start, I may have loads of homework and stuff."

"I'm not. I know you won't forget me. But with Ryan and Amber's wedding and you moving back to the campus all in the same month, I'm feeling a little lonely, I guess. Your father works all day, and the house is so quiet."

"Then you have to find a hobby or get a part-time job, Mom. It isn't good to be alone and succumb to empty-nest syndrome."

"It's not an empty nest yet, young man; not until you find yourself a sweet girl and settle down like your brother."

I hadn't wanted to broach the subject, but it fell together that way. "And by 'sweet girl' you mean 'cheerleader.'" I finished my last bite and wiped my mouth with the napkin my mother had brought out with the plate.

"Of course I mean a cheerleader. You know how your father feels about that."

Just then, my dad walked out on the porch. "How I feel about what?" he asked, walking behind my mother's chair, leaning in to kiss her, and sitting next to us at the glass picnic table. They'd had this same set my whole life. A glass table and six sling-back chairs, which my brother and I moved into the shed every winter, was the setting for many Jackson family conversations.

"Me dating a cheerleader," I reluctantly filled him in.

My dad filled a glass of water from the pitcher my mom had set on the table in case mine ran dry. She was very thoughtful that way. "Of course you're dating a cheerleader. What's her name? Kat? She's a pretty one."

I hadn't actually filled in the blanks last year, and now felt right. "Dad, we were never actually dating. She's just a friend. I told you before, between soccer and classes, I haven't had time."

"Nonsense. A boy your age should always make time to date a pretty girl, especially if she's a cheerleader. I made the time, and look who I found." He leaned over and kissed my mom.

She giggled. "Oh, Henry."

"Charlotte grabbed my attention with her... ah... pom-poms, but she stole my heart with her mind. It was such a thrill to see how large her... brains were." He winked at her and my mom giggled again. My dad hadn't veiled his insinuations in years. I guess as my brother and I got older, he hadn't felt the need. We'd both understood him.

I'd always envied my parents and how in love they seemed. My brother even found true love in Amber, who was also a cheerleader, when he played football in high school. Both my brother and my dad had fallen for cheerleaders in high school and married them after graduating college. Heck, even my grandfather had married a cheerleader he'd met in high school. I guess I should have been glad no one had given me grief for not dating a cheerleader in high school. No, wait…. I *had* dated a cheerleader in high school. Tracy Bonner.

What a disaster that had been.

My parents were nose to nose, giggling and whispering to each other, so my trip to "embarrassing flashbacks from hell" went unnoticed. I could reminisce, and not in a good way, while they shared their moment.

Tracy Bonner was a cheerleader when I was a freshman. Short, scrawny, and shy, I had made the team because they were short players. No pun intended. The following year I had grown six inches, but *that* year I was still little. She'd been a junior and I think on a dare had asked me out on a date to the movies. I hadn't known what to say, and Doug told me to go for it. I did.

She leaned in and I turned my head, not knowing it was Tracy's breath I had felt on my neck. When I did, she planted her lips on mine. I sat there, frozen and terrified, and when she leaned back, she smirked. "Was that your first?" she had asked. I nodded nervously, and that's when she leaned back and murmured, "I win."

I think I blocked Tracy from my memory because most of the time when guys ask "who was your first," I say Candice Zepp. I had always known they meant "first fuck," but I'd never been in the habit of exposing myself as a loser when I was only lying by omission. We'd kissed, and that had been a good enough "first" for me. Fortunately, Candice had never given away my secret, and against strange odds, we'd remained friends even without my telling her I was gay. The guys at school never needed to know I was a virgin, and they seriously didn't need to know it was because I didn't like girls.

It had taken every ounce of energy I had to tell my best friend, Doug, I was gay, but even that courage didn't stick around long enough for me to tell the rest of my friends or my family.

I gazed across the table at the two "teenagers." They were cute. I wanted cute. I wanted to giggle nose to nose and not care who watched.

"What if it isn't a cheerleader, Dad?" I asked solemnly.

He didn't look at me when he answered, "It will be. You just haven't found the right girl yet."

I sighed. "What if it's not a girl?" I admit I said it softly, but that was because part of me was still scared of what they'd think.

"You'll find the right girl. Don't worry," he said before kissing my mom again.

I let out a long breath and rose from the table, taking my plate and glass along with me into the kitchen. I placed them into the dishwasher and went upstairs to my room. They hadn't touched it since the last time I'd been home. I flopped on my bed face-first, lay there a few minutes, and then repositioned myself so my head was on my pillow and I was staring up at the ceiling fan. I'd stared at the thing so many times over the years it had become a source of comfort watching the blades slowly rotate.

I mumbled, "He didn't hear me. I all but said 'I'm gay,' and he didn't hear it. He only hears what he wants to hear. He thinks I'm shy. He thinks I haven't found the right one, but that isn't it. I'm gay. I don't want a girl, least of all a cheerleader. Not that there's anything wrong with cheerleaders, but I don't want any of the ones I know."

It wasn't as if I talked to myself often, but sometimes I felt the need. Hearing things out loud made them more real somehow. "I like Alonzo," I confessed. "I don't know why I've never felt anything for anybody in the past, except that I've only ever hung around cheerleaders and soccer players. I know I'm not the only gay guy in town, but even the few I've met haven't appealed to me. I've never felt a spark of anything. Then Alonzo smiled at me, and I can't stop thinking about him."

I curled over on my side and tucked one hand under my pillow.

What if Alonzo isn't gay? What if all of this is some cosmic joke? What if he's straight and only talking to me because he has no friends? I haven't seen him with anyone and he said he moved across the country. What if he's just happy making a friend, not a potential boyfriend, and I'm reading the signs all wrong?

I closed my eyes and woke up hours later when my mom called me down to dinner.

OUR FIRST official game was tonight, and I was nervous, but I wasn't sure if the nerves were from anticipation of the game or because I'd spotted Alonzo sitting in his spot when I entered the dining hall through the side entrance. I wasn't sure if I should walk up and start talking like last time, or if it would seem presumptuous. What if he didn't want to talk to me?

I hadn't seen him at practice all week, and I wondered if I should mention the time change and our practice schedule now that classes had started. What if he thought it started at 8:00 a.m. and he had a class then? Would he have shown up if he knew it started at 6:30 a.m.?

Now I'm obsessing.

I got food, sucked it down as fast as I could, and then twiddled my thumbs thinking of my next move. How could I get his attention? *Gummy bears!* I dashed out to the vending machine in the corridor by the front entrance and found the gummy bear slot fully stocked. I breathed a sigh of relief. Not only did I like to eat them before every game, but also I had eaten the last bag and been worried they wouldn't restock it by tonight's game. I bought two bags and went back to my table, three tables behind Alonzo.

Now if I can only get his attention without pissing him off.

I opened the bag and chewed a green bear. Alonzo's head was bowed forward, probably a sign he was reading. If I tossed a bear with enough loft, it could potentially fall directly over his shoulder and onto his open page. He'd either think it was funny, or get pissed. I took a chance.

Red bear between my thumb and forefinger, I held it ready like a dart thrower aiming at a bull's-eye. Arm back, calculate the correct angle of trajectory, and release. The squishy, bear-shaped gummy candy sailed through the air and dropped over his shoulder right where I'd aimed.

I'm awesome.

Alonzo didn't react.

Maybe I missed the book and it fell between Alonzo and the table and it's now on the floor?

I crouched down. Only a paper straw wrapper and a few old french fries were under there, so it had to have landed on the book, or at least on the table.

I tried a yellow one.

Logically, I knew the color of the gummy bear had no bearing on its aerodynamics, but I chose a different color just in case. Aim. Toss. Gone. No reaction. *Really?* How about an orange one? I threw six gummy bears before Alonzo turned slowly, eyebrow cocked in my direction, and asked, "Are you done yet?"

I smiled brightly, hoping my happiness would somehow impact his mood. He'd been so serious the last couple of times we'd spoken, despite my slight glimpse of his smirk; I hoped something would give. "Maybe. Depends."

"On what?"

"Whether or not you'll let me join you?" I put forth my best effort to appear calm, cool, and collected, even if I was shaking to death he'd say no… again. Or worse, get up and leave.

Alonzo almost smiled. At least I thought he did before he turned back around. *Shit!*

I sat there a second, thinking of my next move, when a green bear came flying back at me. It hit the floor two feet away. I glanced at it and waited. Another green one flew over his shoulder landing on the windowsill to my left. I picked that one up and retrieved the first one, tossing them into the trash on my way to his table. I sat across from him, hoping to save the remaining bears from a fuzzy, germ-filled death on the floor. No bears in sight.

"What happened to the other ones?" I asked.

He answered without bothering to look at me. "I ate them."

"Why not the green ones?"

Alonzo looked up, that adorable dimple striving furiously to pop into place. "I don't like the green ones."

The needle on this LP screeched to a halt. "What? How can you not like the green ones?" Describing myself in terms of a long-play record probably only made sense to me, but whatever. My mom listened to those on a new-style CD/record player. It was cool; it even transferred records onto CDs.

"They taste funny," he said.

"They taste like strawberries."

"They taste like the artificial flavoring in chewable Meltaways my mom used to give me when I was sick. Besides, strawberries aren't green. Who chose that color to begin with? It's unnatural. Green is for apple, mint, or lime, not strawberry."

I found his rant humorous. He fussed and then went back to his book. *Adorable.* Furthermore, he'd used my same reasoning about cherry-flavored things. "I get it. I guess I'm not real fond of the clear ones."

Alonzo shrugged. "Pineapple's okay. My favorite is the lemon."

I took out a yellow bear and set it on his book, facing forward so the bear knew where it was going.

He reached out, snatched, and ate it.

He was trying to hide his smile again, and I found his shyness charming. As he lowered his face to read, I withheld my comment about reading being rude in lieu of observing him, as I was fond of doing. The tip of his pinkie finger was blue this time. *Interesting.* He was reading *Romeo and Juliet.* A classic, no doubt, but was it a course requirement or personal choice?

He had a leather wrist cuff peeking out from the long sleeves of his shirt, I'd noticed that before, but this time I was able to make out the decorative silver piece on the outside. It looked like Thor's hammer and had an intricately etched design on it. *Pretty cool.* But the cuff was nothing compared to the black leather choker, or collar, around his neck—an accessory that enticed my baser desires.

Does he know how sexy that is?

He glanced up, his black-lined eyes questioning my silence.

I cleared my throat and tried easier questions. "You have an eyebrow piercing. Last time, I recall you didn't have a hoop in it, now you do. What happened? Why did you take it out?"

His eyes twitched and he moved his body back from the table a fraction. Maybe it was involuntary, maybe not, but I noticed it. I'd made him uncomfortable.

"How do you remember that? It was only out a week. It got infected, which is gross, but I thought I'd try a hoop one more time before I let it close up. The same thing happened to my lip, so I don't wear that hoop anymore."

I dropped my gaze to his lips, pink and moist. Below his bottom lip, on the left side, there was a spot that didn't look like a scar, or a freckle, and eventually would have driven me nuts with curiosity. "Is that what that spot is?" I reached over to point it out, but he pulled away before I even touched his face. I withdrew my hand. "Sorry. I guess hanging with cheerleaders has ruined my sense of personal space. They're always touching everyone, including me. I didn't mean to freak you out."

His dimple was gone. His eyes dropped to the table, and I could see his chest rising and falling faster as the seconds ticked. "Not you," he managed to say, eyes darting. "I gotta go." Alonzo snatched his book, bag, and coat and dashed away from me like before. This time I let him go.

I hated that I'd scared him when I hadn't even done anything. I bowed my head and rubbed the back of my neck with both hands, mentally kicking myself for being so forward. I couldn't help myself. I didn't think it was the cheerleader's influence either. I thought it was me. It was my desire to touch him and get to know him that made me act so stupid.

I pulled myself out of the chair and left the cafeteria through the bookstore entrance. Alonzo sat about fifty yards away from the building on the circular stone wall in front of the library, knees on elbows, head in hands. I walked over slowly, hoping my intrusion wouldn't be spurned. I sat quietly, but not too close. "Hey."

"Please go away," he choked.

"But I don't want to. How am I supposed to get to know you if you keep running away?"

Alonzo looked me in the eyes. His were red, but dry. "I'm not worth your time, Chris."

His words stabbed my heart. "Let me be the judge of that. Listen, we have our first official game tonight, at home, in the soccer complex. Come and watch. You seem to like soccer a lot, so maybe it will be good for you, help you relax. I haven't really made *new* friends in a while, so maybe this is all my fault. Maybe I'm doing it wrong. Saturday I have an away game, and then it's back to lecture halls and power point presentations on Monday." I stood up and added, "Give me a chance, Alonzo. I'm not a bad guy. I'll even eat all the green gummy bears when we're together."

Alonzo smirked and looked away.

"I'll take that as a possible maybe." I knew I had a few bears left in my bag so I fished one out while he was still studying the ground. I tossed one at him, and it landed in his lap. A yellow one! How fortuitous. He ate it and smiled up at me. "See? Gummy bears solve everything." I winked and walked away, hoping he was watching me.

If only gummy bears could transform him into a cheerleader then my problems really would be solved.

As I neared my dorm room, I fished out my phone and dialed my brother.

"Hello?"

"Hey, Ryan, it's me."

"Chris. How is college life treating you this semester?" He sounded happy.

"Good. Can I ask you a question?"

"Sure. Shoot."

"If Amber hadn't been a cheerleader, do you think you would have still dated her?" I sat on my bed and toed off my shoes. I had time to kill, and if Alonzo wasn't gonna hang, then I figured I'd chill and chat with my brother.

"Unfair question, bro. She *was* a cheerleader, and now she's my wife. How am I supposed to answer that without sounding like a superficial douche?"

"Okay, I'll rephrase it and you answer yes or no. It's not being recorded; this is for me. I need to know."

"Um, okay, but I'm not sure I like this game."

"Did falling for Amber have anything to do with her being a cheerleader?"

"Yes. Her thighs were so fine I could not look away when she wore that short little skirt."

"If she wasn't on the squad, do you think you would have noticed her?"

"No. I hung with the jock crowd in high school, bro; you know that. Jocks and cheerleaders are natural companions. We have the muscle, and they have the curves. Plus, you know Dad was hoping I'd land one ever since we were old enough to understand how he met Mom. He wanted the same for you and me both. Why are you asking this stuff, Chris?"

"What if I don't like cheerleaders? What if I fall for someone who isn't wearing a short skirt and shaking pom-poms? Do you think Dad will understand?"

"Dude, that's some serious shit to him. I don't know. Have you even tried? I know Candice didn't work out, and you said Kat was a bust, but what about the newer ones? Didn't you say three new girls were on the squad this year? Maybe give it time and ask one out."

I nodded, though he couldn't see it. "Yeah, thanks, Ryan. I'll give it some time. When are you back in town?"

"October, I think. This business trip has been a drag coming right after our honeymoon, and I know Amber wants to look at houses as soon as I get back. She's thankful we can live with her folks, but truth is I want our own place."

"Thanks, Ryan. I hope it all works out soon."

"With you too. Love you, little bro."

"Love you too." I tossed my phone in the general direction of the nightstand. It hit the edge and fell to the floor. My life was not going as planned. I was supposed to focus on school and not worry about relationships for a couple more years. When I was out of my parents' house is what I had promised myself.

Alonzo was not my plan.

Chapter 4
Refusing Hope

ALONZO WAITED for his sandwich to be made in the deli stand of the campus dining hall. He rather enjoyed the fact that the college offered a wide variety of food because he often didn't know what he felt like eating until he saw it. Like today; he'd walked past the soup, pizza, burgers, and vegan selections with no reaction at all. Once he saw the corned beef on display next to fresh loaves of wheat and pumpernickel, his mouth watered.

This was only the third week he'd been on campus and he was starting to notice a pattern in his eating habits. Mondays were burger days. Tuesdays he felt like soup. Now Fridays, he'd had a hankering for deli a couple times in a row. The consistency was comforting. When he sat at the cafeteria table and arranged his plate with his drink on the left, it dawned on him why. Consistency was one of those things his therapist stressed, and without even realizing it, he had fallen into a pattern of what to eat on which day so he never had to think about it.

Mindless choices made his life simpler. College life to begin with was new and frightening, but not for the same reasons other kids had. For most of them, this was a huge step toward independence, but then most students didn't have a conscience whispering to them all day and all night about a past full of overwhelming guilt. Alonzo's shame, at times, seemed almost like a living entity bent on destroying him, one aspersion at a time.

You're worthless.
You're nothing.
You should have died.
No one wants you.

The whispers were always there, but when he was calmly following routines and keeping interactions with strangers to a minimum, Alonzo was able to empty his mind enough to only hear them grumbling. Murmurs were always more tolerable than screams. When his subconscious screamed its taunts, there was nothing to do but curl up in a ball, take his meds, and sleep until they went away.

But not today.

"Hey, you," his sister, Stephanie, greeted him as she set her tray on the table across from him. "I haven't seen you since last Saturday. Where've you been hiding?"

"Reading."

"Hmm." Her disapproval was evident in her nonverbal communication. Eyes hard, mouth firm, she took a bite of her apple and waited.

When Alonzo had told his sister he'd gotten a scholarship to this college, she immediately transferred to be near him. Part of him resented it, as if her move signified her disbelief that he could function on his own. But the other part, the selfish part, knew he needed her, and he was grateful she'd rearranged her life for him.

Besides his mom, Stephanie was the only person who understood him.

"I'm keeping myself busy. I've already gotten most of the reading done for the next two weeks, plus a couple books for my own enjoyment."

"I guess that's good. Reading's good. How many credits are you taking?" she asked.

"Nineteen."

Stephanie whistled. "Good Lord. You certainly know how to put pressure on yourself. I have twelve credits and I'm already worried. Too many papers to write at the same time. I don't like it."

He understood her line of thinking, but school had never felt like pressure to him. Retaining information was easy and articulating his thoughts on paper for the teacher, just as simple. It was *being* in the class that was the challenge, and interacting with other students that had him bolting for the door as soon as class ended. At least that's how it had been in high school. This was college. Maybe it would be different.

"The first week of classes has been okay," he said.

"Mm-hmm," she murmured.

He would have done so much better taking online classes, but his therapist insisted on live ones, where communication and interaction was necessary to get the work done. She had told him he needed "team-building" skills and socialization. Alonzo rolled his eyes. Thinking about his therapist always reminded him of all the things he hadn't achieved, and it was depressing. Going away for college was a big step and one she'd said he was ready for, but he often worried that she'd been wrong.

"Classes aren't pressure, Steph," he responded quietly, taking a bite of his sandwich.

She paused and set what was left of her apple on her tray. She regarded him thoughtfully, and it made him squirm. "Have you made any friends?"

He shook his head and looked down at his food, knowing it was a lie. "Lonnie?"

He looked back up, hearing a tone in her voice that told him she suspected the truth. He darted his attention from her brown eyes, to the pizza sign with the word "pepperoni" spelled wrong, to the red exit sign only twenty feet away. Did he say something now? It was all new. What if Chris didn't really feel the way Alonzo imagined he felt? Then he'd be getting her hopes up for no reason. Or… getting his own hopes up for no reason.

"Fine," he relented. "I met someone."

Her half grin said she was interested in hearing more. "And? Was this a female someone, or male?"

He felt his lips twitch as he glanced down again. This was harder to talk about than he thought. He felt his cheeks getting hot.

She slapped the table. "Oh my God! You met a guy? When?"

He shushed her immediately. "Steph! I don't want the whole building to know."

She leaned closer and apologized quietly. "Sorry. I'm excited for you. It's been a long time since—"

"Don't say it." He cut her off, not wanting to hear the words. "I'm not saying I *met* someone. I'm saying, this guy introduced himself, and he might be interested in being a friend."

"Friend? Or *naked* friend?" She picked up her apple and took the last few nibbles.

"Do you always have to be so crude?"

She snickered, but didn't retract her question.

Alonzo knew she got a kick out of badgering him. He could see it in her eyes—that sparkle of mirth. Gosh, she was so pretty. He loved how she braided her hair on both sides and flared her eyeliner out past the corners of her eyes. Today, the shade was bright pink above the black. Striking. The dramatic flair fit her well, but he knew it would be totally different tomorrow. Stephanie was all about change, and her makeup and accessories always reflected her mood.

Change. Alonzo's life was smack dab in the middle of change right now, and he hated it.

In order to answer her question, he had to think about it. After half his sandwich was gone, he had to admit she could be right. The probability that Chris was only interested in friendship had diminished after he'd winked. And then, good God, the way Chris practically begged him to come watch his game tonight was downright bold. Chris was interested in more than friendship and Alonzo knew it; he just didn't want to believe it.

He gave in and smirked. "Okay, I'm ninety percent certain he's interested in more than friendship, but he hasn't exactly spelled it out in multicolored condoms, so I think you're delusional about the nakedness. He said he wants to be my friend."

Hearing himself admit it out loud made his smile broaden. He felt warmth trail down his chest and swirl in his stomach. Chris liked him. Oh wow! A hot soccer player liked him, and maybe he wasn't doomed to spend the rest of his life alone. Even if it was merely as friends, he could handle it. He hadn't made a friend in years.

Stephanie grabbed his hand, and he flinched. "I'm sorry," she said, pulling back. "Sometimes I forget."

He took her hand and squeezed her fingers. "It's okay. I'm working on it."

"So tell me about him," she said, eyes glowing again. "I want to know who it is that's got you blushing."

"I'm not blushing." Although as soon as he denied it, he felt heat in his cheeks. Yes, he was blushing.

"The hell you aren't. And I haven't seen you smile in ages. What's his name?"

Even if he felt uncomfortable answering her questions, he couldn't deny talking about Chris made him feel giddy for the first time in a long time. "Chris." And hearing his name out loud made his fingers tingle.

"Where'd you meet him?" Her interest made thinking about Chris even more fun.

"Technically, I met him here, in the dining hall. He saw me reading and walked over."

"Really? Like was he interested in the book you were reading, or did he dig your eyeliner?" she jested.

"Neither. He saw me watching the soccer team practicing, and he wanted to know why."

"Was he watching too? Or…." Her eyes grew wide. "No way! He's a soccer player?"

Alonzo felt his face flush again. He grinned. "Yeah. He's the team captain."

Stephanie clamped her hand over her mouth in disbelief. "Oh my God! Chris Jackson has the hots for you?"

Again, he was perturbed at her broadcasting to the entire school something that was not exactly confirmed; especially when he wasn't sure Chris was out. He pulled his hand out of her grasp. "Steph! Shush. God, can't you keep anything to yourself?" He'd never held back his irritation before and he wasn't starting now. He was genuinely pissed that her voice kept getting louder. "Plus, I never said that. We're friends, okay… *friends*."

She looked apologetic. "I'm sorry." She looked around. "I don't think anyone heard."

Alonzo glanced around too. Everyone seemed to be carrying on like normal. Plus, no one sat at the four nearest tables, so it was very likely no one had heard. "Fine. But don't advertise. Nothing is official. If he *is* gay, I don't think he's out, not with the way the cheerleaders hang on him."

"That's precisely why I'm shocked. My roommate Katherine knows him. She said he's totally amazing, but hasn't hit on her like the other guys on the team. She said they sort of dated last year, but he wouldn't make a move so she called it quits. She suspects a bad breakup or something."

"Go with the 'or something.'" Alonzo felt bad talking about Chris behind his back, but he knew he needed to say something or Stephanie could very well blow it for him. "Look, I don't know your friend, but please don't say anything to her. If he's gay like I hope he is, it could really kill our friendship before it starts. You can't say anything to this girl."

"Oh, I won't. I promise. I guess having different last names is a good thing for once. Are you ever going to change yours?"

"To Alonzo Sarzo? Um, I think not." The fact that his sister had decided to officially change her name once their mother remarried was fine, but he wasn't in a hurry to do the same. His father's last name suited him, even if he didn't care for the man.

"Noted," she commented. "Back to Katherine Stewart. They're friends and she's a cheerleader. She'll see Chris all the time. If you're hanging around him, she's bound to ask about it. Your outfit doesn't scream sports fanatic, just so you know."

He heard her attitude creeping up a notch. She was mad. But better to have her mad at him for assuming she'd blab than say nothing and have her ruin everything. "I know I stick out. That's sort of how he noticed me. I was watching soccer practice wearing my coat, and he called me out on it."

"In your coat?" Attitude and her eyebrow arched. "In August? Man, are you dumb."

"No. You know it's because…."

"Because it belonged to—"

He put his hand up. "Don't say it."

Respectfully, Stephanie held her tongue. "Fine. Does the soccer stud know?"

Alonzo involuntarily grinned. He didn't want to, but the way she asked made him picture Chris on the field. Chris *was* a stud. Oh, wow. Chris, the soccer stud, had flirted with him. Alonzo's stomach fluttered. "How do you know he's a stud anyway?"

"Besides your pink cheeks, um, because Kat has a picture of the two of them on her desk. He's seriously hot. It also means they're good friends. So I guess I'm going to the next game with you so I can see for myself what you've gotten yourself into."

Into?

The question made the whole rest of the conversation fade into background noise. *Into* Chris Jackson. Suddenly, Alonzo was imagining what it might be like to be *into* him the way he hadn't been *in* anyone in a long, long while. *Inside of Chris.* Could he? The thought frightened him. He hadn't topped since…. No, that would be too huge. It was terrifying enough to consider Chris might want to kiss him, let alone make love, but the idea of Alonzo doing the deed sent his mind spiraling into itself.

"No!" he exclaimed suddenly, jumping up and almost knocking the table over.

"Lonnie?"

He heard her plea. He heard her familiar term of endearment that only existed between them. No one else called him Lonnie. But even though he could tell she was concerned, he needed to get out of the room. It was shrinking. The walls were tilting and the door frames slid askew with each step he took toward them. Alonzo was having a panic attack, and he needed to breathe fresh air before he passed out—or worse, hurt someone.

A KNOCK on his door. A pause. Another knock. "Lonnie?"

Stephanie had followed him to his dorm room. He pulled the blanket off his face and looked at the clock. Three hours had gone by. Three whole hours. She'd followed, but she had also given him time to calm down on his own. Progress. Maybe she really was giving him the space he'd asked for.

He sat up and swung his legs over the side of the bed.

He opened the door and Stephanie stood there, holding back her tears. He opened his arms and she fell against him. "I'm sorry," he whispered. "I needed to…."

"I know," she cried, burying her face in his chest, holding him tight. "I'm sorry too. I don't know what I said that triggered it. If I knew, I'd never say it again."

Alonzo knew, but he wasn't going to fill her in. He wanted to disappear into the blackness of his drug-induced quiet, but lacked the time. Chris played tonight. Alonzo couldn't escape his pain if he wanted to watch Chris play.

"It's okay," he whispered into her hair, hugging her tight and rubbing her back. "I need to figure out how to cope without running. Just don't give up on me while I work it out. Okay?"

Stephanie pulled back. "Never. I'll always be here for you."

Alonzo smiled softly, cupping her cheek and wiping her tears away with his thumb. "You're going to have to redo your eyeliner," he commented.

Stephanie laughed, though more tears fell as she sank into his arms again.

"If you want to go to a game, Chris plays tomorrow night at Wesley, wherever that is." Chris played tonight at home, but Alonzo wanted to go alone in hopes of working up enough courage to talk to him. He wasn't ready for his sister to meet Chris quite yet. He needed more time.

Stephanie walked over to his bed and sat on the edge. "We could google it. It can't be that hard to find. Are you sure you want me to go?"

Alonzo sat next to her and said, "You're the only one with a car."

She laughed. "True."

"But we're going incognito. No walking up to Chris, and no cheering from the stands. I don't want him knowing I'm there. He doesn't know I checked the college website for the game schedule, and I'm not ready to tell him I've watched several practices."

Stephanie widened her eyes. "Oooh, stalker. And you say you're not into him?"

"Okay, okay. I'm into him. I'm seriously crushing right now, and I hope to God he's gay because if he's straight, I might die."

"Well, let's see what we can do about it." Stephanie stood up and circled his room, poking in his stuff as if looking for something. She picked up the black choker he'd worn earlier. "Did you wear this in front of super stud?"

"Yeah. Why?"

She gaped. "And he *didn't* drop to his knees. Hmm. Maybe he *is* straight, or playing cool." She walked over to him and fingered several long strands of his hair. "I say, get a haircut, lose the long-sleeved shirt, and wear the collar again."

"What's so special about the collar? And you know how I feel about my arms."

She cupped his chin. "I know, honey, but you need to let it go. Your arms are fine. This collar, on the other hand, is more than fine. Without sounding perverted, it makes you absolutely eatable."

He pulled back from her touch. "Really?" he asked skeptically. "He didn't seem to notice."

"Give it another week or two and wear it again without the long-sleeved shirt. You'll have him drooling, I promise." She sat on the bed again and patted his knee. "You are really adorable, Lonnie, and I'm not just saying that because you look like me."

"Thanks. But I'm the oldest, so technically you look like me."

"Whatevs. What time's the game tomorrow?"

"Four."

"Laptop?"

He handed it to her. Alonzo watched as his sister looked up the opposing college and wrote down the address for her GPS.

As soon as Stephanie left, he looked at the desk clock. It read 6:55 p.m. Chris's game started in five minutes. He'd never make kickoff, but if he changed fast enough, he could see most of the game. He sorted through his clothes. *Which one should I wear?*

Green Day: Dynamite

Green Day: American Idiot

Green Day: 99 Revolutions

Green Day: 21ˢᵗ Century Breakdown

Green Day: New Type System

He knew Stephanie disapproved of his wardrobe. She fussed all the time about his lack of color and his need for change. She liked change, he didn't. Maybe one day.

But not today.

He pulled his black Green Day: Welcome to Paradise T-shirt over his head and tossed it into the dirty-clothes pile in the corner of the room. After finding a fresh, black long-sleeved shirt to cover his arms, he worked his T-shirt over it and adjusted the layers of fabric. It was a hassle wearing two shirts, but he hoped one day he'd get over his phobia and relax.

But not today.

Chris's game was about to start.

AFTER THE game, Alonzo paced the sidewalks outside the locker room. He'd seen Chris follow the team back from the field, celebrating their victory, and decided against talking to him in the company of his friends. They hadn't gotten to that stage yet. He'd waited until most of the team trickled out and thanked heaven for the small favor of Chris being last to leave. Chris had asked for "a chance" that morning, and Alonzo wanted to make sure Chris knew he'd have one. Waiting until *next* Friday to talk to him was too long.

There was also something about watching Chris play that made Alonzo long to be near him. He looked so powerful on the field, and Alonzo wanted to be close to that kind of energy even if he was afraid to give in to it.

While Alonzo waited, pacing this way and that, he started worrying about picking the wrong time to inquire what type of friendship they might have. Was Chris really flirting in the dining hall? What if he had a nervous tick and blinked randomly? Why would he wink at Alonzo anyway? Alonzo was nobody. Alonzo was a hopeless loser, addicted to anxiety medication and sports he'd never play.

The taunts started. The whispers, always condemning, swirled around like ghosts in a windstorm, swept in a rapid circle, moving and whipping until the trees lifted from their roots and ripped the ground as they joined the torrent of moving air, crashing and smashing and dashing his dreams to bits. He'd been about to turn tail and flee when he heard his name.

"Alonzo?"

That soothingly familiar voice snapped him out of the nightmare. It was Chris. Freshly showered and dressed in basketball shorts and an orange T-shirt, he strolled up to Alonzo with a huge smile on his face, his normally wild curly blond hair still wet and slicked back behind his ear on one side.

"It *is* you." Chris seemed pleased to see him, although Alonzo wasn't sure why.

"Hi," he managed to grunt. The taunting whisperers, demons, and naysayers remained, but they were hushed by the sound of Chris's pleasant voice. Alonzo tried desperately to ignore them.

Chris walked right up to him. "I'm glad you're here. Did you enjoy the game?"

"Yeah, you played well." He stuffed his hands inside his jeans pockets and glanced around. Students milled about, but were chatting among themselves. No one took note of him or Chris. He didn't have to be self-conscious about people talking. He didn't have to fear their ridicule. No one knew he was gay. Well, maybe Chris suspected, but no one else. He could talk like a normal person. He was allowed to have friends.

"Alonzo?" Chris questioned, waving his hand in front of Alonzo's face. "Are you in there?" Chris was smiling, always smiling. It was hard to concentrate when he was so gorgeous.

Alonzo shook off his thickening stupor, but he was breathing faster than normal and hoped his panic attack could wait until Chris left. "I'm fine," he blurted.

"You don't seem fine. Are you sure you liked the game? You don't have to lie to spare my feelings. If you don't like soccer, you can just say so."

That grabbed his attention. Alonzo pulled his shoulders back and looked Chris right in the eyes. He wasn't going to give in to his growing doubt in the face of an assumption like that. "No, I love soccer," he said. "I've wanted to play since I was a kid."

"Oh," Chris said. Alonzo wondered why he sounded disappointed. "Um, do you... want to walk? Or do you want to stand here and talk?"

"Huh?"

"Walk. Like... perambulate toward the dorms. This seems like an odd place to have a conversation. Walking is nicer. Besides, I worked out in the fitness center this afternoon, after I tossed the yellow gummy bear at you, so I'm a little sore. Between the workout and all that running, I feel like I need to walk so I don't stiffen up. You know?"

"Oh, yeah. Sure." *Stiffen up?* He didn't need the word picture, even if Chris meant it in a different context.

Chris waved his hand toward the sidewalk to Alonzo's right, and they both turned together to walk, side by side, down the lighted path. The game had started at seven, so by now it was past ten. The sky was dark, and people were hanging in groups, laughing, and goofing off. One such group had camping-style lanterns strewn about and their attention was centered on a guy with a guitar, soft tones filtering through the surrounding trees. It was an old campus, with many large trees planted around the buildings. Alonzo loved that about this college.

"So why don't you?" Chris asked, after they'd walked about ten yards without talking.

"Huh?"

Chris chuckled. "You're really off tonight. I'm used to feisty comebacks, not a bewildered space cadet. Let me rephrase my question. Why don't you play soccer, if you've always wanted to?"

Alonzo felt ashamed. How could he explain his psychosis without sounding like a complete basket case? Maybe Chris would understand, but maybe he wouldn't. But talking soccer was at least a neutral subject. He could answer and would only have to reveal a little from his past. He kept his head hung low and his eyes on the ground in front of him. "Um, because I broke my ankle."

"So? Cullen broke his in high school, but he only missed half a season. You see him now. He's really fast."

Alonzo wasn't sure which one Cullen was, but it didn't matter. He glanced at Chris and explained, "No, not once. Three times." He looked back at the ground. Eye contact with Chris was confusing. He was always smiling, and his eyes danced over Alonzo with mixed emotions. Alonzo could have sworn he'd seen desire, glee, and genuine interest exuding from those midnight blue eyes in the collective moments they'd spoken together. Chris couldn't be thinking those things. It wasn't true. It was merely Alonzo's hope yearning to break free of its strangling prison. But hope was a dangerous thing best left starving in the dark.

"Three times?" Chris asked.

"Yeah. The first time was when I was eight. I played on a rec league as a midfielder, if they really have those when a kid is eight. I was fast. I had a clear shot toward the goal, and I remember running and dribbling all the way down the center of the field. My coach yelled for me to pass it, but I tried taking the shot myself. Instead of kicking a goal, my foot went over the top of the ball and I fell backward. My leg twisted as my shoe hit the ground before my body, and I heard a snap. Everyone heard it. I didn't play again until I was ten."

"Did you break your ankle again that year?"

They turned near the library and circled around the large oak tree. Alonzo liked this spot during the day, but being here at night with Chris was even nicer. "Yeah, but not right away. It was in the playoff games. I got shoved from behind. The other kid got yellow carded, but I went down hard and twisted my ankle. And yes, I broke it in the exact same spot. They had to put in a metal plate and eight screws." They made another left.

"Ouch." Chris winced. "This is my dorm." He gestured and they stopped walking.

"Okay." Alonzo could see the fitness center and the gym practically in front of them, suggesting they'd walked a huge circle, when they could have walked straight to Chris's dorm in two minutes. *Did Chris take the long way on purpose?* Alonzo wanted to escape. "Well, I guess I'll see you around."

"No, wait," Chris insisted. "You haven't told me about the third time. Do you want to come up to my room? We could watch a movie or something. My roommate, Doug, said he was visiting his folks tonight, they wanted to celebrate or something, so we'll have the room to ourselves. No pressure. Just saying."

Alonzo shook his head emphatically, chest pounding, hands shaking. "No. I don't think so. I'm not—"

Chris jumped right in, holding out one hand. "Hey, I'm not suggesting anything. I wanted to talk more. We can stay right here if you want." He gestured to a bench next to the dorm. "Look. Sit. Tell me about the third time you broke your ankle, and then we can say good night."

"Okay," he agreed.

They both sat on the bench, and Chris turned toward Alonzo, stretching his arm out along the back of the bench. Alonzo was sitting a good ten inches away, so Chris's arm position might have been for comfort as he turned his body inward. It didn't have to be suggestive in any way, did it? Alonzo's imagination started swirling.

"So tell me."

Alonzo explained, "I was fourteen. I wanted for years to play for a high school team. I knew I was good enough, but none of the kids at my school knew it because I'd only played rec and it wasn't in their district. My mom took me even though my dad thought it was senseless because I always seemed to injure myself. He was right. We were running on the track, warming up for timed laps, when I stumbled. I thought it was on a rock or something, but my friend couldn't find any debris, so I looked like an idiot who'd stumbled over his own feet. Everyone laughed. But when I tried standing up, they stopped laughing when my bone shattered and poked out the side of my leg. It was the most painful experience I've ever had."

"Wow. That sounds terrible." Chris looked honestly troubled for Alonzo's pain. His eyes looked sad as he watched Alonzo intently.

After a minute or so passed, Alonzo felt something on the back of his neck, or rather in his hair. He was about to swat it away thinking it was a bug, but realized it was Chris. He fingered Alonzo's hair, lightly twirling it as anyone might do to his or her own hair while studying for a test. A casual touch—no, an intimate touch. Alonzo wanted to bolt, but he froze.

His eyes fluttered shut. Chris's touch was light, as if memorizing the texture of each strand. Alonzo's whisperers chided him for letting his hair grow to that length. If it had been short, or buzzed up the back like it had been five years ago, then Chris couldn't have touched it. Alonzo was a fool. He had let it grow out until it fell over his shirt collar, to a length this sexy soccer stud could take advantage of, fondle, and enjoy. Maybe even sink his fingers into and twist around his fist as Alonzo....

No! he chided himself.

Alonzo knew the fantasy would die. It always did. His heart accelerated. His breathing increased. His mind whirled. Chris was touching him. Chris had boldly reached over and touched his hair without asking, and Alonzo fought a deep desire to touch Chris as well. His hair always looked so soft and fluffy the way it lifted with any slight breeze. Alonzo wanted to touch Chris's hair and caress his scruff-covered cheek.

But he couldn't. It was too soon. Chris wouldn't understand. Chris didn't know about Kyle. Chris would run in the opposite direction if he knew. Alonzo was better off running first. It would save time. Hope could not win. Hope needed to be destroyed.

Without saying a word, Alonzo bolted for his dorm room, running at full speed in his heavy combat boots, chains rattling with his pounding strides. In only a few minutes, he was in his room and under his blankets, shaking like a leaf. Thankfully, his roommate came in after he'd calmed down and properly undressed for bed. He didn't want to explain his radical behavior. So far, their exchanges had been minimal. Caleb was quiet, possibly even shyer than Alonzo. Alonzo had been grateful for the guy the housing department had paired him with.

ALONZO SKIPPED Chris's practice Saturday morning, and made an excuse to his sister why he wasn't going to Chris's game Saturday night. Alonzo had had a habit of breaking plans with his sister, so he knew she'd understand. He suggested a trip to Albright on Wednesday, and Stephanie seemed satisfied.

He knew he needed to follow through on promises, especially when they caused discomfort associated with his past, because that was one of the things his therapist had stressed back home before he'd left. He needed to heal, and he couldn't do it by constantly running away.

Alonzo really enjoyed watching Chris play, and missing practice and one of his games hurt. He liked the way Chris's long legs moved, graceful yet powerfully so. His quick turns and forward-thinking passes were inspiring. He was truly the best soccer player Alonzo had ever seen; at least for a guy around his age. Pro players had more experience and honed technique, but Chris Jackson was well on his way to becoming the next Cristiano Ronaldo or David Beckham. Alonzo envied him.

By Tuesday, he had avoided Chris for as long as his pride could stand. He felt like an idiot for running away, but not seeing Chris's beautiful smile was more than disappointing. He decided looking foolish was better than drowning. He could wait for him in the dining hall on Friday and hope Chris would show again, but he didn't want to wait until then.

He sat on the grass behind the baseball field fencing on Tuesday morning, occasionally peeking through the gaps in the privacy mesh to watch, hoping no one could see him from that angle since the baseball field was up a hill from where the soccer team practiced.

Alonzo's cell phone rang, and he jumped. Only two people on the planet had his number, so there was a fifty-fifty shot as to who it was. "Hello?"

"Hey Lonnie. What ya doing?" Stephanie asked.

"Watching soccer practice." He didn't want to say, but he knew he couldn't avoid it.

"Oh yeah? How're things going in that department? Did you talk to him the other night? Did he walk you home? Are you two *lovers*?"

"Lovers? Don't be absurd. I've known him for less than three weeks." He hadn't told her about running away from Chris last Friday.

Talking, he'd lost sight of Chris, so he scanned the players for the familiar topknot Chris fashioned every time he played. Alonzo would have to ask him about it because he thought it looked silly. He rather liked Chris's wild mane of fluffy hair. It wasn't overly long, just long enough to create a look akin to Albert Einstein's crazy hair, but much more aesthetically pleasing. Chris's hair was shiny and soft, curly but thin; it stood out on end naturally, without Chris having to stick his finger in an electric socket.

"Are you laughing?" Stephanie asked. "Are you with someone? Are you with that guy?"

"What? No. I'm alone. I'm watching him play."

"Then why were you laughing?"

Alonzo suddenly realized he'd been daydreaming about Chris's hair. Daydreaming. And he'd been laughing softly. That was a first. "Um, I was thinking out loud about something."

"Something about that guy?"

"I'd rather not say."

"Did he show you his Mr. Howdy?"

He jerked the phone away and looked at it as if she'd be able to see his alarm. "Are you insane? You're a pervert, Steph! Is that what you think guys do?"

"I don't know. You tell me. Did he show you his *thang*?"

"No!" he practically yelled into the receiver.

Stephanie must have gotten a clue because she changed her tune. "I'm sorry, Lonnie. I haven't heard you laugh in a really long time so I guess I was making a joke and it didn't come off very funny."

"No, it didn't."

"I'm sorry."

"Look, I have to go. Practice is almost done, and I don't want him to see me watching."

"But—"

Alonzo hung up on her. It might have been a little joke to her, but sex was not a joke to him. Not after….

He stood quickly and walked across the outfield toward the gate. He'd lost his taste for watching. Stephanie's comment rattled him. How could she say that?

His phone rang. He thought about ignoring his sister but answered it anyway. "What?"

"I'm sorry. You know I love you. I'm trying to get back to that place we were years ago, before everything fell apart. You know? That place where we joked about everything, rolled around on the living room floor, and then drank chocolate milkshakes until we puked. I miss that place."

He felt tears threaten, but he couldn't afford to cry right then; he held it in. "Those days are gone, Steph." He hung up and walked through the gate. He turned right toward the grassy area between the trees instead of the path along the soccer field fence, giving up on his silly desire to see Chris. It was stupid anyway. He'd walked six paces before he heard Chris calling after him.

"Alonzo!"

He stopped and waited for Chris to catch up. His mood had been crushed, but he knew he couldn't walk fast enough to avoid him. Chris came around in front of him, and Alonzo reluctantly lifted his gaze to address him. "Hi."

Chris smiled. Of course he smiled; he always smiled. It was like the smile was permanently affixed to his adorably freckled face, as if he'd invented happiness himself. "I haven't seen you since Friday. I hope your classes aren't too hard. Mine are a pain, but whatever. I'll manage. Lots of reading, which I normally don't mind, but it takes up my leisure time."

Alonzo enjoyed his lighthearted rambling, but he couldn't help his negative interjection. "Aren't you afraid your friends will see you talking to me? You're a jock; me, I'm a freaky emo dude, right? Eyeliner and all." He wouldn't define himself as emo; it only seemed that way from outward appearances, which Alonzo wasn't in the mood to explain. If Chris stuck around, maybe he'd tell him where the coat came from.

"What?" Chris asked, obviously thrown by his non sequitur. "My friends won't care. I can talk to whomever I want. I don't need to ask permission to make friends with someone outside the team. What are you talking about?"

Friends. There was that word again. "You're not out, are you?" he spat. Alonzo knew his belligerence stemmed from his irritation over Stephanie's comment, but still he couldn't stop his direct stab at what he'd suspected, even if it was rude.

Chris actually looked hurt. "No," he answered quietly. "But I'm not sure why that matters."

"Because people change, Chris. People who you thought were friends change and hurt you when they find out. What if the team turns on you? Would you sacrifice soccer to talk to me?" The gloom that normally followed Alonzo through life hovered over him. He felt its icy claws on the back of his neck, waiting to dash his hopes again.

Instead, after a slight pause during which Chris's thoughtful eyes danced over Alonzo's features to the point of making him blush, Chris said, "Yes."

Chris winked and smiled his spirited, glowing smile right before he took off jogging toward the gym. He turned and shouted back at Alonzo. "I'll see you Friday!"

Alonzo's heart leapt.

Chapter 5
Reading Signals

I COULDN'T sleep for thinking about Alonzo. Let me rephrase that. Wondering what caused his mood swing and feeling like it may have been my fault from when I touched his hair and he bolted on Friday kept me awake. There had been several occasions where thinking about Alonzo kept me awake at night because picturing his eyes and lips got me horny, and then I'd have to take care of things or my dick would be too painfully hard to sleep. But it wasn't the same since he'd run away. It made me think he didn't like me like that.

On the other hand, his proposition of choosing him over soccer intrigued me. I didn't think he meant it literally, no matter how serious he'd been when asking, but something in his eyes felt wrong. He'd been through something excruciating, and it was up to me to work the details out of him gently. Pain unattended could fester, and I didn't want him to go through it alone.

Plus, he'd directly addressed my closeted state. That meant he knew I was gay and implied he was gay as well.

As far as I was concerned, our friendship was heading in the correct, more than friends, direction.

"YOU PLAYED well today, Chris, even if you didn't look completely engaged." Ellis stepped in beside me as I walked off the field after practice. I had class in an hour, so I couldn't afford to talk long.

"Yeah, sorry."

Doug joined me on the other side and patted me across the back of my shoulders. "Yeah man, your passes were sweeeet."

I grinned at my buddy. "Thanks."

"But I agree with coach here, you seemed out of it. Classes can't be weighing you down yet, can they? I mean… we haven't even had big exams yet or papers due. My first research paper is due *next* week. What happens when we take on Albright tonight and you're all 'Oh man, I'm so tired. I can't focus. I need a burger,'" Doug whined.

I shoved him off me. "Shut up! I don't sound like that."

"Yes, you do!"

I complained, "No. And if you insist on making fun of me, then get it right. It's a double bacon cheeseburger, you dork!"

Doug laughed and jogged off to help Cullen, who had dropped the water cooler twenty paces ahead of us.

"You have good friends," Ellis commented.

"Yeah, they're great."

"You all anticipate each other surprisingly well."

"Some of us have played together for six years. The others fall in as we train them."

"Maybe, but in my experience players don't normally gel so fluidly. This is a really good team, and I'm excited to see how well we fare this season."

"Me too."

"I'm serious. Watching you is like poetry, Chris. I haven't seen a drop shot like yours so precise in a long time. The way you ran down the left side and chipped the ball so it fell right in front of Cedric like that... wow." He seemed in awe of me and I liked it.

"Thanks. But his name is Cullen. Cedric is African-American. Cullen is the one with wavy red hair who just dropped the water cooler," I corrected. "They look nothing alike."

Cullen Rafferty was Irish through and through, from his red hair to his green eyes. I'd had a tiny crush on him in middle school because of those green eyes, but over time I realized how strongly I was attracted to brown. Deep, dark brown like Alonzo's eyes. Cullen was one of my closest friends anyway, so I wasn't keen on screwing up the relationship. Plus—straight. I knew way too many straight guys.

"That's right," he said, snapping his fingers. "Marshall is the one with the mustache, and Josh has the cute little mole right above the corner of his lip. I'll get them all before the last game, I promise."

I almost tripped over my own feet. "Wait... what did you just say?" Surely I'd heard him wrong. We were getting closer to the locker room, and I had the feeling it was not a conversation I wanted to continue where others could hear.

Ellis regarded me, nonplussed. "I was joking about the last game."

"No, the other thing."

"I said Josh is the one with the mole."

I stepped in front of him and stopped him, holding my index finger up in front of his chest. I glanced around and made sure no one was near enough to hear. "No. You said Josh is the one with the cute little mole right above the corner of his lip."

Ellis blanched. "Oh." He took a step back. "I'm sorry. This is going to be awkward."

I didn't like where this was going, judging by his nervous expression. How could he possibly know about me? I wasn't checking out the guys on the field. I hadn't made any inappropriate comments about Cullen's eyes or Taylor's ass. And talking with Alonzo briefly after practice yesterday, even if Ellis had seen us together, didn't mean anything. No. There was no way Ellis Montgomery knew I was gay. "How did you know?" I asked directly. Better to rip the bandage off than to circumvent the obvious.

"Know what?" he asked.

"That I'm gay?" I replied.

He narrowed his eyes and his anxiety transformed into confusion. "Wait… what? What are you talking about? I didn't know you were gay; I was talking about *me*. I thought Mr. Mathews had filled you in. I was open about my sexuality when I applied so it wouldn't become an issue later."

Now I was confused. "You're gay?"

"Yes. That's what I was trying to tell you. I thought you knew, I thought the team knew, and I didn't mean to sound inappropriate when I made that comment about Josh's mole. I do think it's cute, but a comment like that could get me fired. I hope you won't say anything. I'm really sorry. I was out of line."

Ellis was gay. *Ellis* was gay. He'd made the comment by accident and now was nervous about what I'd say. He was nervous. He hadn't known about me. I sucked in a sudden breath. *Oh shit.* I blinked at him while a cold sweat broke out on my forehead. "That means… I just came out to you."

"I guess so. Does that bother you?"

He didn't look bothered at all, but I, on the other hand, was on the verge of hyperventilating. "A little," I peeped pathetically.

Then he smiled and placed a comforting hand on my shoulder. "If I'm the first one you came out to, I'm flattered. Let me know if you need any sort of support. I'm here for you. I promise. I won't say a word. Okay?"

"Okay." I was overwhelmed, for sure, but for the first time it didn't feel so scary. When I'd told Doug, I thought he'd clobber me, but he hadn't. Now Ellis knew and he looked completely supportive. I took a few deep breaths as I calmed down. "You aren't the first, but you *are* the second. And... I feel sort of... relieved. Wow. It feels good."

"I remember that feeling. Do your parents know?" he asked, sounding all grown-up-like.

"No. But I always figured I'd tell them if I ever had a boyfriend. So far it hasn't been an issue, but maybe soon. I don't know."

"My advice is to tell them way before they walk in on you having sex. That's never good."

I suddenly broke out laughing. "Oh God. I could not imagine that. Wow. That would really suck. My dad would probably have a heart attack. No. No way. I would definitely tell them before anything like that happened." The way he *wasn't* laughing made me stop myself. I cleared my throat and steadied my voice. Something wasn't right. "Did that happen to you?" I broached.

Ellis nodded and sighed. "Yup. For a few minutes, I thought I would have to commit my mom to a psychiatric ward. She freaked."

"I can't imagine that."

"Don't. Tell your parents before it gets messy. If you need support, we'll be there for you."

"We?"

"Cole and I."

"Who's Cole?" I had no clue.

"My husband," he said, and I swear he blushed. God, he was cute. "I'm sure you've seen him at the games."

Then he fumbled for his wallet and took out a photo of two guys in tuxes looking mighty sharp. Ellis was standing next to another guy, their hands clasped, both beaming like the sun. "This is Cole," he explained. "We were married in June. Isn't he adorable?"

Ellis was head over heels. The way his voice hushed and he smiled so softly looking at the picture. I could also tell sharing his special day meant a lot. I got that. It wasn't like straight guys sharing their wedding photos and setting their wives' pictures on their desks. Sharing could be daunting because you never knew the reaction you'd get. With me, Ellis could be himself and say what he wanted, and gosh, his expression as he gazed at the picture made me so covetous of what he had. I wanted that too. Bad.

He fumbled for another picture. "Here's another. This one was taken in front our new house. See, he's pointing to the Sold sign."

"You bought a new house? How? I mean, I'm sorry if that's rude, but if you teach one class, how can you afford it?"

"I don't mind answering. I knew it would come up eventually, but I thought it would be with my neighbors. Cole's parents put a huge down payment on it so we could afford the mortgage. They like me." Ellis grinned. His expression grew softer, and I wondered if he was reliving some memories as he flipped through the six or so pictures he had in his wallet. "This one's funny."

His husband, Cole, looked angry in that one. "Why is he pointing a pair of tongs at you?"

Ellis smirked. "Because I was trying to help in the kitchen and dropped a pitcher of lemonade. Our friend Rob was over, and he always laughs when Cole tries to scold me for the messes I make. He snapped the photo."

"Why does he get mad? And why don't you seem upset about it? He looks pissed. Don't his reprimands bother you? You've only been married a few months—isn't fighting bad?" I wondered because I rarely saw my own parents fight, like ever. Right now, Alonzo was upset for some reason, and I didn't really know how to handle it. What was so different about Ellis and Cole that made Ellis grin about it?

"It's not fighting, and I'm not bothered because I know he doesn't mean it. Cole's a control freak and a germaphobe, but he's also easy to placate if you know the right strategy."

"Which is?"

"First, I let him clean my messes *his* way. I never do it the way he wants anyway."

"Second?"

"Are you sure you want to know?" he asked with a twinkle in his eye.

I looked down at my feet. "I guess not. I think I can figure that one out. But"—I brought my gaze back up—"can I point out that 'germaphobe' isn't really a word? Spermatophobia, or spermophobia, is the fear of germs." I didn't like correcting my coach, who was an English teacher, but the know-it-all inside my brain couldn't let it slide.

"Not to be confused with spermophile."

My brain flipped through its database. "Ground squirrel?"

Ellis's jaw dropped. "Dude! How'd you know that?"

I shrugged. "Just another category of useless information I soaked up at my parents' dinner table. I memorized hundreds of rarely used words."

"I find that hilarious."

"And don't forget about spermatium and spermatozoid. I can kick your ass in Scrabble any day."

He laughed. "Thanks, but no thanks. Cole might take you up on the challenge, though. He also pointed out to me that germaphobe isn't in Merriam-Webster, but it *is* in the Urban Dictionary. Added, I suppose, because so many people use it. I can't bring myself to say spermatophobia because it makes me think of a fear of sperm. Cole absolutely does not have a fear of my sperm."

Shocked? Yes. I stepped back and gave him my best look of surprise. "Annnd now we're done." I started turning away.

"My bad. I'm sorry." I took a few steps away and he called, "Chris!"

I turned back around and chuckled. "I'm just messing with you. I'm shocked you'd say that in front of me, but I also think it's funny. I never thought about it sounding like a fear of sperm." I chuckled along with him. I wished Doug and I could talk openly like this. It was really nice, and kind of nerdy.

After the laughter subsided, I prodded, "So back to my question about his annoyance with you…. If he's angry, I mean really angry, then how would you know the difference?"

Ellis tilted his head and pursed his lips. "Good question. I think it's the way he looks at me. Cole has a temper, but when he's yelling at me, I see right through it. I see his quirky behavior and his irrational obsession with cleanliness, and I just want to kiss him… among other things." He grinned. "It's all about knowing him. I *know* Cole. When we're together I *feel* him in the room, even if we're not touching."

If Kat were here, she'd probably tear up. I thought Ellis's description was beautiful. I wanted to feel that same comfort with Alonzo, I needed to. Every time he'd been near me, I wanted to kiss him and more, like Ellis said.

"How do you know when the kisses are welcome, or when making a move will make things worse?" I didn't know who else to ask. Ellis had been so open, and I knew Doug would pester me for details I wasn't ready to share.

"When you spend enough time with someone, I think you learn the signs. Go slow, and maybe even let him lead until you're sure."

I thought about it and nodded slowly. *Let him lead.* That would take some self-control. "I guess I can do that."

"If you're not a follower by nature, I think you'll both sense it and figure things out, but if he's shy, then don't jump in the deep end like a cannonball. Ease into the pool from the shallow end."

I laughed. "This is getting thick with idioms and metaphors, but I get your drift. I'll take it slow and let him lead, maybe. I'll try."

"All you can do is try."

"Congrats on getting married, by the way. I look forward to meeting Cole. I've seen him watching the games. I can't believe I didn't know he was your husband."

"He's not a big people person, so he hates crowds. The noise bothers him. He normally leaves right after the game. He'll be at our home game on Saturday."

"Cool. Well, I gotta head." I pointed my thumb over my shoulder and nodded as I turned away.

Ellis was a really great friend. I think it was the fastest bonding I'd ever done with another human being. I'd known Ellis for all of three weeks, and I'd told him more about myself than I had my best friend. Maybe Doug needed more of my attention? I suddenly felt bad for excluding him when I had personal stuff to work out. I was used to doing it alone. Perhaps I needed to change. Except Ellis seemed to have all this knowledge. I wanted to know if he'd always been like that, or if his maturity occurred after graduation.

Ellis said good-bye, and I headed to the locker room showers.

FRIDAY MORNING after practice, I had difficulty getting out of eating with the guys. They were famished and headed right for the cafeteria, the same place I'd seen Alonzo several weeks in a row. I was hoping I'd catch him a fourth time and maybe get to talk a little more, but with the team around, I thought they'd poke into my business before there was any.

My worry was for nothing. As soon as they each caught a whiff of garlic and onions wafting through the air, they all charged like lions on the hunt. No one looked back to see that I wasn't following. I found Alonzo in the same side nook he'd been in last time. The way the room wound around, only three tables and three booths fit in that space, and the wall blocked the view from the main dining area. It really was a great spot because it had some privacy in a place where privacy was limited with the number of people revolving in and out.

Alonzo was reading when I strolled over and sat across from him. No gummy bears this time. When he didn't look up, I reached over, placed my hand on top of his book, and slid it away from him. Oddly, he paused before fussing.

"Why?" he asked, eyes harder than they needed to be.

Ellis was right. If I looked past Alonzo's glare, I saw hesitance. He hadn't snatched the book back. He hadn't grumbled that I sat without asking. Alonzo—wow, I didn't even know his last name—enjoyed my company, but he didn't want to trust it.

So I ignored it. "Mary Shelley's *Frankenstein*. Cool. You like the classics, don't you?"

His eyes darted, and he suppressed a smirk. I was learning to read his signs. Alonzo didn't like showing his emotions. He also didn't like direct eye contact, or maybe he liked it too much? I handed the book back.

"Look, I'm going to get something to eat. Please don't disappear on me before I get back. I want to spend time with you, and if fifteen minutes on Friday afternoons is all I get, then I want *all* fifteen minutes. Okay?" I stood next to the table and waited. I spoke softly, so he wouldn't take it as a command, but as a request.

Alonzo looked up and nodded.

I smiled and winked before walking away. I couldn't say I'd ever winked so much in my life, but it felt so fun to wink at Alonzo. I knew he liked it. And making him smile felt so good. I needed that feeling to carry me through until he smiled again because I had a suspicion he didn't smile often.

Cullen bumped into my shoulder and made me stumble sideways. "Hey, are you eating with us? We've got a big table over there."

He pointed and I followed his gesture. Doug, Marshall, Isaac, and Taylor waved, but so did Jill, Mindy, and Kat. *Argh.* I groaned to myself.

I didn't want to lie, but I also didn't want to explain the whole truth. I said, "I've got plans, but maybe tomorrow."

"Okay."

Luckily, he didn't press me for details. He walked over and sat, Doug gave me hand gestures and a weird face—he didn't look happy— and Kat blew me a kiss. Was she flirting, or being nice? Did girls blow kisses all the time, or was it only at me?

I didn't want to know.

I grabbed my double bacon cheeseburger, fries, and a drink, and headed back to the secluded spot on the other side of the wall. I breathed a sigh of relief when Alonzo was still there.

AFTER I ate and watched him read, I asked, "Take a walk with me?"

"Where?" he questioned.

"Does it matter?"

He closed his book. "I guess not."

His silence during lunch wasn't bad. In fact, I rather liked how comfortable it felt to be near him, even if he wasn't talking.

He slipped the small paperback into the pocket of his long coat and we left.

We walked around campus and then down a few streets that led away from the college and into the adjacent neighborhoods. When we'd successfully walked about four blocks away without the exchange of a single word, I felt the overwhelming desire to touch him. I hadn't tried for more than fingering the strands of his hair last week, but I seriously wanted to. Flirting with our eyes was great, truly, but my catalytic converter had been set at idle way too long. I was going to explode if I didn't move to the next gear. On campus, I was nervous. I got the vibe that he was too. Maybe neither of us was fully out to the world and it was as hard for him to relax as it was for me. I didn't know, but I needed to find out.

While we were walking, and before another ten minutes of hesitation clouded my afternoon, I reached over and touched his fingers. He stopped short and jerked his hand away, much to my surprise and dismay. You would have thought I'd stuck a spider on his hand or a bee up his sleeve.

"What are you…?"

I held both hands up in surrender, not that Alonzo was the enemy. "I'm sorry. I wanted to hold your hand. I didn't think I'd offend you. Maybe I was assuming way too much. I'm sorry." Punctuating both ends of my reason with an apology might have been over the top, but I thought it was needed.

His shoulders relaxed and he asked, "Why?"

I was slightly confused. "Why what?"

"Why would you want to hold my hand?"

Was he skeptical, naïve, or completely flummoxed? "Um, are you seriously asking me *why* I want to hold your hand? You have to know I like you."

"Yeah, but…." His narrowed eyes didn't help me discern his thoughts.

"Alonzo, I like you. I *really* like you." I'd never had to convince someone before. What else would I have to do to prove it?

"You do?" He was still baffled.

I stepped closer and smiled. "Of course! I can't believe you didn't know that. But yeah, I like you a whole lot. I can't stop thinking about you. I've wanted to hold your hand for weeks." I stepped another two inches closer. His eyes were huge.

"But you don't know anything about me."

"No, but I'm trying to. I know you like a band called Green Day because you've worn several different concert shirts since I met you. I even watched some YouTube videos so I'd know what they're like."

"You did?" His reaction wasn't the elation I'd hoped for, but he hadn't backed away.

In fact, the olfactory stimulation of his proximity made me weak in the knees. He smelled so good; it was hard not to think about stripping him here on the street and licking his entire body. I held my needs in check and moved at a snail's pace.

"Uh-huh." I reached out slowly, eyes locked with those brown depths that pulled me in, and slipped my fingers around his. Alonzo closed his eyes, and my smile grew wider than ever. I stepped closer and fully grasped his hand, my palm to his, fingers laced. I licked my lips while his eyes were shut and reached up with my other hand to cup his cheek. His eyes popped open.

We gazed into each other's eyes as if locked in time. I heard myself think it, and almost laughed at how sappy I'd become since I'd met him.

I read adventure novels, not romances, but somehow he'd cast a spell over me only a romance novelist could explain. I was sinking, helpless, trapped in those eyes.

I was breathing hard, thinking I might get to kiss those succulent lips. I wet mine again as I leaned forward, dipping my head to make up for the six-or-so-inch difference in height, but he pulled his face out of my grasp.

"No. It's too soon." Alonzo looked away, probably embarrassed.

I was disappointed, but I was happy he hadn't snatched his hand back. Maybe he was super shy. Or, maybe he'd never been kissed. At this point, we knew very little about each other. What if he'd only kissed girls, like me, and felt it was boring or unnecessary? I'd need to work on convincing him it could feel completely different. I was banking my whole gay life on the notion that kissing boys felt different because celibacy was out. I was a hot-blooded American male hell-bent on knowing someone in the biblical sense, and the female population was not on my "to do" list. I wanted a boy. No, that made me sound creepy. A man? No, I didn't want a daddy. I wanted a guy my age. I wanted *this* guy. Kissing could wait if the whole package was my reward.

I backed off. "Okay, that's fine. But can I ask you something?"

Alonzo nodded.

I tried humor. "Will you tell me your last name?"

He nodded again and ducked his head sideways. I could see him blushing even though he tried to hide his face from me. My heart thudded. I squeezed his fingers.

"My last name is Martin. Alonzo Martin."

He peered up at me shyly, blush tinting his skin, dimple in his cheek. I swear those eyes, in that moment, melted my heart. I would do anything to get him to smile at me like that every day. I tugged gently on his hand, and he stepped closer to me, smile vanishing as if he was caught off guard by my confidence. I took advantage of his nearness by slipping my free hand around his waist; but probably thinking me too aggressive, Alonzo turned his face away. Maybe he thought I'd take what I wanted.

I shushed in his ear and whispered, "I'm not going to hurt you. I'm not going to kiss you unless you ask. I don't know what happened to you in the past, but I'm not that kind of guy."

Alonzo leaned into me. With his face still averted, he put his hand on my upper arm as he dropped his head on my shoulder. I could feel him shaking. I carefully unfurled our laced fingers and wrapped my arm around his back. When he did the same, I held him tight for fear he'd vanish like smoke.

We didn't remain that way long, but holding him was like tasting the first piece of pumpkin pie in the fall. Everything inside me came alive, and I wanted more. I didn't dare make a move. I didn't want to scare him. I simply smiled into his beautiful brown eyes, released him against my natural urge to hold him forever, and motioned for us to walk again. We'd made a loop around the little neighborhood and headed back toward the college before he spoke up.

"Thank you," he said very quietly.

"For what?" If he was going to be quiet every time we were together, then he'd have to get used to me asking questions that required more than a yes-or-no answer.

He stopped walking, so I turned to face him. "What?" I inquired.

Alonzo was standing still, taking deep breaths. Calming his nerves, I assumed. A few minutes passed while I waited. I wasn't sure what I was supposed to do. I didn't know who to call if he had a panic attack or something. When he opened his eyes, he seemed different.

I asked, "Are you okay?"

He blinked at me, stepped into my personal space, and took my hand. He laced our fingers together and smiled. "I haven't been okay in a while, but I will be. I like holding your hand."

My smile took over my face. I mean, I don't think it could get any bigger because I was about to hoot and holler to the world that Alonzo Martin liked holding my hand! "Well that makes two of us." I lifted our joined hands and kissed the back of his. He closed his eyes again, but this time he smiled softly instead of appearing afraid.

"It's been a long time since I felt like this," he admitted. "It may take a while to believe I'm not dreaming."

"I've got forever, so you take your time." Again, I sounded like a sappy cheerleader writing a love sonnet. *Good googamooga.*

He snickered. I actually made him snicker. "Are you always so nice?" he asked.

"Depends who you ask."

"Doug?"

"He'd say I'm arrogant, but gifted."

Alonzo stepped into me again and laid his other hand against my chest. "Kat?"

I quirked an eyebrow. "How do you know all my friends?"

"I pay attention." Then he smirked. "And I eavesdrop. What would Kat say?"

I thought about it. "Hmm. She'd say I was a tease."

"Reason?" I love how his eyes twinkled as he asked. There was a more assertive guy in there begging to get out. I was sure of it.

I explained, "She thought we were dating last year because she doesn't know I'm gay." Since he was resting his palm over my heart, I rested my hand on the back of his hip.

"Do you think she'll be hurt when she finds out?"

"Maybe, but I doubt it. I think if we'd been hanging out at my parents' house all summer, then maybe, but it's been a while. Who knows? She might even suspect." Alonzo had a shine to his eyes I hadn't seen before, and he wasn't shaking. "Can I ask you a question?"

"Besides my last name?"

My turn to chuckle. "Yes. Will you go out with me?"

"Maybe."

"Playing hard to get? Okay. I can deal with that. Will you come to my game tomorrow night? It's at the football stadium this time."

He nodded. "Why there?"

"It has to do with availability. Our little bleachers don't hold many fans, but most of the time they're full. It's the football team's stadium, so they get priority. When they aren't using it, the soccer team can. It accommodates larger crowds and has a concession stand. Plus, the cheerleaders can cheer for us when they aren't cheering for the football team."

"I guess that makes sense."

"Will you come by my dorm room tonight? Maybe we could watch a movie or something? I brought my own television with me, even though the dorm has one in the common room and mine takes up a huge chunk of my space. Doug and I like playing Xbox and having my own TV means we don't have to share."

He shook his head. "I-I don't know. I have research to do tomorrow. Can I have a rain check for a different night?"

"As a matter of fact, I have every Friday night open. We play every Saturday, and either Tuesday or Wednesday during the week. We could have a standing date every Friday night if you want." I lifted my hand and touched his hair, smoothing it out of his eyes. His hair was kind of long for a guy, but clean and soft.

"I think I'd like that."

"Yeah?" I smiled more. I was a smiley kind of guy of begin with, but Alonzo made me smile differently. It felt like anticipatory happiness. Like Christopher Columbus first setting foot in the new world, I had all this energy bubbling up, dancing in place, waiting to explore all the wonders that were Alonzo Martin. Happiness needed a new definition.

"Yeah," Alonzo confirmed, releasing my hand, sinking into my arms, and holding me tight.

He turned his face inward this time, so I could tell he wasn't as scared as our first tentative hug. I could feel the warmth of his hands through my shirt as he caressed my back. His incredible scent—from soap, cologne, or natural, hormone-laden pheromones—washed over me, seducing me into a hazy dream about our future Friday nights.

When I felt his hot breath on my neck, I could have shot a load in my pants.

DOUG GRUMBLED at me as soon as I entered our room late Friday night. "It's about time. You've been in the shower so long I thought I'd have to call the paramedics."

I stopped in the middle of the floor and reminisced. I was mostly dry, with a towel wrapped around my waist, so I could glide my fingers over my bare chest and recall the joys of showering. "Yeah. It was nice."

"You were in there for like forty minutes. How did you even have hot water?"

I closed my eyes and tilted my head back. "I don't know. I don't think I did; my skin's cold."

"Okay. What's with the stupid grin? You look too happy. Are you on drugs?" I heard the disbelief in his voice, but it was hard to scoff when I felt so high. Doug knew better than to question my happiness; I was happy most of the time. He was questioning my new *reason* to be happy. Drugs? Not on your life.

"Oh, Dougie. I was done washing in the first five minutes, and then I came three times in the other thirty-five."

"That explains it."

I moved my hand lower and rubbed my stomach in gentle circles. "Have you ever had a perpetual hard-on? My woody would not relax, man."

"Yeah. I guess." Doug was sitting at his desk in his favorite rolling desk chair. I'd given it to him last year when his other chair broke. He liked being able to roll across the room for things and not have to get up.

I kept talking, dreamlike, remembering the feeling. "I mean, I kept stroking, and before I knew it I was shooting again."

Doug got annoyed. "Okaaay. So what's up with that? Did you meet a girl?"

I snapped out of the fantasy and questioned him. "Are you kidding me? A girl?"

Doug rolled his eyes. "Fine. Whatever. Did you meet a guy, then?"

I grinned again and nodded woozily. "Yeah. I can't stop picturing his hands on me. I close my eyes and I can see his fingers running over my nipples, I can feel his tongue licking down my chest, and his dick touching…. Oh, shit." I grabbed my junk through the towel and squeezed gently. "I'm getting hard again." I did a little wiggly thing with my lower body, hoping I could get my balls to calm down without another release. I didn't want to wear my parts out before they had the chance to perform. "Damn. Ever since I looked into his eyes, I can't stop thinking about him."

"That's nice," Doug commented blandly, rolling back around to his schoolwork.

I walked over to him. "Do you have a problem with me talking about someone? Because you've never held back when *you* met someone."

He turned back to respond, yet made a face and slid his chair backward. "Can you please put on some clothes? Your towel isn't enough to hide that." He fussed, recoiling and pointing at my groin.

It kinda hurt to see his reaction because this wasn't a playful jibe about my tented towel. We'd known each other a long time, and we'd seen each other naked. It was never a problem in the past; even after I came out to him, he hadn't treated me differently. But now….

"This isn't about me being happy. This is about me being gay. You're freaked because I jacked off about a guy, aren't you?" I asked him directly. No sense in skirting the issue if there was one.

"No!"

"It is!"

Doug shot out of the chair and paced. "Maybe it is," he snapped.

I felt gut-punched. I sat on the corner of his desk, mouth agape, careful not to display anything inappropriate as I watched him take five steps, pivot, and take another five. Back and forth. I didn't know what to say. It threw me. "Doug? I—"

"Don't." He stopped, rubbing his face and neck nervously. "I knew something was up. I could tell. You've been moody. You've been happy almost every day since the day we met, and yet I knew something was wrong when you started spacing out at practice. I mean, stumbling on a throw-in? Who does that? You've never done that. So I started watching you. I noticed where your eyes went every practice, and that's when I saw him, that guy in the black leather trench coat. He's the one, isn't he?"

I was speechless for the first time in my life. Doug was angry and hurt; I could tell by the quivering in his jaw. It only did that when he was really upset. Plus bringing up a throw-in that happened weeks ago was unlike him. Normally, I was the one to listen and comfort him, not the cause of stress. "I'm sorry. I should have told you I liked him sooner."

I saw the tears forming in the corners of his eyes before he abruptly turned around, arms crossed tightly over his chest. I jumped off the desk and went to him.

"I'm sorry, Doug. You're my best friend. I should have told you, but we hadn't actually gotten very far. I didn't know Alonzo was even interested in me until today. Before that, it was just a crush on a cute guy I'd met."

He slowly turned to face me. "Really? You didn't know anything until today?"

"No. I swear. He's really shy, and I wasn't even sure he was gay."

"But he is."

That seemed like a dumb question. I answered, "Yes. He's gay."

"But you haven't…." He left it to linger, but I got the insinuation.

I jumped back, offended. "Doug, you freaked out on me about jacking off in the shower and now you're asking if I fucked him? What the heck?"

He threw his arms out. "I don't know! I don't know what I'm supposed to say. Okay? This is weird. You like a guy. If I'd have met a girl, you would have asked me."

He had me there. I sighed, "You're right. And I did."

He nodded and pointed his finger at me. "When I went out with Cathy. The very first thing you asked was whether I nailed her."

I shrugged. "I was curious."

"Can't I be curious?"

"Are you?" I asked because he looked edgy.

Doug was tapping his foot. That wasn't a good sign. "Maybe. I don't know. Shouldn't I be?"

I stepped closer and put my hand on his shoulder. "Not if it makes you uncomfortable." I'd seen the signs in Alonzo to take things slow. Now I saw them in Doug. He wanted to be supportive, like I had been for him in the past, but this was all new. "This is new for me too, Doug. I've never felt like this for another person in my life. He's got me walking in circles, and stumbling on throw-ins, but this would be a whole lot easier if I knew you'd try… for me. Can you try to like him?"

He was jumpy, and his arms were still wrapped firmly around his middle, but he nodded.

"Good," I said, slapping his shoulder and heading over to the closet. I picked out a shirt and a fresh pair of underwear. "I plan on bringing him by next Friday night to watch a movie in our room. Can you handle that?"

He retook his seat at his desk. "I guess. As long as you don't fuck right in front of me."

I huffed. "Could you be more crude? Besides, that's not going to happen. Alonzo's shy. It took me three weeks to hold his hand. I'm not pressing for anything he's not ready for. I'm telling you, this guy does things to my insides. He looks at me and the world spins."

I slipped my shirt on over my head.

"Wow. I never thought you'd fall that fast."

"Fall where?" I turned to regard his incredulous stare. "What? Why are you looking at me like that?"

"Chris, forgive me when I say this, but you are the stupidest guy I've ever met."

Chapter 6
Baby Steps

I KNEW I would have a hard time not seeing Alonzo for a couple of days. I would miss him, but being the positive person I am, I thought I should focus on the bright side and dive into my classwork. Not having his phone number or knowing his class schedule would force me to do my own work because everything else was out of my control. I knew I'd see him Friday, but I hoped he would show up to some of my practices and maybe a game or two. I couldn't dwell on not knowing where he was the rest of the week. I had to do my own work.

So I planned to do it.

I even contemplated completing one project for my Modern U.S. History seminar two weeks in advance. It was only logical. I thought if I got everything out of the way while I was relatively boyfriend-free, then when Alonzo had time to spend with me, I figured I'd have nothing to distract me.

THE WORD "boyfriend" derailed me in the middle of a drill Saturday morning, and I passed the ball to the wrong person.

Cedric yelled, "Yo, Chris! This is a diamond drill, remember? Pass it to Marshall and then run around behind him to intercept a pass from Taylor. Get with it, man. Where's your head been lately?"

"Um, I'm sorry," I said, tapping the ball with my foot, putting it back in play in the correct direction.

After that drill was over, and before Coach Montgomery had us switch groups for the next, Doug cornered me. "Get your head in the practice, Chris. We have one win and two losses so far, and our next game is tonight. I need you in it. If you can't keep focused because of some guy...."

"Keep your mouth shut, Doug," I hissed in his face. "I'm the captain of this team. I will be in the game, whether or not I'm seeing Alonzo. You said you'd give him a chance." I was speaking quietly, albeit forcefully. No one was in earshot, but it still bothered me that we had to bring it up *here*. "If I was dating a girl you wouldn't have an issue."

"You don't know that."

"Don't I?" I gave him some attitude, sticking out my chest.

Doug hissed back, "Well, if it's all me, then why aren't you telling the team about him? How come we're arguing so no one else can hear?"

He was angry, but he respected me enough not to advertise his thoughts to the others. Doug was being a friend even when he was uncomfortable about the circumstances.

"I'll tell them."

"When?"

"When I can at least say I've been on one date. Can I have until then?"

"You haven't been on a date yet?"

"Not officially. I told you last night this is all new. We took a walk yesterday, and I threw gummy bears at him in the dining hall. Do those sound like dates?"

Coach yelled over to us, "Chris? Doug? Do you think you might join us for the rest of practice?"

"Yes. Sorry, sir," Doug answered. He rolled his eyes at me and huffed, "Fine. Go on a date first. I'm telling you, if you're this spaced out now, then kiss playing good-bye if you don't get your head on straight. And that's not a pun." He jogged into position with another group and left me.

I felt the tension, but I got his point. I was letting Alonzo pull my head out of the game, even though I'd convinced myself he hadn't. I wasn't sure what needed to change since I really thought I'd been doing well focusing on soccer and school while we were apart. I didn't want Doug to be right.

WE WON our game Saturday night against Rosemont, but I only scored once. I didn't see Alonzo, but I hoped he was there to see me score. Tuesday we had an away game against Muhlenberg and won, which brought our record up to three wins and two losses. Alonzo hadn't shown up, but it was an away game and I knew he didn't have a car. I should have lent him mine. By Friday morning, I was buzzing with so much anticipation I didn't even hear Doug talking to me until he slapped me on the side of my head.

"Ouch, what did you do that for?"

"Because I asked you the same question three times while you were staring at the wall like you're brain-dead. Snap out of it!"

He'd been irritated with me for almost a week. You'd think I'd have been used to it, but I wasn't. "I said I'm sorry."

"And I said I didn't care. You're an asshole; and until you start treating me like your best friend, I'm going to punch you in the head every time you ignore me." Doug punctuated his tirade by slamming the door upon exit.

I sat on my bed and thought about it. What he said was true, but I didn't know how to change it. He was my best friend, but somehow my uncertainty about my relationship with Alonzo clouded my judgment on everything else. Alonzo had become my only priority, and Doug was left out. This was serious when we hadn't even officially become a couple.

Basically, I was screwed.

I'd have to figure out something to make it up to Doug, but I had twenty minutes before I was meeting Alonzo in the dining hall and I needed to look good. Doug could wait.

WE ALWAYS met at 11:00 a.m. because he had class at 1:30 p.m.; he told me that much. I'd been under the impression he had somewhere to be at noon, but that was an assumption based on him running out on me. No, he explained, he'd been nervous. He had two and a half hours to spend with me, so this time I planned to make the most of it.

I reached across the table for his hand. Alonzo pulled it away.

"Not here. Someone could see."

He averted his eyes again. It was a sign I'd picked up on that he was anxious and maybe fearful. Something about being in public, maybe? I'd figure it out.

"Then let's go somewhere else," I suggested.

"Where?" he asked.

I'd noticed this was the first time he hadn't worn his coat, and he wasn't carrying a bag or his books. If Alonzo didn't bring a book, then he had planned ahead to give me his undivided attention. The knowledge pleased me.

"Come on," I said, waving him to follow me. I walked out of the cafeteria and continued down the sidewalk along the same route we'd taken the week before on our walk. Except this time, I took a left down Main Street instead of crossing Main and following the other road to the neighborhoods I preferred.

"Where are we going?" he asked when we'd crossed Pennsylvania Avenue.

"To a café I know. It's a good twenty minute walk, so I'm glad you aren't wearing the leather coat today."

"Yeah, I thought I'd try leaving it in the dorm. I sort of hoped we'd take a walk."

I smiled at him. "Yeah? Do you like walking?"

"I like the outdoors. I like the openness. Inside, with all those students, I start feeling claustrophobic after about fifteen minutes."

I walked at my normal pace, taking long strides, and I was pleased Alonzo kept in step with me. It wasn't like I was racing, but I wanted to get there as quick as possible so we could relax before heading back.

Knowing that lecture classes lasted more than fifteen minutes and usually had upward of a couple hundred students per class, I asked, "What about lectures? How do you stay in there with all the students?"

"I sit in the back. If I start to have a panic attack, I slip out without anyone noticing. I talked to the professor and he said he understood."

"That's pretty cool. It's nice that they're understanding. Not many professors are. You pay for the class, and many don't really care if you fail."

We crossed John Street and kept on walking. His casual tone and relaxed gait told me walking together was going to be the best way to get him to open up. This was Friday afternoon on the main drag through town; we weren't the only ones on the sidewalk, but here, Alonzo seemed comfortable. He even held the door for a lady coming out of a shop with too many bags. I didn't believe it was people Alonzo was afraid of, perhaps only their judgment.

"I didn't pay for my classes, the college did," he told me.

"Scholarship?" I asked the obvious.

"Yeah. I chose this college because they gave me the most."

"Sweet. So where are you from?"

"Nebraska."

"Wow. I've never been out there. I bet the mountains are gorgeous. Here, you have to drive like three hours west to even find elevation over eighteen hundred feet." We stopped and waited for the light to change at Center Street. "Did you ever go skiing?"

He gave me a look, which made me smirk because he was letting the walls down enough to glare at me, and not in the same ways he'd glared before. I could tell the difference. This was because I already knew the reason, and he was telling me I was stupid to ask. "Okay. Right. Broken ankle, compound fracture, plate and screws—the works. So you can't do any sports? What a bummer."

"Tell me about it," he grumbled. We crossed over Center Street and he continued. "Where I'm from everything is flat, so to answer your question, no—skiing is out. I think the closest ski resort is in Iowa, but I don't know. As far as sports, I can't do anything that requires pivoting or sharp turns because subconsciously I baby it. The doctor said it's psychosomatic. He thinks I fall all the time because I've talked myself into believing it's going to break again. I can't say if that's true, but I haven't been able to run much unless it's in a straight line."

I couldn't help pointing out his reaction when I touched his hair. "Like when you ran away from me the other week?"

Alonzo looked down. He'd been watching the street and sidewalk in front of us and turning his head to make eye contact with me as we spoke. Now, he was either ashamed or embarrassed. "Yeah," he said.

"Alonzo," I said, touching his shoulder and stepping in front of him. He stopped but didn't look at me until I lifted his chin. I stared into those fathomless eyes and rubbed the sparse hairs on his chin with my thumb. "Don't look away. Please. You don't have to answer anything you don't want to, and if the reason is embarrassing or stupid, I'm not judging you. I want to know you. So please, give me a chance."

Since I was gazing so intently into his eyes, I saw them watering before he turned away. He wiped his eyes and sniffled before turning back and moving in the direction we'd been walking. "Where are we going?" he asked.

I caught up the few steps and pointed. "See that tree with the lights wrapped around it? Birdie's Café is right there."

In another few minutes, we were there, but Alonzo stopped me from opening the door. "Is my eyeliner okay?"

I grinned. Not a question I hear often from a guy, but I had plenty of experience inspecting eyeliner on cheerleaders. I checked the black lines under his eyes. "Looks fine to me." Of course, I also had to caress his cheek while I had the opportunity. Then I opened the door. Inside, we walked down a little hallway that led to the order counter in the back. The walls were painted with murals, and Alonzo was looking all around. When we stopped at the counter and smelled fresh coffee brewing, he turned wide eyes my way. I knew he'd seen their pride flag on display next to the Human Rights Campaign symbol.

I nodded. "Yup. The owner declared it a safe zone." I winked.

I was betting on Alonzo's comfort level coinciding with his surroundings. No people meant no eyes watching and judging him for his actions. Here, ridicule over his sexuality was unlikely. Before we even stepped up to order, Alonzo slipped his hand into mine.

"Can I help you?" the bearded barista asked.

It took a second for my brain to catch up to his question, because as soon as I felt Alonzo's hand in mine, I pictured shoving him up against the wall and latching my mouth on his throat. Not in a blood-sucking fiend sort of way, but in a horny I-want-to-make-you-beg way that made my heart thrum and my mouth water. I heard the guy ask again before I blinked away the image, swallowing hard.

"Um, yeah, ah… I'd like the Councilman with a sweet tea."

"What size tea?"

"Large."

"What's that?" Alonzo asked. He was reading the menu, which was displayed on two sections of wall behind us, so I pointed to the listing. "That sounds like a ton of meat. Salami, capocollo, *and* pepper ham?"

"Think of it as a cold cut, but yummier because it has two kinds of cheese and banana peppers." It was my favorite. The coffeehouse offered many different coffee drinks, smoothies, and tea, as well as sandwiches and soup.

"Yeah. I guess. Can I have a BLT with avocado please?"

"What kind of bread? We have white, wheat, sourdough, and my personal favorite, pretzel rolls," the guy behind the counter asked in a sweet tone that snagged my attention.

Alonzo's voice went up. "Oooh, a pretzel roll, please, and a water."

"There's water on the counter over there." He pointed.

The guy was tall and slim, with a kind face and a large section of his hair dyed green. I'd seen him working in the coffeehouse several times, but I'd never engaged him outside normal business conversation. I thought his name was Lance, but I wasn't about to ask. He'd always been polite, but now he was smiling rather coquettishly at Alonzo—something I did not appreciate! I cleared my throat and gave him a hard stare. He shrunk back, knowing he'd been caught, and apologized. "I'm sorry. It's just your boyfriend is really cute." Boldly, green-haired barista guy then shifted his gaze over to Alonzo and said, "Your look is very Gerard Way circa two thousand four."

I didn't like the barista's smile, or the way he batted his eyes.

And damn it! Alonzo blushed. "Thanks. You should have seen me three years ago. I was more Billie Joe Armstrong around the same time frame; short punk cut, textured, with the right amount of hair product to spike it like he did. It's grown eight inches since then."

"I bet you were hot," said barista guy, smiling his very smiley smile, which I did not care for. I cleared my throat again, insistently. He coughed and glanced down at the cash register guiltily. "I'm sorry. Was there anything else you'd like?"

I narrowed my eyes, but didn't comment. I paid for our order and then led Alonzo to an area away from the flirtatious barista. "What was that?" I asked, as I sat.

"What?"

"Ah, *you*! Flirting with that guy."

He didn't deny it. Alonzo smirked and his cheeks colored again. "Are you jealous?"

"Hell yeah! I don't even have your freakin' phone number, and somehow this guy gets filled in on the history of your hairstyles. Who the heck is Gerard Way, and what does he have to do with anything?" I was irrationally hot, but I didn't think I'd ever felt a flash of anger so strong before. Jealous? I think I was about-to-punch-someone-in-the-face jealous.

Alonzo's low chuckle of amusement did not help me one bit. He stood up, walked back over to the counter, asked that guy, Lance—I definitely recall someone calling him Lance—a question I couldn't quite make out, and then returned. After he sat in his chair, Alonzo slid a piece of paper across the table to me. "That's my phone number."

I took it. "Oh."

Then he took my hand; a move I didn't expect because he'd been so hesitant up to now. "Chris, you don't need to be jealous," he explained very calmly. "His comment threw me because very few people make the right connections about my hairstyle, makeup, or dress. And no one ever flirts with me, ever, so I enjoyed it a little too much in front of you. But even if I like his smile and his green hair, that doesn't change how I feel about you."

I don't know where my anger went, but it vanished completely when he spoke so seriously and gazed so deeply into my eyes. In the history of our relationship, Alonzo has been shy and skittish, so for him to be so assertive, I really had no recourse but to forgive him for any and all playfulness with the nice-looking barista.

"Yeah?"

"Mm-hmm. He's cute, but…."

I squeezed his hand and encouraged him to finish because I had to know what could possibly be better than cute. "But?"

His telltale dimple appeared on his cheek again as he whispered, "But you take my breath away."

Time stopped right then, like a movie set on pause when the hero was about to leap out of a plane to save his one true love. "Wow." I covered his hand that held mine with my other hand, and then he did the same. So we were sitting there, clasping all hands in a big pile in the middle of the table, staring all googly-eyed at one another, when green-haired barista Lance brought over our sandwiches.

"I was going set these on the counter like we normally do, but you two looked a little busy to interrupt." His smile wasn't as flirtatious as before, like he knew he'd lost.

"Thanks," Alonzo said to him, while gazing at me.

I squeezed his hands reassuringly before letting go and sitting back, relaxed and awash with his adoration. He licked his lips and blushed, and that's when I realized I'd been staring a tad too long. We were there to eat, after all.

I took a bite of my scrumptious sandwich and started a random conversation based on Lance's comment. "Tell me, who's Gerard Way?" Because I surely didn't know.

Alonzo took out his phone, typed something, and handed it to me. It was a picture of a guy I didn't recognize. Textured black hair, styled so it fell across his face in long bangs, possibly razored to get the varied lengths. I knew this because my mom had taken me to a hair salon on numerous occasions to see what could be done about my wild hair. After several attempts, and way too many botched haircuts, we decided letting my hair grow, without restraint, was best. My loose curls were better left to themselves, which suited me fine. It was long enough to pull up into a knot on the top of my head during games, but not so long it fell past my collar. I liked my hair the way it was.

The young guy in the picture had features surprisingly similar to…. I looked up. "He kind of looks like you."

Alonzo nodded. "That's Gerard Way. He's the lead singer of My Chemical Romance, a punkish rock band that broke up in 2013." He took his phone back and typed in something else before handing it back. "This is Billie Joe Armstrong."

"I can see a resemblance here too. You have the same chin. That other guy's was too square."

"Yeah. Back in high school, I got into Green Day big time. I cut my hair like Billie Joe: short, spikey, stylish. I dressed like him. I even wore eyeliner like him. But Green Day is an older band, so not too many kids my age made the connection. I was born in 1996. By the time I was old enough to appreciate good music, Green Day had been around for over twenty years."

"Good point. That's why you wear eyeliner."

Alonzo nodded.

"What about the nail polish, trench coat, and combat boots? Your Green Day idol isn't wearing that in these Google images. He looks clean-cut and sexy in the picture with the red tie."

Alonzo grinned. "Yeah, he's a nice-looking guy. I have reasons for everything I'm wearing, but eventually I want to return to my punk look. I felt the most comfortable like that." He took a sip of his water.

"Punk, huh? You're not really goth *or* emo, are you?"

"No. But I understand why you thought that."

"So tell me… nail polish?" I stroked his fingers.

"My sister. She was painting her nails black one day, and I decided I liked it."

"What about the blue tip on your pinkie, which was red a while back?"

"Again, my sister. I like the black, but she paints the tip of my one finger whenever she changes hers."

"Then I take it she goes to McDaniel."

"Yeah."

"And you two are pretty close?"

He nodded. "In fact, no one has my phone number besides my mother and my sister."

"And now me."

He picked up his sandwich and, after a few bites, started telling me more details about punk bands. "If I asked a random person nowadays about a punk band, or a lead singer sporting guyliner, they'd probably name The Killers, Thirty Seconds to Mars, or Adam Lambert. None of them play punk rock like Green Day, but they all have the eyeliner in common. Some might consider The Killers a postpunk revival band, but I think they sound alt rock, same with Thirty Seconds to Mars. I think Billie Joe was the trendsetter with the makeup, and you often see photos of him with the tagline Real Men Wear Eyeliner."

I smiled and kept eating. I loved hearing him talk.

"Back in high school, Adam Lambert had released his second album, and it hit number one. I wasn't a big Adam Lambert fan because he was more pop and dance than anything else, so I didn't think people would link my look with his, because I didn't look like him."

"You looked like the guy from My Chemical Romance."

"I do now because my hair's gotten so long, but back then I looked like Billie Joe. Anyway, when Adam Lambert's record hit number one, there was talk in school about him being gay. Apparently he was the first openly gay artist to hit number one on the charts. Since I wore eyeliner, kids started calling me a fag. It didn't matter that I emulated Green Day's lead singer. If I'd shown them the picture I showed you, they might have understood."

"Were you out in high school?"

He shook his head. "Not at that time. It happened later, but I don't want to talk about that." He took a drink and washed down the last of his lunch.

I got the impression that high school hadn't been very fun for him. If Alonzo wasn't out and people called him a fag because of the eyeliner, or guyliner as he called it, then I could see why public displays of affection bothered him. I let it go. He could explain more another day. I picked up our trash and threw it in the bin. Before we left, we thanked the barista and then lingered by the door.

I took Alonzo's hand and kissed it. I explained, "Out there I'll restrain myself. In here I'm touching you as much as I can."

"Thanks for understanding."

Alonzo chitchatted the entire walk back to campus. He explained the differences between punk and alternative, pop punk, post punk, punk rock, pop rock, funk, grunge, and punk blues, as if there was such a thing. I didn't understand most of it, but I didn't care. I wanted to hear his voice, so whatever the topic of conversation, I decided I'd take it.

"Did you follow any of that?" he asked after I hadn't commented in ten minutes.

"Not really, but I don't mind listening to the explanation again."

He chuckled and shook his head. "What kind of music do you listen to?"

"Um, I'd rather not say." Thinking of the slip I'd made with Ellis, it was hard for me to admit to liking show tunes. I was a jock. I had a certain reputation to maintain.

Alonzo furrowed his brow.

I felt guilty and apologized. "I'm sorry, Alonzo. I've never told anyone what I actually like. Doug thinks I listen to Shinedown and Nickelback, which I do because those bands are great to work out to, but their music isn't my favorite. Doug likes All Time Low. He even has a poster signed by them hanging on his wall from the concert he went to back in May. I think they're a good band, but…." I stopped in the middle, hearing my own excuses as a whiny tantrum. Why wouldn't I tell him? He kept waiting.

We were back on campus, in the middle of the quad with the big tree, only minutes before we both needed to rush off to class, and he was looking at me with this puzzled expression.

I broke down. "Okay." I let out a breath. "When I'm alone, I like singing show tunes."

He paused and then burst out laughing.

I gave him an incredulous look and spat, "Thanks a lot, Alonzo!" I stormed away.

He rushed around and blocked my departure with a hand on my chest. He glanced around, I guess to see if anyone was watching, and then stepped closer. "I'm sorry. I wasn't laughing at you."

I felt the warmth of his hand through my shirt, and I know he had to have felt my heart thumping against it. "Sure sounded like it." It was hard to remain angry when he was so near.

"I was laughing at the juxtaposition of your characteristics. Not at *you*."

This time, it was me who burst out laughing. With that one word, he totally disarmed me. "Oh my gosh. You just freakin' used my favorite word!" I sighed. "Oh, Alonzo. I wish you didn't have class. I wish I could sit with you for hours and learn everything there is to know about you." I reached up to touch his face, and he stepped back.

My fingers stung as they touched only the air between us.

Alonzo stuttered, "I… here…."

"It's okay. One day at a time. Can we go to dinner? I have a car. We can go to Olive Garden. I think you'll like one of the waiters there." He gave me a look, so I answered his unspoken question. "He's gay."

"Really? There's more than one safe place?" His tone reminded me one more time that not every town was accepting of the LGBT crowd.

"Yeah. I'm not saying this whole town's gay, that would be ridiculous, but I know several people who work here who are. There's a lesbian on the other side of Westminster who owns a business, the guy at Olive Garden, the barista we already met because, besides flirting with you, I remember seeing him holding hands with another guy a couple months ago, and I think there are three homosexual people working at Target. I don't know exactly the kind of town you came from, but I don't think it's the same as here."

The tear in his eye caught me off guard. "For nineteen years, I only knew one other person like me and he didn't even live in my town."

He closed his eyes, and the tear rolled down his cheek. I placed my hand on his shoulder, but he flinched, so I removed it.

Then he said, "Give me time, Chris. I've conditioned myself not to feel attraction or show affection for so long it's hard for me to relax. But I swear… I like you a whole lot. I want…." He paused. I could tell he was breathing really fast, and he darted his eyes from me, to the side, to me again, and then over at the students walking by. "I really… liked hearing the barista call me your boyfriend."

I smiled, huge. "I did too. Alonzo, I—"

"Lonnie," he interrupted. "I like Lonnie. Or Lon."

"Lon?" I questioned.

His eyes grew bright. "Yeah. As in Lon Chaney. Although his given name was Leonidas, not Alonzo, but I don't have time to go into his biography right now, since I need to get to class. But call me Lonnie. Okay?"

"Why Lonnie and not Al?"

He stuck out his tongue. "Ehh! I don't like Al. It makes me sound like a plumber."

I grinned and nodded, "Okay. Lonnie it is." My uncle was a plumber and he made a load of cash, but I got the impression Alonzo wasn't mocking the profession, only his association with the name Al. I was fine with that, and I figured my uncle would be too.

Alonzo sighed. Maybe he enjoyed hearing me say his name? I hoped that was the reason for the bashful smile he gave me. Before I knew it, he said a quick good-bye and dashed off toward his class.

"Lonnie," I repeated to myself, watching him disappear around the building. He was my boyfriend.

WE HAD dinner at Olive Garden, and just like at the café, Alonzo relaxed. I'd figured him out. He was fine as long as he knew no one was going to give us a hard time for being together. After we ate and I drove us back to campus, I suggested a movie in my room, and this time he agreed.

I walked Alonzo to my dorm room, hoping it might develop into more. Ever since that moment on the sidewalk when we'd held hands, I'd wanted to kiss him more than I wanted to play soccer, and I think that had been my problem. The anticipation of progressing into the stage beyond small talk was eating me up. I needed to kiss him.

I stopped outside the door before opening it. Most likely, Doug was inside. If I wanted to steal a kiss, it had to be now, or I'd have to wait until I walked him back to his room, which would probably usher forth jests of how lame I was for walking my boyfriend back to his dorm room only five minutes away.

"Alonzo… I mean, Lonnie?" He smiled as I explained, "My roommate Doug might be in there, just so you know. Are you okay with that? He knows about me, and he said he'd like to get to know you." That wasn't exactly a lie.

He nodded and dropped his eyes to the ground. Lonnie had issues keeping his eyes focused, especially on me, when he was nervous. I figured that out the first day we officially met, and it remained consistent for weeks. I longed for him to be comfortable around me, and I thought we'd gotten to the "comfort zone," but still his eyes darted away every time. I needed it to end.

I hooked my finger under his chin and made him look at me. "You don't need to look at the ground. I won't bite, I promise." As he gazed back, eyes locking on mine, I could feel him shaking even through my slight touch. I rubbed my thumb across his chin and licked my lips. Lonnie looked away again, and it bothered me.

"Hey," I said, lifting his chin again. Only this time, I didn't continue touching him. I dropped my hand. "I know what you're thinking, and you're right; I want to kiss you. But if you're not ready for that, it's fine. I don't want to do anything you aren't ready for."

Lonnie locked eyes with mine again and replied, voice desperate, eyes pleading, "I *do* want to kiss you."

My heart swelled. "You do?" I asked, my voice lifting with the exhilaration of anticipation.

He nodded slowly. "Yeah. I'm just… scared."

I smiled. "Oh. Well, that's fine. We can wait. Just knowing you *want* to kiss me makes me happy. We can go inside and cuddle for a while. There's no need to—"

Lonnie cut me off with a kiss.

I had turned to grab the door handle when I felt his hands take a hold of my face on either side and guide me to him. His lips trembled against mine as I went with his lead, returning kisses for kisses. I slid my arms around his lower back and held him against me as he pressed me gently into the door. The notion that Doug was inside our room whispered in my thoughts, but Alonzo's kisses easily shushed them. The taste of his lips and the saliva that mingled between us tempted me to deepen our kiss, but I didn't. Alonzo was leading. If he wanted more, he could take it. I knew better than to frighten an already ruffled rabbit back into his dark hole of isolation, where intimacy was banned. No. If I wanted Alonzo—and oh God, did I—then I needed to accept what he offered.

After a few minutes, his kisses slowed, teasing and coy. When he pulled back, I had to steel myself from launching my body at him. My stomach flipped and my groin throbbed. "Wow," I said, not thinking clearly enough to say anything more.

"Was it okay?" he whispered.

His voice was so small, yet it zapped my attention back from "tear his fucking clothes off" mode to "slow the fuck down, you asshole!" I blinked and listened to my very savvy inner voice—the one that didn't think with my dick. *What did he say?*

"Okay?" I managed to say, still wading through the fog that was my brain.

He looked down at his feet and nodded, saying quietly, "Yeah? I was wondering because I haven't kissed anyone for a really long time and…."

Alonzo stopped talking when I cupped his cheek and pulled his face up to look at me. "Stop. Please. We're not teenagers." His eyes told me that, yes, he was indeed a teenager and I misspoke. I grinned, trying to ease the tension. "Okay, you are, but not by much. What I meant is… I'm not a kid who's going to text my cheerleader girlfriends and tell them what a lame kisser the punk kid is."

Alonzo pulled back a step. "That's not helping," he said defensively.

I realized what I'd said and the way he perceived it before he could take another step. I reached for his waist and pulled him into my arms. "What I mean is, you have nothing to worry about, Lon. That kiss made my arms tingle and my knees go weak."

His eyes brightened and he smiled, finally. "It did?"

I nodded. "Fuck yeah." *And having your body pressed into mine is making other things tingle.*

"I didn't even use my tongue."

"Tongue?" I swallowed the lump in my throat. The thought of what his tongue might feel like made me shiver. I'd kissed a couple of girls in the past, even passionately, but I knew it was never going to satisfy me, no matter how hard I wanted it to. I'd tried to like girls like Katherine and Candice, but none of them made me quiver like Alonzo did with only a few gentle kisses.

Alonzo grinned. I think he enjoyed my drooling. He touched my face tenderly and stared at each spot his fingers traced—my cheeks, my eyebrows, my jaw, my lips. He had me panting for more.

Alonzo glanced up and down the hallway. "Not many people walk by your room, do they?"

"No. The main entrance is around the corner." Alonzo relaxed comfortably against me, so I slid my hands lower on his waist. Not quite low enough to squeeze his ass, but I hoped he would appreciate my restraint. I told him, "Only the people who have rooms at this end of the floor use the stairs at the end of the hall. Doug noticed how quiet it is on Friday night when the other guys are out, so he does most of his schoolwork now."

"Can I kiss you again?"

"Lonnie, you don't ever have to ask."

His kiss was as gentle as before, only this time he flicked out his tongue. I opened my eyes and watched Alonzo's expression as our tongues slid playfully over each other in the open space between our lips. His face was so serene. I groaned involuntarily, moving my hands lower. I had to. I needed to. I squeezed his ass and pulled his groin tightly against mine, but my action caused him to pull away.

He stammered. "I-I'm sorry. I want to, but…."

"Shhh," I soothed, caressing his cheek. "I'm sorry. Whatever you want, whenever you want it. You say stop, we stop."

He looked so innocent and scared, which gave me an overwhelming desire to protect him. Something in his eyes, though, told me he wasn't afraid of me. It was something else that bothered him.

After a time, Alonzo said, "I think I'm gonna go."

I whined, "Go? I thought we were going to watch a movie. If you're worried about Doug, he won't bother us. He'll be fine." I hoped.

"It's not Doug. I just… I'm worried…. There are so many things about me you don't know."

"I'll wait. You tell me when you feel comfortable. I promise, I'm not going to jump you, even if I'm thinking about it. I can be on my bed with you watching a movie and not do anything."

Instead of timidity, or showing fear as I was used to, Lonnie lifted his eyebrow at me. Challenging. "And who said I was worried about *you*? What if I'm the one who bites?" And then he winked.

I swear my grin could have split my face if it got any wider. I'd not witnessed the playful side of Alonzo, and I liked it. "I like the sound of that. But, I also know you have more self-restraint than that. I trust you." I winked back.

Alonzo's smile was warm and genuine and made my heart explode. He had smiled so very few times since we'd met that each one was like witnessing a shooting star on a pitch-black night. I asked, "Can we give it a try? I promise I'll take my cues from you."

He grinned and agreed, "Okay."

When we walked through the door, Doug was sitting at his desk with his back to us. He said, "I was wondering if you were ever going to come in. I heard a thump against the door and almost opened it." He swiveled his chair around and paused when he saw us come in together. "Oh, hey." Doug waved.

"Doug… Alonzo. Alonzo… Doug." I gestured toward Doug and then back to Alonzo.

Doug got out of his chair, and they shook hands, but Doug looked around the room as if Alonzo had a huge wart on his nose and he didn't want to stare. I'd never seen him so unsure. "Seriously, Doug? I've talked about him all week. You've got nothing to say?"

He immediately stopped darting his eyes around the room and glared. "You're an asshole, Chris."

He snatched a couple of books off his desk and almost made it out the door before I stopped him. "Doug, I'm sorry. Stay. Please. We'll watch a movie with my headphones. I have a splitter so we can each have a set. Like you and I do sometimes when we play *FIFA* so the students in the next room won't hear at 2:00 a.m. Come on. Stay. I know you like your quiet Friday nights. We're only watching a movie."

Doug took a deep breath, turned around, and went back to his desk. Alonzo sat on the bed next to me with our pillows up against the headboard.

"Why does the screen have those funky spots," Alonzo asked and pointed.

Reluctantly, I explained, hoping he wouldn't think of me as an immature idiot. "They're from when Doug and I had a *FIFA* tournament and we threw gummy bears at the TV. They melted and stuck to the screen, and I haven't cleaned the mess off yet. But it isn't very noticeable when watching a movie, I swear."

Doug snorted, and so did Alonzo, but neither commented about our childish behavior. We watched half the movie sitting side by side, holding hands. He scooted closer and laid his head on my shoulder. Another fifteen minutes and I had my arm around his back, and he was leaning against my chest while we rubbed our socked feet together. Ten minutes after that, he lifted his head and gave me this desirous look that just about killed me. Neither one of us knew the movie even ended.

Alonzo glanced back at Doug, who was glued to his papers, his back to us, and then kissed me. This time, it wasn't lazy-lipped kisses and tentative licks. I didn't know why Doug's presence didn't bother him. Maybe he trusted my judgment, or maybe he was as worked up as me, but this Alonzo was very different from the guy who'd kissed me in the hallway.

His first lick inside my mouth had me groaning so loud I thought the neighbors could hear. I turned into his body and encouraged him with gentle tugs to slide down onto the mattress. Once we were both lying flat, we kissed deeply yet softly—my tongue stroking his with all the creativity my inexperienced mind could think of, yet playfully, without the bruising force of urgency. I kept my hands to myself and my hips in check. I could grind against him another time. I promised myself to let Alonzo lead, so I ordered little Jackson to stand down.

I slid one arm under Alonzo's neck and held his hand between our chests with my other. I knew I needed to hold on to something or unconsciously I'd probably move my way down to his dick, unzip his jeans, and before long we'd be naked and fucking, and that wasn't something Doug needed to witness. I had promised him. I had to behave myself.

Technically, this was our first date. Dinner and a movie. I couldn't give in to sex on the first date, could I? It sounded like a slutty thing to do. I wasn't like that. I told Alonzo we'd go slow. No thrusting. No sucking. No stroking. No coming. I could concentrate on the taste of his mouth and the tiny sounds he made. I could ignore his hand on my back, under my shirt. If all he wanted was to touch me there and nowhere else, I could keep our first date PG-13.

Lined up next to each other, bodies touching all the way down our lengths, my leg over his thigh, and his bent knee pressing into my hip, we kissed for what seemed like hours. When we ran out of breath, we disentangled and lay there gazing into each other's eyes until Doug turned off his light. Doug shut the bathroom door, and that was when Alonzo decided it was time to leave for the evening.

"I think I'm gonna go," he whispered in the dark.

"Okay," I said, hesitant to move from his side. "Think of me," I whispered breathily, desperate to remain where we were, yet hoping to subliminally send a message that would carry over into his dreams. "Think of me fondly."

It was silly, but I heard the overture of *Phantom of the Opera* click on in my head—that scene where Christine starts singing and everyone around her stops to listen. It was my one of my favorite musicals, and I guess part of me hoped Alonzo wouldn't think it stupid that my brain did inexplicable things like roll soundtracks in the middle of tender moments. I couldn't help it, any more than I could stop my eyes from noticing details that went unnoticed by others. My mind had always been overactive, unpredictable, and undeniably romantic.

He kissed me one more time and slipped from my arms and out the door.

The following week, our kissing was much less restrained.

Chapter 7
Wind's Change

HE KNEW they were kissing. It was predictable ever since that first night Chris had brought his new guy back to the room. They watched a movie, as Chris had promised, but long before the credits rolled Doug had dropped his pencil, reached down, and caught a glimpse of them locking lips. For a second, he stared. Like a train wreck he couldn't turn away from, he watched Chris leaning over the emo-guy's body, sipping at his lips. Kiss after kiss, and then a tiny glimpse of tongues tasting each other and playing as they licked.

Doug turned away. His stomach churned and he tasted the gastric juices in the back of his throat. He gagged, but held the bile down. Seeing them kiss made him feel queasy because it dredged up memories from long ago when a boy at outdoor school had kissed him. Doug had buried the memory and forced his inexplicable attraction deep, deep down in order to appear normal. He hadn't thought about it for years, even after Chris had come out to him. Now, witnessing Chris and Alonzo together made the memory surface. He didn't want to think about it. He wanted to avoid every thought like that he'd ever had. What could he do now when Chris was his best friend? He told Chris he'd give his guy a chance, but seeing them kiss was too much. If he ran for the RA's office and asked to switch rooms, what would that do to their friendship?

He sneaked a peek again and they'd stopped. Thank God. They were lying on the bed silently and Doug wasn't sure how long he could pretend he wasn't watching. He struggled to get through the last part of his assignment and then he turned his desk light off. Maybe they'd get a clue that he was getting ready for bed and that guy would leave.

When he returned from the bathroom, Alonzo was gone.

SATURDAY WAS an afternoon home game, so that meant a short practice in the morning. Chris was a different guy and Doug couldn't explain his anger about Chris's mood change. When Chris was spacing out during practice and in the games, it was easier to be angry because Chris needed to focus for the sake of the team. This morning, holy crap, he was focused. He was charging the ball, yelling instruction to his teammates, and moving his feet faster than Doug had ever seen.

"Switch!" Coach Montgomery yelled. "Pass it to Jackson!"

Doug watched the team move their positions strategically on the field, pass the ball to the opposite side thereby "switching" as the coach urged, and pop it over to Chris just as he lined up for the goal. Like a crescendo to a great piece of music, Chris faked right and then tapped the ball with his left foot sending it to the far side of the goal. The "home team" won!

Coach Montgomery called all the guys over to the bench and congratulated them on a perfect practice. Doug was sweaty and grumpy, but he listened to the pep talk with as much attentiveness as everyone else. Chris came up behind him when the chat was over and clapped him on the back.

"That was great!" Chris exclaimed, smiling his stupidly happy smile. It made Doug's mood sour.

"One more thing," Coach said before dismissing them. "Even though you did great in practice and our record is three and two, Penn State comes to our field four and one. Don't play confident. Play smart. Let them make the mistakes that come from overconfidence. Let their players foul you. I want sportsmanship and forward-thinking passes. Don't run the ball without knowing you have the shot. Pass it. We've got ten men on the field, plus Steve—use them. Chris and Cullen will take center, with Doug and Marshall completing the front line. Take them by force and pass the ball quick. Keep the other team guessing. Got it?"

"Yes sir!" the team yelled in unison.

As his fellow teammates dispersed and gathered up their stuff, a guy Doug hadn't seen before walked up to the coach. This guy wore glasses and a science-related T-shirt that said something about Einstein, but Doug was too far away to read the fine print. Doug watched as they talked a little too closely and a tad too comfortably. Then the coach waved Chris over and made introductions, which Doug could only hear part of. He thought he heard the word "husband," but that had to have been a mistake.

Chris shook the guy's hand and coach placed *his* hand on the small of the guy's back. Doug's gut squirmed. He had heard the right word. How could their coach be married to a guy? Sure, same-sex marriage had been passed in Maryland a few years ago, but Doug had never met anyone who'd really done it. They both looked so normal.

When Chris looked his way, he knew he'd been caught watching. Chris called him over. "Hey Doug, come over here and meet Cole."

He had to suck it up, bury his insecurities and disgust, and be nice. He shouldered his bag and wandered over to where they spoke on the sidelines. "What is it?" Doug asked, hiding the fact he already knew.

Coach Montgomery smiled and motioned to the man standing next to him. "Doug, this is Cole. My husband." He turned his attention to Cole and explained, "Doug is one of our offensive players. He's a very talented young man."

"Not like Chris," Doug mentioned, he wasn't sure why. Chris's skills spoke for themselves. Something about acting humble toward his own talent made him hope that the conversation would shift to soccer and not where he thought it would go.

"Oh," Cole said. "Well, seeing how I'm not the expert, I'm sure you'd both look stupendous to me. Ellis is the one who plays soccer. I'm not that coordinated."

Chris was standing there with this stupid smile plastered to his face. He was watching them so intently. Chris even felt the need to fill Doug in on some of the conversation he'd missed. "Did you know they met in college? They were roommates. Ellis was Gettysburg's star player a few years ago. I remember seeing his name on a banner in the gym when I was scouting prospective schools." He addressed Ellis, "I heard you were awesome. Why didn't you play professionally?"

Chris asked so innocently, though he had to know only a small percentage of college soccer players advance into professional sports. Doug rolled his eyes, thinking Chris naïve.

Ellis answered, "Because I knew I wasn't good enough to play for the teams I dreamed about." He moved his eyes over to Chris. "Like Real Madrid." Chris grinned and shook his head as if there was something hidden in that comment that only Chris understood. Doug felt left out, again.

Coach continued, "I was rational about it. I was good, but there were better players than me. To be the guy professional scouts noticed, you needed to be the best player no matter who you were playing against. You've gotta be the one player that stands out. I knew that wasn't me. I majored in English and planned to make a life for myself doing something else I enjoyed: teaching."

Cole added, "It also didn't help that he broke his leg during his junior year and didn't get back to running full speed until almost the end of his last season."

Ellis sarcastically remarked, "Thanks, L-D. I'm glad I have you on my side."

Cole said, "Only pointing out the drawbacks of sports injuries."

Doug smirked, and hoped no one noticed. To be caught enjoying their banter might be misunderstood as acceptance. Doug wasn't accepting, he was tolerating.

Of course, Chris returned to the original point. "Either way, I bet you were awesome to watch. Your name was on a banner at the school. To me, you're a soccer legend."

Ellis smiled and looked to the side. He looked embarrassed or something. What was the big deal? So his name was on a banner, Chris was just talking a bunch of nonsense.

Cole asked, "Why don't you show them your moves? You don't get to play enough and you told me this team was really good."

Ellis looked around. "There aren't many guys left."

Doug checked. Preet, Josh, and Cedric were talking at the other end of the field. If Ellis played with Chris and himself they could do a little three-on-three challenge. "There are some guys over there," Doug pointed out. He may not enjoy the thought of Ellis and Cole *together*, but playing soccer was always a plus.

Chris called them over. "Guys, we want to play a game," he explained when they joined the others. "Ellis hasn't played soccer for a while and we thought it would be fun."

"With seven guys?" Preet asked.

Cole said, "Six. I'm not playing."

"Okay," Cedric said. "Three on three. Teams?"

Doug stepped in and offered his advice. This thing was going to happen so he might as well speak up. "How about me, Coach, and Cedric, against Chris, Preet, and Josh? That way we separate Chris and Ellis, and we get the better defender." He glanced at Josh. "No offense."

"None taken."

"We're going to do this?" Coach Montgomery asked, looking around excitedly at the players.

"Heck yeah," Chris said, retrieving his personal ball from his gear bag.

Chris scooped it up with his toe, bounced it on his knee twice, let it drop to his over foot and then passed it to Josh. Josh caught it with the same knee-bouncing action, alternated bounces on either knee and then passed it to their coach. Ellis caught the pass with the inseam of his right foot, jerked it up into the air in front of him, tapped it with his other foot sending it over his shoulder, but instead of turning around he leaned forward slightly and let the ball connect with his heel as he lifted it off the ground. The ball popped back over his shoulder, he kicked it with his toe, and as it came back down Ellis lunged forward so his body was parallel to the ground and caught the ball on the back of his neck.

Cedric gaped. "Coach, why haven't you showed us these mad skills, man? I thought watching you run and pass was incredible, but now?" Then he whistled.

"You can call me Ellis. 'Coach' sounds so formal, especially when I'm not much older than you."

Preet added, "You really need to join in our drills. I think the team would respond better knowing you're the bomb."

Ellis grinned softly. "Thanks."

Chris said, "That was cool, but I want to see you play."

Ellis asked Cole, "You don't mind waiting?"

"Watching you play soccer was one of the things that attracted me to you in the first place."

Ellis blushed.

Preet eyed them curiously and asked, "Attracted? Does that mean you two are... what? Boyfriends?"

Doug thought maybe he had another player who felt like he did, unsettled and slightly grossed out. He waited for the next comment, hoping the other guys would say what he was thinking, that they were disgusting.

Ellis corrected, "No. We met in college a few years ago, and got married this last June." He tenderly touched Cole's back. "Cole's my husband."

"Really?" Preet asked.

"That's neat," Josh said. "My parents met in college too."

"Mine met in high school," Chris added.

"So he's married," Cedric said. "I'm sure Cole's a great guy, but if we intend to play soccer before we have to come back *later* and play soccer, then we best get a move on."

He had a point. They had a home game against Penn State at 2:00 p.m. The guys jogged out into the middle of the soccer field and squared off, Doug standing with them, although thinking about the other players' reactions. They weren't bothered at all. In fact, they went from "oh, you're married to a guy" to "let's play soccer" in the span of three seconds. Doug didn't understand it.

They played soccer, three-on-three-style, for twenty minutes before it was necessary to take a break so they could rest before coming back on the field for real.

Doug walked back toward the gym with Cedric.

"So, Cedric, it doesn't bother you?"

"What doesn't?"

"Coach being… you know… gay."

He shrugged. "Why should it? What he does with his private life is none of my business."

"But what about it morally? Don't you think homosexuality is wrong? Don't churches say that?" Doug didn't understand the root of his own distaste for it, but he hoped talking to Cedric would help.

"Some do," Cedric said. "But there are also churches that don't. Personally, I think it's up to an individual to work out those details with God. It's not up to me to tell someone how to live their life. I don't want someone telling me what I should do. I know plenty of people who give me shit for datin' a Middle Eastern girl. I say, fuck them. I'm happy."

"Dating Kadija is not the same thing as two guys together."

"Sure it is. I remember two years ago, sitting in the high school auditorium, getting the antibullying talk. They had a video and everything. What stood out to me the most was how many of the arguments applied to me. I was dating Amira back then, so Kadija doesn't know about this, but I was hounded all the time about blowing up the school or joining terrorist groups."

Doug was horrified. "What? That's sick! Why would they say that?"

"Because the girls I was attracted to were stereotyped and profiled as Muslim activists or some dumb shit. People are plain stupid, Doug. Amira's parents were Hindu, but she was born in America. I cannot tell you how many times I took the heat because some asswipe thought I was a terrorist because of my girlfriend's heritage."

Doug wasn't making the connection. "But how is that the same as Coach Montgomery? Don't you think he's sick? What if there were other guys on our soccer team who like to take it up the ass? What about then?" He cringed with his own terminology. It slipped out, even though he hadn't thought that deeply on what two guys might actually do. What Chris might do, or had already done.

Cedric stopped walking and faced Doug. "Look. They're just people. Okay? And people deserve the right to be happy. I'm not saying that murderers that enjoy killing should be allowed to do it. I'm not a wacko who thinks pedophiles and sex offenders should be free to do some sick shit that hurts other people, especially kids. What I'm saying is that these guys are consenting adults, who got married for fuck's sake, and they deserve the right to live their lives. Coach is a kick-ass player, Doug. That's all I care about. If there happens to be another gay guy on the team, I don't care. It's his life. If his life contributes to our team going all the way and taking the championship, then that is the part of it I care about. Personal lives are just that—personal."

Doug stood there, speechless, as Cedric poked his long finger into Doug's chest as a way of punctuating his point. Then he turned and walked away. Doug had no rebuttal. Cedric outlined it perfectly. He glanced back and caught a glimpse of Ellis in the parking lot, far away but close enough to make out, carrying Cole piggyback. He could picture Ellis's smile as he dropped Cole next to the car door and kissed him before running around to the other side.

Doug felt bad for judging him so harshly. Maybe he was just a guy who deserved finding happiness, even if it was with another guy.

THE GAME against Penn State was incredible. Chris was thunder and lightning—striking hard and fast without warning. He scored five times with two assists. One goal was on a corner kick that curved at just the right angle, which the goalkeeper tapped but could not deflect. The modest crowd rose to their feet when the ref blew the whistle in three short bursts.

As the fans left the stands of the football stadium, Doug noticed two sets of people waiting for Chris: Chris's boyfriend standing next to a girl dressed in a black concert tee and jeans, and Chris's parents. Doug lingered in the background, but followed Chris to see whom he might address first. Chris went to his parents.

"Hey, Mom. Hey, Dad," he said.

Dressed in jeans and a Ravens shirt, Chris's father was as happy as he always was. "Chris! That was the best soccer I've seen you play yet, boy. Astounding! The movement you put on that ball surpassed David Beckham himself."

Chris got his smile from his mother, but his mirth from his father. They were one of the happiest married couples Doug had ever met. His own parents were happy, but they certainly had heated discussions from time to time. Doug liked Chris's folks. He had a feeling that Chris's new love interest might not go over well, though, as Mr. Jackson had talked for years about Chris marrying a cheerleader. In high school, he pointed out the ones on the sidelines that had the cutest smile. In college, Chris had taken Katherine home many times. Doug knew they assumed Chris had been dating her. This was going to be interesting.

"Chris," Mr. Jackson said, clapping his son on the shoulder. "I saw that blonde you're dating, cheering you on. How come the squad isn't at every game?"

"They also cheer for the football players, Dad."

"See, if you'd played football then your girlfriend would be at every game."

Chris's mom commented, "Honey, I told you they aren't dating anymore. Isn't that right, Chris?"

"Well, no, but we weren't dating before. We're just friends."

"Chris has to keep his options open, right, son. I bet that one over there is a sweetheart. Just look at that smile."

Doug glanced over, as did Chris.

"No, Dad, Mindy's too immature. She only *just* turned eighteen and her vocabulary is seriously lacking. I'm not interested in her like that," Chris argued, but Doug thought Alonzo couldn't be much older than that. Doug knew age was not Chris's issue with Mindy. Doug even heard a hint of whining in Chris's voice.

Then his father pointed out Lilliana. "What about her?"

Doug snorted.

Chris turned and Chris's mom held her arms open. "Douglas, it's so nice to see you. How are your parents?"

Doug hugged her and answered. "They're fine."

"I meant to call your mother last week and have lunch. I'll make sure I do that tomorrow." She took out her phone and most likely made a notation on it.

Doug heard another familiar voice to his left. "Um, Chris. I wanted to introduce you to my sister." Doug turned around at the same time Chris directed his attention to Alonzo. The boyfriend. Doug didn't envy his friend's position at all.

"Um, hi," Chris hesitantly said. He held out his hand, as did the girl.

"Introduce us to your new friends, Chris," Chris's mother said. "I don't believe we've met them."

Chris's ever-pleasant smile vanished and Doug could have sworn his skin looked paler. His voice even wavered as he introduced them, "Mom, Dad, this is my friend Alonzo and his sister…."

"Stephanie," Alonzo offered quietly.

Doug saw the hurt plainly on Alonzo's face. To Chris's parents he probably came off shy, which he was, but Doug was standing close enough to see the shift in his expression. "Friend" was not the word he wanted to hear.

The rest of the small talk continued, short as it was, but Doug zoned out. He felt bad for Alonzo.

Doug stepped away, quietly, and walked back to the locker room to change. It was early, and he figured he could get a bite to eat in town, because he suddenly had too much on his mind to be around people. It was Alonzo. He seemed so withdrawn, and that was coming from a guy who didn't really care to think about what other guys were feeling… ever. Doug cared about Chris, and maybe Cullen, but beyond that he never thought about guys at all.

Doug scoped out women, and studied hard so he could make a lot of money and date lots of women. Everything changed when he saw the look on Alonzo's face when Chris introduced him as his friend.

Doug showered, left the dorm, and walked pensively down Main Street. He wasn't thinking about where he was headed, only that he needed to think good and hard about why he was so grossed out when he'd seen Chris kissing Alonzo. Or when he thought about what they might end up doing together. Chris and a… guy. Together. Touching. Naked.

Fuck. Why was he hard thinking about it?

Doug pinched the waistband of his jeans and jiggled, adjusted himself. He shook his mind clear only to realize he was standing in Chris's favorite coffee house. Luckily he knew where the bathroom was and went right for it. He splashed some cold water on his face and stared at his reflection: short brown hair, hazel eyes, perfectly straight teeth, square jaw, and a dimpled chin. He was a good-looking guy, right? Yet Chris had never shown an interest in him. Chris's eyes lit up over Alonzo, an emo-looking, black-coat-wearing, introverted homosexual, who….

Doug derailed his anger trail. Calling Alonzo bad names wasn't fair. Doug's issues were with Chris. Chris had replaced him with another guy. A guy he could laugh with, snuggle with, and have sex with. Doug wasn't that kind of guy, so why did he feel so jealous?

His hard-on subsided, so he peed, washed his hands, and left the restroom. In the back of the coffee shop were a couple couches and table in between. Many times patrons sat and read or played chess, but tonight, one of the employees Doug recognized was lounging back on one couch. *His name's Lance, I think.* Right as Doug walked by him, another guy walked over and kissed him on the lips before walking off.

Doug continued past him and found a table to collect his thoughts. *Is the whole damn town gay?* It was a silly question, but one he couldn't help asking. He'd been struggling with how he felt about homosexuality for years. He certainly knew what it meant, but it never meant anything to him personally until the last few days. Chris kissed a guy, he liked it, and he was happier than Doug had ever seen him.

Doug needed to accept it, or lose his friend.

He ordered a sandwich and a mocha, and sat at a table by the window away from the gay employee who might know Doug was thinking about him and the kiss he'd witnessed. The guy was kind of cute and Doug liked his beard and his green hair. As soon as the thought flashed through his mind, Doug dropped the sandwich and buried his face in his hands.

Something is wrong with me.

For the first time in his life, Doug pondered the question, "Are people born gay, or are they converted?" *Because I don't understand why I feel like this. Maybe Chris's germs are getting on me.*

IT TOOK Doug a week of avoidance to bring up his frustrations with Chris. Their schedules overlapped and they normally only saw each other at practice. Now this was Friday and Doug assumed Chris would be going out with Alonzo unless the strained introductions on Saturday had caused friction between them.

When Chris entered their room, Doug asked, "Are you seeing Alonzo tonight?"

Chris dropped his towel and slipped on some underwear. Doug would have looked away, but he didn't because he wasn't sure of his reason why. He'd seen Chris naked and it hadn't bothered him until that time recently when Chris described his fantasy in the shower a little too vividly for Doug. Doug hadn't thought about him like that since high school. Back then, he'd developed a secret man-crush on Chris after he'd started growing facial hair and Doug hadn't. He'd been afraid of screwing up their friendship by telling Chris his scruff was hot. Doug had told himself it was jealousy and nothing more. A little curiosity mixed with adolescent hormones, right? Thinking about boys was wrong for straight guys, and Doug didn't do it anymore. Chris was with a guy. Why couldn't Doug let it go?

"Yeah," Chris said, adjusting his waistband and then reaching for his jeans.

Doug nodded. He sat on his computer chair and swiveled it back and forth slightly while he thought about what he wanted to say next. "So…. Alonzo isn't angry about Saturday?"

Chris zipped his jeans. "Why should he be angry? We have away games all the time. I can see him before we leave for Bridgewater."

"No. I meant *last* Saturday. When you introduced him to your parents."

"You heard that?"

"I was standing right there. Your mother hugged me."

"Oh, right."

"I heard you use the 'F' word."

Chris was defensive. "No, I didn't. I'd never say 'fuck' in front of my mom."

Doug explained, "No, idiot. You introduced Alonzo as your *friend*."

"Oh yeah. Lonnie wasn't happy about that." He pulled on his shirt and then fingered through his crazy hair while looking in the small mirror on the back of his closet door. Doug didn't understand why he preened when his hair never looked anything short of a wild mess.

"He seemed upset," Doug said, fishing for details.

Chris sat on the bed and grabbed his shoes. After putting on his white socks, he slipped on a sneaker. "He was. I hurt his feelings, but he was man enough to listen to my reasons. Although, it took until Monday for him to agree to talk to me."

"What did you tell him?"

"The truth. I'm not out to my parents, which he already knew. I asked for some time to work up to it and he agreed. He said coming out hadn't been his choice, so he understood my need for it. I think he's been through some shit. I wish he'd tell me."

"Maybe he wants to forget it. Some people like to bury their past." *Like me. I don't want to think about outdoor school and that boy ever again. What was his name? John? I don't know.*

"Maybe. Listen, are you going to be here tonight? I want to bring Lonnie back to our room. He said he's not keen on snuggling in front of his roommate. He'd rather come here. I don't want to freak you out if we start kissing." Chris stood up and looked at Doug, waiting for an answer.

"I'm not bothered by it."

"The hell you aren't. I saw you watching Ellis and Cole. You looked disgusted. I can't imagine what you'd do if you saw *us* kissing. I don't want to make you puke."

Ironically, that was just how he'd felt last Friday when he'd seen Chris kissing Alonzo, and then again at the coffeehouse with the bearded barista, Lance. The idea made him sick, but it also fascinated him. Plus, how did someone know they were gay? "Can I ask you something?"

"Sure."

Chris was always so relaxed and casual about things. Doug wished he had the same attitude in life. "Um, just don't get mad."

"I'm not."

"Have you always been gay? Or was there this time when you decided to try it?"

Chris snorted and half laughed, but stopped himself when he noticed how Doug *wasn't* laughing. He was dead serious. "Oh, I thought you were joking. You really want to know."

His stomach quivered and he nodded. "Yeah, I do."

Chris sat again, and got serious. "Well, as far back as I can remember I've liked boys. I've had crushes over the years and none of them involved girls."

"Like who?" His curiosity peaked.

"Um, well… don't tell anyone, okay?"

"Okay."

"John Turcotte in third and fourth grade. Michael Irwin in fifth grade. Then in middle school, I used to have a thing for Cullen."

"Cullen Rafferty? Why?"

"I liked his green eyes. I also think Taylor Decovitch has a great ass, but I'm not attracted to him."

Curiosity poked Doug to ask another question. "Have you ever… been… attracted to… me?"

Chris cocked his head. "Why do you want to know that, Doug?"

"Because. You've been attracted to all these other people and I wanted to know if there was something appealing about me?"

"Of course there is. And if you have to know, then yes, I was attracted to you in high school. But you're straight, Doug, my crush was a silly fantasy that wasn't going anywhere."

"Did you ever think about me like you do Alonzo?" *Like in the shower? Or in bed at night?*

"No." His answer came instantly. "Alonzo is the only guy I've thought about this much, this long, and this deeply."

"But you've jacked off in the shower before. Every guy has. You haven't thought about…."

He jumped up, alarmed. "No! I picture Johnny Depp or Hugh Jackman. I've never thought about my friends like that. It's wrong. Doug, is there something you're getting at? Are you…. Are you jealous?"

He hung his head in shame. Chris had figured it out and he didn't want to look at him. Chris kneeled down in front of Doug's chair and squeezed his hand. "Doug, please don't take this the wrong way, but I'm not attracted to you. You're my best friend, and maybe I haven't acted like one lately, but that doesn't mean it isn't true. No one can take your place, not even Alonzo. What I feel for him is completely different. Just because I'm not having sexual thoughts about you doesn't make you less important to me."

Doug looked him in the eyes and forced himself to ask, "What if I was gay?"

Chris gave him a piteous grin. "Not even then. I don't feel that spark when I look at you. Even though you have great eyes and a killer smile, I've never felt for you the same thing I feel for him. It's that simple."

Doug got it. "So you're bringing him by tonight?"

"Yeah. We've had some time to cool off since Saturday. He's no longer mad at me. Tomorrow we're meeting his sister for breakfast. Tonight, I want to hold him against my chest while watching a movie on my bed."

"No sex?"

"No, man. He's not like that. Plus, I think waiting until it feels right for both of us is best."

Again, he nodded somberly as if none of Chris's answers satisfied him.

Chris stood up and walked over to the door. "I don't understand what's going on with you, but I'm not comfortable hanging out here if you're going to act weird when I bring Alonzo. Can you just get your shit together, please? Or tell me and I'll go someplace else."

"I'll be fine. Really. You can bring him by. I'll take off when you get here."

Chris nodded. "Okay."

SEVERAL HOURS later, Doug heard muffled sounds on the other side of the door. He knew it was Chris and Alonzo. He knew they were kissing. It was inevitable and predictable. He approached the door and hesitated to open it. Was he jealous of Alonzo's presence in Chris's life, or did he want what Alonzo had with Chris?

Doug cracked the door like a peeping Tom. Chris had his arms wrapped around Alonzo's slender waist, and Alonzo's arms were around Chris's neck, one hand fisting Chris's hair. Doug couldn't help but wonder if kissing a guy was that much different than kissing a girl. If it was, would it make a difference?

Chapter 8
Getting Naked

I WALKED Alonzo down the hall to my dorm room Friday night after taking him to dinner. I'd texted Doug to see if he planned to go out, and he said he didn't. I thought I'd warn Alonzo about a possible change of plans. "Doug is inside," I explained when we stopped outside the door. "He's been acting weird lately, so if he doesn't seem amicable about having you in our room tonight, then we'll have to go into town to catch a movie. I hope that's okay."

Alonzo was quiet. He'd been quiet all week because of my woefully inadequate introductions last Saturday. I mean, I turned and there he was, sister and all, fifteen feet away from my parents and inching closer like a spilled cup of coffee next to my computer. I had to stop it, imagining the introductions would be as disastrous as coffee on the keyboard.

I leaned on the wall next to the door holding Alonzo's hand. I tugged gently and he relaxed into my embrace. I held him there, silently, reveling in the feel of his arms around my body and his head on my shoulder. I could feel his breath on my neck when I slid my hand up his back to touch his hair as I spoke to him. "I'm sorry about Saturday."

"You said that," he whispered.

"I wasn't going to come out to my parents at one of my games."

"You said that too."

I knew I didn't need to recap Monday's conversation. Alonzo wasn't Kat. Alonzo was intelligent and often recalled things verbatim. After I'd finally gotten a reply text, Alonzo and I met on campus and he listened to my apology. I felt like a turd, but he said he understood and we agreed to try again. Not seeing each other the rest of the week, though, made me doubt his honesty. Dinner had been fine, and he smiled softly as we spoke, but I could tell something was holding him back. We were in public, so I associated his restraint with prying eyes all around us. I knew he needed to be in a place where he felt comfortable to talk. Most places, Alonzo was reticent.

"Will you kiss me?" he asked so quietly I almost didn't hear him.

"What?" Surprised, I pulled my chin back to look down at him as Alonzo lifted his head off my shoulder. I didn't have time to question him again before he pressed his lips to mine. One good, sound kiss and Alonzo pulled back.

His timing seemed odd, as did his question. "Have you had other boyfriends?"

"No." I thought we'd covered that before.

He regarded me as if pondering my response. I guessed I answered correctly as his eyes brightened and a smile gradually curved his beautiful mouth. Then he leaned into me again, lifted up on his toes, reached around my neck, and kissed me. His kiss was strong, deep, and passionate. I didn't have time to think about being in a hallway, or what would happen if Doug came out of the room and found us. Alonzo's slender frame pressed all the way down my body, making me ache to grab his ass, but I held back because of the way he'd reacted the last time I'd squeezed it.

I was getting into this unexpected frenzy when the door opened to my right and Doug coughed. I suspected he knew what we were up to before he opened the door.

I want to say we got naked on my bed after Doug left us alone, but Alonzo's burst of passion fizzled after we turned on a movie. It was fine. I enjoyed holding him, and this time I snuck my fingers under the hem of his shirt so I could rub his stomach. Lucky for me, he's not very ticklish.

ALONZO'S SISTER looked just like him. She used dark eyeliner and had black hair, which she pulled into two ponytails. She wore a black leather choker with a silver pendant of the Eye of Ra that I thought would look sexier on her brother. Alonzo always wore a leather wrist cuff with a silver hammer on it that added to his gothic appearance. Everything about him was a mix of fashion trends; therefore, I had a hard time classifying him into one. Maybe that was his point? Alonzo wore what he wore because he liked it, not to fit into a social group.

His sister seemed equally eclectic. Her black lipstick popped against her pale skin. Her eyeliner was far more dramatic than Alonzo's, and her clothes were more gothic. I never realized how much I liked the look. Hanging with perky pink cheerleaders, whose mission was to wear the latest fashion and curl their hair so they all matched during competition, had conditioned me to see most girls as cover models of *Elle* magazine. In contrast, she could be featured on *Rolling Stone*, and if I were straight, I'd be totally into her.

We met at my favorite coffeehouse and found a table in the front room.

"You remember my twin sister, Stephanie Sarzo?" Alonzo asked.

"Of course." I smiled her way, but his introduction befuddled me. "Why the different last names?"

Alonzo shrugged. "Our mother remarried. Steph hates our real dad. It's a whole big thing. I'll fill you in later."

"Okay," I said. I didn't want to push for family history until he was ready. Especially when I saw the skin tighten around his eyes.

Thankfully his sister changed the subject. "This place is awesome. How did you find it?" Stephanie asked enthusiastically.

"Doug knew a girl who worked here a couple years ago. We came by to visit her, and I kept coming back. He does too. We know some of the employees by name and others by face. I like the coffee and their food, but mostly I like the atmosphere. They have live bands and poets and things like that. It's a cool spot."

She touched her brother's arm as she turned her excitement his way, and I noticed him flinch. I didn't like it. His reaction seemed unconscious, as if her touch was associated with pain or fear, because she hadn't done anything in the last few minutes that would cause him to react like that. He glanced up at me as if he knew I'd seen. Our eyes locked seconds before he dropped his gaze and looked away.

Stephanie pulled her hand back. "Sorry. But don't you love this place? I told you moving here would bring good things into your life."

Alonzo lifted the corner of his mouth, but he didn't comment. He appeared even shyer than normal around his sister, another subject to talk about when she wasn't with us.

Stephanie beamed at me. "I'm really glad to meet you... again... when we can talk. You have no idea how much he's changed since he met you."

I shifted my eyes to Alonzo, who glared at his sister. "Steph, don't!" I didn't like how angry he sounded.

"This is the first white T-shirt he's worn in three years. It doesn't matter that he's still got the long-sleeved one underneath; this is huge.

And no jacket! If I could count how many times the counselor urged him to stop wearing—"

Alonzo stood abruptly. "I said don't!" He stormed toward the door, and Stephanie bolted after him. She grabbed his arm, and he yanked it away. "You don't get to decide how I spill the past. Back off or get out!" He pointed to the door.

She looked around at the few people who were watching from their seats. Her face flushed and she quietly returned to her seat across from me.

Alonzo took one step toward us and decided against it. I heard the little bell dingle as he shut the front door behind him before it registered that he'd left me there with his sister. I rushed out after him, down the steps in one jump, calling his name. Much like he'd done to me when I tried walking away thinking he'd made fun of the music I liked, I stepped in front of him and placed my hand on his chest. He stopped and looked up.

"You don't get to walk away like that," I said. "I don't know what the heck that was, but leaving me in there with your sister isn't fair."

"I hate the way she treats me sometimes," he said.

"Look, older siblings can be controlling. You need to look past it." I tried being positive even though his dark expression was the opposite.

Alonzo grumbled, "We're fraternal twins, and I'm the oldest."

"Oh." My argument died before I could finish it.

"See!" he fussed. "I keep telling her to back off, but she treats me like I'm helpless. I told her not to follow me here, that I'd be fine on my own, but nooo, she has to transfer from Berkeley so she can keep an eye on me."

His claim surprised me. "Really? Your sister was attending Berkeley and came here? Why?"

Alonzo glared. "I told you why."

"But that doesn't make any sense. You're old enough to take care of yourself. And it's not like you have all that much to take care of here since the college feeds us. All you're responsible for is homework, laundry, and showering. Unless you need help showering?" The list tumbled off the top of my head because it made logical sense, but when Alonzo heard the last part, he stuttered.

"I, um, d-don't need… help."

"Holy shit, you're blushing." And I was walking on sunshine because of it. "Are you sure you don't need help showering, because I can think of one person who'd love to slide his soapy wet hands all over your naked body." I waggled my eyebrows and his blush deepened.

"Stop, people will hear." His voice was not distressed this time and I knew he'd been thinking about my suggestion.

I glanced around. "No one's here. We're on the sidewalk, alone, and I want to hear you say it, Alonzo Martin. Have you been fantasizing about showering with me?"

His silence was my answer. I stepped closer, lifted his chin with one finger, and gazed into his nervously darting eyes. "You are so fucking adorable."

He pulled back and dropped his gaze to the pavement. Was he shy, reluctant, or anxious?

"Lon? My beautifully bashful boyfriend…." I placed my hands on his shoulders and tried soothing his nerves. "What can I do to convince you that shower fantasies are welcome anytime?"

The one dimple in the side of his cheek appeared; I about died every time I saw it. "I do, kind of… think about you… sometimes… soapy and… naked."

I felt a tingle run from my chest, take up residence in my groin, and shoot sparks all the way down to my toes. "Oh, man. Can we ditch your sister and go take a shower now?"

"But didn't you just get out of the shower? Your hair was still wet when we left campus."

"Logic? Who needs it?" I squeezed his upper arms. "I want naked."

Alonzo chuckled and blushed again. I couldn't help my need to kiss him. When I cupped his cheek, his mirth dried up. "Chris? You're not…?"

He asked, but he knew the answer. I was going to kiss him in public. One kiss, sweet and soft, placed ever so gently on his lips. I expected him to back away or shake, but he didn't. I placed a check in the win column. "See, a little PDA isn't a bad thing."

He smiled. "No. I guess not. I'm not used to it, Chris. I can't promise the next time you try I won't push you away, but I liked it."

"That's all I can ask for. Now, let's go back in and talk to this overbearing sister of yours." I was about to lead the way when I noticed

Stephanie in the window. "Wow. She's controlling and a tad creepy." I reached for the door. "She's watching us through the window."

"Terrific," he said, but I could tell sarcasm when I heard it.

BREAKFAST WASN'T all that bad, even after the rocky start. I learned a lot about Alonzo, even if it was from what *wasn't* said. I'd hoped for a shower before my game, but that didn't happen. We lost to Bridgewater, but it was not for my lack of effort. I had three goals and two assists, but our teams were very well matched. We lost 6-7 in overtime.

Before I knew it, it was Monday again and I was back in class. Alonzo and I agreed to spend Sundays doing homework so he could come watch my game on Tuesday. After a frustrating tie with Dickinson, Alonzo met me outside the locker room—after my parents went home.

"Hey," he said, calling me from a bench twenty feet up the sidewalk from the locker room door.

I stopped following the guys and walked over to him. "What are ya doing over here? I thought I'd meet you later for coffee or something. I was about to head in for a shower."

This was the first time Alonzo glanced down where I knew it wasn't from being nervous. I saw the dimple on his cheek, so I knew he was grinning.

"Lonnie?"

He slowly lifted his face, revealing a very coquettish grin.

I felt my body waking up at the very notion. "Are you thinking what I hope you're thinking?"

If that look in his eyes didn't get me hard, his sultry voice sure did when he said, "Maybe."

"Oh fuck," I cursed.

"Possibly." Alonzo smiled brightly, revealing his dimple. "But if you don't get your stuff, I might be taking that shower all by myself." Then the little imp winked at me and took off running.

Holy man. I bolted after him, allowing him to stay ahead of me so I could watch his ass move. I could get my stuff tomorrow. I needed his body right now! As soon as I opened the door, he was in my arms, holding me, kissing me, and squeezing my ass. I wasn't sure why he was suddenly so aggressive, but I wasn't questioning it. He moaned into my mouth, and I slid my hands up the back of his shirt, loving the feel of his smooth skin. I tugged, hoping he'd let me slip his shirt off, but he pulled back.

"You first," he insisted.

"Okay!" I whipped my game jersey off and tossed it onto the floor by my bed.

Alonzo gasped and then exhaled, "Wow." He stepped closer and touched me as though I might break, running his fingertips lightly over my pectoral muscles. "You're so… sexy."

The wonder in his voice made me think he either didn't expect me to be so buff, or he knew I was but didn't expect to be so awed by it. At this point, I didn't care. I had his hands on my bare chest. He could study my physique all night if he wanted to.

"I don't have muscles like this," he said, "or the chest hair."

I stepped closer and put my hands on his hips. "Alonzo, don't take this the wrong way, but if I wanted muscles, I'd date Doug. Have you seen his guns? I'm not attracted to Doug. I'm into you. Way into you. You could have a peg leg and a third nipple and I wouldn't care as long as you kept smiling at me."

Alonzo leaned in and kissed my neck. He licked his lips. "Mmm, salty."

"Sweaty," I corrected. I tugged at his shirt. "Please?"

He moved away and slipped both shirts off together, the tee and the long-sleeved one, and laid them on the end of my bed. He turned around, shoulders hunched, with his hands shoved in his pockets as though he was scared for me to see him. I couldn't understand why because he was beautiful. Clean, clear skin with just a hint of black hair between his pecs—I reached for him because I needed to feel him against me. Sure, he wasn't defined like me, but as I told him, that wasn't what I was interested in.

I held him to my chest until he relaxed and took his hands out of his pockets. "You, okay?" I asked.

He was shaking. Was he as inexperienced as me? I'd never done anything like this, but I was enthusiastically jumping in with both feet. Maybe Alonzo needed to ease his way in? "Lon, you asked about me, but have you… have you had a boyfriend before?"

"Yes."

Part of me was disappointed, but the other part reminded me that maybe his hesitance was not from fear of sex. I rubbed his back up and down and kissed his neck and shoulder. "Then, why are you shaking? Are you afraid of having sex with me? Just because I want you in the shower doesn't mean we have to... *do* anything. I'm not a sleazeball. I don't have to fuck you the first time we're naked together."

I felt him tense up, so I let go.

"Hey," I said, holding his chin and gazing into his eyes. "I can take a shower by myself. When I'm done, we can lie on my bed and hold each other all night. I don't like how you shake every time we get a step closer to sex."

"No. I'm not afraid. I want you." His breathing accelerated. "I want you *really* bad. I'm not afraid of sex, Chris; I'm apprehensive of trusting what we have. I'm afraid I'm dreaming and that I'll blink and it will all disappear. I haven't been with anyone in three years, but I'm not a virgin."

"I am," I admitted easily.

Alonzo smiled and his shoulders relaxed. "That actually makes it easier. I don't have to try and impress you."

"What? Why would you think you have to impress me? I'm all for discovering things together." I slid the backs of my fingers down his chest until I hit his nipple. I rubbed it and he closed his eyes. "See. I just discovered how much you like that. You dart your eyes and look away when you're nervous, but you close them when you enjoy something."

I watched his throat bob as he swallowed. "Yeah. I like that," he said breathily.

I bent and kissed his neck, his ear, and his shoulder while I played with his nipple. I kissed my way down his chest and ran my tongue over his nipple, daring to push for a better reaction than I had from my fingers. The skin tightened and his nipple stood erect as I teased him with the tip of my tongue. I glanced up and continued flicking my tongue, watching his facial expressions as he gasped and breathed harder through his open mouth.

He gripped my upper arms firmly, but he made no move to push me away.

I caught a glimpse of the inside of his forearms as I licked him with the flat of my tongue and then pulled back a smidgeon to blow on the moistened nub. Alonzo hissed, so I shot my attention back to his face. His eyes remained shut, and he was now biting his lower lip. I suckled the stimulated area again and then repeated myself with lapping tongue and cool breath. Alonzo made a cute little noise, so I moved over to the other side of his chest.

As I licked and teased him with my teeth, I studied his forearms as best I could out of the corners of my eyes. From the way I was stooping to access his nipples, my face was close, but the angle made it difficult. One, two, three, four... I counted six tiny scars on his left arm, each about two inches in length, running parallel down the center of his arm like tally marks on a chalk board. I swirled the tip of my tongue around his nipple one last time and stole a glance at his other arm. The same kind of scars marked his flesh.

"Chris," he moaned. "That feels so good."

I wanted to chuckle, but it was difficult to enjoy his approval of my simple actions while my mind conjured up all sorts of reasons for him to cut his flesh like that. I may have grown up in a happy family, where self-harm never entered my mind, but I wasn't naïve. I knew things like this happened all the time, but they'd never happened around me.

I casually kissed my way up his chest to his neck, and then I held him tightly so our bare skin pressed together. I nuzzled my nose in his hair and ran my hands up and down his back. I was feeling so emotional with him in my arms, especially after seeing the scars. I wanted to protect him, heal him, and engulf him all at the same time. I sipped the skin along his shoulder and shivered when I felt his hard nipples touching my chest.

It was like sensory overload, and I was transported to a place outside myself where I hovered in a cloud of skin and sun, with Alonzo's fingers massaging my arms and shoulders and his erection pressing into mine. Wait... no. That part was real.

I pulled back to look him in the eyes.

He had the prettiest eyes I'd ever seen. I've always known I was partial to brown eyes because it felt like peering into the fathomless depths of an abyss, seeking mysterious creatures that lived in the realms where no one ventured. Brown eyes were doors for my imagination. Alonzo's eyes were where his pain lurked, pain that haunted and tormented this beautiful man and beat him into submission until he was convinced living in solitude was his only option. Pain from thinking it was wrong to show affection to the same sex. Pain from feeling like the only homosexual on earth.

I smoothed his hair over his ear and suppressed a desire to scream at his pain as if I could will it into corporeal form and chain it to a wall and torture it in the same way it had tortured Alonzo. Whatever he was hiding was bad. I could tell by his hesitance, scars, and the couple of near panic attacks he'd had before. I only hoped that when he told me about his past, I'd be mature enough to listen.

For a while we stood there gazing into each other's eyes until Alonzo asked, "Do you think we could take that shower before I lose my nerve?"

I blinked. Obsessing over his past and what may or may not have happened made me forget what we'd set out to do in the first place. "Oh, yeah, I'm sorry. Feeling you in my arms is… it's way better than I ever thought it would be. I love the feel of your skin against mine."

Alonzo smiled. "Me too."

I took a step back so I could undo his belt. I pulled it through the loops in his jeans and tossed it onto the bed. I looked him in the eyes before undoing his zipper. "Are you sure you're okay?"

Alonzo moved his hands over my chest, shoulders, and neck. "Definitely."

I unzipped his jeans and slid them down his legs, kneeling in front of him. I slipped them off as he lifted each foot, and I faced his last item of clothing—purple briefs with tiny skulls. I probably would have chuckled, but the erection pressing hard to escape the patterned fabric brought my focus to a tight center. I needed that dick in my mouth.

I lifted my eyes to him as I reached for his waistband and carefully let him out. Alonzo closed his eyes. After he stepped out of his underwear, I asked, "May I?"

He gazed down at me looking up at him with my mouth inches from a throbbing erection that bobbed and pulsed in involuntary anticipation. "You never have to ask." His voice was absolutely debauched.

Alonzo gasped as I took a hold of his dick and guided it to my lips. I felt my own body quivering as I suckled Alonzo's mushroom head and licked the vein that ran up from the base. He sank his fingers into my hair and moaned and gasped with each bob of my head as I took him into my mouth as far as I could. He pressed against my skull, encouraging me to suck him in deeper, but I was nearly gagging already. Dude was hung! Or maybe he was just above average, the same as me, and my mouth and throat weren't used to the intrusion? Whichever. I didn't care. I liked how he thrust forward ever so slightly. It helped me know this was welcomed and he wasn't afraid.

But after a few minutes, I had to let go.

I sat back on my haunches as Alonzo reached down and cupped himself. He groaned heavily and said, "Oh, Chris, I was so close."

"Me too." I stood up quickly and stripped, needing to feel him against me. "Come on," I urged, taking his hand and leading him toward the bathroom that Doug and I shared with two other guys from the adjoining room. "I need to come, and I want it to be *with* you in the shower." I shut the door behind us and locked it, then locked the other door. When I turned around, Alonzo was hugging himself, arms loosely crossed over his torso, hands resting on his ribs. He looked freaked again, even if his cock was as hard as mine.

"Lonnie? Look at me." When he did, I reached for him. I took his hand and slowly eased his arm away from his body so I could kiss the inside of his left forearm, over his scars. "If this is what you're afraid of, don't be. These marks don't make me think any less of you, but they do make me wonder about the cause." He swallowed visibly. "I'll listen when you're ready, but please don't pull away from me because you think I'm gonna judge you for the things you've done."

Tears welled in the corners of his eyes, and Alonzo's other arm relaxed away from his midsection. He'd been afraid of me seeing those scars, of the world seeing them, so he'd worn a long-sleeved shirt in summer. I had to help him know it was okay for him to let the walls down. Of course, the only comment that came out of my mouth in his time of need was more of a lighthearted jest.

"The only thing I'd take issue with is if you gouged out these amazing eyes of yours, then I think I'd have to kill you."

Alonzo laughed and choked back a sob at the same time. "That's not really funny."

"Sorry. I'm not good with serious situations sometimes." I cupped his cheek and rubbed my thumb over his clean-shaven chin. "I know you've had a crappy past. You've mentioned therapists and the need to prove to your sister you can take care of yourself. You have scars on your arms, and you've said you fear what we have between us could be a dream. Something has you shaking when we're in public, and I may not understand it all, but I'm telling you I'm not afraid of anything you could say. It won't change how I feel about you."

Then those words I never thought to say slipped to the tip of my tongue, perched, waiting, longing to be uttered. How could I deny them? My parents always told my brother and me there was nothing worse than love left unspoken. So, naked and aching to finish what we'd started in the other room, I pulled Alonzo into my arms and whispered, "I love you."

So soft, so right, so unexpected, my feelings finally made sense once I released those words into the universe. Alonzo pressed himself into me, hugging me tighter than I thought humanly possible given the fact he didn't look all that strong. I hugged him back as tightly, running one hand up and down his bare back. I shushed him, kissing his hair, but the eroticism of the moment caught up to the romanticism of it. We were naked after all. And hard. I dipped my hand down farther and slid it over the globe of his buttocks.

Alonzo giggled and pulled out of my arms so he could wipe his eyes. He sniffled and chuckled, saying, "All right. I've disrupted sex long enough. I want your body, Chris. And saying what you just said means everything to me."

I wanted to hear him say it back, but maybe that was selfish. If he wasn't ready, he wasn't ready. I turned the water on and waited for it to heat up, while Alonzo washed his face of all things.

"What are you doing?" I asked.

He rinsed the soap away and held out his hand. "Towel?" I handed him one. After drying his face and wiping the remnants of eyeliner off, he said, "If I got in with this on, I'd have black streaks running down my face, and I'd probably scare the crap out of you."

"Doubtful." He stepped over as if ready to hop in, but I stopped him. I pointed to his wrist. "Your cuff. It's not good to get leather wet."

He had that look again, and his hands trembled.

"Lonnie, it's okay. Take it off." I knew it hid something else he tried to keep secret. Something painful? Something embarrassing? I wouldn't know until he revealed it.

Alonzo unsnapped the cuff and set it on the double sink, between the bowls. He glanced up at me and then back down. His chest rising and falling, hands shaking, he lifted his arm and held out his hand, palm up. There, on the inside of his wrist, was an ugly red scar where a tattoo used to be. I knew it had been a tattoo because I could make out part of a letter, maybe a K, on one edge and a smidgeon of another letter on the other side of the red, wrinkly skin that appeared to have been sliced off or burned—I couldn't tell. Alonzo didn't need words of sympathy. He needed me to treat him like a whole person without reminders of his pain.

I took his hand and brought his wrist to my lips. I kissed it.

"Chris," he rasped.

I kissed his wrist again. Then I kissed his arm three times and moved my mouth higher and higher until I kissed his shoulder and neck. Finally, kissing his lips, I held the side of his face and plundered his mouth with deep hunger. We'd stalled too long, and I was almost beyond rational thought. I wanted to soothe him and protect him, but I also wanted to paint him with my cum while jacking him off.

We stumbled into the shower and managed to shut the curtain without flooding the floor, although the rug got soaked in the process. It might have been easier to disengage while stepping into the tub, but I was not about to release his mouth until he was good and kissed, which was about five minutes after we'd slipped under the spray. Only then was I able to stop tasting him long enough to grab the soap and lather him up. Shoulders, chest, stomach, inner thighs, balls; I glided my soapy hands all over his body and up his pulsing cock.

He stood there silently, eyes closed, possibly spellbound by my sensual touch, and it thrilled me. Alonzo completely gave himself over to me in those moments. Naked and vulnerable, he allowed me access to any part of him I wanted to touch.

I moved in close and took both of us in hand, pumping my firm fist slowly so I could get used to the rhythm without one of our dicks slipping free. I wanted them touching and rubbing so we'd get off together. While I pumped my fist, I slipped my free hand around his lower back and over his ass. I teased up and down his ass crack until my fingers dipped in and ran across his opening. Alonzo gasped but kept his eyes shut. He had his arms around my neck, and when I touched his hole, he leaned his forehead against my chin but made no move to pull away.

"I'm getting close. How about you?" I whispered.

"Mm-hmm," he managed to squeak. "Chris...."

I pulled my shoulders back suddenly so I could look him in the eyes. In doing so, I startled him out of his trance. "What's wrong?" he asked.

I kept stroking. "Nothing. I want to look at you. Keep your eyes open for me."

His lids fluttered. "I can't."

"Yes, you can," I insisted. "I want to look into your eyes when you come. Look at me."

He was breathing as hard and fast as I was, but his ability to focus was severely diminished.

I licked his mouth with the flat of my tongue, trying to zero his attention. "Kiss me," I said, licking at him again, wet and sloppy as the shower spray trickled down our faces and washed the saliva away as quickly as it accumulated. Our tongues clashed and teased, but Alonzo's ability to kiss was overridden by my stroking hand.

"I… can't. Chris…. Oh…."

"Then look at me. Keep your eyes open. Lonnie. Please." I stroked harder.

Alonzo did as I asked no matter how hard his struggle to comply. My eyes desperately begged to close, but I was determined to come for the first time with my boyfriend and watch the ecstasy wash over his face. He gripped my hair as he groaned, eyes rolling back slightly. Alonzo came two seconds before I did. Our splooge coating my hand, I kept stroking until every last drop oozed out.

Alonzo cried out in a long moan and then fussed, "Stop, stop, stop."

I wrapped both arms around him and kissed his shoulder. We were both breathing hard, but after a couple of minutes, he started laughing. I let go so I could ask what was so funny. "Why are you laughing?"

Alonzo grinned. "I don't know. I feel so great." He touched my face and traced my lips with his fingers before he kissed me. It was the perfect kiss to end with.

I turned off the water and grabbed a towel from the hanger on the back of the door. I handed it to Alonzo. "You first."

"Okay." He took it and dried his hair with a good rub, followed by his chest, groin, and legs. Then he handed it back. "Here."

I dried off the same way and watched him looking at himself in the mirror, fingering through his hair and wiping under his eyes.

"I didn't think this through," he commented. "I forgot about redoing the eyeliner after we took a shower. Now I'm gonna have to go without it the rest of the night."

I dried my legs last and stepped out. Yes, the carpet was pretty wet, so I set it in the tub. I could wring it out later.

"Does it matter?" I asked. "With or without it, I'm still going to drag you into my bed and ravage your body with kisses."

He turned around abruptly and leaned against the sink. "Oh yeah?" he asked, smiling.

I ran my hands over his shoulders and down his arms. "Oh yeah! I found out how sensitive your nipples are, so I'm going to lay you down in there and have a little more fun with them."

"Yeah?" Alonzo's fear and hesitation must have washed down the drain with the dirt and sweat from my skin because he was bright-eyed and affectionate as we caressed each other.

I opened the door and peeked into the room. No Doug. I pulled Alonzo from the bathroom across the floor and into my bed. We hit the mattress and rolled together until Alonzo was on top of me. He had his hands in my hair while he kissed and kissed me. I felt him tilt his hips, grinding against me, signaling that his need was at least as strong as mine, which was a good sign since I wasn't sure how far and how fast we should go on our first try.

Alonzo moved his mouth down my neck and latched on. I've never had a hickey, but from the intensity with which he vacuum sealed his lips onto my neck, I figured I'd have a mark large enough my parents could see it from the stadium seats when I played soccer on Saturday. I had to say, though, the sting on my neck sent ripples down my body, and I was hard again in no time.

"I want to suck you," Alonzo rasped into my ear, nibbling on my earlobe.

"Go for it."

I let my arms go limp and flopped, spread out, onto the bed. I surrendered. I couldn't catch my breath as he had every inch of me throbbing for whatever he desired, so why fight it? Lying still while he explored my body conserved my energy for later. I wanted to play with his nipples, and I wasn't about to forget that.

He giggled and got to work, kissing down my chest until he reached my dick. I groaned loudly as he engulfed me with that hot, wet mouth of his. It only took a few seconds for me to understand what I'd done to him before we'd gotten in the shower. No wonder he'd almost come while I was sucking him. Blowjobs were fantasmical.

"Oh…. Oh…. Oh fuck, Lon!" I panted. There was no way I could last long with the way his mouth felt on me. "Shit! Lonnie, I'm…. Fuck!" No talking in logical sentences when every muscle in my abdomen tightened and electricity shot sparks straight through my balls.

"Holy fuck, stop," I insisted, shooting buckets down his throat. Slapping at his head, unable to move my arm with much control, I finally dropped it limply on the bed again. "Holy man oh man," I continued, gasping for breath as he released me when I was done.

Alonzo crawled up my body and snuggled against me. "There's a wet spot on your comforter now. Sorry."

"I don't care." I pulled him close with one arm because I needed Alonzo as close to me as possible. I needed him plastered to me in order to feel every bit of him as he left tiny kisses on my neck and jaw and nuzzled me with his nose. "That was the best feeling I've ever had in my life," I told him.

"I'm glad," Alonzo sighed. "But do you think it makes me a slut if I have sex with you after only dating for two weeks?"

"Two and a half, but if you're a slut, then so am I. Plus, I'm an *easy* slut because I gave you my virginity without protesting at all. What does that say about *my* willpower?"

"Not all of it. There's still… you know."

"Don't say it. If my dick hears the words, I swear little Jackson will be pounding on your back door without any assistance from me."

Alonzo leaned on my chest so he could look at me. Then he quietly said, "That wouldn't necessarily be a bad thing."

I groaned and rolled us both over. "Oh, Lonnie, you say the most thought-provoking things." I kissed down his neck and managed to blow him one more time before Doug texted he was heading back to the dorm. We didn't have anal sex that night, but I daresay we were getting pretty good at the other interpretations of sexual intercourse.

Chapter 9
Desperate Need

THE NEXT couple days were a blur. Doug mumbled something about my hickey, but I couldn't concentrate long enough to remember his comment. After having my mouth on Alonzo, and his on me, concentrating on schoolwork was damn near impossible. I found myself several times doodling sketches of Alonzo in the margins of my notebook instead of taking notes. Luckily, I knew people in most of my classes, so I copied their notes. I'm not exactly an artist, so my renderings of Alonzo always resembled those big-eyed stuffed animals popular nowadays. Mainly, I got his hair right and maybe the chin and mouth, but those eyes always made my portraits look like those caricatures done by artists at theme parks.

I finished class and meandered around the buildings, sort of heading to my next class, but not with much heart. I heard familiar laughing and giggling behind me, and I turned in time to see Kat and Candice, cheek to cheek, smiling for a selfie. I kicked myself for not thinking of doing that with Alonzo. I had zero pictures.

I texted: *Hey, Lonnie :) Can you take a selfie and send it to me? I need a picture of you to stare at all day. I miss you.*

You saw me this morning for ten minutes before practice.

I know, but I can't stand being away from you. I want to touch you. I never thought it would feel this painful.

You can touch me after class.

A second later a picture came through. He was sticking out his tongue in protest, with his eyes squinted shut.

I huffed and texted back: *Really? You had to close your eyes? You know how much I adore them.* I was standing in the middle of the sidewalk, so I decided to avoid becoming a traffic cone for others to sidestep by walking over to a bench nearby.

Alonzo texted: *Fine.* Another picture came through. He was smiling just enough to see a hint of his dimple.

Thank you.

Where's mine?

I'm half tempted to unzip my fly and send you a picture of the parts that miss you the most.

You better not!!!!! What if someone walks by when I open it and sees your penis on my phone?

No one but you knows what my penis looks like. Except maybe Doug and Cullen but they've never seen it look the way YOU'VE seen it. I only get hard for you, baby.

Chris! You know what I mean. What if someone sees me looking at a penis? Before I responded, he texted again: *No one's ever called me "baby."*

Do you like it?

I don't know. Maybe. I'll have to think about it. You'll have to say it again when we're snuggling in your bed. Naked. ;)

My dick throbbed as I read his text. I wanted to reach down and rub it though my jeans, but I was sitting on a bench by the library with people walking past all around me. I couldn't. But I had to think of something because waiting until this evening to get my arms around him would probably do me in.

I flipped open my notebook and looked at his class schedule. He had Principles of Biology in the science building right now. In five minutes, I was supposed to be heading to the building in front of where I was sitting to learn about the early Roman Empire, but then I'd be in class when he got out. Our schedules sucked because nothing meshed. Every class was on opposite sides of the campus and at conflicting times. I would certainly make sure next semester's classes matched up or were at the very least near each other so we could walk to class together—holding hands, of course.

Alonzo's comfort about public displays of affection was improving. When we'd said good-bye this morning, I could have sworn he was about to kiss me even though there were people around. He didn't, and that had been fine because I could see the longing in his eyes that told me my patience would soon pay off.

I snapped my fingers. "And I know a little something to help him on his way."

I grabbed my backpack full of books and notes and ran off toward the science building, hoping to catch Alonzo right outside the door. I hid behind a bush, and when he exited the building, I called to him, "*Pst!* Lonnie. Over here."

He turned, eyes searching until he spied me. "What are you doing?" he asked, walking up to me but slowing as if sizing up my illogical behavior. I'd never hid behind a bush before.

I grabbed his hand and pulled him swiftly into my arms. I kissed him, but he struggled to break free. "Chris, stop."

I did, but only to relieve him of his bag. I took the strap off his shoulder and placed his things next to mine on the grass before turning his body and pressing him up against the brick building behind us. "No one can see." I kissed him soundly, tilting my hips into his and grinding slowly. Much to my surprise, he responded in kind by holding me tight around my back and snaking one hand downward to squeeze my ass.

"Chris, I have class." Maybe he was trying to convince me to stop, but his breathy request, coupled with tiny moaning grunts, wasn't cutting it.

Between kissing and nibbling his neck, I said, "Forget class. Doug's at Exercise Psychology; let's go take advantage of the next forty minutes."

"No. I have a better idea. My room's closer, and Caleb's at his chem lab."

I'd never met his roommate, but then I also hadn't been to his room. He'd told me during a conversation about our class schedules, and when and where we could fit in time together, that his roommate's name was Caleb and he was a computer science major. Other than that, I hadn't pressed about Alonzo's apprehension of being in his room while Caleb was there. Maybe Caleb was a religious person who shunned homosexuals. Or maybe Alonzo was simply not the kind of guy to share personal facts with a person he barely knew.

I pulled back and peered around the side of the bush. "No one's looking," I said, stealing one last kiss before snatching my stuff and leaping over to the sidewalk as if nothing were amiss. I casually narrated my actions under my breath. "Just walking on the sidewalk like any other student on campus. Nothing to see here. Carry on with your personal business." I whistled and scanned everyone in sight: one girl reading, one dude talking on his cell and laughing out loud, one group of girls sitting in a circle on the grass talking casually. "Nope. No one suspects a thing."

I took out my phone and texted: *All's clear.*

Already twenty feet ahead of you.

I looked up and saw Alonzo make a face at me as he jetted past the sociology building. "Oh, you little minx."

I took off running after him and followed from a safe distance until he waved me into his room. When the door shut, I dropped my stuff and got down to business. I kissed his mouth and neck while trying to undress him and walk him toward the bed with a Green Day poster hung next to it—a strong indication as to which bed was his. He tripped, and I caught him before he went down on his back. "Gotcha!" I smiled into his eyes, holding him in my arms as if we'd been dancing and I'd chosen to dip him in the middle of the floor.

"Thanks. I'm not good at multitasking, I guess." He stood up and yanked off his shirt.

"I think it's the singular thought we both share that's overridden our ability to walk and kiss at the same time." I undid my belt and zipper.

"Probably. I can't believe how desperate I feel to be with you." He pushed his pants down and kicked them off.

I tossed my shirt next to my jeans and stepped over to take him in my arms. I glided my hands all over his skin. "I know what you mean. It feels like day and night. Before we showered on Tuesday, I thought about sex all the time, but I never had trouble carrying on with the rest of my responsibilities. Now, holy man, I can't think of anything else. I want your skin, Lon." I kissed his neck. "I want your flavor coating my tongue." I shoved him onto the bed—not that I needed to be aggressive—and kissed and licked my way down his chest and stomach until I reached his seeping head. I sipped his essence from his oozing slit. "Ambrosia," I sighed.

Alonzo stroked my hair but protested. "But I want some too, and you're too far away down there."

I let go and repositioned myself so we were stretched out alongside each other, but opposite. "Sixty-nine, baby. Problem solved."

Alonzo snickered and took my dick into his mouth.

After another mind-blowing—pun intended—session, we had fifteen minutes to snuggle before heading to our respective classes. I loved how he enjoyed being in my arms—as much as I didn't want him in any other place. I kissed his hair. "I wish we could do this every day."

"Ditch class for sex? Yeah, it sounds good, until you fail and I lose my scholarship. We can't, Chris." Alonzo rubbed my chest in lazy circles. I think he liked my blond chest hair. "But I know what you mean. It's been a long time since I've been with someone, and I don't remember feeling this urgent. I physically hurt when I woke up this morning, and I almost started crying because I missed you so much. I know that makes me sound pathetic, but I can't help how I feel."

I rolled him over so I was the one leaning on his chest, looking into his eyes. "Don't apologize. Do you know how many couples could save their relationship before it's doomed if they only communicated more? I learned that from my parents. They've been married twenty-seven years, and my mom always told me it was because my dad was a great communicator. I want to hear what you feel." I kissed his neck up to his ear. It wasn't easy withholding kisses when his skin tasted so good. "I want to know what you think, what you feel, what you like, and what you want me to stop doing."

I kissed my way down to his nipples because Alonzo's body turned to Jell-O when I sucked on them. I swirled my tongue around one and moved my hand down to play with his balls. He spread his legs, bending one leg at the knee and flopping it limply to the side. I took that to mean I could venture farther, maybe to those parts we hadn't gotten to. He gripped the sheets along the edge of the bed when I ran my finger over his hole, but he didn't clench his ass. He cooed softly. So I kept licking and suckling his nipple while circling his opening.

"You like that?" I asked.

"Mm-hmm."

His eyes were closed, so I kind of knew he enjoyed my touch. I sucked my finger, wetting it really good. One thing we needed to buy was lube and condoms, but I'm so lame I hadn't thought about it until we needed them. I guess I figured it would take a few more weeks, but each of us fed off the other's zeal for more.

I eased in one finger, and Alonzo quietly moaned. He kept making little sounds as I probed and twisted my finger. It felt odd, feeling his squishy inner parts clamping down and then relaxing alternately, but his facial expressions and accelerated breathing said I was doing everything right. When he whimpered, I knew I'd hit that special spot, so I wiggled my finger over it again.

"Ohhh, Chris. More!" he begged, arching his back slightly and pressing his ass down onto my probing finger. I added another.

He needed more lubrication, and I didn't want to hurt him, so I moved down, settled myself between his thighs, and spit more saliva on my fingers, watching as I pressed them inside again. I rotated my wrist while jutting my fingers in and out.

"You're sure this feels good?" I asked. I knew it was a stupid question. Alonzo only nodded and bit his lip. His cock was very red and full, seeping from the tip. It seemed only logical to stroke him with one hand while I pumped his ass with the other.

"Chris! Fuck, yes. Ohhh. Don't stop. Shit."

Alonzo was writhing on the bed. He grabbed the headboard behind his head and panted, his stomach going taut. A few more stokes and he was shooting ropes up his chest. As he regained speech, I snagged a T-shirt off the floor, wiped my fingers, and then wiped his chest and stomach.

"Thanks," he said between deep breaths. "That was seriously intense."

I smoothed his sweaty hair off his forehead and then propped my pillow next to him. "It looked that way. I've never seen a more erotic sight than the look on your face when I was doing that."

"It's never felt so incredible."

"Even with that other guy?"

Alonzo looked away. I knew I shouldn't have asked. It was rude and intrusive and no matter the answer, Alonzo was with me, not that other guy. So why did I even have to ask? I caressed his stomach and apologized. "I'm sorry, Lonnie. I shouldn't have asked. Lon, look at me."

He scowled. I could bounce a quarter off his cheeks they were so tight. "Kyle and I were young. Sex never had a chance to be like this, even if you and I haven't done everything. He went to another school, so I rarely saw him."

I wanted to say "And?" but that seemed equally rude. Alonzo didn't need pressure from me, so I waited. He sat silently, closed off from our previous closeness because of my stupidity. As I gazed into his hard eyes, the hurt slowly drained away and light returned. I touched his face, delicately tracing his cheek and lips as the silence stretched into minutes. Tears formed in the corners of his eyes right before he leaned into my chest and held me.

We sank back onto the pillows, wrapped around each other. It took some adjustments, but soon we lay there comfortably, Alonzo's body pressed snuggly against me, my arms securely around him. His ex was named Kyle. That explained the *K* on his wrist that was practically flayed off. *What did that guy do to him?*

I knew the longer we lay in his bed, the more likely we'd fall asleep. I'd catch an earful from my English professor, but fuck it, Alonzo needed me.

FRIDAY AFTERNOON we started walking toward Birdie's Café, where we'd had a couple of enjoyable lunches thus far. I'd suggested skipping lunch in lieu of sex, but then my stomach growled so loudly that Alonzo laughed at me. So I was hungry? I thought I could risk starving in order to get naked, but he suggested we eat anyway. Later it was my job to pick up the necessary supplies so we could make use of them this evening. Alonzo even waggled his eyebrows when he'd suggested it, so I was fine with lunch now, knowing what was going to happen later.

Additionally, the barista who'd flirted with Alonzo the first time I'd taken him to my favorite café had talked to us both the last time. Logic reminded me that Lance was a nice enough guy. Not that I knew him very well at all, but I'd frequented the place he worked for years. I'd never noticed anything untoward about him in the past, so I decided he deserved a second chance. He had a nice voice and a gentle smile, and he didn't actually seem like he was out to steal Alonzo away from me. I knew that was my jealousy talking. Yet even my jealousy dwindled as Alonzo and I grew closer.

We stopped walking at Longwell Avenue and waited for the light to change.

"I really want to hold your hand," Alonzo admitted.

"Then do it." I could see the strain in his eyes as he thought about leaping over this next hurdle. Could he?

"What if people criticize us? What if they throw things, or worse, ambush us? What if someone decides to plaster our pictures all over the campus website? What if—"

I cut him off and added a few of my own. "What if a satellite falls from the sky and lands on us? What if the sky turns to pudding and pours whipped cream into the streets? What if pigs start talking and tell us bacon is really made from armadillos? Lonnie, what ifs don't do any good unless it's 'what if I don't study; will I still pass my exam?' Stop being paranoid." I knew I was being harsh so I tried tempering it. I smoothed his hair back over one ear. "I know you don't need scolding or rebuke. I'm sorry. But look around. This isn't like the town you grew up in."

He glared and pointed out, "It isn't Los Angeles either."

"True, but I think you'll find little things like holding hands aren't going to set people on edge. As long as we aren't protesting naked in the streets, I don't think anyone will say a word. If you're worried, then we'll ask Lance. I'm ninety percent sure he has a boyfriend, so we'll ask his opinion. Okay?"

He nodded and looked down. The light had changed and was now back to red, so we had to wait for another cycle unless the traffic dispersed.

"Lonnie?"

I knew I could be an outspoken asshole sometimes. Doug had pointed it out on numerous occasions, but I didn't want to treat Alonzo that way and have him think I was callous. I had strong opinions and had never held back before, but then again, I'd never had a boyfriend. I didn't intend on hurting his feelings, and Alonzo seemed rather sensitive.

"I'm not trying to be a jerk, really. I think it would be interesting to hear his opinion. Maybe it will help you relax."

Alonzo reached out, took my hand, and smiled. His nonverbal response was perfect, because that dimple of his popped out and I knew he was okay. I couldn't help but beam back with the biggest smile I had. I stole a swift kiss before he knew what hit him. Alonzo gasped, but only snickered afterward.

As we finally crossed the street, he asked, "Have I ever told you that I feel about your smile the way you talk about my eyes?"

"Nope." I hopped on the curb on the opposite side of the street, feeling a little more skip in my step than usual.

He explained as we walked. "Your smile makes me feel like I did when I was eight years old. My mom's friend from work had a litter of puppies, and she took me and my sister over to see them. All I remember was lying in the grass and being attacked by six husky puppies, tongues licking, feet pouncing, tails wagging. It was the most incredible feeling of my childhood. I couldn't stop giggling. My sister was so jealous, but she didn't want to lie in the grass. She had a thing about bugs. So when I did, all the puppies ran over to me, and my sister griped about it for days. I remember rolling side to side as they hopped all over me. It's the happiest memory I have."

I opened the door to the café. "Sounds fun." He stopped walking, which pulled me to a stop since he was holding my hand. "What?"

"You don't think I'm childish, do you? That analogy wasn't exactly deep." His voice sounded hurt and his eyes drooped.

"Maybe a little," I answered honestly, exacting a disappointed frown from Alonzo. "Hey," I asserted, lifting his chin. "Haven't we covered this? Stop looking down as if something you say is going to nullify my feelings. I love the memory about the puppies. It sounds awesome." I pulled him over to the nearest table by the door so I could talk to him without blocking the door. We sat and I held his hands across the small table. "If my smile reminds you of snips and snails and puppy-dog tails, then yay me! I don't give a fuck about you sounding childish. I know damn well how much of a man you are." I grinned and winked. He had always responded well to my wink.

Before he had the chance to say anything, more of my thoughts tumbled out. "I don't see you as a child, Lon. I see you as a man I want to fuck into the stratosphere every fucking day, but I've been holding back because I didn't want to seem demanding or desperate when I barely know anything about your past. I told you I'm not afraid of your scars, but that's not completely true. I'm scared of what that guy did to you. I'm scared to know some guy's memory has such a strong hold on you that you're afraid to tell me about it." I flipped his arm over and pointed to his cuff. "This isn't funny. This is some serious shit. You said his name was Kyle." I undid the snaps as he tugged to pull free from my grasp, and then I rubbed the remaining ink on the edge of his scar. "I'm not blind. This was a *K* for Kyle, wasn't it?"

I was observant enough to see his chest rising and falling rapidly. If his previous episodes of rapid breathing were indicators of impending panic attacks, as I suspected, then I was pushing him toward one now. It wasn't planned, but maybe this was as good a time as any to confront some things. On campus, there always seemed to be loads of people, even in the dorms. Mine was mostly quiet on Friday nights while everyone was out. Not so much during the afternoon. Alonzo also relaxed more when we'd been away from campus, even more so in this café. If he was going to open up, this was probably one of the safer places.

His lips were trembling and tears were forming. I squeezed his hands tighter and urged, "Breathe, baby, just breathe. I'm here. I love you. I know I'm a jerk sometimes, especially with what I just said, but I'm not used to sugarcoating things. I've always been assertive. The only thing I've ever feared was coming out to my parents because of my dad's obsession with tradition. I'm telling them soon, I promise. This thing between us is too good to deny. I want everyone to know."

Alonzo pulled his hands away so he could wipe his tears, and then he stood up and came over to sit in my lap, wrapping his arms around my neck and laying his head on my shoulder. "Thank you."

I rubbed his back. "Everything will be okay, you'll see."

He spoke quietly, but I heard every little whisper because his mouth was close to my ear. "I admit I'm scared of too many things. You don't know what it's like thinking you're the only gay guy on the planet. It's terrifying. I had the Internet. I knew my fear was bogus, but what I didn't know at the time was that I'd be able to leave Nebraska and go to school in another state. I hated Nebraska. Even when gay-marriage bills started getting passed, my state was one of the last ones, resisting with an iron will, which made me fear being alone forever."

I'd never thought about it like that before. "It must have been awful growing up like that. I can't imagine." I continued rubbing his back and arm, soothing him in the only way I knew how. I hugged him, thankful he was daring enough to sit in my lap this long. "Even though I've been apprehensive about coming out to my parents, it was never because I felt marginalized. I've avoided the whole sexuality talk for years because it never mattered. I wasn't in a relationship, so I put it off. You've seen my dad. What you don't know about is his obsession over cheerleaders. All the men in my family have married cheerleaders."

"I could be a cheerleader," he suggested innocently.

I chuckled, but it wasn't from mirth. "If only it were that simple."

Alonzo sat up and looked at me. "I promise to let go of my fears, one at a time, if you promise to tell your parents about me by the end of soccer season."

"I can do that."

Alonzo smiled and caressed my face with both hands. Then he kissed me, right there in the coffeehouse! His tongue dipped inside my mouth in between kisses and it made me think he simply needed to know he was tethered to solid ground. I wasn't wavering, I wasn't waffling, my stance was firm. I was in this.

"Aww," gushed a familiar voice.

Alonzo ended his kiss but didn't move away. He rested his forehead on mine and tilted his face toward Lance. "Sorry," he told Lance. "I couldn't help myself."

Lance waved him off. "No, you're fine. I was wondering when you'd feel comfortable enough to kiss him in here."

Alonzo sat up straighter, like students do when teachers demand their strict attention. "Why do you say it like that? 'Wondering when'? How could you tell I was uncomfortable?"

Lance shrugged shyly. He wasn't an overly extroverted person by my observations. Before flirting with Alonzo, I'd always found him to be quiet and businesslike. He walked over to us, looking slightly embarrassed. "I don't know. I think it was the way you reminded me of myself a couple of years ago. I used to be very shy and never wanted to kiss in public. I also didn't like talking to strangers."

I pointed out, "Um, you work in a coffee shop. Don't you deal with strangers all day long?"

"True, but the level of conversation is often limited to drink orders or recommendations. I'm not forced to be social, just congenial. My boyfriend used to visit me every day before going to work, and I refused to kiss him in here for months."

"What changed?" Alonzo asked, standing up.

I followed suit because I didn't want to be the only one sitting. Besides, we needed to order lunch before we ran out of time. Only, when I stood up, there was this awkward silence. I glanced at Alonzo and then back at Lance. "By all means, don't stop talking on my account. I'm the one who suggested you knew about stuff like this."

"Stuff like what?" Lance inquired, his eyes turning serious.

"Stuff like public displays of affection. Alonzo's concerned about hate crimes and ridicule. I suggested asking you since I was pretty sure you had a boyfriend."

His pleasant smile returned. "I do. Jason should be here shortly. I can introduce you if you like."

"That'd be great," I said. I turned to Alonzo. "See, there are other gay couples in this town."

Lance nodded. "Yup. Were you concerned about being the only ones?"

Alonzo tucked his face against my shoulder and held my arm. "Yes."

"He's from Nebraska," I explained.

"Oh jeez. I guess that's pretty bad. *Pft!*" Lance made a noise and rolled his eyes, waving his hand dismissively. "Well, you don't have to worry about that in Westminster. You aren't alone." His casual tone must have eased Alonzo's nerves because he loosened his grip on my bicep. "Come on. Let's get you guys something to eat and we can talk some more."

Lance led the way toward the back of the building, where the register was. After taking our orders and handing me my change, he continued our previous conversation. "You asked what changed?"

Alonzo nodded.

"This place." Lance gestured to the building around us. "Working here has changed my life so much. Over time, of course, but working for a person who accepts others for who they are is so freeing. I mean, I remember this one time when Jason asked for a kiss before he left, and I told him 'No. I'm working.' The owner spoke up and told me to kiss him if I wanted to. She didn't have a problem with it, and if anyone else did, then she told me she'd ask them to leave."

I questioned, "Leave the café?" It seemed a bit strong. "Wasn't she worried about losing a customer?"

Lance shook his head. "I asked the same thing. She said she'd rather have patrons who respected other people. She didn't want bigoted customers who complained about a kiss. When she said that, it made me think about the way people treat each other. Nobody bats an eye over two people kissing good-bye, *unless* they're a same-sex couple. It just seemed wrong. So one day, I kissed Jason good-bye when he left for work. No one reacted. Then, over time, it became a habit, and I found myself kissing him more often when we were other places."

"So…." Alonzo worked up his nerve to ask, "Do people ever give you a hard time for being gay?"

"Sometimes. But I can't please everyone. I've come to feel pretty good about my life. I like who I am, and I have supportive friends and a terrific boyfriend; I can't control other people's reactions or opinions. I am who I am. If they don't like it, they don't have to be my friends."

Alonzo told me softly, "I wish I was that strong." He asked Lance, "But what about if they try to hurt you or they treat you like shit because you're in love with another guy?"

Alonzo pressed closer to me. I had my arm around him as we stood next to the counter anyway, but I think he needed to feel safe. I pulled him tighter to me and he locked his fingers together on the other side of my hips.

Lance answered, "I try not to think about it. I mean, I've never had anyone try to hurt me personally, but I did know a girl in college who got mugged once. It wasn't over her sexuality, but I saw it as a sign that bad things happen whether or not you're gay. She's fine by the way. I guess I could move and live in a more liberal town, but I like Westminster. The fact that times are changing is pretty awesome, and people in Maryland are becoming more and more accepting. Besides, all my friends live here. I don't want to be forced to leave. I try to live my life as best I can, and that's really all any of us can do, isn't it?"

I gazed down at Alonzo. "The man speaks truth."

"Thanks," Lance said, blushing at my compliment.

"Kiss me," Alonzo said.

I did as asked but also wrapped both arms around him and lifted him off his feet, which made him giggle. I set him back down and kissed him one more time before we took our sandwiches and drinks into the dining room to eat.

When we were finished, I thanked Lance and shook his hand. I really liked the guy, and so did Alonzo. Lance's talk helped because during our walk back to campus, Alonzo held my hand almost the entire way.

LATER THAT evening as I got ready for my standing Friday night date with Alonzo, I called to Doug from the bathroom sink. "Do you think I should shave?" My facial hair was blond and untamed, much like the hair on my head. I hardly ever touched it with a razor. I was scruffy most of the time and my mother gave me crap, but it was such a pain to shave when it grew slowly and never got very long. Plus, when I shaved it off, I seemed to lose five years. Alonzo didn't need to date a kid.

"Never mind," I told Doug before he could answer. I strolled back into the dorm room and closed the bathroom door. "I like my look. Besides, I think Alonzo likes it too. He's always touching my face."

"Uh-huh," he grunted without turning away from his computer.

"Are you even listening?"

"Yes. By the way, I'm bringing Debbie back here tonight, so you'll have to go to your boyfriend's dorm if you want to fuck."

I gaped. I didn't like how he was so crude when referring to Alonzo, even if he'd always been that way. "What? But I—"

"You've had the room for the last couple Fridays," Doug contested, swiveling his chair around to face me. "It's my turn. You don't get to be the only guy who scores."

He caught me off guard. "What Alonzo and I have isn't just sex. It's deeper than that. You barely know Debbie." Debbie was a wannabe cheerleader who didn't have enough brains to say no when it came to sex. I didn't care what other people did if it was consensual, but I never thought of Doug as the kind of guy who'd date a girl just to screw her.

Doug refuted, "So? What do you care? You don't talk to me about anything anymore unless it's about soccer."

"Not true."

He stood up. "Yes, it's true. You carry on like he's the only one on the planet. You even skipped class for him, and that's totally out of character. It's like I don't know who you are anymore."

I took a step forward. "Doug, that's unfair. You know I've never had a boyfriend. I spend all my time with Alonzo because I want to know him. How do you know I skipped class anyway?"

Doug gesticulated. "I saw you the other day, chasing after him by the sociology building. From the giddy looks on your faces and the laughing, I would think the whole campus knows you're gay by now. You might as well tell the team, unless you're embarrassed by it."

"I'm not," I protested. "I'll tell them."

He stepped closer. "When? Because I don't like secrets."

"Why are you getting so bent out of shape over this?" I asked. I'd never seen Doug so belligerent.

He got up in my face. "Because... because...." He stopped and stared at me. He turned away suddenly, rubbing his face—from frustration, I assumed. "I don't know what I want anymore. Watching you is confusing."

"Why?" I didn't get it.

He whirled around and threw his arm to the side. "Because I want what you have!"

"Oh."

Doug tightened his fist at his side, shaking his head and clenching his jaw; he was wrestling with something. I only hoped it wasn't about my sexuality, like I'd thought the last time we'd fought. I couldn't afford to lose my best friend. "Doug?" I asked.

"I don't understand how I feel." His eyes implored me, but I didn't understand what he was asking. "At first, I thought I was jealous over you. I thought about you in ways I never have, but my feelings aren't *for* you or *about* you." He stepped into my personal space and carefully touched my face, much like Alonzo did, with the delicacy of a lepidopterist. He studied me tenderly, and I felt guilty for enjoying it.

Doug whispered, "You don't know what it's like: dating girls, having sex, wanting more, yet feeling empty."

I shook my head with the very slightest of movements. Doug was not himself, and I was at a loss of how to help.

"I keep thinking, what if… what if it isn't a girl?"

"Who?" I asked.

"The person I fall for who makes me smile like you do when you look at Alonzo." He squeezed my shoulder. "I want what you have, Chris. Lately I've been thinking, what if I'm looking in the wrong places?"

I finally got what he was implying. "Doug, you're not gay."

"How do you know? Aren't there people who live years before it sinks in that they're not happy because they married the wrong gender? What if that's me? What if I go on dating girls until one day the condom breaks and I have a kid with someone who doesn't make my heart soar? I can tell Alonzo does that to you."

I lifted the corner of my mouth in a slight smile. Alonzo *did* make my heart soar. Knowing Doug saw in me exactly how I felt without me explaining it felt good. He knew me so well. The "what ifs," however, always yanked me into counterarguments. It was my nature. "Doug, what if you have sex with a guy and regret it because"—I stressed the last part—"*you're not gay!*"

"What if I am?"

"What if you're not?" I leaned closer.

"I think I am!"

I moved forward, but before our lips touched, I turned away. "Shit." I ran my hand thought my hair. "Dude," I addressed him from a safer distance across the room, "I almost kissed you."

"Why didn't you? Maybe it would help."

I huffed. "I'm not cheating on Lonnie."

He nodded, considering my reason. "Okay. But, Chris, I still don't understand how I feel."

"Maybe it's like a crisis—a sexual crisis, only without impotency. You can still get it up for girls, right?"

"Yeah, mostly at inappropriate times. Kind of why I wanted to bring Debbie back here tonight. I wanted to see if I could come after all the shit I've been thinking the last couple weeks. She's easy."

Debbie was not the choice I'd make for him, but I understood his underlying logic. Doug had had several girlfriends, but he hadn't slept with all of them. Debbie was kind of a slut, and she'd been around more than a few times. My biggest fear with her was the broken condom scenario. "Will you at least be careful? You don't want a kid with her."

Doug snorted a chuckle. "God no." He grew serious. "I'm sorry I gave you shit before."

I shrugged. "It's okay." I reached into my pocket and held out a quarter. "Can we at least flip for the room?"

"Fine. But you already know who's most likely to have sex tonight."

"Shut up!" I grumbled, shoving his shoulder. "Way to make a guy lose hope."

He laughed and snatched the coin from me. "Call it."

"Tails." Because I wanted Alonzo's tail in my bed.

The coin landed in Doug's hand and he flipped it over onto the back of his other. "Heads."

"Crap!"

"Sorry, buddy."

I let my head fall back when I breathed out a long sigh. I told Doug, "Don't gloat. And make sure you cover up Doug junior. You've got me worried about random pregnancies now."

"But that doesn't apply to you. You've got it made."

"No, I don't. It's still not an excuse to go bareback. I drove over to Target to buy condoms before I came back here to change my clothes. I want to be safe too, ya know."

"Good." Doug quieted down and turned back to his studies. He seemed occupied, so I grabbed my keys and headed to the door. "Chris?" He stopped me there.

"Yeah?"

He strolled over to me. "Don't.... Don't say anything to anyone, okay?"

"About what?"

"Me... thinking I might be gay or something."

I patted his shoulder. "Doug, wanting to fall in love is a good thing. Even if I don't think you're gay, the fact that you're open to the possibility *the one* could be a guy is good. I promise you, when you fall in love, you'll know even if you don't realize it's happening. Love is like an avalanche, tumbling down a hillside with no end in sight."

"I hope so. Now get out of here." He shoved me out the door, and I headed over to Alonzo's dorm.

His entire floor was throwing a party near his end of the hallway, and he told me his roommate, Caleb, had a couple guys over to play some role-playing game. He met me by the stairs. We went to dinner and talked as long as we could, but it was obvious we weren't having sex that night unless it was in my car. Neither one of us was thrilled about it. We hung out in the parking lot and kissed awhile, but he headed back to his dorm, alone, around eleven.

SATURDAY AFTERNOON, however, was a whole other ballgame. After Alonzo had breakfast with his sister and I finished up soccer practice, Alonzo agreed to meet me in my dorm room. Doug promised to be gone all afternoon. We had a home game at 4:00 p.m., leaving several hours for naked fun before I had to hightail it to the locker room.

When I heard a knock on the door, I practically yanked the doorknob off opening it.

"Hey," I greeted him with a huge smile, gesturing for him to step inside.

"Hey," Alonzo said, giving me a half smile. He stepped into the room with his hands in the front pockets of his jeans, looking around the room as I closed and locked the door.

I walked up to him, giving his shoulder a little squeeze. "Are you sure you're okay with this? I know we were all gung-ho yesterday before Doug spoiled our plans, but... you don't look so hot right now." I asked, because he looked anything *but* fine. Alonzo was visibly shaking as he stood in front of me.

He nodded nervously. "My sister, she... bugs me."

"I noticed. So what did she say?" I ran my hand down his arm and worked his hand with my fingers until he lifted it out of his pocket. He might feel uncomfortable for some reason, but I wasn't going to allow him to remain closed off while standing in front of me. I smoothed his bangs to the side so I could look him in the eyes as I held his hand.

"She had to make a big deal about my shirt. It irked me. Plus she's always saying things that are so crude. I'm not like that, and she assumes things that…. Ah! I don't know," he whined in frustration.

"Hey, it's okay," I said, caressing his jaw and kissing his forehead. "We can sit on the bed and talk about it if you want. I like your shirt; it's white, but it's still Green Day." I caressed his cheek with the backs of my fingers. Anything I could do to help him relax.

"I'm not…." He darted his eyes again and started taking deep breaths. "I'm not wearing the long-sleeved one underneath."

"Oh wow! You're not. That's great." I ran my hands over his arms and down to each hand, celebrating slightly by swinging his arms out to each side. He looked embarrassed, but that telltale dimple that only popped out when he smiled spoke for him. "What?" I asked. "Don't you like me swinging your arms around like a human octopus? I can think of better uses for them."

"For my arms?"

"Yeah." I laced our fingers together and then moved both his hands behind his back. I stepped closer, my legs and chest rubbing against his. I kissed him several times, but Alonzo started laughing so I pulled back. "What so funny?"

He smiled shyly, blushed, and looked away. "Not funny ha-ha, but funny ironic. I can't be tense with you around. I guess I laughed because I've never felt like this."

I brought his hands around from behind his back so I could kiss them. "I'm glad. Me neither. So what did your sister say?" He hesitated, so I coaxed him over to the bed. We sat and I rubbed his thigh as I waited for him to answer me.

"She's the kind of person who enjoys inappropriate humor. She used to make butt jokes all the time, and now she makes penis jokes and her conversations are full of sexual innuendos. When I told her about you in August, she asked if we'd fucked yet."

My eyes twitched involuntarily, and I made a face. "She did? That seems rude. I barely knew you." I cocked my leg on the mattress so I was facing him. That way I could touch his back and play with his hair as we spoke.

"That's what I said. Then she made another comment shortly after that about your penis and if I'd seen it yet."

"Oh my gosh! Doug practically said the same things. As soon as I mentioned you, he asked if I'd nailed you. I kind of got angry about it, actually."

Alonzo scooted closer, sliding his arm around my back and slipping his hand under the hem of my shirt. "She did it again today. She had to point out all the smiling I do now. I know I'm happy; I don't need her making me paranoid about it by reminding me.... Never mind."

"No, I get it. I think Doug was acting the same way. He knew I was into you even before I told him. He gave me shit about not telling him sooner." I sunk my fingers into the hair at the back of his neck and rubbed the base of his skull. "My plan has always been to wait until I was out of college. *You* were definitely not my plan."

I liked how Alonzo was touching me while I was touching him. He'd gotten so relaxed around me this week, and it made me feel all fluttery when he looked at me like he was. He ran his hand up my leg and back down and asked, "Is that okay? Do you regret anything?"

"Oh heck no!" I exclaimed. "Alonzo, I'd never trade you for a cookie-cutter ideal." I kissed his cheek, his nose, and his lips. "You weren't planned, but I want this. I want you." I stroked his jaw and kissed him again. "I think about sex all the time, but I didn't ask you out just to nail you. I worry about us moving too fast."

"We aren't."

"But... Lonnie, you're always shaking and looking away as if you're scared to touch me. See, now you're breathing hard again. I've seen you on the verge of a panic attack numerous times since we met. I don't know what I'm doing wrong."

He sighed and laid his head on my shoulder. "Nothing. It's not you, it's me. I've been working on my triggers for a while, and sometimes I can't even figure out what does it." He took my hand and clasped my fingers tightly. "With you, it's trusting that it's real. Like I told you, I've only ever known one other gay guy in my life. I come here, and I see you on the soccer field, and then all of a sudden you're walking up to me in the cafeteria. It was surreal. I never dreamed a guy like you would even look at me, let alone talk to me, so I got scared. But I want this too, Chris."

"Yeah?" I ducked my head to glimpse his face.

He lifted his head off my shoulder. "Yeah." Alonzo was no longer shaking. In fact, his eyes darkened and he moistened his lips.

So I went with it. If Alonzo wanted me, I was more than willing. He and I had been so desperate for each other all week. I didn't want the bump in the road from last night or this morning to disrupt our flow. Whatever his sister's deal was I could figure out later.

I kissed Alonzo, running my fingers slowly down the center of his chest. I slipped my hand under the hem of his shirt so I could rub his stomach, knowing Alonzo was partial to being touched there. I loved the texture of his tender skin and the way he sighed every time I rubbed the sheen of soft hair trailing south. I dipped my finger inside the waistband of his jeans and ran it from one hip all the way to his other. We'd done a few things together. We'd showered and blown each other, but this was the first time we would be completely intimate, and I wanted Alonzo to take some initiative too. Especially after entering my room with the look he'd had on his face.

Alonzo must have sensed my hesitance because he reached over and rubbed my erection through my jeans as we kissed. I groaned, of course, and he gently pressed me back onto the bed, rubbing my crotch and thighs before fumbling for my belt. I tried helping him, but he pushed my hand away.

"I'll do it," he insisted, using both hands to undo my belt and unzip my fly.

I went still, watching him slowly divest me of my jeans, moving them inch by inch, pushing the fabric down my thighs. I think he knew how excited I got when he led. When my pants were almost over my knees, he stopped and placed his hands on either side of my hips, straddling me.

I thought he would slide my boxer briefs down next, but he didn't. Alonzo leaned forward and nuzzled his face into the cotton, rubbing me with his nose and breathing in deeply. He caressed my hardened rod with his whole face, like a cat might do under its owner's chin. Alonzo breathed me in again, and I could feel his breath through the fabric. It felt so erotic, he had me panting with anticipation.

Alonzo flicked his tongue out, licking my inner thighs and kissing his way down. It tickled but also sent waves of indescribable sensations throughout my legs and groin. He finally slipped my jeans off the rest of the way and massaged me through my briefs. I was steel hard by then, but his careful attention was so erotic, I didn't mind the torture. I wanted more.

Holding still was near impossible as he bent forward and ran the tip of his nose up and down the length of my hardened cock while slipping several fingers inside my underwear to caress my balls. My stomach muscles jerked involuntarily, and I slapped at the mattress.

"Lon," I begged with ragged breath.

He looked up and smiled coyly, as if it had finally dawned on him how much I needed to progress our actions. "Oh, sorry." He uncovered my cock and removed my underwear.

Once freed, I jumped at him, pinned him to the bed, and kissed him like crazy. That thing he'd done with his face in my groin had jolted me into overdrive. I moved my hands all over him. I nearly ripped his shirt off in my need to taste his skin. I shed my shirt in seconds and removed his pants, taking delight in how wonderful our bodies felt together.

He ran one hand up and down my back while grabbing my ass with the other. I never imagined someone's hands on me could feel so empowering, but it was like every caress from him was a green light to explore our wildest desires together. First and foremost, I needed to stick my dick in something before I erupted like a volcano. My body hummed with the intense buzz of a high-powered electric line. I wasn't able to contain this much energy without completely overloading, and I'd be damned if I was going to explode all over his leg like a horny dog. I wanted inside that ass!

I fumbled for the lube sitting on the nightstand and only disengaged my lips and tongue long enough to pay attention to what I was doing. I rolled to his side and snapped the cap back on once my fingers were squishy. I didn't ask. Alonzo was assertive enough to stop me if he wanted to.

I gazed into his eyes as I reached between his legs. Alonzo's eyes fluttered shut as I pressed my fingers in, but he didn't ask me to stop. His face twitched in reaction as I pumped my hand and twisted my fingers. I went slowly, but the way he flinched, relaxed, and then sucked in a breath only encouraged me to want to try different rhythms and movements. When he moaned, I knew I'd hit his prostate, so I grinned.

I retracted my hand and climbed over his leg, positioning my hips between his open thighs. I pushed his knees to his chest and pressed my cockhead against his opening. This was it. No going back.

As if knowing I needed his approval, Alonzo whispered, "Please."

I pressed forward, sinking in slowly. I gasped. Alonzo was so tight and warm that part of me wanted to disappear into his body and stay there forever, but it was the other part I listened to, that voice in my balls that growled with an authoritative hiss, commanded me to pump and twist and thrust in and out of his tightening hole as if I'd die of exsanguination without the encompassing friction to force the blood back up my shaft.

"I want to hold you," I explained, moving his legs out to the side so I could press my chest to his. The angle had been good, but I needed to be closer. When he wrapped his legs around my hips, I slipped my arms under Alonzo's body and latched my mouth onto his neck. I rammed him with expectant undulations and listened while he cried out my name.

I knew it was coming, I felt it, I needed it. More. Deeper. Harder. Faster. The tingling built with every plunge until I couldn't contain it. I grabbed his hand. Lacing my fingers with his, I squeezed tight as I thrust and grunted my release. When I finished, I registered Alonzo's whimpering cries and fear shot through me. For a spilt second, I thought I'd hurt him—until his eyes met mine, tears leaking out of the corners, and I realized his cries were from ecstasy, not pain or fear. I might have fucked the living shit out of him, but it was in a good way, a deep meaningful way, and in that moment I knew Alonzo was the most precious thing in all the world to me.

I clutched his sweaty body tightly to mine as Alonzo squeezed my hips with his thighs. I kissed him on his lips, chin, and throat and then nuzzled his ear, nipping and licking until he giggled. I delighted in the sound that, to me, rivaled angels' songs. Alonzo laughed and I joined in, and before we knew it, we were crying together in this completely vulnerable way that said everything our hearts felt. He was mine.

Chapter 10
Bad Timing

SOCCER HAPPENED late Saturday afternoon, as it was prone to do, and our profound moment was cut way too short. Pulling out of him was like losing state finals in overtime. A pit of sadness tightened in my stomach, making me queasy. I had to leave him with not nearly enough kisses. He and Stephanie would be at my game, thank goodness, because I needed to know he was watching.

After warming up on the field, I caught sight of him in the stands. He was near enough to see, but too far away to touch. I saw my parents in the stands as well and immediately put on a fake smile. I had to smile or they'd know something was wrong.

I had expected them, since they came to most of my games and rarely missed a home game, but seeing them made me realize I'd have to divide my time after the game in order to talk to them.

I texted Alonzo: *My parents are here.*

I saw them.

I'm not sure how to handle it.

Don't worry, Chris. I'm not mad. I gave you until the end of the season; you have at least a month.

Thanks, baby. I owe you. Speaking of, can we meet later? I want to hold you. It's like someone cut off my arm and I'm bleeding to death without you.

No. I don't know where we could go. We were lucky Caleb was out, but I don't want to risk it. I'll have to ask if he can stay at a friend's dorm so I can have someone over. Maybe you can stay the night soon. That is… if you want to.

Hell yeah! Doug probably wouldn't appreciate it if you stayed at my place, although he does go visit his parents sometimes. Maybe I can convince him to do that overnight one night. This sucks. You're all I can think about, Lonnie. I want to make love again. What are you doing tomorrow?

I need to study. Remember? We agreed no Sundays.
I know, but....
Coach gave me a look and I texted my good-byes to Alonzo.

THE TEAM played well, but so did our opponents. By the half it was tied two-two, and Coach Montgomery stressed quick passes and switching often. I took a swig from my nifty water bottle and glanced over to where Alonzo was sitting, way up in the corner of the stands next to his sister. Heat rushed thought my body, so I closed my eyes briefly. *He's here*, I reassured myself. I could get through this. Only a couple of hours and I'd kiss those lips again.

I went back out onto the field with renewed energy.

Swarthmore's players were relentless. They scored, we scored, and when the ref blew the whistle at the end, it was tied four-four. This meant overtime. It felt like déjà vu since the game against Dickinson had gone to overtime earlier in the week and we'd ended in a tie.

Coach called us in for a huddle. "Okay, guys, we have two ten-minute halves to score. It's sudden death, so make those shots count. I don't want to end in a draw like Dickinson. Okay? Chris, Marshall, Cullen, Doug, aim for the corners. Keep your eyes on the net and where you want the ball to drop. Do *not* focus on the goalkeeper. Got it?"

"Got it!" we cried in unison.

"Cedric. You, Terry, and Isaac keep that ball up front. Preet, I want you, Josh, and Taylor to mind the defense and make sure nothing gets remotely close to Steve."

"Yes, Coach!" Preet answered.

When directed by the ref, the team walked out onto the field. Since Doug and I were the highest scorers, the rest of the team would try to feed us the ball whenever possible. The best scenario would be *me* dropping the ball back to the midfielders as soon as the clock started, Cedric running the ball down the left sideline and then switching with a pass to Marshall on the opposite side of the field, who would then chip it in front of Doug as he neared the box. Being the sneaky player he is, Doug would draw the defenders away by showboating a bit before passing the black-and-white over their heads to me as I snuck in from the other side, taking my place by the goal post. Score. Game over.

But that was in a perfect world, and so far nothing had been perfect. The game had come down to sudden death. Each team would select their best players regardless of exhaustion or injury. The best would take the field, and those players would line up in front our team and strive to achieve the very scenario that ran through my imagination. Shot for shot, pass for pass, our teams would go all out.

From my position near the midfield line, I saw Swarthmore's striker fake a pass as he headed toward the goal and slip around Josh. That was my favorite move! With two minutes left in the second half of overtime, he shot the ball and hit the goal post on the edge, sending it spinning back onto the field. My gut clenched, and I breathed a sigh of relief as Josh closed in and kicked it away.

Our guys ran it back toward their goal, Swarthmore stole it, and then Cedric sent it through Swarthmore's offensive player's legs in *my* direction, much to that guy's embarrassment. Like a tennis match in slow motion, the ebb and flow of momentum transferred from our team to theirs every other second. In what I figured had to be the last two seconds of the game, my feet found the ball and I broke toward the goal. I neared, I aimed, and I got shoved to the ground—fouled in the box.

I didn't think it could have gone any better than that for my team. I mean, yeah, my leg hurt, and I would probably have a huge bruise because I was fairly certain the other guy cleated me, but this meant a direct free kick on the goal. Just me against the goalkeeper. If I scored— we won. If I missed, we tied—again!

I took a deep breath as the ref set the ball twelve yards away from the goal, the designated distance as specified in the rulebook. I could do it. Alonzo was watching. I walked up to the soccer ball and flipped it over, rotated it with my fingers, then placed it back onto the grass in almost the same position, having gained confidence through touching the leather. It was something only soccer players understood. Touching the ball made a connection.

This wasn't football. Football was measured and precise; the ball was placed exactly where the referee wanted it, and no one was allowed to touch it before the snap. Soccer wasn't about the meticulous placement of the ball as much as whose ball it was. For foul kicks, the ball got tossed in the general direction of the point of contact. Only when the player picked it up, rotated it, and repositioned it much like I had, but placed it two feet closer, did the referee make the player move the ball back.

I knew the rules. I wasn't going to try to inch the ball closer to the goal during a free kick. I simply liked to touch the leather surface of the ball to make my connection. The ball and I were one. I would channel my energy, tap the bottom edge, and flip it over the goalkeeper's shoulder into the net. My plan in theory; I only had to make it happen.

I flipped and rotated the ball again and set it back on the grass.

Another six yards back, I took my position to give myself room to build momentum for the kick. Standing tall, drawing long breaths in through my nose then exhaling through my mouth, I searched for that zone my soccer mentality naturally fell into, but a tiny piece of my heart still yearned for Alonzo's support.

I flicked my eyes over to where he sat, needing a mental connection with Alonzo as badly as I did with that black-and-white ball waiting in the grass. As soon as I turned my head a fraction, Alonzo lifted his shirt, flashed me, and swiftly returned to his seat before anyone around him noticed. Did people in the stands across the field see? I didn't know. But if Alonzo was bold enough to do something so out of character for my benefit, all I could do was chuckle. I did it professionally, of course, snorting under my breath, tightening my cheeks and lips so my normally huge smile wouldn't burst forth like the noonday sun, making others around me think I was a raving lunatic. Free kicks in the last two seconds of the game were supposed to be serious, not a comedy routine.

My Alonzo. He never stopped surprising me, and I loved him for it.

I regained composure before my allotted time ended. I signaled to the ref, aimed, and shot for the upper corner of the net. The goalkeeper had anticipated I'd kick with my right, but not with the outside of my foot. My inner sole kick was stronger, but my outside tap duped the goalkeeper into diving in the wrong direction. I practiced it all the time. All I did was connect at the right angle, like lining up a cue stick and ball with the pocket on a pool table, and the soccer ball bounced past the goalkeeper's feet as he dove and landed in the grass facing in the opposite direction. Score!

Cheers erupted from the people in the stands. Normally I didn't hear them. Cheering was background noise when I was on the field, except for now. The jubilation of parents and friends washed over me with a different kind of joy than ever before. Coach Marks had been so right about the grandeur of playing in this stadium. Playing here tripled the emotion.

It wasn't that this was an especially important game, or that it would have been my fault if we'd tied; I think my joy came from knowing Alonzo was in this great stadium watching me. This afternoon had changed things between us, and I felt so elated I almost floated across the grass when I took that shot.

Nothing could bring me down.

"What is my dad doing talking to the cheerleaders?" Elation zapped, illogical exchange underway, I blindly walked through the line, congratulating other players and accepting pats on the back from my team. I heard "great shot" and "way to go," but my attention was suddenly zeroed in on my dad smiling at the cheerleading squad as they gathered around. That could not be good.

After the coach gave us a rundown of his observations from the game and I'd gathered my stuff, I left the field with the others and made my way to the steps leading up to the wellness center. The locker rooms were only a short trek across the parking lot, past the visiting team's bus. Parents were there to greet us, mine included.

"Great game, Chris," my mom said, hugging me.

"Thanks. Why was Dad talking to the cheerleaders?" I had a sneaking suspicion it was not a reason I'd appreciate.

"He wanted to tell them how great a job they did cheering. They weren't at the last game, and you know how your father likes cheerleaders."

"Mom, saying it like that makes him sound like a dirty old man."

She waved her hand at me dismissively. "You know what I mean."

I gave her a fake smile. *No, I don't. He's up to no good, and I know it.* "Well, I gotta go get a shower and change."

"That's fine. Will you come to Sunday brunch tomorrow? We haven't seen you in a while."

I didn't want to. I wanted to spend the day with Alonzo, but I knew what he'd say. "We agreed no Sundays." I'd have to study at my parents' house, which was fine. If I couldn't be with Alonzo, then their house was as good as my dorm room or the library.

"Okay. I'll be there around eleven, I guess."

"Thank you, dear." She kissed me and walked off to fetch my dad.

I spotted Alonzo hanging in the shadows by the fence as I left the stadium. I hesitated about following the rest of the team until he made a hand gesture that I should go. I grinned at him and jogged after Cullen.

Once I reached my locker, I opened my phone. Alonzo had texted: *I'll meet you at your dorm room, okay?*

I replied: *Are you kidding me? I'd die if you didn't.*

I SKIPPED a shower and rushed back to my room. Some of the guys wanted to celebrate, but that usually involved drinking and I wasn't into that. Besides the fact I was underage by eight months, alcohol also added unwanted calories and inhibited my sense of control. I didn't care for it.

Alonzo hopped into my arms as soon as I neared my door.

We kissed as I held him around the waist one-armed and lifted him off the floor, scrambling to unlock the door with my other hand in order to enter the room before anyone saw us in the hall. I was beginning to think our "secret rendezvous" weren't as secret as I'd like, but believing the fantasy kept the paranoia at bay. I shut the door and fell onto the bed, landing on top of Alonzo with my gear bag still over my shoulder. We kissed like that for a couple of minutes before he confessed, "I can't breathe."

I got off him. "I'm sorry. I got swept up in the moment."

"That's fine. How long do we have?"

"Um, I don't know. Twenty minutes. Maybe more. Doug was talking to Preet in the locker room about the paper he had to finish because he was doing something with his parents next week. I think he's taking a shower and then heading back." I climbed off the bed, dropped my bag, and started shedding my clothes.

Alonzo unzipped his pants and took them off. "Why doesn't Doug shower here?"

I paused and cocked my head. "Do you hear that?"

Alonzo slipped off his underwear, socks, and shirt. "Sounds like water running."

"Because it is. We share that bathroom with two other guys."

"Oh. That seems strange because my dorm isn't set up like that. We have a community bathroom on each floor."

"Yeah. I think all the residence halls are set up differently. I'd almost like sharing a huge bathroom with a bunch of guys if there was more than one shower stall. There is nothing like coming back sweaty from a game and wanting a nice hot shower only to find it occupied by one of the guys next door." I removed my jersey and got back on the bed with my lover.

"What about now? You aren't bothered you didn't get a shower?"

I slid my arm under his back and leaned over him before raising my eyebrow. "What do you think?"

He gave me a whimsical smirk. "I think I like the taste of your sweat."

I let out a hearty chuckle and devoured him before Doug returned. Making love the second time was even more earth-shattering.

I PULLED into my parents' driveway the next morning and parked my car. I needed to tell them this wasn't a phase, a tryst, or a one-night stand. Alonzo was my guy, and I needed to come clean with my parents before they showed up at my dorm room while we were in bed together. Ellis's warning was valid, although improbable. I opened the door and made my way into the kitchen.

My mother was talking to someone. *They didn't tell me Ryan was home.* A girl giggled. *Amber's here?* I liked my sister-in-law, but her presence wasn't going to help me explain why I *wasn't* marrying a cheerleader.

I entered the kitchen and put on the brakes. Full stop. I was staring at Katherine. "What are you...?" I started to ask, but it was useless when Kat leapt out of her chair, flung her arms around my neck, and kissed my cheek.

"Uh... hi."

"Great game last night, Chris," she complimented me, standing way too close for my comfort, but also making me feel preemptively guilty for metaphorically backing away from a girl who was 1) obviously my friend, and 2) invited here by my dad. I could pretend it was both of my parents playing matchmaker, but I knew it was all Dad. My mom was patient enough to let me choose for myself. My dad? No. He'd hit it off really well with Kat last summer, and I should have known he wouldn't let her "slip through my fingers" without a good hard try.

"Thanks." I gave her an uneasy grin, and she stepped back. I think she could tell I was surprised, and not in a good way.

"I'm glad you're here, Chris. I just finished making the waffles," my mom said. "Sit down. Your father should be here any minute. Pour Katherine some juice, will you?"

Kat asked, "Didn't your dad tell you he invited me to breakfast?"

"No."

Katherine's gaze dropped to the floor and she reached for her coat, which was hanging on the back of the chair. "Oh. Then I won't stay where I'm not wanted."

"Not wanted?" my dad questioned, entering the room beaming from ear to ear. "Nonsense. Of course you're wanted here, right, Chris?"

The ball was back in my court, and her blue eyes pleaded for a lie. I relented. "Stay, Kat. It'll be nice to chat without all the other girls around. I feel like we haven't talked in weeks." It wasn't a lie. We hadn't had a moment alone, and maybe this was a good icebreaker to ease me into telling my parents I was gay. I could start with Kat.

My dad took his seat at the head of the table. "See. It's all good. I told you my son was just shy." My dad took a couple of waffles off the stack my mom had set on the table.

I sat down at the table and fussed at my dad. "Dad, I'm not shy."

"Of course you are." He dismissed me and reached over to pat Kat's hand. "He's shy. I blame myself for instilling in him a desire for higher education. I think being so smart makes him self-conscious around the ladies." He winked at her, and Kat giggled.

Oh jeez. This is not going well.

"I don't mind being smart," I said. "I have plenty of smart friends. You know Doug is going to be phys-ed teacher or physical therapist because of me. He tells me all the time I pushed him to be smarter. And my friend Alonzo, he—"

"How are your parents, Katherine?" my mom asked in the middle of my sentence.

Kat set her glass of juice down and answered, "Fine. I told them I got an eighty-seven on my exam last week, and my mom was thrilled." It's like I wasn't even in the room. They carried on a conversation without me. "They're so happy for me. My brother dropped out of college after meeting his girlfriend at a party. I think they are pulling for me to finish so they can rub it in his face."

"Oh?" my mom said. "What does your brother do?"

Kat took a bite of sausage. After she chewed and swallowed, she answered, "He's in between jobs right now. His girlfriend is a cashier and pays their rent. He told my mom things are really tight right now and asked for some money. My mom hung up."

I could see my mom's disapproval. She sat back and lifted her hand as if to cover her mouth in shock, but she didn't. "Oh dear. I can't imagine hanging up on either of my boys, no matter how I felt about their decisions."

"My mom and dad paid for three years of college. He dropped out and moved in with the girl without telling them first. I think they're pretty pissed." Kat ate some waffles, and my mom nodded.

My dad added, "Our boys wouldn't do that. Ryan consulted me before asking for Amber's hand. He knew it was polite even though Amber had already been accepted into the family. She was a hard one to resist with her pigtails and chirpy laughter." Dad chuckled.

"And her cheerleading outfit helped," I pointed out.

"Of course! Nothing complements the masculinity of an athlete like a curvy blonde in his arms. Ryan knows how to pick 'em." He picked up his mug of coffee and sipped.

Yeah. He knows how to pick them, so my thin, noncurvy brunet doesn't stand a chance.

Katherine touched my hand. "I think we look cute together, don't you?"

I didn't know where this was all coming from, but I felt as if speaking up would hurt Kat's feelings and make my dad angry. I simply nodded and shoved more waffles in my mouth. I needed to get her alone and tell her everything. Katherine was a nice girl, and if I'd been straight, I guess I would be very happy with her—but I wasn't. She needed to know it wasn't about *her* so the next time my dad asked her over, she'd be able to decline without feeling guilty.

The rest of breakfast was quiet. Thank God.

AFTER HELPING clean up the dishes, I asked, "Is it okay if Kat and I go up to my room? We're just going to talk, I promise. Nothing inappropriate going on."

My dad smirked. "Of course, son. You do what you need to do. Your mother and I will be doing the crossword puzzle in the sunroom." He winked again and turned away.

I think I got my habit of winking from him.

I led Kat to my room and closed the door. "Why does he have to make this so hard?"

Kat circled my room, examining all my stuff. Most of it was from high school. I tended to purge my crap every couple of years because I didn't like clutter. My most important things were with me in my dorm room. Kat picked up a picture.

"Is this you and Doug?"

I walked over to her and took the picture from her fingers. "Yeah. This was tenth grade."

"Who's the other guy in the picture?"

"Cullen."

"That's Cullen? Oh my gosh! He looks so different without hair."

I chuckled. "Yeah. He made a stupid bet with Doug and lost, so he had to shave his head."

Kat smiled at me and suddenly I didn't like having the door shut. What did she think was going to happen? "What was the bet?" she asked.

"Cullen bet Doug I'd lose my virginity first." Of course, at the mention of virginity, I instantly thought of Alonzo. I'd give him everything if he wanted it.

"What?" She gaped. Maybe she thought guys didn't make bets like that because her face was priceless.

I chuckled more. "True story. Doug's got a way with women, I guess." I set the picture back on my dresser.

"You do too, you know," she said, turning to me and placing both hands on my chest.

I backed away, slipping out of her intended embrace before it became all-encompassing. "Um, yeah, I think we need to talk about something." My heart accelerated as I moved over to the bed. I sat, but as soon as Kat sat next to me, I was up and pacing the room like a trapped animal, even though there wasn't anywhere for me to go.

Katherine watched me curiously. "Chris, it's all right. I understand."

I stopped abruptly. "You do?" *How could she?* But as I had told Alonzo, she probably suspected, so maybe it was true.

"Yes. And it's fine if you want to ask Kara out. I understand."

"One of the triplets? You think this is about Kara?"

"Isn't it? You've been acting weird since before school started, so I figured it had to do with Kara's text back in June."

"That was *her* text?" I asked, returning to my seat next to her.

"Yeah. Didn't you know?"

"No." I'd gotten a weird text about "liking me more than as friends" back in June before everyone went home for the summer. I didn't know who it was from, so I ignored it. Kara was one of the three girls Doug and I had dubbed the "gossip triplets" back in freshman year because they were always together and their names rhymed. Sara, Kara, and Lara weren't actually triplets. They came from different states but gelled instantly on the cheerleading squad. They also seemed to always get the scoop on the latest gossip. I guess I should have been glad my "secret" about being gay hadn't made it into the college newsletter.

"Then if this isn't about Kara, then why do you look like you're going to be sick every time you're with me? Do I repulse you that much?"

Why did girls always assume everything was about them? I hated that. "No, Kat. This isn't about you at all. You're fine. I like you as a friend."

I felt her pull back, even if she didn't physically move away from me. "Oh."

There wasn't an easy way to say it that would make her happy. She liked me. I knew it. Not telling her the real reason we'd never be a couple, was wrong at this point. I took her hand. "Kat, I can't be your boyfriend because… I'm gay."

She stared at me, unblinking.

"Kat, did you hear me?"

She slipped her hand free from my grasp. "I, um, did you just say…? I had to have heard that wrong."

"Katherine, I'm gay. That's why I haven't been interested in dating you, or any of the other cheerleaders. I like you as a friend, but it will never be more than that."

She stood up and paced my room. I couldn't read her. She was somewhere between shock and amusement, judging by a quirky little grin that appeared on her face. She took three steps, paused, looked at me, and then continued pacing. "This is so funny."

"Funny? How?" I didn't think it was funny.

"I was talking to Candice about you, and she suggested you were after my roommate, Stephanie."

"Why would Candice say that?"

"Because you're always heading over to the bleachers after the game to talk to her."

Talking to her roommate? Why would Candice think…? "Oh wow. Your roommate is Stephanie Sarzo!" It clicked. I hadn't remembered his sister being around that often, but I suppose she was. My focus had always been on her brother.

"Yeah." Kat retook her seat next to me. "Candice thought you had a crush on Stephanie, and I told her she was being ridiculous even though I couldn't explain why you kept going over to her after the games and not talking to all of us like the other guys on the team. But it was never about her. It was that guy she's always with."

She was smarter than I gave her credit for, albeit a bit slow. "Alonzo Martin," I confirmed. "He's Stephanie's brother. Alonzo explained to me they have different last names because his mother remarried and he didn't care for Alonzo Sarzo. He told me he kept his father's name, but explained his sister legally changed hers. I can't believe Stephanie is your roommate. Small world."

"Oh my God!" she exclaimed, smacking my chest. "You're gay!"

I winced at the volume she used. Although if she announced it to the world, then I wouldn't have to do it. I confirmed, "I am."

She reiterated it more quietly. "You're gay. You're not attracted to me because you're gay."

"Exactly." I wasn't sure what else there was to say about it.

"What does it feel like?" she asked, tilting her head and eyeing me curiously.

"What does what feel like?" If she asked me about sex, I was going to ask her to leave. She wasn't Doug, and what I did with Alonzo really was not her business.

"Being gay?"

I narrowed my eyes, not from anger as much as from an uneasiness that she was stupid enough to ask. "Um, normal, I guess. I'm not sure what you think it should feel like."

"How does it feel liking someone who has the same parts as you? Isn't it boring? There isn't any discovery and adjustment to finding out what the other person likes. You both have a penis. Isn't that boring?"

I snorted at her absurd question. "No. Kat, just because Alonzo has a dick, there's still the joy of discovering what he likes and how I can please him. I have as much fun during sex as you do. It's about being in love and wanting nothing more than to make him happy in every situation, whether it's in bed or walking down the street hand in hand."

"Ohhh," she cooed. "You're in love?"

Sidetrack, rewind, step over to the left. "Yeah, I am."

"That's so sweet," she gushed. Apparently my declaration of love was more important than explaining how sex wasn't boring. That was one thing I liked about dating a guy—Alonzo's thoughts never jumped track. His thoughts were linear.

I did agree with her, though. "Yeah, he's extraordinary. I've never felt like this with anyone before."

Kat repositioned herself, scooting closer and pulling one leg up on the bed, tucking her foot under the other knee. "So where'd you meet him?" she asked enthusiastically.

"The cafeteria."

"What's his major? Does he have any classes with you? Does Doug know you're in love with him? How are you going to tell your dad? He doesn't know, does he?" She asked a bunch of questions in rapid succession, but they were all valid. Unlike the "what does being gay feel like" question. That one was odd.

I answered each question as succinctly as I could. Kat nodded and kept her eyes glued to me. When I told her I hadn't told my parents yet, she said, "You really should tell them."

"I know. I came over here this morning hoping to, but then you were here."

"I'm sorry, Chris. I didn't know. I thought it was cute how your dad was helping you along. I really did think you were shy. I had no idea you didn't like girls. It's weird. These last couple years, I thought you didn't know how to talk to girls. Doug had the swagger, and you have the innocent charm. Wow. I think I'm still shocked."

"But you aren't upset?"

She smiled softly. "No. I'm actually glad. I was getting really jealous of Stephanie the last couple games. Knowing you have a thing for Alonzo makes it easier. I won't have to put glue in her shampoo."

I laughed. "Wow. Girls do that?"

"Girls do worse."

We laughed, and after a while we decided to do some homework together, like old times. My mom came up to my room to let us know dinner was on the table. I glanced at my clock in surprise. It was 5:00 p.m. *Where did the day go?*

Chapter 11
Feels Right

I PARKED my car later that night and lumbered heavily across the pavement, shuffling my feet toward the dorm. My visit with my parents didn't go as expected, and now I felt guilty, as if Alonzo had been watching through the window the whole time wondering what the heck I'd been doing on my bed with Kat, and worse, why my tongue twisted in knots when I talked to my parents at the dinner table. I couldn't explain why I was afraid. I just was. It was like generations of Jackson men were pointing their accusing fingers at me because I couldn't carry on the family tradition.

"I'm such a loser," I moaned.

My phone chimed with a text. I fished it out of my pocket and smiled. Alonzo said: *Hey. Caleb left a note on the dry-erase board that he'd be out all night. Something about a tournament. So… I thought… maybe… if you wanted to…. *This is me looking down at my feet and your cue to lift my chin so I'll look at you.**

I texted back: *And what would I be prompting you to ask?* I wasn't sure, but I thought he was asking me to swing by. I wanted him to spell it out.

Will you come over? And maybe bring your books and stuff so you can spend the night?

I leapt off the ground and cheered in the silence, my whoots echoing off the buildings. I texted: *Oops. What happened to the no Sundays rule?* I was already racing to my room to grab a change of clothes. No need to dawdle when I could be lying next to Alonzo in less than ten minutes.

Alonzo texted back: *I rushed through my homework and stuff. I miss you.*

"Well, hot diggity dog!" I opened my door. Doug was at his desk, as usual. I swear the guy needed a hobby or a girlfriend—or maybe even a boyfriend—because he seriously did nothing but study. I knew he wasn't as quick with the retention as me, but still he studied way too much.

Twenty-year-olds were supposed to be living life, right? Not hiding in their rooms afraid to make mistakes or meet people.

Although I do admit I'd rather have him here than with Debbie.

"Hey," he said quietly.

"Hey, Doug. Listen, I'm spending the night with Alonzo. I'll see you at practice in the morning. Okay?" I grabbed a shirt and my toothbrush and a clean pair of underwear.

"Sure."

The one-word answer stopped me from leaving. I turned and waited. Nothing. "Doug? Do you have more to say?"

He shook his head, so I opened the door. He said, "I didn't sleep with Debbie." I stopped and shut the door.

"Why?"

He shrugged halfheartedly.

"Doug, I don't have time for your 'I'm gay now' speech."

He yelled, "Fine! Just go. I don't need you to help me figure anything out." Doug swiveled his chair around so I couldn't see his face.

I didn't like how quarrelsome he'd been lately. It was exasperating, seeing as how we'd never fought so much in the entire history of our relationship. I stormed across the short space and shoved his shoulder. "You don't need to be so shitty with me."

Doug whirled around and smacked my arm away.

I held my hands up. "Hey! I'm not looking for a fight, but if you hit me like that again for no reason, I might have to explain a thing or two."

He stood up and puffed out his chest. "Oh yeah, like what? Will you explain why you dumped me like a one-night stand because you fell in love?"

He might as well have kicked me in the balls. That statement hurt like a bitch. "Doug! No, I didn't. I wanted you to get to know Lonnie, but you're always acting like a jerk when I bring him around. Plus you mope like you can't handle me being friends with anyone other than you."

"No, I don't."

"Yes, you do!" I raised my voice and stepped closer. "You're always acting like this! Remember that time in high school when Cullen spent the night and you couldn't because your parents had that thing and made you wear a suit? You moped about missing out on guy's night for two months. He told me he didn't want to hang with you anymore if you were gonna act like a jealous girlfriend every time we did stuff together."

"He did not!"

"Did so. You always act like a whiny little bitch when you don't get your way!" I hissed in his face and poked him in the shoulder.

He sneered. "Don't poke me, Chris. You know I hate that."

"What are ya gonna do?" I poked him harder. "I'm never the jealous one. It's all you. I don't care what you say, I *am* in love with Lonnie. I've never loved someone so hard in my life. I can't breathe without him, I can't think, I can't function. He's it for me."

He shook his head in disbelief. "Nice one, Chris. The first guy you meet and suddenly, after three weeks, you've settled on Alonzo being *the one*." He made quote marks in the air and laughed hysterically at my expense. My face burned with anger, but he kept on making fun of me. "Chris, it's lust you feel, and you're feeling it through your dick."

I shoved his shoulder. "That's enough. You don't know how I feel. You don't know what it's like to look in his eyes and feel like the world fades away and he's the only one left. You don't know how my heart skips a beat when he touches my face, or how kissing him makes my knees go weak and my gut all squiggly. You don't know anything because you sit inside every Friday night doing homework! What guy does that?"

I expected him to yell, but instead he swung at me, his fist colliding with my chin. As pain shot through my face and neck, I ducked the next punch and went for him. I grabbed ahold of his shoulder and pulled him around, attempting to throw him to the floor in the middle of the small room. He's as fast as I am, so he sidestepped my maneuver, knocking me off balance before wrestling with me, arms locked, teeth gritted, head to head, in the space between our two beds. We swayed in one direction and then the other, before he cheated and hooked me around the back of my ankle. He took me down in one motion, over his leg and onto my back.

He always won in a wrestling match, so I knew I'd end up on the floor. He had a black belt, for goodness sake. Doug straddled me and pinned my arms above my head.

His eyes had never looked so hateful. Why? Because I'd fallen in love? If he made me choose, I already knew I'd pick—

Doug's mouth came down on mine. His lips searched for my response, but I couldn't give him what he wanted. He kissed me several times, but I refused to kiss him back. I lay still beneath him, hoping he'd understand how much he'd crossed the line between us. This wasn't cool. Friends didn't act like this.

He pulled back after a minute, and I could see the tears forming in his eyes. His face contorted and he choked back a sob before jumping up and bolting out the door. "Doug!" I called after him, but it was no use. Doug's humiliation needed to work itself out.

I felt bad not running after him, but Alonzo was waiting. I grabbed my stuff and left.

I KNOCKED on Alonzo's door and he answered it by peeking through the crack.

I smiled. "It's me. I'm alone. You can let me in."

Alonzo whispered through the crack, "I did something today, and I didn't tell you before I did it." He came off scared and that was not an emotion I wanted to relive tonight.

I joked, "You bought sex toys?"

He snorted and laughed, "No." Alonzo opened the door and greeted me with a smile and a new, shorter hairstyle. "Do you like it?" he asked, eyes drooping as if expecting a no.

I stepped into the room and shut the door, dropping my stuff on the floor. "Heck yeah, I like it." I touched his hair on either side of his head, sizing it up. It was short, layered, and spiked in several directions on the top, much like…. "It's like that picture you showed me of Billy Joe Armstrong. I love it."

"Are you sure? There's not as much for you to play with."

"That's okay." I really didn't care about the length because he was adorable no matter what.

"I used to have it this way years ago. I really like it. I hope you're not mad I didn't tell you. I walked down Main Street and found a salon that was open on Sunday. I wanted to surprise you."

"I'm surprised." I leaned in and kissed his neck. He was also wearing the black choker I'd seen on him a while back. The choker that did things to me. "I like your hair, Lon, but this choker has me all kinds of horny." I nibbled his neck to emphasize my point.

Alonzo giggled. "It's actually a collar."

I growled deep in my throat, lifting him off his feet and carrying him over to the bed. We weren't in a rush, and there was something to be said about partial nakedness ramping expectations, but I was also fine with stripping down and exploring his skin without the cumbersome clothing. Alonzo did not complain while I divested him of his.

I left the collar on.

After we made love a couple of times and cleaned up, I held him against my chest under the blankets, enjoying the sound of our breathing together. I had never experienced such deep and utter peace as I had when he was in my arms. Being inside of him was also a deeper connection than I'd realized it would be. Sex had been fun when we started out last Tuesday, but before I knew it, I had tumbled down into an endless well of sensual bliss, which took over my body and molded it into whatever was necessary to achieve the greatest orgasm of my life, over and over. Somehow, fucking transformed from carnal pleasure into a living entity that wrapped around the two of us and formed something new, something beautiful. Maybe it was from having our bodies joined in a way that was meant for couples. That was how my dad had explained sex. He said it was meant to be beautiful between two people who sincerely loved each other.

Alonzo hadn't said the words yet, but I waited patiently because I saw how he felt in his eyes.

Perhaps it was the exposure I felt in his presence, but I found myself asking for the same connection he'd given me. I wanted to give myself to him. "Alonzo?" I asked, using his given name as a sign of importance.

"Hmm?" he sighed. I think he was daydreaming while playing with my chest hair.

"Will you…," I whispered, pausing as I formed the words. "Will you make love to me? I want to feel you inside."

Alonzo stiffened in my arms and rose up on his elbow. He swallowed hard. "I don't know if I can do that."

I stroked his cheek to soothe him. "Hey, shhh, it's okay. I've heard some guys don't like to top, and that's fine. I only asked because I wanted to feel what you experience. Being inside you is indescribable, and if you don't want to…."

"I do, but…." He paused, eyes going wider as he turned away.

I reached for him. "Lonnie." I caressed his arm and kissed his shoulder as he faced away from me.

"It's not that I don't want to, it's that I haven't since…." He didn't finish his sentence. He tried again. "I haven't done that since… since Kyle."

The ex. I felt so jealous all of a sudden. Kyle had had something with Alonzo that I never would unless he stepped past his fear and tried. "Lonnie, I understand. I don't want to push you. I just wanted to feel you inside of me." I kissed his shoulder several more times, moving my lips up to his neck. I licked the rim of his ear as I reached around his body so I could fondle his nipples. If he wasn't going to take me, then I knew he'd at least allow me another round before we fell asleep.

I felt him shaking, and I wasn't sure if it was from nerves or excitement. I'd caused him to shake a number of times over the last several days, and it was all in a good way. Now, I wasn't so sure—until he turned in my arms and pressed me back onto the other pillow, leaning over me with a look of determination.

"No, I want to. I can do this." He kissed my neck and took hold of my semierect penis, stroking me into full-blown begging in no time.

"Lonnie…. That feels good, but I want… oh…."

"You want more. I know." He slipped down and took me into his mouth, and I gasped. He worked it for a minute but pulled off. He answered my unspoken question. "Penetration hurts more if you come first. Relax. I'll take good care of you. I promise."

Alonzo grabbed the lube and a condom. He worked me open in much the same way as I'd done to him, with slick, probing fingers, before pressing his dick slowly inside. White-hot pain surged through the lower half of my body, and I gritted my teeth, but Alonzo was there, leaning down, shushing me with soft sounds, rubbing his nose over mine while holding still until I relaxed. He told me to breathe. His deep brown eyes lulled me, and soon the stinging pain was replaced by tingling sensations that rippled and mounted with each small thrust. Out, in, out, and back in.

I moaned softly, and Alonzo picked up his pace.

My legs seemed misplaced and awkward propped up on his slender shoulders, and something in the way I was trapped like that between his body and arms multiplied my sense of helplessness. With my legs pressed against my chest, my ass was exposed even more than simply being naked on the bed. Under him, taken by him, subject to him, I became a slave to his desires, powerless to assert my will as Alonzo's body undulated. Jutting his hard cock in and out, connecting with those mysterious places inside, Alonzo rhythmically rocked me into a space beyond myself, where my fingers lost sensation and my toes disappeared.

I arched my back, tilting my head and moaning in a voice I'd never heard before, allowing Alonzo access to my neck, which only pushed my floating body over the cliff's edge. Lightning struck my balls, and the fingers I couldn't feel gripped his back with bruising force.

Like gravity being turned on with a light switch, my thoughts returned, zeroing in on all the nerve endings that had seemed numb seconds before. I felt all of them now, dancing and screaming and howling in delight from the pain that wasn't as painful as it was enlightening. My nerves sang to my heart about how incredibly gratifying it was to be consumed by Alonzo in this way. He groaned and thrust violently into me before collapsing, boneless, gasping for breath.

I gripped the short hair on the back of his head and hauled him to my mouth before he could break our connection and slip free of my body. My lips needed his attention more so in that moment after release than at any other time I'd been with him. If I thought I'd been desperate for his touch in the past week, I knew without a doubt I'd shamelessly beg to make love again after tonight. Nothing in heaven or on Earth could possibly satisfy me like that again.

Afterward, when we'd cleaned off the cum and our giddiness had subsided, Alonzo curled up against my side, his arm across my chest and his head nestled between my shoulder and my neck. I thought to say "thank you," but it seemed superfluous. Instead, I kissed and nuzzled his hair and stroked his arm. I'd never been happier in my life.

THE NEXT morning I awoke to see Alonzo's sleeping face, peaceful and silent. His hair was mussed, but it wasn't long enough to cover his eyes anymore. Though his eyes were closed, I still delighted in the way his lashes formed dark crescents above his high cheekbones, and in the shape of his perfect nose. Alonzo was beautiful, and my fingers were drawn to him.

I gently caressed his hair, over his ear, down his exposed neck and bare shoulder. He sighed but didn't stir. In those moments of captivation, I knew without a doubt I'd never love anyone else. Moreover, I had to tell my parents. Yesterday had been an exercise in futility. I wasn't ready, and Kat's presence had distracted me. Today, my conviction was set.

Caleb's desk clock read 5:15 a.m. when I peered at it over Alonzo's shoulder. I still had forty-five minutes before my dad left for work. If I hurried, I could talk to both my parents while my gumption was still in charge. If I waited too long, chances were good I'd chicken out again.

I kissed Alonzo's forehead and climbed out of bed without waking him. If I was lucky, I could talk to my parents and return before he awoke.

"Shit, soccer practice is at six thirty." Ellis would understand if I was late, right?

I grabbed my jeans off the floor and pulled them on, scooped up my shoes and a shirt, and was out his door as quietly and quickly as possible.

From the parking lot, I texted Alonzo in case he woke up to find me missing: *I love you. I went to my parents' house to tell them. They need to know I'm gay and that I have an amazing boyfriend. Last night was incredible. I still feel you inside of me. My ass hurts, but only in a way that wants more. I can't wait to be in your arms again. <3*

Telling my parents was the singular focus of all my thoughts and the culmination of everything Alonzo had taught me about myself.

I texted Ellis before pulling out of the parking space: *Hey, I might miss practice. Sorry. I'm coming out to my parents while my conviction is strong enough.*

A minute later, as I stopped at the parking lot entrance, Ellis responded: *Really? Good for you. Let me know if you need any support from us. Cole said he's happy for you.*

Thanks. I think I'll be okay. It feels right.

Okay. Let me know how it goes. See you later.

Having supportive friends meant so much to me. I wondered about Doug as I drove. Would he be supportive? I had to admit I wasn't sure where his mind was lately. He'd been fine for years, but he obviously couldn't handle seeing me with Alonzo.

I sighed. I couldn't dwell on that now. I turned down another street.

My arms tingled. My skin crawled, itched, and tickled as if seconds from sliding off my body. "I'm really going to do this." I took a deep breath and exhaled at the next light. This wasn't a dream. I was about to tell my parents I was gay and that I had a boyfriend. "Holy man."

I lifted my shaking fingers off the steering wheel. My hand was literally shaking. I couldn't say I'd ever been so nervous. Alonzo? Totally. He was nervous all the time. Sometimes his hands shook, sometimes his whole body shook, but I couldn't say I'd ever felt this much anxiety over one little phrase in my life. "I'm gay," I practiced from the safety of the driver's seat. "Mom, Dad, I'm gay. I hope it doesn't change anything between us, but it's something I've been wanting to tell you for a long time."

Running over it in the car felt a tad saner than talking to myself in front of the mirror in the bathroom. I used to do that. I'd been fourteen and had admitted to myself I had a crush on Cullen. I'd thought that telling my parents before asking him out was a good thing, so I practiced what I would say. Of course, the whole situation became moot when he'd texted about a date he had with Sheri Michaelson. My hopes had been dashed, and even though it had been a long shot that he'd been gay too, I'd cried a little after reading that text.

It symbolized for me a metaphorical wall I would have to climb every time I had feelings for another guy. I remember picturing myself at the base of the Green Monster at Fenway Park in Boston, staring up at the thirty-seven-foot, two-inch wall baseball players strove to hit home runs over. If you could crack a ball hard enough to clear the top, you were the bomb!

Baseball wasn't my thing, though, neither were football or lacrosse. I had tried out for all those sports in high school, and nothing ever felt as natural as soccer. For my dad's sake, I tried out for several teams during the school year in ninth and tenth grade. By eleventh, I think he had figured out those other sports weren't a good fit, and he had stopped asking if I was going to make the team. He'd let me do my own thing.

My own thing, however, was about to butt heads with that family tradition of dating a cheerleader. I was nervous about how my dad would react.

I pulled into my parents' driveway and parked next to my brother's car. My mom had told me he'd be back from his business trip on Tuesday, so this was an added surprise. I could tell them all at the same time. A few more cleansing breaths in the car and I finally turned off the engine and headed in.

I heard my mom call from the kitchen, "Ryan, go tell your dad breakfast is served. He'll be late if he doesn't start eating soon."

"Already done, Mom," Ryan told her, standing next to the kitchen table with a plethora of carryout selections he'd lined up in the middle. My mom didn't like eating takeout from the bags or cartons. She always said that plates were more civilized.

She turned to face him. "Oh, well then, who came in the front—oh, Chris, honey, had I known you were dropping by, I'd have gotten more breakfast sandwiches."

I smiled from the kitchen entryway where I'd been watching them. I planned to see how long it took for anyone to notice me in the house, but she'd seen me right away. My brother and I used to do that as children because we'd both been silent as ninjas, sneaking around. Sometimes I would stand right behind my mom for several minutes before she'd see me, jumping and screaming when she did, of course. Childhood had been fun.

"It's fine, Mom. I can eat cereal. I didn't expect Ryan to be here."

He opened his ham, egg, and cheese and discarded the wrapper. "Yeah. I drove straight here from Atlanta. I was done. I'm not sure I want to keep this job if they send me on trips like that. I thought I'd bring breakfast by and talk to dad before he left for work. I don't want to bother Amber until I think this through. So why are you here so early?" Ryan took a bite of his sandwich as my mom poured me a cup of coffee.

"I was going to ask the same thing," she said. She set the pot down and glanced at the kitchen entryway, looking for my father. "What is he doing?" She huffed and walked away. "Excuse me, boys. I'll be right back."

Ryan took a sip of coffee. "Little bro, you got something to say, or are you about to puke?" He lifted his eyebrow at me.

I took a deep breath and blurted, "I think I'm gay." Telling Ryan first was actually easier with our parents out of the room, but I still studied the color of the tablecloth instead of looking him in the eyes.

"You *think*?" His skeptical analysis of my wording gave me some courage. He didn't sound mad. His tone was more... amused.

I looked at him directly and corrected myself. "I'm gay. I have a boyfriend who can attest to the fact. Although he might be pissed that I sort of ran out on him this morning after making love last night."

He squinted his eyes at me. "Wait. You had sex?"

Heat flushed my face and chest. Maybe I shouldn't have said that. "Yeah. With a guy."

Ryan chuckled. "Oh thank God. I thought you were one step away from joining a monastery or something."

"Didn't you hear me? It was with a *guy*. I'm gay." I was freaking out about why my brother wasn't freaking out.

"Yeah. So? Do you love him?"

No sweeter question could have touched my ears. Ryan was being really cool about it. I nodded and smiled. "I do. I love him so much. I feel incredible when I'm with him. I only wish we had more time to spend together. He's not in any of my classes, and I practice with the team more hours in the week than I spend with him."

"He's not a soccer player, then? What's he like?" Ryan ate his breakfast and carried on the conversation as if it were normal.

I sat back and relaxed my shoulders. He was making this so easy. Had I known, I would have said something years ago. *How do I describe Alonzo?* "Emoish, sort of, or punk. I don't know. He wears black most of the time and paints his nails. He wears eyeliner and has a couple piercings. Um…."

He grinned. "Nothing like you, then."

I grinned and probably blushed. "Shut up."

Ryan smiled softly. He seemed really happy for me. "What's his name?"

"Alonzo Martin. He's a biochemistry major. He's really smart. He likes to read. I think we've read many of the same books."

"So he's passed the vocab test?" My brother knew my list of standards.

"Absolutely. I think Dad will like him."

"Is he a cheerleader?" he asked, taking a sip of his coffee.

"No."

"Then your chances of approval are slim."

"But—"

"No, bro. I'm telling you, I know Dad. He's the Rock of Gibraltar. Why do you think I married Amber?"

My gut squirmed like a wiggling worm in the beak of a robin in spring. "You said she had great thighs. You said you loved her." I tried to remember every other thing he'd said when I asked him about it before.

"She was a cheerleader. I wasn't going to break tradition. Are you kidding me? Dad told us year after year about the"—he broke into a fake dad voice—"generations of Jackson men who married cheerleaders."

"Yeah, but…."

"No buts, bro. This is not going to end well." Ryan stood up and took his mug to the sink.

I heard what he was saying, and I hoped he was wrong. Dad could learn to like Alonzo, couldn't he? At that moment I heard my parents coming down the steps.

"But it's phenomenal, Charlotte. Did you see the date on the picture?" my Dad asked.

"Yes, Henry, I saw it. Now sit and eat the breakfast Ryan brought this morning before you have to take it to go. I can't believe you frittered away all your time looking through that old shoebox. I swear I need to install surveillance cameras in our bedroom to keep you on track in the mornings. Now sit." My mom was stern, but I knew it was because my dad got sidetracked easily. He'd always had umpteen million projects going on, and apparently getting out of the door for work in the morning was no different today from any other day of the week.

"Chris!" he greeted me, clapping me on the back and taking a seat across from me. "What brings you here so early? Did you see the picture?"

My mom chimed in, "How could he, dear, when you just found it?" She took a photograph from Dad and handed it to me. "This is what your father's talking about."

It was an old-time photograph of a football player in shades of brown rather than black and white, frayed around the edges. He had his arms around a girl with long hair who was wearing a cheerleading outfit. "Is this granddad?" I asked.

"Nope. Look at the date."

"Ryan!" my mom exclaimed, pointing at my brother, who had nearly finished his sandwich. "You couldn't wait five minutes until we came down?"

"Sorry," he said, not looking sorry at all.

I turned the picture over. "Nineteen eighteen." I whistled. "Wow. I didn't know they played football in the dinosaur ages."

My dad ignored my sarcasm. "Nineteen eighteen, Chris. He's too old to be my father. That's my grandfather. You know what that means?" He was frightfully elated, and my stomach grew queasier with each passing second. "Four generations of Jackson men have married cheerleaders."

I tried thwarting his logic. "You don't know that they were married, Dad. It's a picture. It doesn't say 'John and Suzy, married—1921.' Maybe they were just friends."

My father wouldn't hear it. "Nope. They were married. Which means the tradition dates back almost a hundred years." I handed the photograph back. "This is so exciting." He sipped his coffee as my mother sat down with us. "So what brings you home, son? Exciting news? Are you finally seeing someone?" His lips curled up on the edges. "A blonde someone, perhaps, who may or may not have been here recently?"

"Not blond," I admitted feebly.

He slapped the table. Instead of disappointment or anger over my not choosing Kat, he reasoned, "You've done it! You asked out that new girl—what's her name—Mindy? I'm sorry about inviting Katherine. Had I known it was Mindy you were set on, I would have asked her."

I shook my head. "No. I told you, I'm not interested in Mindy or any of the other cheerleaders." There was no way around it. He had to know.

"What about a cheerleader from an opposing team?"

"What?" His illogical conclusion jolted me. "No! I'm not dating a girl from another school."

"Who, then? It must be important if it brings you home before practice. What's her name? Is it Kara? I heard Kat mention a girl named Kara had a crush on you." My dad opened his sandwich and took a bite. He wasn't bothered at all yet, but I knew he would be. His matchmaking was driving me nuts, and I had allowed it to go on way too long.

Ryan, who had sat down after my parents joined us in the kitchen, suddenly stood and patted my shoulder. "Well, I think I'm gonna head over to Amber's parents' house. She's probably awake by now. It was a long drive back from the conference. Mom, thanks for letting me stop here first and grab that box I left. I need those papers."

Dad questioned, "Aren't you staying for your brother's big announcement?"

"No. I got the lowdown while you were upstairs. I'm good. I'll call you at lunch about my other concerns. It's fine. Chris has bigger issues."

"Thanks a lot, Ryan." I was not thankful at all. He was bailing on me before I plunged the theoretical knife into my dad's chest.

"Anytime, little bro." He winked at me. I was not amused.

"Tell Amber we said hello. I'd like to have the two of you over for dinner next week."

"Okay. See ya." He kissed my mom and left the room, so of course their attention zeroed back in on me.

I had to go it alone. "Okay, so you know my friend Alonzo?"

Dad squared his jaw. "The emo kid with the equally strange-looking sister?" He didn't look thrilled as he asked. I think he suspected where I was going with it.

"Yeah. Sort of. But they aren't strange looking."

"Whatever." He blew it off. "I'm not sure I want to hear more."

I continued anyway. "Well, you see, the thing is, I've been seeing Alonzo."

He slumped back in his chair. "I knew it. You picked a weirdo goth chick over a cute, blonde ponytail."

That assumption was worse than his first one. "What? No, Dad! I'm not dating Stephanie. Alonzo is her brother. I'm dating a boy."

"I...." He stopped dead with his mouth hanging open. "But you... I...." My dad stuttered and blinked at me for two minutes straight. I think drool was about to run out the corner of his slack lips. "But...." I knew he was alive, but the sounds he produced weren't intelligible. Then, without another sound, my dad got up from the chair, picked up the picture of my grandfather, and walked it over to the trash. He tossed it in, and my mother had to fish it back out.

"Henry, that wasn't necessary."

"It was tradition," he mumbled.

"I'm sure Chris wasn't trying to snub family tradition. I bet he cares for the boy. Don't you, dear?" My mom was sympathetic, but she wasn't getting through to my dad as she rubbed his back.

He walked off silently.

"Man, actually," I mumbled sheepishly. "'Boy' makes me sound perverted. I prefer the word 'guy' more than anything."

My mom sat next to me and took hold of my hand. "*Guy* it is, then. Tell me about him. Is he nice?"

I nodded. "Do you think Dad will talk to me before I graduate?" I had another year and a half, but his expression was very discouraging.

"Give him time. He's very wrapped up in family history, and finding that old photo this morning really got him going on all the possibilities. You know he's very sentimental."

"About cheerleaders."

"No, about tradition. Generations of men in his family have married cheerleaders, that's true, but I think he'll come around when he realizes the tradition still continues with Ryan. Your father needs to see that you aren't the same person as your brother."

"Do you think he'll give Alonzo a chance?"

She nodded. "Eventually. Your father loves you. I'm sure he'll see how happy you are and let go of his disappointment. You are happy, aren't you?"

Happy didn't touch how I felt, especially now with my mother holding my hand and gazing at me with genuine care. "Yeah, Mom. I love him so much. You have no idea how long I've wanted to tell you I'm gay."

"Why didn't you?"

I shrugged like a little kid who'd been asked why he'd eaten the last cookie. "I don't know. I always figured I'd tell you after I moved out. I thought it would be easier."

"Did you think I'd think less of you?"

I could tell her answer was that she wouldn't. My mom always showed her feelings in her eyes. She couldn't lie. She'd also never held back from telling my brother and me how she felt about everything. He thought it was annoying through the years, but I considered it a blessing because I'd always known where I stood with her. I think that's why I pushed so hard for Alonzo to express his feelings. It worked for our family, so I hoped it would work for him and me.

"Maybe," I said. "I've never felt anything like this before, so I figured it didn't matter. But after meeting Alonzo…. Mom, he sets my world on fire."

She had no words for that. My mom flung herself into my arms and crushed me. I heard her sniffling, which prompted tears to form in my eyes. "Will you bring him over sometime so we can meet him properly?" she asked shakily, pulling back to dry her wet cheeks.

"Yeah. I'll ask him when I get back to campus." I could not have scripted the conversation any better, barring my father's reaction. For now, I would cling to my mom's belief that Dad would come around. Support from two out of three family members was an acceptable percentage.

Chapter 12
Coming Clean

STEPHANIE HAD texted three times. It was unlike Alonzo to ignore all of them. Even when he was angry about something she'd said, he would have still texted back to tell her. So when he hadn't shown up for coffee before his first class, Stephanie thought to seek him out. She suspected Chris was his reason, but it was better to be safe than sorry.

She'd been like a mother to Alonzo for years. Their own mother worked two jobs to support the family while Stephanie and her brother were still in high school. She'd even worked some overtime to pay the medical bills after Alonzo had been committed in 2012. Those had been terrible years, and Stephanie blamed her father for bailing on them after Alonzo had come out. Their mother assured them they were better off without the "narrow-minded bastard," but Stephanie had played the what-if game many times in the past few years.

What if her father had loved Alonzo the way he was?

What if her mother had been home instead of working?

What if Alonzo had been able to talk to someone about the bullying Kyle underwent?

What if someone had contacted the police before he died?

What if they hadn't lived in Nebraska?

She knew it was futile, but it was hard not to wish things could have been different. She wanted a better life for her brother than he'd been dealt.

Stephanie walked down the hall and stopped in front of Alonzo's dorm room. As she raised her hand to knock, she heard Caleb's voice behind her. "I have a key if you want to go in."

She smiled at the shy gaming geek. "Thanks."

Caleb was cute, in his own awkward way. If he weren't Alonzo's roommate, she'd consider asking him out. But if things didn't work out, or conversely, if they turned out too well, then she wouldn't be able to hang with Alonzo in his room without making things uncomfortable.

Maybe once the semester ended, Alonzo could switch rooms, and she'd be free to flirt a little more overtly. She had a sneaking suspicion Caleb wouldn't mind at all since he blushed more times than a newly married Amish girl.

Alonzo was asleep in his bed, sheets bunched at his waist. She could see the hint of sweats sticking out, so at least if she woke him up, she knew he wouldn't flash her any of his naked bits.

"I've never known him to sleep in so late," Caleb mentioned, setting his things on his bed.

"Me neither. That's why I came over here. Alonzo's never late for coffee." She sniffed the air and made a face. "Eww, what is that stink?"

Caleb took a whiff. "Smells like sex."

"Oh, gross."

Caleb gave her a weird look. "Wait. If Alonzo didn't do you last night, then who'd he sleep with?"

Stephanie eyed him in utter shock. "Eww. Why the hell would you think he was doing me? He's my brother."

"Oh. Wow. My bad. Yeah, I thought you were a thing, ya know? I always see you together when he's not hanging with that soccer dude."

On second thought, maybe she wouldn't ask him out. Caleb didn't seem all too swift. "That soccer dude is his boyfriend, Chris."

"Wait. Alonzo's gay?"

Her face warmed as she realized she'd just outed her brother to his unsuspecting roommate. "Yeah. He'll be pissed that I told you, but I'll take pissed any day over passed out. Do you know if he was drinking last night?" She turned back to Alonzo. "Why are you still sleeping?" Stephanie stepped closer to the bed and touched Alonzo's bare shoulder.

"He's not gonna do anything while I'm… asleep, right?"

She snapped at Caleb. "Seriously? Do you know how insulting that question is? Has my brother done anything to suggest he's a rapist, or has somnophilia?"

"Somno… what?"

"Philia. Sexually aroused by unconscious people."

"That's a thing?"

"Yes. Look it up. But did you hear yourself? Has my brother done anything to suggest he'd be that kind of pervert?"

Caleb shrugged uncomfortably. "No."

"Then think before you speak, asshole. Liking boys doesn't make him immoral."

"Then why didn't he say?"

"Maybe because this is the kind of reaction he gets. He wants to be accepted like everyone else. Alonzo's had a hard time in the past. He doesn't share his personal stuff easily."

"No kidding. I didn't even know you were his sister. I thought you were his girlfriend."

Her jaw dropped again. "How dense are you? We're twins. Can't you see that?"

He narrowed his eyes, studying her face. "Yeah, maybe. I guess."

"Oh my God," she swore, wondering how the heck their conversation hadn't stirred Alonzo from his deep slumber. She gently shook him. "Lonnie? Honey? Wake up. It's me."

He stirred and lifted up on one elbow, glancing over at the empty pillow next to him. Then Alonzo whispered, "Kyle?" and lightning could not have struck her heart with more pain.

"Kyle?" he asked more urgently, searching the empty bed, lifting the pillow, and pulling at the sheets.

"Who's Kyle?" Caleb asked.

Alonzo turned an angry face her way and screamed, "Where did you take him?"

Stephanie reached for him as he jumped out of bed, knowing what he needed, fearing where this episode might lead. She pulled his body close and held him tightly as he struggled for freedom.

"Where is he? Where's Kyle?" Alonzo shouted, twisting around in her arms so he was facing the bed again. "It's all your fault, you bitch! Where'd you take him?"

He thrashed in her arms, writhing like a mad creature wrestling to break free. Stephanie held him securely around his waist, trapping his arms against his sides, making it harder for him to slip away. If she held him until the flashback ceased, she could talk him down and soothe his fears. Until his mind cleared and he knew where he was and whom he was with, there was no use trying to reach him.

"Kyle's his ex," she explained, holding Alonzo tightly as he flung her around like a wild monkey on his back. "He's dead. Sometimes the nightmares feel too real, and Alonzo doesn't remember Kyle's gone."

Alonzo kicked at the bed frame, and the two of them stumbled across the floor.

"Alonzo. Stop thrashing and calm down!" she urged futilely. Alonzo kicked at the chair and sent it skidding into the wall. "Lonnie, stop!" They wrestled and squirmed until Stephanie almost found her feet again.

"What the hell's going on in here?"

Stephanie met Chris's gaze in the doorway, but she didn't warn him quickly enough to stand back. He rushed into the room and took a swift kick in the stomach, sending him to the floor in one direction as Stephanie and Alonzo fell to the carpet in the other. Chris grunted and sat up in time to see Alonzo break free and bolt out the door.

"Alonzo!" he called, scrabbling to get up as he clutched his stomach. "Alonzo!"

Stephanie stopped him. "Let him go, Chris. He's never been gone more than an hour."

"Gone where? What's going on? I need to go get him!"

"No, you don't! You need to hear his story first," she asserted.

"Hear what story? I don't know what you're talking about. Why did he run out of here like he didn't know me?"

"Because he doesn't. Not right now. You slept here last night, didn't you?" She knew she was being rude, but she had a hunch what had triggered Alonzo's behavior.

"Yes. But I don't know why that's any of your business."

"Because the last time he woke up alone, it was because of me, and it triggered a flashback."

Chris shook his head and backed away. "I don't think I want to know why you were sleeping with him."

"I'm not perverted, Chris, so get your mind out of the gutter. Alonzo had bad nightmares after Kyle died, and I slept next to him for months. The one time I left before he woke up, Alonzo had a panic attack like none I'd ever seen. He didn't know who I was, and he went searching for Kyle all over the neighborhood."

"Oh. That's awful. I didn't know Kyle died."

Chris's expression softened, and she felt sorry she had to tell him like this. "Sit down," she told him.

"Shouldn't we run after him?"

"I appreciate your desire to help him, but he needs to calm down on his own. He's probably embarrassed for kicking you. Give him some time and I'm sure he'll come back. He'll get cold out there without a shirt or shoes on anyway. My brother isn't stupid—he's just frightened."

Chris sat on the bed next to her and asked, "So what happened?"

Stephanie took a cleansing breath to clear her mind. She had to tell the story again, and this time to someone who was all peaches and cream and probably never heard a story like this. She only hoped it didn't scare the happy-go-lucky jock right out of her brother's life.

"Alonzo met Kyle in a chat room online when he was fifteen," she began. "I remember how thrilled he was that there was another gay boy close enough to date. He went to a neighboring school, and they could only see each other when our mom agreed to drive Alonzo to meet up, but in the beginning, things looked pretty good for my brother."

"In the beginning.... Why does that sound so ominous?" Chris asked.

"Because nothing good can last in a town where folks openly target gay people. The two of them talked all the time, but Kyle wasn't out to his parents. Alonzo thought coming out to ours would help, so after they 'virtually' dated for three months, Alonzo sat our parents down and told them he was gay. I'd always known, my mom had had a suspicion, but our dad went ballistic. He called Alonzo any number of horrible things and forbade him to see Kyle. Not that they could see each other anyway, living forty-three miles apart, without a parent driving them."

"Oh man. I don't know how I'd deal if my dad ever did that. So far he's gone silent and walked away." Chris's shoulders sagged, and Stephanie could feel his grief. "Poor Lonnie."

Stephanie knew it was only going to get worse. Chris used her brother's favorite nickname, which signified to her their deep connection. Alonzo hadn't let Kyle call him Lonnie. She continued, "To condense my parents' history into a sentence, my mom supported Alonzo and my dad didn't. He left shortly after Alonzo turned sixteen."

"Shit," Caleb said from where he had retreated to his computer chair. "That sucks."

"Yup. My dad's not a nice guy. He left us with nothing. My mom worked several jobs to keep the roof over our heads while we were in school. Anyway, times were tough, but they only got tougher when

Kyle started driving. They met up whenever possible and made videos together, sort of like documenting their forbidden love. A couple more months passed, and somehow a boy from Kyle's school found their YouTube channel."

"Oh no," Chris muttered.

"Oh no is right. He outed Kyle to the whole school. It wasn't pretty. Alonzo told me several times Kyle feared for his life. We didn't know what to do. Alonzo talked to our mom, but she said the police refused to interfere in family business, and since Kyle's parents hadn't lodged a complaint, it was none of my mom's business."

"Why didn't Kyle's parents do something?"

"Because they thought he was getting what he deserved for being gay." It felt awful to be so blunt, but Chris needed to hear it all before Alonzo returned.

"That's sick. Did the kids at school beat him to death? Is that how Kyle died?"

She swallowed the lump in her throat. "It would have been easier if they had," she whispered. "The kids at his school beat him up several times, and no one stepped in to help. Alonzo said Kyle told him he screamed for help and no one came." She saw tears leaking from the corners of Chris's eyes.

"Then how did he…?"

"One night, Kyle stole his parents' car and snuck over to our house. The two of them came up with a plan to be together forever. While everyone was asleep, they pulled a Romeo and Juliet. They took a mixture of drugs and overdosed. Only Alonzo didn't die. No one, even the doctor, was sure why."

Chris stared and blinked and clutched his mouth as he dropped to his knees over the wastebasket. He heaved into the small trash can, and the sour stench of bile and half-digested breakfast filled the air.

Stephanie waved her hand in front of her nose to disperse the noxious smell. She handed him a tissue when he was finished. "Stay down there. I'm not finished."

"I don't know if I can hear any more," Chris confessed weakly, wiping his mouth.

"You have to. You need to know it was *me* who found them. You have to hear it was *me* who woke Alonzo up, only to have him stare into the face of his dead lover, vacant eyes, froth leaking from his lips. You have to hear that it was *me* who held Alonzo firmly around his waist while he kicked and screamed, watching the paramedics remove Kyle's body from his bed. He doesn't like me touching him because every time I do, he sees Kyle's body on a gurney covered by a sheet."

She felt sorry for Chris, but she had to admit, this was far more than she'd imagined he could take. His voice shook as he rasped, "Then why aren't we running after him?"

"Because he needs time to come back down. His adrenaline is off the charts. Once his heart rate slows down and he realizes where he is, he'll come back and we can talk about what happened."

"You think I triggered his flashback?" Chris asked.

"Maybe. If you slept here last night and left without him knowing… maybe. I've only seen him act like this one other time, and it was with me."

"And you said he doesn't like being touched by you. Maybe it isn't my fault. Last night was unbelievable. I can't imagine anything we did causing this kind of reaction."

"Where did you go?" she accused.

"Home. I came out to my parents. I texted Alonzo, but I guess he didn't get the message."

Stephanie picked up her brother's phone where it was plugged into his charger and pressed the button on the bottom. "Nope. It's still unread. How did talking to your parents go?" she asked.

"Okay, I guess. My mom is fine, and my brother is happy I'm not a monk. My dad's sad because he was set on me marrying a cheerleader. My mom said he'd come around, but I don't know. You should have seen the disappointment on his face. It was like I told him he had two weeks to live."

Stephanie leaned forward and stroked Chris's arm. "I'm sorry."

Caleb, who'd been quiet through the whole explanation of Alonzo's past, asked quietly, "So you're gay?"

Chris answered, "Yes." He got off his knees and stretched.

"Huh. Okay." Caleb stood up and pointed over his shoulder to the door. "I'm gonna go get some breakfast in the dining hall. You want me to bring you guys back something?"

Stephanie looked at Chris, and he looked at her; then she said, "No thanks. We'll eat later."

"Okay. Text me when Alonzo comes back. I never told him, but I think he's really nice." He held his hand out to Chris. "But not in a gay way or anything."

"That's fine. I'm not worried."

Caleb nodded in an uncomfortable sort of way. "Okay. As long as we're clear on that."

As soon as Caleb left, Stephanie and Chris burst out laughing. "I think I like that guy," Chris said.

"He's different," she said.

"So how did you know I spent the night? It's still early. I could have been stopping to take him to breakfast."

Stephanie appreciated his slightly defensive tone. He was perhaps defending their intimacy or politely saying "It's none of your business, lady." Either way, she was glad her brother had him, because he seemed strong. She pointed. "You're wearing his shirt."

His face twitched. "So? I snatched the wrong one. I hadn't noticed until I got to my parents' house. They're both white." He leaned down and snagged his white Nike swoosh shirt off the floor. "I was in a hurry, and I knew I'd be back."

"Yeah, but I know my brother wouldn't consciously let you wear that shirt."

"It's a shirt."

"No. It's Lonnie's vintage Insomniac concert tee he purchased off eBay," she remarked. "That one's rare, and I haven't seen him wear it for years."

"Oh." Chris looked guilty. "Well, he was wearing it last night. I guess maybe I'll change it, if you think it'll be a problem." He pulled off Alonzo's shirt and laid it on the bed.

Stephanie casually appreciated her brother's taste in men. "What's your tattoo say?"

After pulling his own shirt on, Chris lifted the hem to expose the Latin phrase along his ribs. He touched it and smiled, realizing how meaningful it really was, and then dropped the hem back down. He said, "This above all: to thine own self be true."

"*Hamlet*, act one."

Chris smiled. "Yeah."

"Good choice."

"Thanks. I thought Alonzo would appreciate it, but he's never asked what it said."

Stephanie could tell it bothered him by the sound of his voice. He didn't need to worry unnecessarily when there were worse things to be upset over. She informed him, "Alonzo reads Latin. I'm sure he noticed it."

"You think?"

"Yup." She thought he looked pleased.

Chris was clearly deeply troubled. She watched the way he picked up Alonzo's shirt off the bed, turned it over in his hands, and then held it to his nose, breathing in Alonzo's scent. The action spoke volumes. She understood how much her brother meant to Chris. She could make a joke about Chris being a werewolf, needing to pick up the scent trail, but this was not the time to talk about her obsession with *Teen Wolf*. Chris was seriously worried.

Chris pointed at the clock. "It's been thirty minutes. How long are we gonna wait?"

"Another thirty."

Chris shook his head. "I don't like it. He shouldn't be out there alone. This isn't his hometown. We've only walked down a few streets. What if he gets lost?"

"He won't. Lonnie's probably sitting at the bottom of the steps in one of the dorm stairwells thinking about what happened."

"Okay, but what if he's reliving it all? Don't you think he should be with someone?"

She took out her phone and searched her contacts. "I'll call his therapist."

Chris went to the door. "While you do that, I'm searching the building. I'm not leaving him alone."

When Alonzo failed to return, Stephanie and Chris spent most of the afternoon searching the entire campus: every building, every field, the parking lots, the locker room, even the neighboring dorm buildings. Four hours later, they faced each other in the quad by the big tree. Stephanie knew Chris was angry.

"I'm sorry," she said.

Chris squinted his eyes shut and clenched his jaw. "We shouldn't have let him go."

Stephanie had nothing to say. He was right. Her brother was gone, and it was all her fault.

"Hey. What's going on, man?" someone asked.

They both turned as a guy Stephanie had seen on the soccer field walked up to them. Chris turned his face away and wiped his eyes, and then he told the guy, "Nothing, Cedric."

"Nah, man, you don't get to pull that shit when it's plain as the tears on your cheek it ain't. Coach told us you wouldn't be at practice, and I didn't see you in class. Where've you been?" Cedric looked at Stephanie. "And who's the pretty lady?" He winked.

Chris wiped his eyes again and took a breath. Stephanie could tell he was not ready to answer questions like that. "Um, yeah, Cedric, this is Stephanie. Stephanie… Cedric. He plays midfield on the team."

"I've watched you play. You're good."

Cedric grinned. "Thanks, but Chris here's the star." He tapped Chris on the chest. "So where were you, man?"

Chris looked nervous and unsure where to start, so Stephanie answered for him. "My brother's missing. Chris and I have been looking around campus trying to find him."

"Maybe he wants a little privacy. I know I dodged my sister every time she was in the house. She always wanted to know my personal business. I got tired of it and hid in the garage. I even built a fort in the corner so it would be like camping or something every time I went out there."

Stephanie laughed. "That's funny."

"So maybe your bro needs his space."

"No, he doesn't," Chris said, zapping the humor and bringing them back to the gravity of the situation. "Alonzo had something happen to him, kind of like a panic attack, and he took off. We need to find him."

"Alonzo? Isn't that the guy you've been hanging with?"

Chris hesitated, then nodded.

Stephanie felt the tension tighten around them. Chris's friend was looking at him rather oddly.

"Chris, can I ask you a question?"

Chris answered, "Yeah," but Stephanie could tell the unspoken part was "but I'm not sure I want to answer it."

"Don't take this the wrong way, okay, because I don't mean anything bad by it, but are you gay?"

Stephanie held her breath. What would Chris do? This was obviously his friend, but she could tell by the sudden flush over his cheeks he was bothered by the question.

Chris averted his eyes when he answered, "Yes."

Cedric's reaction, however, was not what either of them expected. Cedric clapped Chris on the shoulder in a friendly sort of way and said, smiling, "That explains it! Doug's been all weird about Coach being gay, and not too long ago he went on and on about 'what if someone else on the team was gay' and shit. I didn't know why he was talking like that, but now I get it—he meant you!"

Chris answered quietly, "Yeah. It's me." He licked his lips nervously. "I'm gay."

Stephanie wasn't sure if Chris was out to anyone, but the way he spoke to Cedric, it sounded like he wasn't.

"Chris, man, you don't have to worry about it. We've been buds for a while, man. We're teammates. Compadres. I don't care if you're gay."

"You don't?"

"No. Is Alonzo your boyfriend?"

Chris nodded.

"And you say he's missing?" Cedric sounded concerned.

Stephanie explained, "Yes. He had a panic attack and took off. We're not from Westminster. Alonzo got a scholarship and only moved here two months ago. If he went too far, and can't find his way back, I'm really scared of what could happen. He wasn't wearing shoes or a shirt."

"What about a cell phone?" Cedric asked.

"Nope. He ran out, and it was still plugged into the charger," Chris said.

"I'll help you look. Have you told Doug? The more people, the wider the search area?" Cedric asked innocently.

Stephanie appreciated his calm voice and nonjudgmental expression. Chris was still unsure. His eyes drooped and his lips were tightly pressed together as if he could not believe his friend was being so nice. When Chris didn't answer right away, Cedric placed his hands on both of his shoulders and turned Chris to face him.

"Chris, look at me." When he did, Cedric added, "If you're worried about the guys, don't be. They all know about Coach and they're cool with it. Marshall keeps some distance when Coach gives a talk, but he isn't rude. I think living in this area over the last couple of years has proven that people *can* be accepted for their sexuality. Marshall is uncomfortable, but it's not like Coach is the only gay man Marshall knows. I'm confident he'll be fine hearing about you. Who knows, maybe knowing you're gay too will help Marshall see it's no different than being straight. Love is love, right? If Alonzo is your man, then we need to get him back here. Explaining that to the team could really help."

Stephanie watched Chris. He was worried, she could tell, but after thinking about what Cedric proposed with his gaze lowered, Chris straightened up, nodded, and smiled. "Thanks Cedric. I think you're right. I've been avoiding the subject for a long time. I told my parents this morning. If you think the rest of the guys will accept me, then telling them now is as good a time as any. One thing, though. Doug's been acting weird over more than Coach Montgomery. I think he's having his own personal crisis."

"Yeah?"

"Yeah. Something happened last night between us, and he took off. I haven't talked to him about it, but I'm sure he's still upset."

"Yeah, maybe. He wasn't running hard, and he barely said a word all practice. He kept looking around for you, I think."

Chris gave a slight grin. "Nice to know I was missed."

"Always. So let's get this search party started. I'll do a group text and have everybody meet us right here. Okay?"

"Okay."

STEPHANIE ENTERED Chris's dorm room and sat on the bed as he went into the bathroom. Even after the whole team had been apprised of the situation and given instructions about who to look for, hours of searching had still proved fruitless. Chris was angry, but also sullen. She knew he blamed her, and she couldn't argue.

Chris came out of the bathroom. "So what do we do now?"

"I don't know. Dr. McKenna is catching the earliest flight available. I told her to text me her flight information."

"What about the police? Don't you think they could help?"

"I've been avoiding the police because I don't want to make it a legal thing. Besides, don't they need to wait until he's been missing for twenty-four hours?"

He exhaled loudly in frustration. "I hate this!" Chris walked over and flopped, face first, on Doug's bed. He pounded his fists on the mattress and wailed into the comforter. When he was done moaning about it, Chris rolled over. "Did you tell your mom?" he asked, staring at the ceiling.

Stephanie answered, "No. I don't want to worry her. She and our stepdad are trying to sell the house while looking for a new one near here. She found a job in Pennsylvania so they could live somewhat closer to us."

"Alonzo didn't mention your parents moving."

"She didn't tell him. She knows change is hard for him, and she wanted to give him time to settle in here without worrying about her moving. I wish I knew why Alonzo hasn't talked to the new therapist. Two months is a long time for him not to work on grounding techniques." Chris rolled onto his side and watched her with his arm propped on his elbow. She asked, "So you told your parents about Lonnie?"

Chris nodded. "Yeah, but I'm not sure how my dad is taking it. He got quiet and walked away. He's been so set on me marrying a cheerleader for years, like all of the men in my family have done."

"They've *all* married cheerleaders?"

"Yup."

"Wow. It's gotta feel strange."

"Yup."

Stephanie wasn't sure what more there was to say. "Well, it's getting late. I think I'm going to go to my room and get some sleep. I have to pick up Dr. McKenna at the airport early tomorrow morning. If Lonnie shows up tonight, please text me."

"I will."

She squeezed his arm. "He'll be fine. I have to believe that. But if he doesn't show by nine tomorrow, I promise I'll file a missing person's report. Okay?"

"Okay. I'm gonna try to do some homework."

Stephanie hugged Chris and then left his room. The weight of her brother's disappearance made sleep difficult, but she had to believe he would be fine, because the alternative left her sick with worry. He was stronger than he'd been in years. Alonzo would be fine. He had to be.

Chapter 13
Living Proof

By 10:00 p.m. I was still doing homework, although I'd not gotten very far. My concentration was shot. I checked my phone every ten minutes, hoping Alonzo would have returned to his room and texted me, but nothing came through. Not knowing where he'd gone was driving me insane. I'd never seen such a look of terror on his face, or anyone else's for that matter, as when he'd kicked me. I'd never been around anyone who'd died like Kyle; I figured it had to have been terrifying. No wonder he hadn't told me about his past, about Kyle, or about his nightmares. We'd only known each other a short while. I couldn't blame him for not trusting our relationship.

I took out my phone and flipped through the pictures I had of Alonzo: one of him smiling, one of him sticking his tongue out at me, and one of us at the coffeehouse together that Lance had taken. I had to believe he was okay, but I didn't know how he could be. Where would he go? What would he do? He'd run off half-clothed, and it was chilly outside.

"Maybe I'll go look some more," I told myself, shutting my book. As I reached for my desk light, the door opened. It was Doug.

"Hey," Doug said.

I returned in the same bland tone, "Hey." I swung my feet over the end of the bed and sat there watching him.

Doug set his backpack on his bed and took something out. He held it behind his back as he stepped over to me with a really weird expression on his face. Discomfort, maybe, but it was nothing like I'd seen before.

I couldn't tell if he was going to yell or cry or what. As we stared at each other for a few minutes, I kept thinking I hadn't done anything wrong. He'd been the one to cross the line, and I didn't need to apologize for anything. Just as the stalemate was getting ridiculous, Doug revealed what he had in his hand. It was a carton of chocolate milk.

My breath hitched.

"I'm sorry for everything," Doug said. "I've been a mess ever since you and Alonzo hooked up, and I'm not sure I can explain it."

I stood up and took the carton of milk. "You don't have to." I set the carton on my nightstand. I turned back to my best friend and hugged him tighter than we'd hugged in a long while.

We'd been friends for years, and even though we were generally affectionate, our hugs were normally the kind where you grab the other guy around the shoulders, give him a good hearty pat on the back, and release without lingering body contact. It was a standard, manly kind of hug and acceptable with teammates, casual friends, and male family members. Most of the guys I knew never bear hugged their friends and held them close for any length of time. Those were the kinds of hugs girls gave each other, or mothers and aunts. Full-body-contact hugs were an unspoken no-no.

Probably because other guys would call those guys gay. Well, I'm gay, so....

Doug hugged me back as tightly. "Thanks," he whispered. "I'm not sure what I feel."

"Give it time," I whispered back.

Doug squeezed me and then released his hold. He took a deep breath and said seriously, "Another thing, besides feeling bad about kissing you and stuff, I know where Alonzo is."

I nearly leapt out of my skin. "What? Where is he? How'd you find him?"

"My friend Ariana knows Lance. She called me."

Lance? That I-want-to-punch-you-in-the-face jealousy came surging back again. "What does Lance have to do with anything?"

"Lance and his boyfriend, Jason, picked Alonzo up this afternoon when they spotted him on the side of the road. Ariana said she would have called me sooner, but she was working and only just got the message."

"What?" I grabbed my shoes and sat on my bed to pull them on. "When did they find him? Where do they live? Is he okay?" My mind was going a hundred miles an hour. I had to see him. I needed to know he was safe, not assume so because he was with acquaintances from the coffeehouse. Notice how I said "acquaintances" because I was not ready to acknowledge Lance as a friend until I knew his intentions.

Doug sat on the edge of his bed. "Lance told Ariana they picked Alonzo up around eleven."

"Four hours," I muttered.

"What was four hours?"

"That's about how long he was alone."

"I'm really sorry," Doug said. "I got Cedric's text, but I wasn't ready to talk to you. I called Cedric, and he told me what was going on. I drove around the neighborhoods between here, Monroe Street, and John Street. I kept thinking about how I'd feel if I were you." Doug got off his bed and crossed the room to sit next to me. He took my hand. "Thinking about how scared you must be made me see how selfish I've been. I don't know why I kissed you. I guess I'm lonely, and I realized all the girls I've dated have been a waste of time. None of them made me feel a tenth of what I see on your face when you look at Alonzo. I guess I want what you have, and I acted stupid. I'm sorry."

I hugged him again. "I forgive you." When I sat back, I grinned at him. "But if you don't tell me soon where Lance has Alonzo, then I might have to punch you. I don't trust that guy."

He tilted his head toward the door. "I'll drive you there."

LANCE LIVED close, so we arrived at his place ten minutes after leaving our room. I pounded rapidly on Lance's door, thinking how closely the thumping represented my heartbeat—an urgent succession of forceful thuds that threatened to splinter the door if he didn't open it immediately. When he did, I pushed my way in and demanded, "Where is he?"

Lance immediately shushed me and grabbed my arm, preventing me from searching his apartment. I looked down at his hand and then glared. "Do you want me to kill you?" My blood boiled as he stood firm.

Lance ignored me and tugged again. "No, but if you think I'm going to let you barge in here at this hour and wake up the whole building, you've got another thing coming. We should talk first," he insisted. He led us down a hall and into a small bedroom.

Doug followed us in and closed the door. "What's going on?" he asked.

"Nothing." Lance's calm gaze infuriated me, but at least he'd let go of my arm. I wasn't used to his serious tone, nor was I the kind of guy who let people direct my actions. I was the one in charge. Lance was merely the flirtatious barista who had no right to keep me from seeing my boyfriend.

I sat in the chair he offered, piercing him with my gaze. I figured if I was made to listen, then he was going to feel my wrath pouring from my eyes like molten lava. He cleared his throat nervously.

Good. I'm getting to him.

"Um, I wanted to let you know that Alonzo isn't okay."

"Duh! That's why I'm here. I need to get him back to the dorm and talk this through."

He paused, collecting his thoughts. I really was intimidating him, and I cannot deny how empowering it felt. Lance said, "No, I mean, this is beyond simple amnesia or getting lost in an unfamiliar town. Alonzo needs professional help. Jason, my Jason, is a nurse. He worked in a psychiatric ward for three years before transferring to Carroll. He's studied all kinds of behavior problems and mental illnesses. He thinks Alonzo shows signs of PTSD and social anxiety."

I slid to the edge of my seat and straightened up. "Exactly! His sister explained what happened a few years ago. Alonzo has videos online and everything. His previous boyfriend killed himself."

"What?" Doug asked.

Lance covered his mouth and gasped. "Oh, that's horrible."

I looked at both of them and filled in some details. "I know. It's pretty bad. Apparently his ex, Kyle, was bullied at his high school. The two of them had a YouTube channel and someone outed him. When they couldn't take it anymore, he and Alonzo decided to die together if they weren't going to be accepted for loving each other."

Lance said, "Like Romeo and Juliet."

I nodded. "Kyle died, and Alonzo woke up next to him. They were sixteen. Now, Alonzo has a history of panic attacks and nightmares, but his sister said he hasn't experienced anything this severe for eighteen months."

"Did you tell Stephanie where Alonzo is?" Doug asked.

"Oh shit! I forgot. I wanted to get here as fast as we could. I didn't think." I took out my phone and reconsidered. "She *did* say she was going to get up early and pick his therapist up from the airport. Maybe I should wait."

"I'd want to know," Doug offered.

Lance said, "It's late. Jason suggested he sleep here for the night anyway."

I stood up and protested, "Oh hell no. He doesn't get to tell me what to do."

"Yes, I do," said a guy who entered the room and shut the door behind him. "Are you Chris?" he asked.

"Yes." I eyeballed him.

This guy was nothing like Lance. As soon as he walked into the room, I could feel his presence. I was an assertive person and very sure of my leadership skills. I'd never been challenged on or off the field for my authority, whether that be in the classroom for group discussions or projects, or on the soccer field as a team captain or stand-in coach. Everywhere I'd gone since I was ten, others followed *my* lead and never challenged me—until this guy.

I straightened my stance.

Jason was shorter than me, but every bit as muscular. He wore a sleeveless tank that showed off his biceps as well as several tattoos. He carried his shoulders back and his chin up. His eyes were set and firm—not wavering. He knew this was his house, and he was not going to take orders from any outsiders. He was in charge.

"Lance told me you're Alonzo's boyfriend."

"Yes. I want to see him."

"Not tonight."

I stepped closer, peering down my nose at him and sticking my chest out. "I want to see him."

Jason took a step toward me and glared. "No."

I stepped closer, bringing us within inches of bumping our chests together.

"Whoa. Whoa. Whoa." Lance inserted his hands between us, pushing us apart. "Let's not get out of hand. Remember this is about our friend, Alonzo."

"Agreed," Doug said, taking a hold of my arm and pulling me back into the chair.

I yanked my arm free and jumped out of the chair. "No. I'm not sitting down. I want to know why this tough guy thinks he can boss me around and tell me I shouldn't see my boyfriend."

"Because he's had a rough day," Jason said.

I threw back, "I know. We've looked all over the place for him. He had a panic attack this morning, or a flashback of some kind, and took off. I've been worried out of my mind and yet you insist I stay away. Not happening!"

Jason held up his hands. "Okay, okay. I get it. I'll let you see him as long as you promise not to wake him up. He needs some sleep. When we found him he was scared and freezing and—"

"And he wouldn't even look at me," Lance finished the sentence.

His voice was small and pained. I flicked my eyes at him only to see the hurt on his face.

Lance continued, "His eyes were so wide, but he wouldn't focus. He kept turning his face away. Jason was the one to get him in the car and convince him to come inside and put on a shirt. He wouldn't even take a glass of water from me. Jason had to do it. His mind's cleared since this morning, but now I think he's embarrassed. Like we're judging him or something. He still won't talk."

Jason added, "I got him to lie on the couch and I covered him with a blanket. I think if he can rest, maybe he'll talk in the morning." Jason asked me, "You mentioned a therapist flying in, but why didn't he have one locally? Something that traumatic, if it's left lasting effects, shouldn't be ignored."

"You heard that?"

Jason gave me a look. "I was in the hallway, and you are very loud."

I felt stupid for asking. "Oh. Well, Stephanie said Alonzo was given a recommendation but hadn't made an appointment yet. She doesn't know why."

Jason offered, "If he's been relatively stable for eighteen months, he may have assumed he was fine. Pride can talk people out of getting help."

"Whatever the reason, you found him and he's going to get help." I held out my hand. "Thank you."

Jason shook it and nodded. "Anything for one of Lance's friends."

Friends. I guess we were. Lance and his boyfriend had taken care of the person who was the most precious to me and didn't seem to be in a rush to get rid of him. They sincerely wanted to help.

I toned down my attitude. "I just want to see Lonnie. I won't wake him up."

Jason agreed and led me quietly into the darkened living room. Alonzo was asleep on the sofa, so I crouched down next to him. I felt my emotions surging but held them in. I reached out slowly and touched his hair very lightly. When I'd touched him that morning, he hadn't woken up, so I was pretty sure that if I didn't make any noise, I could touch him carefully and he'd remain asleep. I leaned in and nudged his hair with my nose, smelling him. His scent reassured my brain he was fine, he was here, and he was safe. I kissed his hair and stood up, following Jason out of the room.

By the door, I thanked him again. "Call me if anything happens. I'll be back again tomorrow."

We said our good-byes and Doug drove me back to the dorm. I texted Stephanie, but she didn't reply. I figured she was sleeping. Doug had nothing to say verbally, but he was there for me with reassuring pats on my back and half smiles that told me he didn't know what to say, but he was there to listen if I needed him. He was a good friend.

It was after midnight when I finally fell asleep.

IN THE morning, Stephanie called me from the airport to hear what Jason told me. She wasn't concerned about Alonzo, saying he was safe enough, and she said she'd text me when she got back.

I intended on skipping practice again, but Coach told me I couldn't play in the game this evening if I didn't go. I reconsidered and showed up. The guys all approached me at once, circling around.

"Did you find your boyfriend?" Preet asked, his discomfort plain in his darting eyes.

"Yeah. He's safe for now." I didn't know what else to say.

Cedric had been the one to hit the team with the specifics when we organized the search party; I'd merely been standing there listening in. He'd started off with Alonzo running off and finished his speech with, "By the way, Alonzo is Chris's boyfriend, so this is personal." This was the first time we'd had the chance to stare at each other. Preet, Josh, Marshall, Cullen, Conner, Isaac, Donald, Terry—all of them hesitant to say anything.

Cullen spoke up. "I don't know why it took you so long to tell us, but I'm not freaked or anything. I was yesterday, after Cedric told us, but I hope you know you could have come out anytime before now and I would have still accepted you."

I bowed my head. I felt guilty for keeping them in the dark for years, especially Cullen. "I'm sorry."

Cullen stepped closer, and I looked up. He grinned and then hugged me. The rest of the guys joined him, and it swiftly became a group hug, with everyone laughing and patting each other and swaying back and forth in a giant huddle, until Josh joked, "And now we're all gay."

The huddle hug broke up, and we were all smiling at each other. My eyes caught Coach grinning at me from outside the circle, and I grinned back. It felt wonderful to be accepted for who I was, and the team was living proof.

As I turned, thinking we'd break up into squads for drills, I saw Katherine approaching with two other girls. She walked right up to me. "Jill found out and didn't believe it."

"Found out what?" I asked.

Kat rolled her eyes. "About Alonzo, duh! She was in my room last night when Stephanie got back."

"I think it's cool you're gay," Jill said.

I lifted my eyebrow. "Okay. Um, thanks, I guess." It seemed like an odd thing to say.

"It's not a novelty, Jill," Doug said.

"I know," she said. "But now I can tell my friends I know a gay guy, and I won't be left out of discussions."

"Way to inadvertently define 'novelty,'" I said.

"What does inadvertently mean?" she asked.

Doug snorted and she huffed at him.

"Never mind, Jill," Kat said. "Let's leave the guys for practice. We'll be cheering at the game tonight. Will Alonzo be there?"

"No. I think he needs some time to sort some stuff out." I wasn't sure what Stephanie had told her, but I wasn't randomly sharing information about Alonzo. "I gotta practice."

"Okay. I'll talk to you later."

Katherine waved good-bye and left with her friends. I hoped Alonzo would be okay with them knowing. He was nervous enough about holding my hand on the street; I couldn't imagine how he'd handle being outed to the whole team, plus the cheerleaders.

WE PRACTICED hard, and afterward I showered quickly and went by Alonzo's room to grab some things for him. Caleb let me in, and Stephanie called to say she was back from the airport. I'd given her

Lance's number, and Dr. McKenna had talked to Jason and decided she would go by to see Alonzo this afternoon. Before that happened, I was determined to see him.

I knocked on Lance's door and waited.

When he answered he smiled softly and gestured for me to enter.

I apologized, "I'm sorry about yesterday. I didn't mean to be a jerk."

He shrugged. "It's okay. I think I'd have acted the same if someone had told me I wasn't allowed to see Jason."

"You're a really nice guy," I said. Lance ducked his face shyly and shrugged again, which made me smile. I had to ask. "Last night wasn't normal for you, was it? I mean, ordering me around and dragging me into the other room. You're not bossy like that, are you?"

He blushed and glanced away, shaking his head. "No, but Jason was here, and I knew he wanted to talk to you first. I can be aggressive if I need to be."

I held out my hand, and he looked up. "Friends?"

He shook my hand and smiled. "I'd like that. I know you're jealous of Alonzo, but you don't need to be. I love Jason. We're planning to get married and everything. See?"

He held up his hand, showing me the diamond ring on his finger. "That's cool. So where is Jason? Is he here?"

"He's playing chess with Alonzo."

I sucked in a sudden breath. "He's awake?"

Lance stopped me from rushing off. "Chill. Alonzo hasn't said anything yet. Jason doesn't want you overwhelming him. He knew you'd be by to visit and suggested you sit with me over by the breakfast bar and wait for Alonzo to go to you."

Self-restraint was not my strong suit, but I agreed, "Okay. I brought Alonzo some clothes and stuff from his room." I held up my bag of goodies. "I know he's self-conscious about his makeup. I brought his Green Day: Welcome to Paradise T-shirt and his eyeliner."

"Cool. What's all the other stuff?" he asked, leading me into the other room.

"Supplies," I explained.

As soon as I entered the room, Alonzo pulled a blanket over his head and shrunk down into the sofa. He remained like that for a few minutes and only relaxed when I didn't approach him. Jason smiled in approval and winked as I spoke casually to Lance, doing my best to pretend Alonzo wasn't in the room. The sofa faced in the other direction, so I hoped Alonzo would relax while his back was to me. Jason sat on a hassock facing me, opposite the coffee table where the chessboard rested, which made facial communication easy.

I asked Lance about the photographs and watercolors hanging on the walls, and he told me he'd done them. I commented about the décor, and Lance blushed happily, explaining that he'd been the one to decorate the apartment. Lance was so laid back he made conversation easy. We talked about his hobbies, how he and Jason had met, and even about his family.

I also watched Alonzo out of the corner of my eye. He'd uncovered his head, glanced in my direction, and resumed playing chess where he'd left off. Jason moved his piece next without missing a beat, and I grinned at him. He was doing a good job making Alonzo feel comfortable without making him talk.

After a while, Lance made fresh guacamole and offered me some chips while we waited. I got out my bag of gummy bears and amused myself.

"What are you doing?" Lance asked.

"Arranging them," I told him, turning one red bear upside down and setting it on top of a green one. "They were lined up having a battle, but I got bored with that, so now I'm doing this."

Lance studied my handiwork. "They look like… oh, my! Are those sexual positions?"

I chuckled. "Yeah."

"Now I've seen everything. Jason did that once with my friend Kelsey's stuffed animals, but I've never seen it done with gummy bears."

Alonzo snickered, and I glanced over. He hadn't looked my way yet, but snickering was a good sign. I took out my next prop and slipped it over my head.

"Oh my God, what's that thing for?" Lance questioned, stepping back with his hand over his heart. "It's hideous."

"It's for Lonnie," I said, turning around hoping he'd notice.

"But it's weeks before Halloween."

"I know." I could only make out half the living room, but it was enough. All I needed was to see Alonzo, the rest was a bonus.

"Are you staying for lunch?" Lance asked.

"I guess so. I e-mailed my professors to let them know I wasn't going to be in class. I have an away game at four, so I can hang around here until two. I have all my gear ready."

"It's really hard to take you seriously in that thing."

"Kind of the point." My phone chimed. It was a text from Stephanie. *Dr. McKenna said she'd like to get settled in her hotel room as long as Alonzo is okay. She wants to call the other therapist to make an appointment to meet and discuss his case.*

I read it and showed the text to Lance. If he was kind enough to watch over Alonzo, then he deserved to know what was going on. He nodded when he finished reading.

Texting with a mask on was not easy. I had to tilt my face down and hold my phone up higher to see the keys. *Fine. Alonzo is playing chess with Jason. He hasn't talked to me yet, but he did snicker at something I said.*

Good. That's good. I'm sure he'll be fine. I bet getting lost was more traumatic than having the flashback.

I hope so. Let me know if you need anything.

I will. I put the phone down. "So what are you making for lunch?" I asked. "We could order a pizza if you want. I'll pay for it."

"No, that's okay." Lance was filling a glass with iced tea and turned back to hand it to me. He jumped suddenly. "I forgot you had that thing on for a second. It's so creepy. Do you want a lemon for your tea?" The way he asked reminded me of being in the coffee shop.

"No." I pulled the bottom of the mask to shift my eyeholes. "It's hot in here."

"I guess so. It's made of rubber and covered with fur. What if he doesn't notice? Are you going to wear it all day?"

I *had* considered his question. I knew I wouldn't be able to wear it all day. It was too hot, and I wouldn't be able to eat with it on. Even drinking didn't work. I lifted the bottom, took a sip of tea, and then pulled it back down. "No. I have a plan." I picked up a gummy bear and turned around, leaning against the breakfast bar as I aimed.

Just as Alonzo moved his pawn to another square, I tossed the yellow bear over his shoulder and onto the chessboard. Jason glared at me, but I tossed another one anyway. Jason moved his knight around the bear, Alonzo moved his bishop, and Jason removed Alonzo's castle from the board without either of them commenting about the four bears I managed to position in the middle. It was the fifth one that got a rise out of Alonzo.

He snatched it off the board and turned to wing it at me. "Would you stop!" The sight of my mask silenced him. "Wh-what… are you doing?" he asked.

"I'm Lon Chaney," I explained, curling my fingers like claws as I growled at him. "Grrr!"

Alonzo sort of smiled, but his mouth curved downward and he covered his eyes and turned away. I thought I'd upset him and went immediately to his side, kneeling on the floor next to where he sat on the couch, lifting the mask from my face.

"Lonnie, I'm sorry. I didn't mean to make you upset. I was trying to be the Wolf Man and make you laugh. Lon?" I touched his knee and pleaded, "Please look at me."

Alonzo wiped his eyes and then grinned at me with one of those smiles that was half-happy and halfway on the verge of sobbing. He attempted to laugh as he took the mask off the rest of the way and looked it over. "Lon Chaney played in *The Phantom of the Opera*, just so you know. He was a master makeup artist. His son, Lon Chaney *Junior*, was the Wolf Man."

I got off my knees and joined him on the couch. "Do I get points for trying?"

"Yes."

Slowly, I leaned in and kissed him. I had to. I missed those lips. I could ask him about *The Phantom of the Opera* later because I was definitely a fan. Alonzo kissed me back, steady and sweet, our lips falling into the dance as naturally as breathing.

When the kiss ended, he leaned into me. I pulled him into a tight hug and rubbed my nose and cheek in his hair. I said quietly, "I was worried sick about you yesterday. I looked everywhere. Lonnie, had I known you'd be upset, I wouldn't have left."

"Why did you leave in the first place?" Alonzo asked, his voice tiny and shaking.

"I told my parents I'm gay."

He lifted his face from my chest. "You did?"

"Yup. My mom and brother are fine, but my dad seems really disappointed. He walked off and wouldn't talk to me. My parents don't always make away games, but I'm hoping they'll come tonight. I'd like to talk to my dad."

Jason, who had been sitting on a hassock next to the coffee table, smiled approvingly. He stood up, walked around the back of the couch, and patted my shoulder. He left Alonzo and me to sort things out.

"I don't think I'm up for…." He started to panic as if I'd asked him to come meet my folks.

"It's okay. I didn't expect you to come to my game tonight. You've had a rough couple days. I'll come back later, if Lance and Jason don't mind."

"Fine by me," Jason said, walking over to Lance in the kitchen. He took out a glass and filled it with fresh iced tea.

I shifted my attention to Lance to make sure he was on board with my visit. He answered, "No, I don't mind. Jason works tonight, so it'll be nice having company."

"See," I told Alonzo. "Everything will be fine. You're not alone."

"It's so hard to believe."

His life before moving to Westminster had to have been hard, but I hoped he would start trusting now that from here on out, it would be different. I caressed his chin as I gazed into his troubled eyes. "I got you, baby. I'm so sorry you were lost. Next time, I'll wake you up and take you with me."

"I was so scared," he whimpered. "I couldn't remember how I'd gotten there and where the school was. I was so disoriented. I didn't even know what day it was."

"I know. I know. Shhh." I coaxed him to lean against my chest again so I could stroke his back. "I wish you would have told me," I whispered. "I had no idea until Stephanie said—"

He jolted upright and gave me his full attention. "Stephanie told you?"

I nodded.

Alonzo tried to hide his face from me so I wouldn't see the tears forming. He yanked at the edges of his blanket, but he was sitting on it. He couldn't disappear, and I was glad, even if it agitated him.

I grabbed his hand.

"Don't! Don't try to hide from me. Lonnie, please? I'm not going anywhere. I'm scared, but only because I want *you* to be all right. Stephanie called your therapist. She flew in to see you."

"She did?"

"Yup."

"Y-you're not… ashamed to be with me?"

"Nope." I pulled his hand to my chest and held it over my heart. "I told you before, I love you. What happened in your past is hard for me to understand, but it's a part of who you are. I'm here for you. I'm not running away. I want to help you." Alonzo started crying harder, and I held him until it all came out.

LEAVING HIS side was more difficult than ever. I could understand why couples moved in together, sometimes after only dating a short while. The separation anxiety was a killer. My heart ached, and my mind wouldn't focus. I'd never truly hated anything in my life as much as I hated being away from Alonzo. I wanted to help him, even if I knew there wasn't much I could offer. He needed to see his therapist. I was the guy who wanted to kiss away his problems, which went deeper than the scars on his forearms.

Life sucked sometimes, and I had a soccer game to play.

It was an away game at Franklin & Marshall College, and we were on the bus for over an hour. I sat next to Doug, as always, and watched him play the *2048* game on his phone. He played one game forever, and I couldn't understand how he got such a high score. My best was 10,364. Apparently that wasn't very high. My game was *FIFA*. I think Doug enjoyed knowing there was at least one game he could beat me at.

What I liked most about this bus trip to Lancaster was how Doug seemed to be his old self again. He was smiling a lot more and talking to me without a strained hesitance in his eyes. He poked me, and when I questioned why, Doug stuck his phone out in front of us, leaned into me, and said "Smile" before snapping a selfie. He grinned and set the photo as his background.

Doug amused me. I looked at my phone. *Why hadn't I thought of that?* My background was the Manchester United team crest. I scrolled to the pic Lance took of Lonnie and me in the café and set it as the background and my lock screen. Now that everybody knew, there was no sense in hiding it. I wanted to look at Alonzo's face every time I opened my phone.

I got a text from Coach: *Got a minute?*

Yeah. What's up?

Join me up front.

I stood up and squeezed past Doug. I always sat by the window, he always sat in the aisle, and Cullen sat on the seat opposite. We had our routines.

I slipped into the seat next to Coach. "Hey."

"How ya doing?"

"Good."

"Anything you want to talk about?" he asked.

I sat there thinking. What was he hoping I'd say? "Um, I don't know?"

"Chris. Yesterday you skipped practice to tell your parents. Don't you think that's significant? How did it go? Are you okay?"

Ellis was a really caring guy. He was right, telling my parents would have been huge except Alonzo's disappearance had overshadowed it. I nodded. "Yeah, it went fine. My mom and brother seem very accepting, but my dad's not really speaking to me."

"Give it time." He patted my knee.

It's what everyone said. I lost track of how many times I'd heard that in two days' time. *Give it time.* Perhaps it was the only answer people could offer. They say "time heals all wounds," so maybe this was one of the invisible wounds that would scab over in enough time and heal. I hoped so.

"Will your parents be at the game?" he asked.

"Maybe. They don't always show for away games, but I'm hoping to see them. If my dad cheers like he always does, then it will give me hope."

"How are other things in your life?"

Cedric hadn't included him in the group text. I didn't think he knew about the campus-wide search we did for Alonzo. He'd been at practice, so it was safe to say he knew I was out to the team, but he hadn't said anything this morning. He'd watched the huddle hug, and probably overheard Kat and Jill, but he and I hadn't talked about it.

"I came out to the team," I said.

He nodded. "I surmised from the comments this morning. That's good. Has anyone given you a hard time?"

"No. I think having a gay coach squelched potential protests. There really isn't anything left to say. Ya know?"

"Maybe, but there's still a difference. I don't play on the field. If someone didn't like playing for a gay coach, at least they knew I wouldn't be anywhere near them. With you, you're right there. They could avoid passing the ball to you or cleat you or shove you from behind."

His arguments were valid in a greater context, but not with my guys. They were my friends. This morning's huddle proved that. "No. Not these guys. I don't have to worry. I'm confident that they're supportive. I guess the big test will be seeing me with Alonzo. That had been the kicker for Doug."

"Doug had an issue?" He looked concerned and I appreciated it.

"Yeah, but we're good now. He's working through some personal things, and I don't think it was about *my* sexuality as much as something deeper."

"Good. That's good. So do you think you and Alonzo might like to come to dinner at my house sometime?"

"Dinner?" I questioned, because his offer threw me.

"Yeah. As in… another couple joining my husband and me?" Ellis sighed and then explained. "We just bought a house together, and I'd like to have you over for dinner. You have no idea how much Cole likes to show off. He loves to entertain. We haven't had a dinner party in a long time. My best friend Rob went to graduate school in Missouri, so I haven't seen him since the wedding. My other friend Russell has been in Japan for almost two years. Cole and I need to make friends, especially now that we're settling down in Westminster."

It took a few seconds for my brain to compute his proposal.

This wasn't a coach-player conversation. This was a friend-to-friend conversation. Ellis was asking me and my boyfriend to come to dinner. "You have no idea how much this will mean to Alonzo. Thanks. We'd love to. I'll have to ask him when is a good day. He's never had so many friends before, so I don't want to overwhelm him."

"Sure. Just let me know when. Cole makes a delicious beef Wellington."

"I don't even know what that is."

Ellis chuckled.

I headed back to my seat, and we were at the stadium in no time.

As promised, Katherine and the other cheerleaders were there. Jill gave me a little smile and wiggled her fingers down by her side as if we had a special sign or handshake between us. I'd told Ellis that the team was fine with my gayness, but maybe it wasn't the team I had to worry about. What would happen if all the cheerleaders knew?

I groaned.

We warmed up on the field as usual, and after coach gave us a speech on tactics and strategy, I surveyed the visitor stands for my parents. I spotted Ryan and Amber walking back from the concession stand with drinks and hotdogs in hand. I scanned the people in the direction they were walking and caught sight of my mom. Alone. Ryan and Amber joined her, and when all three sat, there were no empty seats next to them. My dad wasn't there. While it wasn't unusual in general for my family to miss away games due to long drives, my mother showing up without my dad *was*.

The reason for my dad's absence could have been any number of things. Maybe he had an early appointment and couldn't afford staying out late? Argument number one was shot down when I remembered another game that started late and then went into double overtime, and he stayed for the entire thing even though he had to get up extra early to catch a flight. He told me nothing was worth missing a playoff game. But… *this* wasn't a playoff game.

Reason number two for my dad's absence: leprosy. He had contracted leprosy, and for fear of spreading the disease to the rest of the soccer fans, he opted to remain at home.

I turned away. I couldn't think about it anymore because the real reason was too painful. My dad hated me, and no amount of facetious conjecture would change it. I toed a soccer ball and flipped it up in front of me. While I waited for the coach to send us onto the field, I'd juggle the ball. Knee bounce. Knee bounce. Toe kick. Knee bounce. Reverse over my shoulder. Heel kick. Over the shoulder again. Knee bounce. Juggling a soccer ball was easy and required zero thought. I needed zero thoughts. I needed a clear mind to play soccer and forget every tiny feeling associated with my dad's absence. I had soccer. I didn't need him.

Doug came over to me and stuck his foot out as the ball descended. He stole it and popped it over his shoulder, turning away and juggling it on his knee with three short bounces.

"Hey!" I protested.

Doug grounded the ball and stepped on it, turning to me with a serious look. He squeezed my shoulder. "I saw your mom and brother," he said, saying everything without being specific.

I hung my head.

Doug said, "It doesn't mean anything. He probably had to get up early for a meeting and couldn't drive this far."

Doug's near echo of my own rationalization floored me.

I covered my face. I wasn't going to cry because I think I'd cried enough in the past couple days to last a while, but I still felt the emotion surging. I didn't want to admit my dad didn't show because I'd told him. Doug hugged me briefly and then coach charged us to run onto the field.

Emotions had to wait.

AFTER THE game and before I boarded the bus, my mom and brother met me outside the gate. "Congratulations, Chris," my mom said. "Great game."

"We still lost," I reminded them.

"Chris, you were spectacular," Mom stressed. "This team has always been good, and losing doesn't negate your playing."

"Yeah, little bro. I liked that rainbow kick over the defender's head for your last goal. Nice one!"

I loved my family. They knew how to help me see the silver linings. I smiled. "Thanks. I was proud of that."

My mom stepped forward. "I'm sorry that your father—"

I stopped her, holding up my hand. "You just made me feel better about my game, so don't start making excuses for Dad. We both know why he isn't here. I'm thankful you all are here."

She hugged me and then asked, "I want you to bring your boyfriend to dinner sometime, or maybe Sunday brunch. I'd like to get to know him, if you think that's okay."

I nodded.

"Yeah Mom. I think that'd be great. I'll ask Alonzo when I see him." They didn't need to know Alonzo wasn't used to so much attention. Between Ellis's offer, and now my mom's, he was about to find out how accepting his new hometown could be. I hugged my mom, and said good-bye. Riding back gave me time to close my eyes and think. So much going on, and yet so little I could control. Once Alonzo had a chance to sort himself out, I'd ask him about visiting my folks. Dinner with Ellis would be easier.

Chapter 14
Fag Hags

THE NEXT couple of days were a blur. I went back to class and discovered I hadn't missed very much in the two days I'd skipped, which was good. Alonzo skipped class on Wednesday but had returned to his routine by Thursday. Doug was back to being himself without the strange distance, and I found it nice to be able to talk to him about Alonzo without his ridicule. Stephanie told me the therapist had talked to Alonzo three times already and had set up a schedule so he'd be able to go regularly to try and pinpoint exactly what happened to trigger his reaction. He still couldn't remember running away, but he wasn't afraid of talking about it with Dr. McKenna.

Friday after practice I habitually ended up in the dining hall. I hadn't seen Alonzo on campus in days because we both had work to catch up on, and I guess I hoped he'd be there, sitting at our table in the corner. He wasn't. It was some girl with her papers spread all over the table. She'd been there a while.

I turned around and caught sight of the cheerleaders waving me over to their table in unison. I groaned but trudged over.

"Hi," I said, setting my tray on the table across from Kat.

She jumped up and circled around the table. "That's no way to greet a friend." She hugged me and then kissed my cheek before heading back to her spot. I lifted my eyebrow at her.

I sat next to Candice, and she proceeded to hug me from the side and kiss my other cheek. When Jill attempted to do the very same thing from my other side, I stopped her. "Whoa. What's going on?"

Kat answered, patting my hand across the table, "Nothing."

I narrowed my eyes at her. "No, this is something. Why are you all smiling at me, and pity-kissing me as if I hadn't gotten any goals in the last game?"

"We're not," Kat said.

"Yes, you are," I insisted. These girls weren't clever enough to hide it from me.

Candice said, "Chris, we're trying to treat you like you deserve to be treated, as if nothing has happened and we're still your friends."

I didn't like the sudden incongruity. Who were these people, and where were the vapid cheerleaders? These were imposters. I amended that assessment—they were still vapid, but now they appeared to be caring individuals, instead of self-centered narcissists. "But nothing *has* happened and you *are* my friends. Saying it like that makes me feel like I got red-carded for cleating someone on purpose and you're all pretending it didn't happen. What the heck's going on?"

"Kat told us all about your boyfriend," Mindy said.

I felt sick. It was one thing for Kat to know because Stephanie was her roommate. Jill's knowing was reasonable because she'd heard it from Stephanie, but telling the whole squad? It really did make me feel like a novelty to be petted and put on display. Suddenly I was the trophy gay man. I grumbled, "Oh jeez."

"Don't sweat it, Chris," Candice said. "It's no big deal. So you like dick? I do too. We have more in common than I thought. At least it explains why you and I never got to second base."

I wanted to die. I beat my forehead on the table a couple times, but that only made Candice pat me on the back like a puppy. I lifted my head off the table and glared.

"Is it true that the hot coach is gay too?" Mindy asked, ignoring my obvious discomfort.

I flicked my eyes over to her. She looked sad, and I knew the news wouldn't help. I opened my mouth, but Jill answered for me, "Yes. It's so dumb that all the cute ones are gay."

"Bummer," Mindy pouted, literally sticking out her bottom lip.

"Tell me about it," Jill said.

Natalie asked, "But don't you have a cute boyfriend, Jill?"

"Yes, but that's not my point. It's irritating how all the good-looking guys I know bat for the other team. Hot coach, Chris, that guy in the Boscov's, Doug—"

"Doug's not gay," I interjected.

Candice snickered. "Well, if he can't get it up for Debbie, then he ain't completely straight."

"That's not an argument," I tried reasoning. I didn't like them talking about me, but somehow talking about Doug was worse when he wasn't there to defend himself. Though I found it interesting that he hadn't mentioned his inability to perform. *Hmm.*

Mindy sulked and crossed her arms over her chest. "I guess I'll have to hope the new player is built like the coach." She crossed her arms and turned around.

Some girls were so irrational.

I thought Mindy was silly, but what she'd said grabbed my attention. "New player?" I asked. If it was true, then at least it was a better topic than me and my boyfriend, or Doug and whatever *really* happened with Debbie.

"Yeah," Kat said, poking her salad. She was looking for the black olives and stabbed one as soon as she uncovered it. "Didn't you hear?"

"No. When did this happen?" *And why hadn't I heard about it from the coach?* I took a bite of my burger and waited to hear what the girls had to say.

"It hasn't happened yet," Sara explained. "Kara works in the administrative office part-time and overheard the admissions liaison for transfer students talking to the English department chair. She said that he said the student was transferring from somewhere and asked if it was possible to audit classes halfway into the semester, and if he could join a sports team."

I was used to the girls' gossip, and I even found it fun sometimes. Sara, Kara, and Lara were the ones who knew everything.

"Did the administration approve his request?" I asked. "Because what about tryouts and practices? Coach doesn't let *us* play if we miss practice that morning. How can this new kid get away with playing when he hasn't been practicing with the team?" I was irritated about so many things, and I guess it all came out against this new guy and his special privileges. I'd never heard of a transfer like that, especially in the middle of a semester.

"Jeez, chill, Chris!" Kat said. I guess she thought I was being ridiculous, but I didn't think so.

"Yeah, wow, what got up your ass?" Jill asked, immediately reconsidering her phrasing. She covered her mouth and giggled. "Oh, sorry. I guess that was Alonzo." She laughed some more.

The girls knowing wasn't so funny anymore. I stood and picked up my tray. "Okay, I'm out of here."

"Oh no. Don't go, Chris. I'll stop," Jill apologized.

I hesitated but sat back down. Something told me I'd regret it by the looks on their impish faces.

Jill shrugged and took a sip of her soda. "Besides," she mumbled, "it's not a big deal. I don't know why you're so upset. I like butt sex too."

"Jill!" I cried.

"I'm just saying. Everybody does it."

I didn't care for her rude comments. "Jill, maybe so, but I'm not discussing my sex life with you."

"If I was Doug you would," Jill proposed.

"Maybe," I said. "But it doesn't matter. Doug is my best friend. You're not. I don't even think I'd tell Kat if she asked, and I've known her longer."

"Really? You won't even talk to us a little bit?" Mindy asked, still pouting but now pointing her pout at me.

"No! Why would you think that?" I didn't know for the life of me what had changed so much that these girls would assume I'd start spewing personal details.

Sara answered, "Because you're gay."

"So?" If she'd been a guy, I might have punched her. Seeing how Sara was a girl, I only growled slightly, reining in my anger.

Sara did a little head-flippy thing to convey her incredulity. "So... gay men have their posse of women friends. We're yours. So you have to share shit, like relationship details and sex tips. We can go shopping and do lunch as a group like other people."

"What other people?" I think I was momentarily stunned into a stupor. As the seconds ticked by, my brain realigned and told me this was not where I needed to be. These girls had it in their heads that I was suddenly a completely different guy. "You know what, I'm done." I stood up and looked each one of them in the eyes so that nothing would be misunderstood.

I told Sara plainly, "I hate shopping. I hated it before I knew I was gay—at the ripe age of eight—and I still hate shopping. Unless you're taking me out to buy new cleats or a car, my answer is a resounding no!"

Then I turned my attention to Jill. "You are the rudest girl I know. Whatever possessed you to think that we'd suddenly talk sex because

I'm gay is sickening. I will never talk to you about anything I choose to do with my boyfriend. It is none of your fucking business."

I looked at Mindy. "I find it interesting about the transfer student and potential player, but for his sake I hope he's everything you girls hate. I'd feel bad for him to get here only to be descended upon by a bunch of selfish, hypocritical gossips who have nothing better to do than squeeze juicy details out of their gay friend under the guise of 'everybody does it.' Everyone *might* have sex, but I'm not talking about it with any of you.

"As for you, Katherine, I can't believe you're their leader and you'd allow this. It's insulting. I'm gay; I'm not a pig. My *guy* friends don't even talk like this. Doug and I talk about our personal lives, but he's my best friend, and he's never been flat-out rude." *He'd been rude lately, but that was between the two of us.* "Gay guys might stereotypically have girlfriends they hang with, but I'm *not* stereotypical. I'm me. I like Doug, Cullen, Cedric, and the other guys on my team. I understand them. They belch and goof off and don't give a shit about shopping. If you can't treat me the way you used to before you knew I was gay, then I think I'll be better off without you."

I turned on my heel and made a dramatic departure. I was pissed, but really I knew deep down they were all very shallow. My speech would either jolt them out of their self-centeredness or prove my point. I dumped the rest of my lunch in the trash and stormed out. I needed Alonzo.

I texted: *Hey. Where are you? I missed you this afternoon. Can we have lunch, or dinner? I just need to see you.*

Hi Chris :) I miss you too. I'm with Lance. He has to work tonight so we went out. We're headed back to his apartment now if you want to meet us there.

Sure. Okay. But where did you go? "And why were you with Lance?" I fussed out loud as I hit send.

My battery is at 1%. I'll talk to you soon. <3 <3

I wanted him to explain it to me now. I glanced at my watch. I still had almost two hours of free time. I could meet them. If I was late to class, or missed it, so be it.

I didn't enjoy the thought of Alonzo shopping with the cute, flirtatious barista—the one with enough balls to boss me around. I abhorred it.

I KNOCKED on Lance's door, but no one answered. Somehow I'd managed to beat them back. I waited in the hallway like an idiot and leaned on the wall next to the door. I texted Alonzo, but he didn't answer, which meant his phone was dead. I didn't like the disconnect. Even when we'd been in class during the week, I'd still sent a couple of texts throughout the day.

I tapped my foot and examined the floorboards in the hall. It was an older building if I could judge by the hardwood floors. Weathered and uneven, the dark mahogany would probably cost a fortune to put in nowadays. I liked it. If Alonzo and I ever bought a house, I'd want hardwood flooring. My parents had some put in a couple of years back, and I liked the way it looked. Plus, hardwood went with everything. You could even add in a throw rug for color to liven things up.

I heard voices and laughing coming up the stairs.

Alonzo's laughing. He's never laughed so heartily for me.

"Oh my God, I know! That guy was so gross" Lance was saying as he reached the landing. "Oh hi, Chris." He greeted me with a smile, setting his bags on the floor to fish out his key.

"Hey, you," Alonzo said, smiling ear to ear. "I missed you." He kissed me before I could reply. I'd never seen him so relaxed, which was a complete opposite from the way he seemed at the beginning of the week.

A girl appeared behind him, and I nearly tripped myself allowing her to follow Alonzo inside. Lance set his bags on the breakfast bar, and the girl put hers on the floor next to the couch. Alonzo set two on the floor and some on the chair I'd sat in on Tuesday. "How much did you buy?" I asked, inspecting his bags from Kohl's, H&M, and Forever 21.

"Not too much. I haven't had new clothes in years. I'm a college man now. I can't wear the same old T-shirts every day." Alonzo smiled at me, stopped rummaging through his things, and stepped up close. "I'm glad you came by." His eyes were so bright, I would have never guessed he'd been so frightened only days before. He kissed me again, but this time it wasn't light and fleeting. He wrapped his arms around my neck and pressed his lips firmly to mine. It wasn't as all-consuming as it might have been in my room, but it was much more engaging than his swift peck in the hall, and Lance was standing right there!

"Wow," I said to Lance, holding Alonzo around his back. "Where did you find this guy? He looks exactly like my boyfriend, but my Lonnie isn't so bold."

Alonzo play slapped my chest. "Stop! I can be bold. You have no idea what this week has been like for me." He stepped out of my embrace and picked up two of his bags. "I want to model something for you. Do you have time?"

"For you? I'll wait all day."

He kissed me one more time before turning to leave, but something about his hands attracted my attention, so I took one, which stopped him in his tracks. He didn't seem to mind, though, when I kissed the back of his hand before looking it over. "You have different color nail polish."

His eyes twinkled. "Lance did it."

"Lance?" I questioned, moving my eyes over to him. I didn't glare; I merely eyed him with more interest than before. Lance blushed and turned away.

Alonzo chirped, "Yup. He suggested a change and I said okay. Wait until you see the shirt I bought to go with it."

"Isn't it supposed to be the other way around? You buy the nail polish to match the shirt?" I was almost positive that's what Jill would have said.

"Maybe, but whatever." Alonzo took his things and disappeared down the hall. I watched the empty space, hoping he'd pop back around the corner and wink at me or something, but he didn't.

"This is my friend Kelsey," Lance said, reminding me there were more people in the room and I was being impolite. "Kelsey, this is Chris."

"Hi," I said.

Kelsey held out her hand. "It's so nice to meet you. Alonzo's talked about you all day. He's such a sweet guy."

I shook her hand courteously. "Thanks. I think so."

Lance tipped his head to the side in his usual manner, which was both charming and shy, and said softly, "You don't need to be on guard every time you visit here. I swear I'm not out to steal your man. We're friends, that's all."

Kelsey snapped her attention from her new items to Lance. "What?" She turned her shocked expression my way. She was either a dramatic person by nature, or Lance's comment truly bothered her. "Lance can't be serious. Chris, if you'd heard Alonzo today, you would never be jealous of anyone. Alonzo is so completely in love with you it's adorable."

"He is?" *Because he's never told me, even if I believe it's true.*

She waved her hand at me. "Totally!"

Alonzo called from the other room, "Lance? Can you help me? I think I need scissors. And hair gel."

Lance snickered and swatted his wrist in Alonzo's general direction. "He's so funny. I already told him I haven't used anything for a while because my hair's too short." He shook his head and rolled his eyes, smiling as he weaved around the bags on the floor and down the hall.

I spied a bag of gummy bears as soon as I sat down at the barstool next to the breakfast bar. "Gummy bears! Cool. Maybe Alonzo does love me," I mumbled, flipping the two-pound bag over, inspecting it.

"It wasn't Alonzo's idea," Kelsey said. "Lance saw the bag in the candy store and asked Alonzo if he'd mind if he bought it for you."

"Lance?" I questioned. Every time I got jealous of him, he did something else that was selfless and kind. I heaved a sigh. My shoulders sagged. I really did need to get over myself and accept his presence in Alonzo's life. Alonzo needed friends, and Lance was probably going to be one of the best if I only looked past my irrational jealousy. It had no place or evidence to support it; the jealousy only existed in my stupid imagination. Lance was a great guy. Alonzo was lucky to find someone like him. Plus, they'd gone shopping together, and I had to admit I was glad it wasn't with me. I hated shopping.

I set the gummy bears down and walked over toward the hall when Lance came around the corner. He shooed me away and said, "Step back. Step back."

I did.

Lance announced, "Now introducing, here directly from Podunk, Nebraska, the new and improved Alonzo Martin. Drum roll...." I started making a drum-roll sound in the back of my throat and Lance gestured to me. "You don't actually have to make the sound. It was rhetorical."

I stopped and waited.

"Alonzo Martin.... Yay!" he exclaimed, clapping and holding out his arms to sweep my attention over to the part of the hall where Alonzo was to appear, except he didn't. Lance dropped his arms. "Alonzo?"

"Make Chris turn around," Alonzo insisted, hissing it to Lance quietly, but loud enough for me to hear.

"I can hear you, Lon."

"Turn around," he said.

I did.

Lance announced again, "Now introducing the new and improved Alonzo Martin!" He clapped and hooted for show, and I had to chuckle to myself.

Kelsey was smiling at me, and I saw her expression change when Alonzo had obviously stepped around the corner of the wall. I turned and sucked in a breath. "Lon," I uttered, drinking in his beauty on a whole other level. "Wow."

"Do you like it?" he asked, the coy little smile on his lips making that dimple pop on his cheek.

Alonzo was wearing a purple button-down shirt that matched his nail polish but also contrasted with his brown eyes in a way that made me salivate. I stepped closer and ran my gaze all the way down his body. I took his thin, slate-gray tie between my fingers and ran them down its length, noting how perfectly it complemented his dark gray, pinstriped, skinny jeans. I licked my lips and then ran my fingers over the shell of his ear, appreciating his hairstyle: spiked on the top, slicked back on the sides, with a tad pulled down across his forehead for accent. My man was fuckin' hot!

"I like it," I growled deep in the back of my throat, guttural and full of lust. I tugged his tie and Alonzo took the hint, stepping forward and tipping back his head. I pressed my mouth on his and devoured him, pulling his body tight against mine, lifting him off his feet.

"Yay," Lance quietly cheered us on, clapping softly. "They're so cute."

Alonzo started giggling into my mouth, which hindered my kissing, so I moved over to nibble on his ear. "I want to fuck you so bad right now," I whispered, licking my way down his neck and nipping his throat with my teeth.

Alonzo chuckled.

I pulled back. "I don't see what's so funny."

"You." He grinned. "Lance told me when I tried this on, you'd probably blow your load in one glance."

I dropped my jaw and turned to look at Lance, who was sitting on the armrest of the sofa, grinning and shrugging—guilty as charged.

"You said that?" I asked incredulously.

"Yes. Sorry."

He didn't look sorry. He stood up and walked back over to us. "Come on." He waved Alonzo to follow. "You need to show him the other outfit."

Alonzo slipped out of my arms and skipped off to follow Lance.

I called, "I like your black leather dress shoes, by the way."

Alonzo poked his head around the corner of the wall and winked. "Thanks."

It was nice to see him in something other than combat boots, although I kind of wanted him naked at the moment, so really any shoes were merely another article of clothing I would have to remove. I sighed. I wasn't going to have him naked, so I might as well enjoy my time. I turned around and joined Kelsey in the living room.

"So have you known Lance a long time?" I asked, plopping down on the sofa next to her.

"Seventeen years. We lived in the same neighborhood growing up. I got a new bike one year, and he thought it would be fun to ride around with a rabbit in the basket, so we spent all summer trying to catch one in my backyard."

"Wow. Did you?"

"No, but Lance gave me a stuffed one for my birthday, and we've been best friends ever since. He's thoughtful like that."

I glanced over at the gummy bears. "He is." Suddenly I found myself fighting tears. I didn't know why, and I blinked several times, willing the surge of emotion to end. Whether by luck, chance, or destiny, Alonzo and I had made friends with people who were genuinely kind and completely different from the other people I was used to hanging with.

I looked around. This wasn't a dorm room. It was a well-decorated apartment, warm and inviting, with paintings and photographs on the walls and vases on the tables. Lance and Jason had a bookshelf lined with books and curtains to match the rug. There was a framed snapshot of the two of them—smiling and posing in front of a waterfall—sitting on a long, narrow mahogany table by the door. An Ashington console table, my mom called the style. She had the very same one, with pairs of shoes sitting in a row underneath like Lance and Jason did.

My sudden swell of emotion was because *this* was exactly what I wanted. This was what my parents had when they'd been younger. My mom told me they'd had an apartment filled with things they'd bought together, which progressed into a buying a house and having children. Lance and Jason were building a life, and I wanted to do the same thing with Alonzo. It didn't matter that I'd only known Alonzo a few weeks. I loved him with every muscle in my body and no outside influence could change that. My dad would have to suck it up and deal because this was the guy I wanted to spend my life with.

"How long have you been with Alonzo?" Kelsey asked, pulling me out of my daydreaming.

"Hmm? Um, a couple weeks." It was a short answer because I was still restraining my emotions. I didn't need to cry in front of a stranger, no matter how nice she seemed.

"I would have thought it was longer the way Alonzo talked. That's cool, though. Was it love at first sight, then?" She had a sweet voice. Not too high-pitched, but light like a bird.

I smiled. "Pretty much," I replied, knowing it was precisely like that for me. "I think I knew the first time he gazed at me with those amazing eyes of his I'd lost my heart."

"Aww, you are so sweet," she gushed.

Something in the way she looked at me made me think of the girls I knew and whom I'd spoken with that morning. Was Kelsey anything like Kat or Jill? "Can I ask you something?"

"Sure."

"Don't take this the wrong way, okay? I'm just wondering." I hoped she'd see my sincerity. I didn't intend on ruining the friendship before it started.

"No worries." So open, so unguarded, Kelsey smiled pleasantly.

I took a deep breath. "So would you consider yourself one of those girls who likes being friends with gay men?"

She laughed. "You mean like a fag hag?"

I felt guilty for asking. "Yeah. I guess."

"Maybe." She laughed some more as if my question was hilarious. "I've never thought about it."

"Why?"

"Because Lance and I have been friends forever. It was never about him being gay. It was never about him being gay. We were friends back when we were eight and not thinking about sexuality at all. Back then, it was about who we enjoyed being around. If you want to define it, then sure, I'm his fag hag, but to me that term has a negative connotation suggesting I'm only friends with him *because* he's gay, which is untrue."

She had a point. The term *did* sound derogatory and not toward the "hag," but rather the associated "fag." I didn't like that word. It made my stomach churn. I'd never been called a fag, and I certainly didn't want any of my friends slinging it around as if the label were acceptable. To me, it wasn't.

"Do you... ever talk to Lance about sex?"

She snorted and covered her mouth with her hand. When she recovered from laughing, probably because I wasn't joining in, she said, "Oh God, no! Why would I want to know what they do in bed? That's so lewd."

"That's what *I* thought." I put the emphasis on "I" and she picked up on it.

"Did someone ask you that?" She sounded appalled.

"Yeah. The girls I know who dubbed themselves my fag hags. They made me mad. I told them it wasn't any of their fucking business what we did together."

"Good for you!" She reached over and patted my arm.

All I could do was smile weakly. Kelsey gave me much to consider. I wasn't so happy with my "girl" friends.

"Attention, ladies and gentlemen," Lance announced. "Back for his second appearance at Lance's house of fashion is Alonzo Martin." He clapped and gestured. "Yay!" Lance was such a boisterous person around his friends. I could see why Alonzo enjoyed his company, even if I was a tad jealous.

Alonzo stepped around the wall, and my breath hitched a second time. He was wearing a black button-down dress shirt with a red tie and tight red jeans, which had black pinstripes. I jumped up and inspected his attire up close and personal.

"Turn around," I instructed. He did and I took advantage of his exposure by rubbing his ass. "I like these jeans."

He smirked. "I knew you would."

"You have a thing for stripes, I notice."

"Yeah. Is that okay?" he asked.

"Lonnie, why do you keep asking for my permission? You did that with your hair, and you're doing it now with your clothes. I already told you I love you. I can't think of anything that would change that. Just be yourself, and I'll love it, I promise." Alonzo looked down as if thinking it over very seriously. Lance wore a serious expression too, which told me maybe there was more going on. I took Alonzo's hand and led him to the couch. We sat, and Kelsey left the room with Lance.

"Alonzo, what's going on?"

Alonzo said very quietly, "I told you before, I had a hard time trusting *us*, and thinking I must be dreaming." I remembered him saying something along those lines, so I nodded. He continued, "Other than not remembering what happened to make me run off, this week has been amazing because for the first time in my life I have friends I can be myself around."

"Yeah, I was thinking the very same thing. I'm happy for you. So why do you seem so worried?"

"I'm worried because my original therapist is going to start some deeper exercises next week. We're going to the new person's office, and they're both going to work together so Dr. Hewitt is brought up to date on my past. Dr. McKenna said she was going to do some hypnosis and work with recorded sounds and voices to see if I react to different stimuli. I'm worried because she said she was going to call you and ask to record your voice."

"Why is that a bad thing? I thought you liked my voice." I grinned, leaned close, and whispered in his ear. "I thought you liked it when I told you the things I'd like to do with you, like how I want to get you naked and lick your asshole."

Alonzo gasped and pulled back to look at me. "You do?" He was shocked.

I gave a shrug. "Sure. There's a first time for everything." I touched his cheek and licked my lips seductively. "I want to make you beg, Lonnie. I want to have you come unglued. I want to know every part of you." I leaned in and kissed him.

Alonzo rubbed my thigh with one hand and touched my face with the other, but his kisses were reserved. He sat back and sighed. "I suppose I'm most afraid of finding out that *you* triggered my reaction on Monday. What if it *was* you?" he pleaded with sad eyes. "Do you really want to be stuck with a guy who can't remember running away and getting lost? What if that happens again? You don't know about all the time I spent in a mental institution, Chris. I don't want to go there again."

I was surprised and concerned, but only because I didn't want to think of him as someone who was broken. "You did?"

"Yes. That's why I'm starting college at nineteen. I missed a year of high school because I couldn't handle Kyle's death. I guess I still can't handle it if I slept with you and freaked out the next morning. Do you really want to get involved with that? With me? What if they can't fix me?"

I had to set him straight on a few things, so I turned my body and got comfortable with one leg folded under the other. I took both his hands and said, "Look at me." When he did, I explained, "I admit I was thinking some of the same things, but I can't now. If you're worried about being broken, then I have to be the one strong enough to hold you together. I *want* to know what happened to you. I'm in this. Look around you." I gestured to Lance's place. "I want this. With you. I was sitting here almost in tears waiting for you to get done changing because all I could think about was building a life with you. Call me a romantic sap, but it's true. You can probably blame my mom. No, my dad! He's a sentimental fool sometimes, hence the cheerleader obsession. I want what my parents have, what Lance and Jason have. I want a relationship with you and if that means sticking it out when your brain isn't all there, so be it. I'm here for you."

"Ohhh," Lance sobbed.

I glanced over, and he was fanning his face while reaching for a tissue. I grinned and turned back to Alonzo. "See, we have a support group."

Tears started rolling down his cheeks. He said, "Which is why this week has been so incredible for me. I've never had friends like this." He choked on his emotions, and I pulled him into a hug.

"You *do* have good friends." I rubbed his back until he was done.

He sat up and wiped under his eyes. "My eyeliner is messed up, isn't it?"

"No. It's fine."

"Thanks for bringing it here for me the other day. You know me so well."

"No problem." I kissed him and stoked his jaw. "Speaking of good friends, Ellis and Cole want to have us over for dinner."

His eyes widened, and he turned his head toward Lance. "Did you hear that?"

"Hear what?" I asked.

"I did," Lance answered.

Alonzo explained, "Lance asked me the same thing earlier today. He wanted to know if you and I would come to dinner on Sunday."

"Brunch," Lance corrected.

Alonzo repeated, "Brunch."

"Cullen's having a pool party, but I'm sure he'll be fine if I skip it."

Lance asked, "Isn't it too cold for a pool party?"

I agreed, "Yes, but that's the whole point. They normally close their pool the last Saturday in September, but something came up and they left it open. His dad is having a fundraiser challenge for anyone willing to take a swim before they close it."

Lance shivered. "Brrr. I think I'd just donate without jumping in. What's the cause?"

"Um, autism, I think. They have a friend whose daughter is on the spectrum. Their family is always raising money for different causes. I guess they're true humanitarians." Cullen did have a great family, and I was glad to know people like them.

Alonzo asked, "So can we come over for brunch? Lance was telling me about this Indian dish he makes that sounds incredible."

I was glad to see his tears dry up. "Yeah," I responded. "We can have a meal with our new friends, and I'll tell Ellis we'll go over his house sometime too."

Alonzo did a happy dance in his seat. "Yay! Thank you." He wrapped his arms around my neck and squeezed. When he was done hugging me, he jumped up and said, "I have one more thing to show you. I'll be right back."

He dashed off, and I went over to where Kelsey and Lance stood in the kitchen. "So, Lance, you like to cook?"

He shrugged casually. "Sometimes. I mostly like to spoil people."

I picked up the gummy bears. "Like with their favorite candy?"

He grinned and blushed. I wasn't sure who was more modest, Lance or Alonzo. They both blushed often with compliments, though on Lance it was harder to notice because of his beard.

"Alonzo really had fun shopping, didn't he?" I changed the subject.

"Oh yeah," Kelsey said. "You would have thought he'd never been to a mall before. His eyes were wide as saucers the whole time."

I thought about it. Maybe he hadn't. How big was his hometown in Nebraska? I didn't know. He didn't seem to have had many of the same experiences as me growing up. Maybe he wasn't exposed to big malls and hundreds of stores. Stephanie did say their mom worked several jobs. How could Alonzo afford all this now? "Where did he get the money for all this?" I asked casually, trying not to come off wrong.

Lance explained, "He was talking to his mom this morning and said she wanted him to get some things for himself, so he asked if I'd take him. He used her credit card."

That jealous streak of mine stood up, ears cocked. "This morning?" I questioned.

"Didn't Alonzo tell you? He's been staying here all week in the guest room." Lance said it as if it was no big deal, but it was for me.

"All week? And Jason doesn't mind?" I asked, hearing the edge in my voice and hoping Lance couldn't hear my resentment. I didn't know why I brought Jason into the conversation, but perhaps I knew subconsciously if Jason didn't mind, then maybe I shouldn't either.

Lance shook his head. "No, Jason likes Alonzo. I'm not very good at playing chess, so having Alonzo around this week gave Jason a challenge. Plus, Alonzo's read half of the same books as Jason. Alonzo has things in common with both of us, so having him here's been fun."

"Oh. That's good, I guess." Suddenly I felt left out.

Lance knew it. He walked around the breakfast bar and placed a hand on my shoulder. "You're doing it again."

"Doing what?"

"Acting jealous. If you believed half of what you told Alonzo earlier, you wouldn't behave like this. Stop getting jealous and go see the last thing he bought for you." Lance suggested with a tilt of his head that I should walk down the hall.

"For me? I thought it was another outfit for him?"

He grinned. "Yes… and no. Go see." He shoved me, and I went with it.

"Alonzo?" I called, peeking into the empty bathroom. "Alonzo?" I cracked the bedroom door. "Are you in here?"

"Close your eyes." I did. He took my hand and led me into the room and shut the door. Then he said, "Open them."

My heart palpitated. Alonzo was wearing nothing but skimpy black underwear. "Oh wow." He turned around. The underwear had no back. "What the…? It looks like a jockstrap for sports without a cup."

"It is. You like?"

I drew closer, inspecting the absence of material by cupping his rear. "I like."

"I have a few more things, some shirts and a sweater, but I thought you'd like to see this the most."

I growled in the back of my throat and scooped him off the floor.

Alonzo was not the shy introvert I'd met in the dining hall weeks ago. He was a vivacious person trying desperately to break free of a haunting past. The real Alonzo was bold and flirtatious and willing to buy a jockstrap while shopping with his friends to wear for his boyfriend. He wasn't all that shy. He was hesitant, because of growing up the way he did, so as he learned life could be better, I had the feeling I would discover a completely different person on the inside.

Was I ready for it? Oh, heck yeah!

Chapter 15
Slow Progression

I COULDN'T bring myself to have sex in Lance's apartment, but I didn't mind lying on the bed with my virtually naked boyfriend, kissing for half an hour. He had removed my shirt, but I felt too out of place to allow Alonzo any more access to my skin. He was so much more confident and responsive the more we made out—touching me, kissing me, and looping his leg over mine—that I could not help but ponder his initial guardedness.

We whispered about it in the quiet of the room as we kissed and explored each other with no other goal than to feel. It wasn't about sex, and I think he opened up even more because he believed what I'd said in Lance's living room. Alonzo told me he'd been scared to fall for someone after losing Kyle, which I completely understood. He'd said finding out he could live *openly* in his new town felt surreal and meeting me had been a dream come true. The pinnacle of his week had been making friends with Lance and Jason, so much so it made him see his blackout as a blessing. Everyone needed friends, and Alonzo responded so positively to circumstances that could have been a burden to anyone else.

I left their apartment late Friday afternoon feeling content for the first time in my life. We were a couple, and we had "couple friends" like my parents had. I was elated.

After class, I went back to my dorm room to clean up. Alonzo said he'd swing by, as we had done several times before, to watch a movie, and I wanted to be shower fresh and ready for anything. When I opened the door, Doug was at his desk as always.

"Hey Doug."

"Hey. How's Alonzo?" he asked. I also appreciated his tone of voice because it sounded like genuine concern and not bland interest.

"He's good. He's coming by later to watch a movie. Is that all right with you? We can pick something we all agree on if you want to watch with us." I was trying.

"No. That's fine. I was planning on going bowling with Cullen and Josh. Cullen's got family coming over this weekend. You heard about the pool party, right?"

I sat on my bed and removed my shoes. I was happy about Doug going out because I couldn't remember the last Friday night when he did. "Yeah. I can't go. Lance invited us to brunch Sunday. He and Alonzo are pretty good friends. I was jealous at first, but I think I'm over it. Lance is a really nice person."

"Oh. Okay."

"Besides, Cullen will understand. I've been to his dad's 'pool closing charity events' before." I took off my shirt and threw it into my dirty clothes pile.

"Yeah, Cullen will be fine; although, you'll miss meeting his cousin. Cullen's aunt's family is visiting from Iowa, or something; Cullen wasn't clear on the specifics. He said to show up with twenty dollars and eat burgers. I was cool with that."

I chuckled.

Yes, Doug liked burgers almost as much as I did. I shed my pants and rifled through my stuff for clean underwear. I took out a new T-shirt and headed to the bathroom. After turning on the water, I heard a knock, so I opened the door. "Yeah."

"We're cool, right? You and me?" Doug sounded worried, and his puppy-dog eyes didn't help either.

I tapped his chest with my fist. "Yeah. We're good." When his expression didn't lift, I said, "Come here," and pulled him into a hug. He patted my bare back and then released me.

"Thanks, Chris. I promise to give your boyfriend a chance. I haven't been a very good friend. I know that now."

"I understand. And Doug, if you're gay or bi or whatever, I'll support you. Just don't do anything without thinking. Okay? I mean, don't have sex with any random guys to figure it out." I was concerned he'd do something rash.

He shook his head. "I won't. I'm not that desperate to understand myself. I guess I've seen your relationship as something to consider. Like, I'm more open-minded than before. If I fall in love with a guy, I think I'm okay with that. I've been doing a lot of thinking in the past two months, and I've researched some stuff on gender identity, sexuality, and what drives sexual impulses. Did you know there are *asexual* people?"

"No." I'd never heard of asexuality.

"Yeah. People who don't experience a sexual attraction to anyone."

"Huh. Interesting. Look, man, I'd like to chat, but I really need to take a shower. Let me know how it goes. I wouldn't mind talking about it later sometime."

"Okay. Have fun tonight."

"Yup." When I gestured toward the shower, it was like the light clicked on that I was in my underwear and he had interrupted me. "I'm sorry," he apologized. "I'll catch up with you later." Doug backed out the door and left me to get ready for later.

MOVIE NIGHT with Alonzo was awesome. Doug went out for the night, leaving no fear of him walking in on us, so it didn't take much coercion to make love. I turned the movie on, pulled him into my side, and slipped my hand under his shirt. Seconds later, Alonzo had his hands under my shirt. Then we started kissing, which progressed quickly to groping hands and hungry groans. I had Alonzo moaning my name in ecstasy in no time.

The next morning, after practice and breakfast, we did it all over again.

"ARE YOU coming to my game later?" I asked as I held him. We were still naked and sweaty, but I wasn't in a hurry to disengage. I needed him wrapped around me.

"I guess so. Do you think I could invite Lance and Jason to a game sometime? Jason said he used to play soccer."

"Yeah, sure. You can always invite your friends." I rubbed his arm and shoulder while nuzzling my face in his hair. I never thought of myself as a cuddler, but I was sure turning out to be one.

"You're not jealous anymore?"

I knew why he asked, and I was confident in my answer. "No. After being around Lance and getting to know him, I like him too. Plus, the guy bought me gummy bears. How can I hold a grudge against him? He's always been there for you with advice and support practically from the first day you met him. I wish all my friends were like that."

Alonzo leisurely traced my collarbone with his fingers. "They are, aren't they?"

He had me there. "Okay, you're right. Most of my friends are supportive. My dad isn't."

"Hmm," he mumbled, readjusting his position so he could reach my neck. Alonzo kissed me, and nibbled his way up to my ear. It tickled.

I giggled and tried to get away from his mouth, but he persisted. He snickered as he climbed on top my body, pinning me in place. He suckled harder on one spot, and I felt a sting.

Alonzo was the kind of lover who could surrender everything to me in one moment, yet take what he wanted in the next. No one mentioned anything about my hickey last week, but now that they all knew it was Alonzo, I was certain someone would notice. And... it didn't bother me.

I *thought* he wanted to make love again, but he stopped kissing my skin after giving me a hickey. He straddled me, still holding my arms down, and asked, "Can we go for a walk?"

"Of course," I said, knowing it was unrealistic to think we'd remain in bed all day.

After getting dressed, we took a walk down Main Street—holding hands.

OUR GAME was against Hood College. Their record was the same as ours, so the pressure was on for a win. I followed the team into the stadium, immediately scanning the spectators for my personal cheering section. I saw Alonzo sitting with his sister in their normal spot in the top right corner. I was glad to see them together because things had been awkward after the incident earlier in the week. Stephanie seemed overbearing, but after what I'd witnessed, maybe it wasn't without reason.

I dropped my gaze to the front row of the bleachers where my parents normally sat. I saw my mom and my brother, but my dad was missing. Amber joined them seconds later carrying items from the concession stand, so I thought maybe my dad was in line getting snacks. I could only hope.

BY HALFTIME, I still hadn't seen my dad. Then, after our victory, I didn't want to hear my mom's excuses as to why he hadn't come. She hugged me, but the look in her eyes told me more than if she'd given a long exposition. Luckily when the awkwardness between us was getting ridiculous, Alonzo walked up.

My mom immediately opened her arms.

"Alonzo! I'm so glad to meet you." She proceeded to hug him, which I didn't think he liked, judging by the stiff expression on his face, but at least he hugged her back.

"Hi," he said.

"Mom, you met him before, remember? He was with his sister. The one dad thought I was dating."

"Yes, I remember." She dismissed that with a shrug. Turning back to Alonzo, she said, "I only mean it is nice to meet you again, after finding out you're dating my son."

Alonzo smirked and looked away. I could have sworn I saw a blush wash over his face.

My mom then said, "I'd like the two of you to come over for dinner sometime, okay?" She touched his upper arm. "I want to get to know you. Chris hasn't said very much, but if he's in love with you, then our family needs to welcome you into our lives."

"Mooom," I moaned.

"Shush," she warned. "We didn't get to meet Amber until your brother was practically engaged." She turned her stern gaze toward Ryan. "He dated her for years in secret, and I felt very excluded."

"That was not my fault," Amber said.

Ryan sighed, "I apologized already. I'm sorry, okay? I was a stupid kid. I didn't know you'd be mad when I didn't bring her home."

She leaned in to me and whispered, "I've forgiven him, but a mother never forgets. For years it felt like I'd lost my son because he never came home." She moved her attention back to Alonzo. "I'm glad I'm getting the chance to develop a relationship with you early on."

Alonzo smiled and looked down in that shy way he does. "Thanks. My mom wants to meet Chris too."

"Oh? And where does your mother live?"

"Nebraska, but she's moving to Pennsylvania in a couple months. Our house is up for sale, and she said she and my stepdad have had several offers."

"Oh good. I'd love to meet her after she moves."

Alonzo smiled wider. "She'd like that."

My mom turned back to Ryan. "See, *this* is how people do things."

Ryan groaned. "Okay, okay." He looked at me. "Thanks, Chris! Way to be the benchmark so all my deeds fall short."

"Any time," I gloated with a grin. "For once it's nice to outshine you."

Ryan stilled, staring at me, and then lunged forward, clamping his arm around my neck and pulling me down so he could give me a noogie.

"Ahh," I cried. "I give, I give."

He released me with a hearty laugh. "That'll teach you to be a perfect son. Stop ruining it for the rest of us."

I rubbed my aching head where he'd dug his knuckles in. It hurt. *Bastard!*

Alonzo snickered behind his hand.

SUNDAY WAS good. I enjoyed hanging out with Lance and Jason much more than I anticipated. Lance was a talented cook despite his modesty, and Jason was really smart. I liked smart people. They challenged me intellectually, and that was something my father always stressed when I was younger. He'd say "smart friends make you smarter."

MONDAY MORNING, though, was tough. I stayed up late doing homework Sunday night and thought about Sunday brunches becoming an issue if we did them too often. We'd have to share our Friday nights with other people if we kept getting invited to dinner. The semester was only half over. I'd need to prioritize or my grades would drop.

TUESDAY, AFTER practice, I shut my locker and noticed Doug sitting there—texting and smiling. It seemed odd because he rarely texted anyone outside the soccer team and something from his mother wouldn't make him smile so bright. I shouldered my bag and stepped closer.

"Who're you texting?"

Doug looked up and smiled wider. "This girl I met Sunday."

"Weren't you at Cullen's house?" *And what happened to Debbie?*

"Yeah. She's his cousin."

I thought about the cousins I had met in the past. Doug and I had known Cullen for a long time. Doug had met the same cousins I had, and none of them grabbed his attention before, so I wondered what had changed. "Which one? Judy?"

"No."

"Carla?"

"No. Her name's Sam, which I'm guessing is short for Samantha. She's from Iowa."

"And she gave you her number?"

"Yeah." His phone chimed again and he grinned, reading the text.

"Wow. I haven't seen that expression on you before. You must really like her."

Doug finished typing and answered, "Yeah, I do. There's something about her. I felt drawn in. When I kissed her, I—"

"You kissed her? You just met her. Does Cullen know? He might kick your ass." Cullen was normally protective of his cousins, even the slutty ones. I didn't think he'd appreciate Doug kissing one.

Doug shook his head. "I don't think he knows. It was one kiss. We were playing this Truth or Dare game and—"

"So you kissed her in a game? I guess that's different."

"No. Stop interrupting." He bristled. "We played the game, but it ended before I got a chance to kiss her. Later we were talking and she asked me something, and it came out in the conversation that I really wanted to kiss her. She got all cute and blushed, and she asked if I wanted a kiss. So we kissed."

"And that's all you did?"

"Yes, Mother," he moaned. "I didn't take her back to my place, nor did I drag her behind a bush and bone her. We kissed once and I left."

I know badgering him was unnecessary, but I had my reasons. "Okay. I'm just asking. You said you were taking Debbie out to nail her, even if you decided not to. I had to make sure you weren't after this girl for the same reason because Cullen would be pissed."

His hand shot up like I was swearing him in for a trial. "I'm not. I swear. I've never felt like this. She's... *different*. My heart was beating like crazy the whole time I was with her. Even now, every text makes my heart race. I can't wait to see her again."

I felt happy for him. "When's that?"

"Friday. I'm taking her out before she goes back to Iowa."

"Goes back? Like you may never see her again?" The prospect didn't sound very good for my buddy. He was setting himself up for heartbreak.

"Maybe. I don't know. She's enrolled in an online college right now and wants to find a college that will accept the credits once she transfers. She said she's applied to several colleges and is waiting for three more responses before making a decision."

"For your sake, I hope she decides to go somewhere in Maryland."

"Me too."

"I guess, then," I broached carefully, "you're not gay."

He shrugged resignedly. "I guess not. But… I have to say… there was this moment on Sunday, during the dice game, when I had to kiss this other guy. I did it, and it wasn't like kissing you."

I held my tongue to see what he'd say. We both knew kissing me was a bad idea.

"Kissing you was just plain stupid. Kissing that guy was… weird. I thought I'd be grossed out because I didn't know him. He was one of Cullen's parents' friends' kids, and I hadn't seen him before. Anyway, when he said he was gay when we all introduced ourselves, I thought it would be an interesting experiment. After I kissed him, I didn't feel anything. It was like kissing my brother or something. It was no big deal, and I really didn't care."

"I'm glad it didn't make you sick."

"No. Not at all. It was just a kiss."

"But not with Samantha?"

He shook his head emphatically. "No. When I kissed her, I felt light-headed, like I couldn't breathe."

I liked how Doug's eyes lit up when he talked about her. It made me happy, and I hoped it would all work out for him. But I missed Alonzo. "I think I'm gonna head out," I said.

"No shower?"

"Maybe later… with him." I lifted my eyebrows, and he shoved my arm.

"Get out of here. Tell Alonzo I said hello. Maybe we could kick the ball around sometime. Didn't you say he likes soccer?"

It made me feel good that Doug had paid attention to the details I'd spilled here and there in the dorm. He really was a great friend. "Yeah, maybe. He has a bum ankle, so playing might be out."

"We'll think of something."

"I'll see you at the game tonight," I said.

We slapped palms and bumped knuckles and I winked at my friend before heading out. I made it out of the building before my phone rang. "Hello?"

"Hi Chris. It's me, Lance. Could you come over?"

I stopped walking. "Um, sure." I felt uneasy about the call. "When?"

"Now, if you can. I have to work, and Alonzo is still in bed. Normally I'd leave him, but I'm worried about him because he isn't usually lethargic. Depression I understand, but this feels different."

Alonzo didn't mention sleeping there again. I thought he'd gone back to sleeping in his dorm room. But I also knew he'd had a therapy session yesterday, so lethargy could be a side effect from mental exhaustion.

"I'll be right there," I told Lance and took off running toward the parking lot.

I DROVE straight to Lance's apartment.

"He's in the guest room," Lance whispered after letting me in and shutting the door. "Although if he keeps staying here, Jason said we'd have to make a sign that says Alonzo's Room to hang on the door." Lance giggled, but I did not.

"Thanks for taking care of him," I said, patting his shoulder.

"Any time. I have to go to work. Text me and let me know how he is."

"I will."

"Alonzo has a key. Make sure you lock the door when you leave," he instructed, slipping on a light jacket. He left the apartment and quietly shut the door.

I dropped my stuff by the mahogany table and took off my shoes. I slipped into the guest room where Alonzo slept and knelt by the bed. I touched his hair. "Lonnie, baby, are you okay?"

He turned his head over so he was facing me, opened his eyes, and nodded.

I stroked his hair. "Lance was worried about you. I thought you said the session went well yesterday. What happened?" We hadn't seen each other because I had papers to catch up on, and he'd told me he was fine. Obviously he wasn't.

He rolled onto his side but didn't speak.

Instead of asking more questions, I got off the floor and slipped into the bed beside him, taking him into my arms. After a while, Alonzo found the courage to open up.

"My therapist figured out what triggered me," he confessed softly.

I wanted to jump up and shout, thinking it was good news, but his quiet tone subdued me. "Uh-huh," I responded, holding in my excitement because the thought occurred to me: *What if I don't like the answer?* I rubbed his back and waited.

"You know how she recorded your voice?"

I swallowed hard. "Yeah."

"She recorded other voices and sounds too, like dogs, cheering crowds, my mom, and my sister."

A chill ran down my spine. Was he going to say it was me? I really am the one who triggered his flashback/blackout episode that morning after? I whispered, "And?"

Alonzo sniffled. "It was my sister."

I waited. "Your sister what?" *Found out that I triggered your panic?* "I don't understand."

Alonzo lifted his head off my chest and looked me in the eyes. "My sister's voice. It was my sister's voice that morning. She woke me up, and I flashed back to waking up next to Kyle. She'd been there then also. That's why I flinch when she touches me, and why I couldn't remember anything when Lance found me." Tears streamed down his face as he collapsed back onto me and hugged me tight. "The doctor thinks we need a break from each other until I can work through it," he sobbed. "Dr. McKenna suggested that I've been stable for so long because my sister had gone to California. Being around her again made the memories flood back."

"If she triggers a reaction that strong, then I think your doctor is right."

"I know, but I missed her so much when we were apart."

"Really? I thought you were annoyed with her most of the time?"

"I am, but we're twins. I'm closer to her than anyone else. I feel connected to her. I missed her terribly when she was at college while I was home making up the year of high school. I thought being here together would help me adjust to a different life, but I guess I was wrong. I don't know if I can say good-bye again."

I held him and caressed his back. I didn't know what I could say to that. I loved my brother, but we weren't twins. I knew the bond between twins was very different from other siblings. I felt bad for Alonzo, but it was all out of my control. I thought holding him was the best I could offer. Alonzo grew silent and tucked his face against my neck.

I HELD him for the longest time and just when I thought he'd fallen asleep, he commented, "You stink."

I chuckled. "I guess so. I had just finished practice when Lance called. I came straight here."

"What about class?"

"I skipped it, but I do have a game tonight. We've only got a couple more hours until I have to go."

"Thank you." He lifted up and looked down at me, leaning against my chest. "I feel better with you here."

"Yeah?"

Alonzo nodded. "I might feel even better if you let me take a shower with you before you have to leave."

I felt his suggestion in my groin. "Are you serious?" *Or am I dreaming?*

A mischievous twinkle appeared in his eyes. "Yes."

"Oh hell yes!" I exclaimed.

Alonzo got up, and I followed him into the bathroom.

I closed the bathroom door and took off my soccer jersey. "You don't think this is weird, do you? I mean, this isn't our place. What if Lance comes home?"

"He won't." Alonzo turned the water on and removed his clothes.

I stepped out of my shorts and underwear and joined him next to the tub. I cupped his ass as we waited for the water to get warmer, rubbing his curved flesh with gentle strokes, daring to run my finger up the crack.

Alonzo giggled.

"Ticklish?"

"No," he said, his eyes growing frightfully wicked. He rubbed my chest and absently fingered my chest hair. "Your fingers touching me there reminded me of something my sister used to say." He pulled back from our embrace and stepped into the tub.

"Am I going to like what she said?" I followed, closing the curtain behind me.

"Maybe," he said. "She always called me the dumbest things growing up." He grabbed the soap and proceeded to lather up my chest.

I grabbed the shampoo and applied a dollop to my hair. I casually asked, "Yeah? Like what?" as Alonzo soaped up my dick and balls.

"Cadaver."

"Isn't that a dead body?" I was trying to play it cool because showering together was suddenly my number one favorite thing in the world. I could do it every day. Plus, I wasn't sure if he wanted to have sex. Alonzo could have asked to shower with me as foreplay. It was working. I was rock hard and ready to jackhammer my way through concrete.

"Yup," he said. "Steph said it all the time."

"What else?"

"Buttfinkosaurus."

I laughed. "Sounds like an unfortunate dinosaur."

Alonzo lathered up my chest and washed my nipples meticulously. "Yeah. I think she had a butt fetish. She called me Butthead, Buttfinkosaurus, Boney Butt, and the nickname I thought about a minute ago: Buttmunch." Alonzo ran his soapy hands down each of my legs.

I chuckled. "That's a funny one." I gasped as he relathered my balls. Now I *knew* he was using the shower as foreplay, because my balls were clean the first time.

Alonzo turned me around so he could wash my back. He spread the suds all over my shoulders, down my spine, over my ass, and yes, up and down my crack. He added causally, "Buttmunch *is* funny, but it's also interesting because she called me that when we were five, before I ever knew I was gay."

"So?" Playing it cool was increasingly difficult when he rubbed my asshole. I gasped again and unconsciously widened my stance.

"So," he explained, sliding his fingers up and down, over that spot, making me desperate. "I've been thinking about my sister a lot lately. Her name-calling and lewd jokes aside, I lay awake last night thinking about the word 'buttmunch.' 'Why would anyone want to munch a butt?' I thought. Then, I remembered what you said a while back about licking my asshole."

My dick was already throbbing from his seductive wash job, but with that one phrase he had me on the verge of coming from the anticipation of what he'd say next. "Y-yeah?" I panted, hoping he'd continue. I never thought talking about his sister would get me so fucking horny.

As an answer, he slipped one digit into my hole and stroked.

"Lon," I gasped.

He snickered, the little tease, and instructed, "Put your hands on the wall."

My heart raced as I did want he wanted. Alonzo adjusted the spray so it wouldn't fall directly on his head as he knelt behind me. Was he really going to do this?

Alonzo kneaded my ass and then pushed his finger in a little farther. I grunted and spread my legs as far apart as the tub allowed, hoping to encourage him to do more than probe with one finger. He knew I liked it.

He stretched me with his hands on both sides of my butt, pulling both cheeks out to the side. When his tentative tongue licked my private area, I babbled unintelligible noises at a pitch I'd never heard come from my mouth before. My thighs felt like rubber as he licked and wiggled the tip of his tongue in ways I'd never imagined would feel this tantalizing. I rested my face against the cold tile and cried in tiny panting grunts. "Oh… ah… um… eh."

Alonzo leaned back, and I nearly groaned in protest. "You like it?"

He had the nerve to ask me after I all but collapsed before him? "Lon," I rasped in a most desperate voice.

He understood me fine and dove forward, giving new meaning to the nickname "buttmunch." Munch my butt he did. He pressed his face completely into my crack and licked me fervently. I thought I might have felt teeth nipping at my most sensitive skin, yet I could not complain as my only compulsion was to grab my achingly hard cock and tug.

I was so close I couldn't utter a word when he stopped licking me and manhandled me around to face him. I couldn't see anything but stars as white lightning shot upward from my balls and electrified my body, but I distinctly felt Alonzo's mouth descend over my cockhead as jets of cum exited my body. His hands moved mine away and pumped me until every drop was secreted. I leaned heavily on the wall, fearful of sliding boneless to the bottom of the tub, but Alonzo stood up and held me.

When I had enough breath, I asked, "Do you think Lance will get pissed we did this in here?"

Alonzo snickered.

As if right on cue, we heard the bathroom door open, and we looked at each other.

"Hey," Jason said. "I thought you had to work today?"

We heard the toilet seat hit the toilet tank and then the sound of pee streaming into the bowl. I opened my eyes wider and quirked my lips in a mock-panicked expression. I knew this was about to be embarrassing.

Jason continued casually, "I saw Alonzo's shoes in the living room. Did something happen with him after I left last night?" He paused as if waiting for an answer. "Lance? Are you all right? I thought I saw Chris's stuff too. He didn't do anything stupid, did he? Lance? It's been a long shift and I just want to relax and—"

Jason pulled back the shower curtain and found us in each other's arms. His eyes locked on me and then Alonzo before he pulled the curtain back in place. He flushed the toilet, and the water went hot momentarily. We both screamed and jumped out of the spray.

"You deserved that," Jason said. "And you're scrubbing that tub before you leave." He shut the door soundly.

I turned the water off, glanced at Alonzo—who was plastered as far from the water as he could have gotten—and we both burst out laughing. Jason was right… we deserved it.

Chapter 16
Dinner Parties

ALONZO NEVER thought he could be any more nervous than when he'd agreed to go to dinner with Chris's friends. Okay, maybe agreeing wasn't the nerve-wracking part; it was showing up at Chris's dorm, knowing they'd drive over to his coach's house any minute. He wanted to make a good impression on Ellis and Cole.

It had been a rough week, with the therapist's discoveries and recommendations, but finally making progress had been worth it, even if he knew it wasn't over and wouldn't be for a while. Knowing his triggers was better than being in the dark—literally. Chris had been around as often as he could be, and no longer showed signs of jealousy over Lance, which Alonzo was thankful for.

Making friends with Lance and Jason had proven to be one of the best things about moving to Maryland, aside from meeting Chris. He hadn't been so good at making friends in the past, but his life was different now. Alonzo found he could be himself in more ways than one, and having dinner with Ellis and Cole was his next big step.

Alonzo took a deep breath and knocked.

Chris opened the door with his typically gigantic smile in place, quelling Alonzo's anxiety. Alonzo loved that smile because it lit up all the dark spaces in his soul and chased his fears away. He wanted to gaze into Chris's dark blue eyes every day and kiss his smiling lips, all the while clinging to the fragile hope growing inside his skeptical heart. He had to trust Chris, even if he doubted himself. Chris loved him.

"Hi," he said, quietly, forcing his lips to smile.

Chris scowled. "What's wrong?"

"I'm nervous," Alonzo explained, stepping into the room and closing the door behind him. "What if they don't like me?"

Chris grabbed him by the hips and tugged him into a hug. "Stop," he said. "They'll love you."

"Are you sure? I'm not an interesting person." He wasn't in the habit of self-deprecation, but if Chris insisted on loving him, then Chris would have to learn about all the cynical parts too.

Chris cocked his head to the side and lifted his eyebrow. "Oh really?" he challenged. "I can think of some very interesting bits." He stepped back, tugging Alonzo by the hand over to the bed.

Alonzo smirked. "I'm not showing any of *those* bits to Ellis and Cole."

Chris took him in his arms and flipped him over, pinning Alonzo under his body.

"You're going to wrinkle my shirt," he pointed out, but Chris didn't seem to care as he kissed his neck while unbuttoning his dress shirt.

Chris slipped his hand inside and fondled his nipple, which Alonzo liked. He kissed his way down to Alonzo's belly button. He licked and Alonzo squirmed.

Chris glanced up. "Oooh, so you *are* ticklish." He flicked his tongue over Alonzo's indented navel, rousing a wiggle from him. Chris chuckled wickedly and closed his lips over the area, laving him relentlessly.

It was funny at first, and it tickled like mad, but as Chris continued, Alonzo felt all his other parts taking notice. He sunk his fingers into Chris's hair and tilted his pelvis.

Chris chuckled deep in his throat. He repositioned himself and proceeded to undo Alonzo's belt and jeans. Alonzo attempted to protest breathily, "Chris… we shouldn't…." He couldn't think as Chris pulled his jeans down only enough to get access to his now-hard cock. Freeing it, Chris took him into his mouth and went down.

Alonzo's stomach muscles quivered. His balls drew up and his toes tingled. Chris knew all the right ways to tease with his tongue and suck until all Alonzo's nerve endings surged in one collaborative rush toward a colossal explosion. Chris wrapped his hand around the base of Alonzo's cock and pumped his fist in time with his undulant mouth—plunging, slurping, cajoling Alonzo to that perfect pinnacle of powerful paroxysms that would ultimately drain him of stress, worry, and care. He felt it building as he gripped Chris's hair, grunting and moaning on the bed under Chris. White-hot lava shot from his dick, and Alonzo shoved Chris down as he lifted his hips off the bed. He held him there as he dumped endlessly into Chris's throat.

Spent, he let go, and dropped his arms to the bed. "Oh, Chris," he sighed.

Chris coughed hard when he sat back, and Alonzo opened his eyes. Chris's eyes were watery. "Are you okay?" Alonzo asked, propping himself on his elbows.

"Yeah," he said, coughing again. "That was… intense." *Cough.* "And a little painful. I don't think I've taken you back that far. It felt like I was swallowing your whole dick."

Alonzo's face got hot and he reached for Chris. "I'm sorry. I didn't know. I wasn't thinking." Alonzo squeezed his hand. "I'm really sorry."

"It's okay." He coughed with less force. "I'll be fine." He went over to his mini fridge, took out a bottle of water, and downed the entire thing in three swallows. He cleared his throat one last time and assured Alonzo, "I like making you feel that good. I'm just not used to swallowing my bananas whole." He sat on the bed again and winked.

Alonzo giggled and kissed him soundly as a way of saying thank you. The thought of reciprocating ran through his mind, but he knew if he did, they'd be late. He didn't want to explain the reason to Ellis.

After Alonzo buttoned his shirt and pulled up his pants, the two of them headed out to Chris's car.

THEY ARRIVED at Ellis's house right on time, even after the earth-shattering blowjob. Chris took Alonzo's hand after ringing the doorbell. As they waited for the door to open, Alonzo allowed his eyes to wander. Ellis and Cole's little house was cute, with a wraparound porch, a swing, and flower boxes filled with mums on the front steps. Alonzo thought it looked so normal. His mother always wanted a house like that: typical and very much "small town Americana." This house blended in with all the rest of the historic houses that lined the street, except it was owned by a gay couple.

Alonzo felt his emotions surging. Ellis and Cole, a gay couple, lived here, and yet there weren't eggshells on the porch and streaks of dried yolks running down the siding. The flowerpots weren't broken, and no one had spray-painted their sidewalk. This house was more proof that gay couples could live normal lives like everyone else. Alonzo choked back a sob.

Chris eyed him. "Are you okay?" he asked with concern.

Alonzo nodded, keeping his eyes averted.

Chris turned toward him and wiped his tear away. Alonzo hadn't noticed one escape, but it had and Chris saw it. "Lon, we don't have to be here if it makes you that upset. Really. I don't like seeing you cry. You've been through so much lately. I guess I wasn't thinking when I agreed to come here tonight."

Damn Chris and his caring heart! The traitorous tears tumbled down his cheeks, and he tucked his face into Chris's neck, folding his arms against Chris's chest. Alonzo heard the door open, but he didn't look up. Chris whispered "One second" toward the house. *Great.* That meant someone was standing in the doorway witnessing Alonzo's embarrassing display. Alonzo pressed himself into Chris, trying to disappear as Chris rubbed his back.

"I got you, baby. It's okay. If you want to leave, just say so."

"No," he squeaked in the tiniest of voices. Chris continued to console him, even if Chris didn't know what was going through Alonzo's mind. Alonzo asked quietly, "Is Ellis watching me from the door?"

"No. He closed it. We can go in whenever you're ready, or leave. Whichever."

Alonzo took a cleansing breath and stepped out of Chris's comfort. He gazed into his eyes and found the strength to explain. "You know how you said you wanted what Lance and Jason have?"

He furrowed his brow as if recalling his comment from before. "You mean their relationship and their apartment and stuff?"

"Yes. Well… I want that too." He took another deep breath, absorbing joy and happiness from Chris's huge smile. "I was looking around at Ellis's house after you rang the doorbell, and it hit me. I want this. I want a house and a yard and a cat—"

Chris interrupted with a grin, "A dog. You mean a dog, right?"

Alonzo giggled and wiped tears off his cheek. "A dog *and* a cat."

Chris nodded. "Deal."

Alonzo reiterated, "I want this. I want a place I can call my own, where no one cares if their neighbors are gay or straight, but whether they like hostas or pachysandra. I want a normal life." Alonzo paused as he gazed into Chris's beautiful eyes, knowing exactly where he saw his future. "I want a normal life… with you. I want to come home to you after talking to my therapist about triggers I can't pinpoint and blackouts I can't remember." Alonzo smiled so Chris would know it was a joke.

Chris grinned. "I want that too." He leaned in and kissed him several times. "Ellis said he met Cole in college, so they're living proof relationships can start young." He kissed him again. "So we start now, and maybe in five years we'll be where they are. You game?"

Alonzo nodded. It certainly seemed like a great plan.

"Awesome!" Chris pecked his lips one more time and then reached for the doorknob.

"As long as I get my cat," Alonzo mumbled.

"I love you." Chris laughed heartily and shut the door behind them. "Ellis? We made it inside," he called.

A different guy than the one Alonzo recognized from the soccer field came through a doorway to the left. "Greetings. Mi casa es tu casa," he said. "That means 'my house is your house,' but if you actually started speaking Spanish in reply, I wouldn't understand anything, so forget I said that."

Chris's coach came up behind Cole and squeezed his shoulders. "Don't mind him. Cole's nervous about meeting more of my friends."

"And *telling* them I'm nervous in front of me is going to make me relax so much faster," Cole snarked.

Chris slipped his arm around Alonzo and whispered in his ear, "See, you're not the only nervous one." He kissed his cheek and smiled at his friends.

Ellis commented, "Not all of my friends are loud and crazy, Cole."

Cole replied, "No. Some of your friends are lewd and obnoxious."

"Cole," he warned, his tone conveying the "don't you dare" without voicing the words. "I haven't seen Kevin or Marcus since the wedding. They were both drunk. You have to get over it."

Chris piped in, "I promise not to get drunk. Really. I'm not in the habit of drinking anyway, and I don't think my friends would describe me as lewd. The lewd people I know are cheerleaders, and they weren't invited."

Ellis suggested, "Why don't we all go in the living room and sit down. Dinner is almost ready; Cole just has a few things to put together."

As they started moving in the direction Ellis directed them, Alonzo stepped up next to Cole, mustering up the courage to say, "I like your shirt, by the way." It read "Particle Physics Gives Me a Hadron," and Alonzo's previous tension drained away. He understood the principles behind particle physics, which meant he and Cole apparently had some things in common.

Cole stopped and looked down, pulling the T-shirt away from his chest. He smirked. "Thanks. I'm fond of this one. I had the same one for six years and it got too ratty to wear, so Ellis bought me a new one for my birthday. He's good to me. So… you understand it?"

Alonzo nodded. "I'm a biochemistry major."

"I studied physics, but apparently I'm only qualified to sling burgers because I can't get a job."

Ellis warned, "Cole, we talked about your negativity. You have a *great* job."

"Not in my field."

"What do you do?" Chris asked.

Ellis answered before Cole could. "He's a sous-chef for an upscale restaurant, which we should all visit sometime when he's working."

"A chef?" Alonzo asked happily. He liked eating, so knowing a chef seemed beneficial.

"No, not chef and not sous-chef. I'm the assistant to the sous-chef," he stressed. "The sous-chef gets all the credit, and I do all the work." As if sensing Alonzo's query as to how he got into cooking after taking physics, Cole explained, "I graduated a year before Ellis. I applied for several jobs, but no one was hiring, so I took a few cooking classes and completed a program, blah, blah, blah. Another person in the class mentioned an opening where he worked and presto, I'm an assistant to the sous-chef until she quits, which I hope will be soon. I like to cook, so it really isn't that bad. I only wish I had thought about my career before spending so many years studying physics. I'd love to work for the John's Hopkins Applied Physics Lab, but they may never have an opening while I'm still young enough to care. In the meantime… I cook."

"And he does it really, really well," Ellis said, kissing Cole's cheek.

Cole changed the subject and asked Alonzo, "How much do you know about physics?"

"I'm only a freshman, but I've read about particle physics in Brian R. Martin's book."

Grabbing Alonzo by the upper arm, Cole cried, "Oh my God! I have that book on my bookshelf." Then he qualified that statement with less enthusiasm, releasing Alonzo's arm. "Or rather, I *had* it on my bookshelf in our old apartment." He glared at Ellis.

Ellis said, "We'll unpack your books as soon as the library gets painted."

"If you'd have let me paint it, it would have been finished by now," Cole grumbled.

"Not when you climb up on the ladder and drop the paint bucket."

"One time."

"Twice! And the second time the paint got on one of my textbooks."

"It came off."

"Cole," Ellis said with finality. "I don't think they came to hear us argue." He waved them on, and everyone finally walked into the living room.

Alonzo took a seat next to Chris on the sofa. He leaned in against his side and draped his arm over Chris's thigh, feeling as comfortable here as in Lance's apartment. It was awesome. He commented, "I don't know. I kind of like it. It seems so normal."

"Fighting?" Ellis questioned.

"Yeah. Kind of. Although you don't look angry. You look amused."

Ellis chuckled and Cole sneered as he sat down. Cole said, "He never takes me seriously. One food fight that ends in great sex and suddenly he never takes me seriously." He crossed his arms and looked away.

"Because this isn't really a fight, Cole." Ellis explained to Chris and Alonzo. "He gets irritated because he thinks he's coordinated enough to climb up on a ladder and paint the ceiling, but he's not. So when he spilled the paint—" He paused and glanced at Cole. "—twice, he got doubly angry at himself because he wouldn't listen to me when I told him not to. I'm normally the messy one, so he thought he'd do a better job. Cole is stubborn." He emphasized the last word and gave Cole a goofy expression, popping his eyes wide and crinkling his nose.

Alonzo smirked and flicked his eyes over at Cole, who had taken a seat in a big comfy chair that almost swallowed him up. Cole was blushing. A subtle thing like that helped Alonzo absorb the true comfort the two of them had with each other. They weren't arguing. They were discussing a disagreement with sarcasm, but also with the underlying knowledge that they weren't actually angry at one another.

Alonzo looked at Chris. "Will we argue like that?"

He seemed confused. "Um, no. I'm not very sarcastic, and you've never given me the impression you're messy or uncoordinated. Why would we?"

Alonzo shrugged and looked down. "I don't know."

Chris turned his body to square off with Alonzo. He grabbed his chin and made him look up. "What we're going to fight about is your lack of self-confidence. Lift your eyes and look at me. I'm not giving up on you. I'm gonna fuss every time you look down as if your opinion isn't valid. Speak your mind, Alonzo. Tell me exactly what you think. My parents have been married twenty-nine years by sharing their thoughts and I want our relationship to last as long or longer."

Alonzo actually appreciated Chris's confidence in him. He needed Chris's strength. "My parents used to hit each other," he muttered.

Chris's eyes went wide. "Do you think I'm gonna hit you? Because I would never…."

Alonzo shook his head. "No! I know that. I'm just saying I haven't seen a very good example of what marriage can be like. My father wasn't supportive or kind. My sister hates him and calls him an asshole. My stepdad's okay, I guess; I haven't been around him much to form an opinion, but Stephanie likes him."

Chris took his hand. "Oh, Lonnie, you don't have to worry about us turning into that. I will always be supportive of you. I want you to succeed. I want you to learn and grow as a person. And I want it to happen together."

"I'm going to go put the food on the table," Cole said, exiting the room abruptly.

Alonzo watched him leave. "Did I ruin this? I didn't mean to. My thoughts about my father just came out."

Ellis moved over and sat on the coffee table in front of them. "No. Cole is sentimental. He got teary-eyed and didn't want you to see."

"He did?" Alonzo asked.

"Yeah. I think he likes you," Ellis said. "He's wanted other couples to do things with, but we haven't really settled down until now. We were living in Pennsylvania near Cole's parents, and our neighbors were pretty cool, but when we moved here, he got dour and cynical about 'never finding other couples to do things with.'"

Alonzo giggled as Ellis made fun of Cole in a fake voice and mock facial expression.

"I heard that," Cole complained from the other room.

Ellis laughed and patted Alonzo on the knee. "He likes you. The fact that you know something about physics was a hit. But the clincher was probably the comment about you fighting like we do. I told him how much I liked Chris, so I bet Cole knows he'll like you just as much, and he's realizing he didn't have to be cynical about moving. I told him we'd find people to do things with and you two proved my point."

"I heard that too!"

Ellis laughed, and so did Chris.

"I was worried about making a bad impression," Alonzo said.

"You don't have to worry at all. Except one tip I'd give would be to never shake the salad dressing bottle without checking the lid first. Cole's not fond of salad dressing on the ceiling."

Alonzo snickered. "Neither am I."

They all headed into the dining room and sat. Cole had prepared a lovely dinner, and Alonzo laughed often at their snide remarks to one another. It was never malicious; it was simply who they were. Alonzo found himself daydreaming during dinner, thinking over the possibilities with Chris. They wouldn't be the sarcastic type—no. Alonzo would be the reluctant one, and Chris would push him to try new things. But what could he be for Chris? He'd have to think about that one awhile.

HALFWAY THROUGH dinner the front door opened and shut, and all four of them eyed one another. Cole asked, "Did someone come in through the front door, or was I imagining things?"

"Nope, not imagining things, Cole. It's just me," announced the newcomer.

Alonzo watched as Ellis jumped up and hugged him immediately. "Rob! It's great to see you. Why didn't you tell us you were coming?"

Cole grumbled to himself, "And why didn't anyone lock the front door?"

Rob wagged his finger at him. "Uh-uh-uh, Mr. Doom and Gloom. You don't get to shut me out so easily. Your husband already gave me a standing invite to Casa del Montgomereid. He even mailed me a key." Rob held up a key and gloated.

Cole turned to Ellis. "You sent him a key?"

He shrugged helplessly. "I didn't know he'd use it this fast!"

Alonzo smirked. The scene was like watching a comedy show at a dinner theater. He reached under the table and placed his palm on Chris's thigh. Chris smiled at him and squeezed his hand. He didn't understand the argument going on in front of them, but it didn't matter when Chris made Alonzo feel so completely happy. He leaned his head on Chris's shoulder, thankful their chairs were close enough to lean that far, and watched Ellis, Cole, and their friend Rob.

Rob gesticulated wildly and pointed at Cole. "I heard that, Cole! You don't get off the hook so easily. Last time I saw you, I said I wanted a dance, and you conveniently forgot."

Cole protested, "I did not. The reception ended and the DJ wanted to go home."

Alonzo only registered half of what was said. Chris was stroking his fingers under the table, and the warmth spreading up his arm from that small action made most of the commotion in the room fade away.

"That's no excuse," Rob argued. "You were the bride, and I was the best man. It's tradition that we dance to one song."

"It would have been weird. You're not gay. Weren't you worried about what people would say?"

"People who? Your parents people? You danced with Jonathan to 'Endless Love,' and no one cared."

"Which is a good thing because I told him not to request that song!"

"It doesn't matter, Cole. Like I'm trying to tell you, there weren't any people to worry about, and since Russell was in Japan and decided not to show, I was alone. The least you could have done was dance one time with me."

"Did you come all the way here tonight to tell me that?"

Rob stilled his dramatic posture and pulled a chair out and sat. "No," he said quietly. "My dad broke his foot and my mom couldn't handle him on her own. I'm here for a couple weeks." His eyes lit up and he reached for a bowl on the table. "Is this Thai peanut sauce? Oh, Cole, I've certainly missed your cooking." He took a red pepper off Ellis's plate and dipped it in the sauce, helping himself.

"Would you like to join us?" Ellis asked.

"Don't encourage him to stay. We have guests," Cole fussed.

Rob looked over at Chris and Alonzo. "Oh, hello. I'm Rob McAvoy, Ellis's best friend and the brother he never had." He reached over and shook Chris's hand. Like that the entire conversation shifted. Rob wasn't mad at Cole, and they were on to a new topic. Alonzo thought it funny.

Ellis protested, "I have a brother."

"Oh, right," Rob said. "How is good old Benjamin?"

"Ben's fine." Ellis gestured toward Alonzo. "These are my friends, Chris and Alonzo. Chris is one of my best players on the team. I'll grab you a plate."

Cole held one up. "I already got one. But Rob eats on the plastic ones, not my fine china."

Rob placed his hand over his heart. "Ouch." The plastic plate Cole sat in front of Rob had Disney princesses on it. Alonzo snickered to himself.

Cole stuck his tongue out. "Don't be theatrical. I know you're not offended." He sat and offered Rob a bowl of rice. "I bought it for you specifically."

"You're so good to me." Rob took it and took a large helping of food. "Is this Thai curry? Oh by gosh, by golly, I really missed you guys."

"Where have you been?" Chris asked, helping himself to more shrimp pot stickers, or jiaozi as Cole called them.

Rob said, "I've been studying worship arts at a seminary in Missouri. I transferred to complete my masters because my sister just had a baby and needed help with the twins while her husband was at work, so I moved after graduating with Ellis. Russell, my other best friend, abandoned me for a job in Japan, of all places, so I figured the South would be a good place to live for a change. It was, but then I realized how much I missed my buddy El, so as soon as my dad was settled for the night, I headed on over to surprise him."

If Rob's visit was unwelcome, then these guys didn't know how to express themselves. Their words had barbs, but Ellis's shining smile told otherwise. Rob fit in like family.

Ellis said, "I am surprised. You'll have to come watch a game. We play at Haverford tomorrow, if you want to hitch a ride with Cole."

Cole groaned, "But it's a two-hour drive."

Rob started jumping in his seat. "Oh, oh, oh, we could sing show tunes!"

"Or not," Cole suggested.

Then Rob did something Alonzo was not expecting, especially given that Rob didn't know either him or Chris. He jumped up and started singing the song "Don't Rain on My Parade" by Barbra Streisand, from *Funny Girl*. Alonzo remembered seeing the movie with his mom years ago. He probably should have told Chris he liked old movies, but he could mention it later.

Rob grabbed the lit candlestick from the table, blew out the candle, and then started using it as a microphone. Alonzo heard Chris mutter, "Oh my God." He turned his attention from Rob to look at Chris. When Alonzo realized Chris was mouthing the lyrics, it dawned on him how dead serious Chris was when he said he liked show tunes.

Rob thrust the candelabra in front of Cole's face. "Sing it, Cole!" A trail of smoke still rose off the wick.

"No thanks," he grumbled.

Rob did a twirl and belted out another line without faltering. He sang with more passion than any man Alonzo had ever heard. True, he'd seen things on television like this, but he'd never seen a real person break out in song and dance. It was truly inspirational.

And then Rob turned toward Chris and pointed. He made his way around the table and interrupted the lyrics to say, "Sing it for me, Chris!"

To Alonzo's surprise, Chris sang into the makeshift mic that Rob thrust in front of his lips. He even rose from his chair and sang the rest of the song as a duet. It was spectacular. Alonzo knew Chris was a showman who loved that spotlight, but he'd never shown such passion toward singing in front of people. It was a discovery about Chris that Alonzo cherished.

When they finished, Rob and Chris bowed and everyone clapped, even Cole.

Chris took his seat next to Alonzo as Ellis asked, "You miss singing with Russell, don't you, Rob?"

Rob held up his hand like a stop sign. "Don't get me started on Russ." He sniffled and pretended to wipe a tear from his eye, even though Alonzo hadn't noticed any. Rob composed his fake sadness and regarded Chris. "Do you care to sing another, oh melodious master of merriment? Your audience awaits." Rob swept his hand toward the rest of the party.

Chris, again shocking Alonzo as to how congenial he could be, jumped up and bowed with the same sort of flourish as Rob. He took the "mic" from Rob and said, "See if you recognize this one." He winked and began singing.

Rob gasped and covered his mouth. He started jumping up and down. "Oh wow! 'All I Care About' from the musical *Chicago*. You're now my new favorite person in the whole wide world." He turned his head briefly to Cole. "Sorry, Cole." He then started whistling as Chris sang. It was like eating in one of those diners where the waiters sang to the customers. This Rob guy was the most dramatic person Alonzo had met, and he loved it.

ALONZO LISTENED intently all night, but barely spoke himself. He didn't feel the need to. The shenanigans of Ellis, Cole, and Rob were enough to carry the evening. He held Chris's hand and let the warmth of their friendship wash over him. He had great friends, and even if he needed to see a therapist to sort out the rest, he knew he'd be fine. He wasn't alone anymore.

CHRIS WALKED Alonzo to his dorm room.

"Do you want to stay?" Alonzo asked.

Chris lifted an eyebrow. "Really? What about Caleb and the thing that happened the last time we did this?"

"I think Caleb would be okay as long as we were only sleeping. I'm tired, so I didn't think I'd want to do other stuff."

Chris grinned. "I think I could muster up enough energy for the other stuff." He winked.

"Chris!" Alonzo rolled his eyes and stepped closer. Chris cupped his jaw and kissed him softly.

"If I stay, I promise not to leave until after you wake up."

"Okay. Tomorrow is the first time I won't be having breakfast with Stephanie. She spoke to the therapist Thursday, and we agreed to follow her suggestions for a while. Steph is going back to California." He laid his head on Chris's shoulder, and Chris pulled him in close. "I'll miss her."

"I'll be here for you."

"Thank you," Alonzo whispered, more thankful than ever for Chris's presence in his life.

SATURDAY'S GAME was a win for the team, but a loss for Chris. His father missed another one. Alonzo knew how disappointed he was even if he didn't say. So when Chris's mother invited them to brunch on Sunday, Alonzo accepted the invitation before Chris had time to decline.

"We'd love to come, Mrs. Jackson," he said.

Chris looked at his sharply. "Lon, really? Are you sure? My dad is…."

Alonzo knew where he was going even if he didn't finish the thought. They had spoken several times privately about it. "Chris, it's fine. Like your mom said, we need to give your dad time. I'm sure he'll understand if he sees us together."

Chris smiled and held out his hand. Alonzo took it and stepped to his side. They were standing by the gate and Chris would have to board the bus back to campus soon, but this was the first time he was showing affection of any sort at a neighboring school. He held Chris's hand as people walked by, yet no one taunted them. Alonzo wanted to pinch himself.

SUNDAY BRUNCH was at 11:00 a.m. at Chris's parents' house. Ryan and Amber were to be there as a buffer, which made Alonzo more confident. Chris's brother had been very nice to him the few times they'd seen each other at Chris's games.

While they were in the car riding over, Alonzo thought it was a good time to bring up something from Saturday night. "I saw you talking to that cheerleader, Kat. My sister roomed with her. Did she mention Steph?"

"What?" Chris asked, glancing over. "Um, no. She wanted to apologize for something she did the other week. It was nothing."

"It looked like something. I was talking to your mom, but I had my eyes on you the whole time. You were shifting your weight from one foot to the other. You only do that when you're upset."

Chris stopped at the stop sign at the next corner and smiled. "How did you know that?"

"I watch you."

"Oh, yeah?" He stepped on the gas and turned down the next street. "What other scandalous details have you picked up on?"

"You like to kiss me with your eyes open."

Chris gaped. "How do you know that? Your eyes are always shut."

Alonzo shrugged. He didn't feel the need to expound upon his sixth sense. He'd always known when he was being watched, as a child and later as an adolescent. He could feel a person's eyes on him. It was his fear of being found out for what he was that scared him into hiding it as long as he could. If Kyle's school hadn't found out from that one boy, then Alonzo's secret would have been only theirs for years, until they had the chance to move away somewhere safer.

Alonzo had dreamed of living somewhere safe where he could be himself and love a man without shame. In Westminster, he thought he'd found such a place. Whenever the two of them were together, Alonzo never felt the hair on his neck stand on end. He never experienced a looming weight of dread that signified he was the subject of some onlooker's curiosity. No. The only time he felt eyes on him was when Chris kissed him.

If their first time together in the shower was any indication, Alonzo knew Chris liked to watch his expressions, hence the open eyes. Alonzo had been paranoid for too many years to count, but being near Chris, held in his arms or simply by his side, Alonzo knew his life had changed. He could allow himself to feel.

They pulled into the driveway.

"Now… my dad might behave badly, but I want you to know that isn't how he's always been. Okay?" Chris explained rapidly. "My dad and I have always had a great relationship. It was only since I came out and told my parents about you that things have been strained."

Alonzo nodded. "You already told me that."

"I know. I'm nervous." Chris took Alonzo's hands and squeezed them. "I love you," he said and then kissed Alonzo reassuringly. "Let's do this."

Chris let go of his hands and got out of the car. He zipped around to Alonzo's side even before Alonzo had the chance to set one foot onto the driveway. Alonzo gave him a look and stared at Chris's proffered hand. He wasn't used to being assisted from a car.

Chris stepped back and bowed his head. "Okay, okay. I'm overdoing it. I'm nervous!"

Alonzo snickered at his cuteness, but only on the inside. He knew not to make things worse by embarrassing Chris. He shut the car door and stepped up to Chris, slipping his arms around his waist. "Hey, it's okay. I'm here. I'm supposed to be the basket case, remember? You're the strong one."

"Not today," Chris said, settling one arm on Alonzo's shoulder while caressing his face with his other hand. "You have to be strong for me, I guess. I'm worried this brunch will make things worse. My mom thinks he needs time, so maybe I should have given him more than two weeks."

"Stop overthinking it. Your mom invited us, so maybe we need to trust she knows what she's doing."

"I guess."

As they walked up to the house, Alonzo realized how calm he was. At Ellis and Cole's, his heart had been racing. Here, for some reason, he felt the steady rhythm of normal breathing without the sensation of drowning. They stepped onto the porch with no signs of a panic attack brewing under the surface of his skin as Alonzo would have expected. His hands were steady. Maybe it was knowing how nervous Chris was that grounded him. Chris held his hand tightly, keeping Alonzo firmly planted by his side. Chris was genuinely worried that his father would reject him again.

Before Chris opened the door, Alonzo turned and stopped him with a hand on his chest. He gazed intently into Chris's beautiful, questioning eyes, and whispered, "It'll be okay." Chris tried to smile, but his doubt overshadowed his bravery. So…. Alonzo kissed him, soft and sweet and final. Chris would have to believe him.

"Thank you," Chris uttered.

When they entered the house, Alonzo felt the tension like a rubber band being stretched too far. The smiles were almost fake in their pretense, and the hugs weren't as spontaneous.

"Chris! Alonzo! We're so happy to have you here," Chris's mom's high-pitched greeting was more dramatic than Alonzo thought normal.

"How's it going?" Chris's brother Ryan asked, coming over to shake Alonzo's hand.

"Good," he replied, seconds before Amber swooped in and hugged him. "Uh, hi." She'd never hugged him before.

She stepped back and apologized, "I'm sorry. I get overenthusiastic sometimes."

"When?" Chris asked with an edge to his tone.

She seemed hurt when she replied, "Sometimes. I don't know."

Ryan said, "Chris, chill. Amber's happy for you. Can't you be civil?"

"I am," Chris said. "Since when does Amber hug people she barely knows? I've known her for a couple years, and she's never hugged me like that."

Amber turned into Ryan and buried her face in his shoulder. Ryan said, "Thanks, Chris."

"What? I didn't do anything."

Ryan glared and Amber was crying. The whole moment was crumbling before any of them even tried. Chris had been worried, and it was turning out as he'd feared. Alonzo had to fix it. Chris had been so supportive of him recently, it was only right for him to reciprocate.

"Chris, your father isn't here yet—some emergency at work."

"On a Sunday?" Chris asked.

Ryan answered, "That's why Amber's upset. We came over to help Mom get ready for you guys, and Dad was rude to Amber, grumbled something about you, and stormed out."

"But that's not my fault," Chris replied.

"We're not saying it is, honey," his mom said.

Alonzo didn't like the tension. Unlike the argument at Ellis's, this one made him queasy. The looks in their eyes weren't warm like Ellis as he fussed with Cole. Chris's family was on the verge of biting off each other's heads because of Mr. Jackson. Alonzo suggested, "Maybe we can all sit down, get some coffee, and get to know each other. How does that sound?"

Chris's mom placed a hand on his shoulder and nodded. "Good idea."

IT DIDN'T take long for the tension to settle and for them to find something to occupy their time. Ryan suggested a game, so for two hours they played a word game called Balderdash. Chris seemed surprised Alonzo could play so well, and although he could have taken offense at Chris's assumption, he knew it wasn't an argument worth having. Alonzo's IQ was rather high, and it seemed conceited for him to belittle Chris, especially in front of his family. Chris would find out through daily interaction how smart Alonzo was.

But being in a room with equally intelligent people was fun. The word game proved challenging, and Alonzo truly enjoyed the company of his potential in-laws. If he and Chris really did get married in the future and buy a house and all, he knew that being a part of this family would prove to be amazing.

Chris was amazing. Alonzo flicked his eyes over to him. Chris felt his gaze and glanced up and winked. Alonzo smiled. He was beautiful, vivacious, and life-giving, and Alonzo knew without a doubt that no matter how this "meeting" with his dad went, nothing could destroy how he felt. Alonzo loved him.

TWENTY MINUTES later, Chris's dad walked in and the temperature in the room dropped. "Oh jeez. *He's* still here," he mumbled, crossing the room to take a glass out of the cabinet.

Chris jumped up and approached his father huffily. "Dad! That's so unfair. You don't even know him. How can you be so cold?"

"Don't start with me, Chris."

Chris's mom joined them by the sink. "Henry, please, sit down with us. We've been waiting for you for hours."

He pointed at the table and the empty dishes. "Seems as though you only waited so long and ate without me."

She scolded him. "Henry! I texted and called, yet you refused to answer. I'm not making the kids wait when their father is being ridiculous. You could have come home and joined us. Alonzo is a very nice boy. If you only took a moment to talk with him—"

"Stop. I told you I'm not ready." His eyes burned as he glared at his wife. Alonzo didn't like it. As when his own father would get angry at his mother, Alonzo wanted to defend her. Chris's dad had no right to yell.

"Ready for what, Dad?" Chris pressed.

Ryan and Amber got up and quietly slipped from the room, leaving Alonzo alone to watch the argument play out. Only Alonzo knew Chris would feel less defenseless if he was standing with him and not sitting across the room.

He approached and listened as Chris argued, "Ready to accept that you have a gay son?" Chris's voice grew louder with each question. "Ready to realize I'll never be the son you want? Ready to acknowledge that I have a boyfriend, *not* a girlfriend?"

"Chris, that's not—"

Chris declared, "I love him, Dad. Can't you just be happy for me?" Alonzo slipped his hand into Chris's sweaty palm. He squeezed it to give him strength as he continued, "Can't you love me the way I am?"

"No! I can't," his father said with finality.

Alonzo pulled his shoulders back and proclaimed, "Then you're not the man Chris told me about. He said *his* father always supported him. He said *his* father was strong and smart and encouraging. If you can't accept him for loving another man, then—"

Chris's father snarled. "This isn't about his sexuality... *Alonzo*. This has to do with his disregard for tradition." The man controlled his tone, but Alonzo could still hear the hurt and see the strain in his eyes as he explained his side. "I never said I didn't love my son, but I can't simply let go of our family history in the span of two weeks. What I *can't* do, Charlotte, Alonzo, Chris"—he eyed each one of them— "is move past my disappointment. You might be a great guy, Alonzo, and my son might very well love you, but you're not a cheerleader. Therefore the tradition ends with Ryan, and I'm not ready to get over the hurt this causes me."

One tear slipped out of the corner of his eye. "I love you, Chris, but I can't forgive you yet." He took in an enraged breath and stalked off.

Chris's mom reached for him, and he hugged her briefly, turning back to Alonzo for consolation. Chris cried quietly, his body shaking even as he tried to stop.

WHEN ALONZO was back in bed, alone, thinking over the week's events, he couldn't help but muse over what might happen if he took the initiative and did something daring for Chris. Standing at Chris's side was step one, but if he was going to give into the relationship as much effort as Chris, Alonzo knew he needed to think of something grand. Chris might get upset if it backfired, but not taking initiative would hurt Alonzo more. He needed to, he wanted to, for Chris.

Even with the many bad scenarios zipping through his mind, Alonzo still picked up the phone and called his sister. She hadn't left yet. Her plane departed on Friday morning. He risked flashbacks to talk to her for Chris. Alonzo wasn't allowing Stephanie to transfer without one more favor.

"Hey Steph," he said when she answered her phone. "Are you still friends with that cheerleader, Katherine?"

"Yeah, I guess. We're not enemies, or anything."

"Then can you ask her to meet with me tomorrow? I have a plan, and I need her help."

Chapter 17
Grand Gestures

SUNDAY NIGHT, it didn't take much persuasion for Alonzo to make love to me. I think he knew I needed it. I swear I never thought it would feel so good, but Alonzo was more confident this time, loving on me with gentle caresses and nipping teeth, while plunging rhythmically into my body. He had me panting and writhing, arching my back, and gripping the sheets as I came with sticky ribbons up my chest. His domination left me spent, so my mind couldn't obsess over my dad's disappointment. Sex made me sleepy.

Everyone else loved Alonzo. Why couldn't my dad?

After Alonzo kissed me good night and left, I fell asleep quickly and dreamed about the past when my father rallied behind my decision to play soccer, and all the times he'd been proud of my academic excellence.

MONDAY MORNING I showed up at practice the same as every other day. We ran warm-up laps around the track and then did passing drills on the practice field. Doug was in an exceptionally sour mood. In fact, I'd noticed Doug's mopey mood during Saturday's game, but I'd been distracted by my own troubles then. And when my outlook remained the same on Sunday, I hadn't thought about not seeing Doug around. Now, though….

"Hey," I said, clapping him on the back. "Why aren't you texting that girl you met?" I asked because he was sitting on the grass holding the phone and staring at it.

"I don't want to talk about it." He frowned and put his phone back in his bag before taking another mouthful of water.

"Dude, what happened? Last week you were all gung-ho, and now you look dejected. Did she turn out to be different than you'd hoped? I know sometimes after you get to know people, personalities don't always click."

"Yeah. Sam was definitely different on Friday."

"You never did tell me about your date. Was it just dinner or was there sex involved?"

"Definitely no sex, just dinner. Sam turned eighteen."

"Eighteen? Isn't that a bit young?" Because we'd discussed the age thing before when referring to Mindy.

"No," he said tersely. Doug glanced around nervously, but we were the only ones at this end of the field. "Look, do we have to talk about this? I'd rather forget all about it."

"Okay." I walked over, squatted, and placed my hand on his shoulder because this was the first time I'd known him not to want to talk about a date. "I never thought you'd clam up over the details. Was the date that awful?"

Doug wouldn't look at me. "Sam's not a girl."

I thought I heard him wrong. "What?"

He lifted his gaze from the grass and looked me dead in the eyes. "Sam's a guy."

What he said did not compute. *Guy?* I thought he had to be joking. I snorted and asked, "What are you talking about? How could Sam be a guy?" I was all but belly laughing when Doug punched me in the arm.

He glared. "Don't, Chris. Just don't! I feel like a complete idiot already, okay?"

He was serious, so I changed my tune. "I don't understand how you didn't know."

Doug's face sagged. He was clearly upset, and I felt bad for laughing. "It had to do with the stupid thing Cullen's cousins do every year."

Cousins? It clicked for me. "Oh wait. That thing where they draw straws and then one of them dresses like a girl and waits on them and shit." I chuckled. "That is so funny. Remember when Cullen had to dress up two years ago?" I snorted. "He was so pissed when we hammed it up and called him Cullenita for days."

Doug wasn't laughing. "Yeah. Funny. Except I forgot about that part when I saw Sam. He looked like a real girl, boobs and everything."

"Boobs?"

"Padded bra."

"Shit."

"Cullen spent most of the time talking to his uncle, so I wandered off and found a group of cousins playing the dice game. I wasn't thinking."

I followed his thought processes and connected the next dot. "Which means you asked her out not knowing she was a he."

He slumped forward, resting his elbows on his knees. "When we went out on Friday, Sam showed up wearing jeans and a T-shirt. She looked different, but with the same hair and soft smile. It took me ten minutes to realize Sam was a guy, but by then we had already ordered pizza and he was laughing at something the waitress said."

I grinned. "So you stayed? You went out and stayed on a date with Cullen's *male* cousin?"

"Yes."

I had to ask, "The one you kissed?"

He huffed, "Under false pretenses. I thought Sam was a girl."

"But you said she made you feel light-headed."

"I also said I didn't want to talk about it!" Doug snapped, standing up and storming away from me. Yet he only took a couple of steps before he stopped. After a few silent seconds he grumbled, "How are things with you and Alonzo?"

Subject shift. Doug was too pissed to talk about himself, but not too pissed to talk about me. I let it go. "Good," I sighed. Were there really words to describe how I felt?

Doug turned around and lifted the corner of his mouth. "I heard you singing in the shower this morning." I didn't respond because I was worried about which song he'd heard. Doug crooned some lyrics, mimicking me in a singsong tone.

I jumped at him and covered his mouth with my hand. "Doug, jeez, can you sing it any louder?"

He chuckled and pushed me off him. "Nobody's gonna know it's from *Rent*. I ribbed you before about being in love, but it's really true. This isn't a joke or a lust-induced delusion. You really love him."

I sighed, "Yeah. Doug, he's like fairy dust. When I'm with him, I feel like I'm flying."

"Does he feel the same way?"

"I think so, but he hasn't said. Given his past, I think he's scared to say it out loud. But I know he wants to be with me and plan a future together. That's something, right?"

"Totally. And your parents?"

"Not so good. We went to brunch yesterday, and my dad argued and said he couldn't accept me. I don't think he'll ever forgive me for not dating a cheerleader."

Doug didn't have an answer for that. He only clapped me on the shoulder and joined the group, slipping seamlessly into the drills until the coach dismissed us.

WE WENT to the dining hall after showering in the locker room and ran into Mindy, Candice, and Jill.

"You can sit with us," Mindy said, gesturing to the seat across from her. I hadn't hung around the girls since they'd insulted me—even though Kat had apologized, I still felt out of place.

When I hesitated and looked to Doug for support, Jill pleaded, "Please? I know we were all out of line treating you like the trophy gay. You're not a trophy to be put on display, Chris. You're our friend, and we forgot to treat you like one. Please, sit with us."

Doug and I consulted each other in the nonverbal way we've always done. One glance, our eyes locked, and we both knew what the other was thinking. I sat down and heaved a sigh. "Fine. But one derogatory word about my sexuality and I'm gone."

"What about that guy's sexuality?" Jill asked, pointing to someone we didn't know across the room.

"No one's sexuality. Okay? It isn't right," I told her. I took a bite of my hotdog as a few of the other cheerleaders joined us, followed by Cullen, Josh, and Cedric. They each sat, thereby doubling our group.

Kara was the first to comment. "How many hotdogs are you eating, Chris?"

I looked down at my little stack. "Eight."

Doug snickered.

Sara did a verbal inventory of my tray. "How can you possibly eat eight hotdogs *with* buns, two bags of chips, an apple, and a large soda? Your stomach can't be that big!"

I shrugged. "I'm hungry." To prove my point and astound the lot of them, I picked up another hotdog and shoved the entire thing, bun and all, into my mouth.

Mindy cringed. "Eww, that's repulsive."

"Whaaa?" I asked with my mouth full of hotdog. Little bits flew out, making the other girls shrink back in disgust and the guys chuckle. As soon as I swallowed the last crumb, I picked up another one and did the same thing. The girls made faces and looked away.

Cullen asked, "Where's Kat? I haven't seen her all day."

Jill answered, "She'll be here in a minute. She was arranging something for Chris."

"For me?" I asked before eating another hotdog.

Then, as if I were asleep in some dream mash-up of reality and my obsession with gummy bears, I heard the actual gummy bear song come on over the campus radio. "What the...?" I glanced up at the ceiling and then around the room searching for Tim Burton, who *clearly* could write my life's musical.

A giant gummy bear appeared around the corner of the wall from where Alonzo and I normally sat. It gestured and danced in time with the tune. Wiggling its huge green butt, and spinning on its oversized, white plastic tennis shoes. I had no idea where anyone would find a bear suit that large, and I was unaware of any school with a bear mascot. This was unreal.

I caught sight of something coming at me from the side and glanced where it hit. A yellow gummy bear had landed on my hotdog. I looked at Josh. He shrugged. A green bear landed on my drink lid, and Mindy studied the ceiling as quickly as I shot my attention her way. Then a red one landed on my chips as the dancing bear sang, "I'm a gummy bear...."

I recognized that bear's voice. It was a sweet and high-pitched soprano, and singing in a bear suit was her way of apologizing. It meant so much more than the thirty seconds she gave me the other day. When the song was over and she was done, Kat removed the bear head with help from Kara and Mindy.

"Damn, that thing is hot in there!"

I stood up and walked over to her. "Thanks, Kat. That was pretty cool." I kissed her cheek and chuckled.

"You're welcome. I am truly sorry for the way I've treated you. You deserve so much more from me than that." Just when I thought she was going to get sentimental and blubbery on me, she turned to the rest of the group and ordered, "Now!"

Everyone fired at once, throwing gummy bear candies at me. First, it was individual ones, which ricocheted off my head and arms as I covered my face. Second, they showered me with small bags of gummy bears for my later consumption. I laughed even as I was pelted by their unusual display of affection.

When they were through, I dropped my arms. "You guys are weird." Everyone started laughing.

Lilliana joined us at the end of the table and looked around as she pulled a chair over from an adjacent table. "What did I miss?"

"Kat singing the gummy bear song and everyone throwing gummy bears at Chris," Mindy explained.

"Is that why Kat's in a bear body? What happened to the head?"

Kat held it up. "Right here. But I need to change. Lara?"

Lara followed Kat, and I retook my seat. My friends were stupid yet hilarious. Although it was a shame some bears were sacrificed. *Gummy bears.* I sighed. I felt a hundred times better.

Candice turned to Kara and asked, "Where'd you get that top? I love it."

"At rue21. I love that store," Kara said.

"Me too!" Jill said, gesturing to Kara with a flop of her wrist.

Suddenly, the girls all started chitchatting like they always did. Sara said something about her nails, which prompted comments from Mindy and Jill on the color she'd gotten. Candice explained how her aunt had coupons for Applebee's if a group of us wanted to go one night because there was no limit and the coupon was for buy one, get one free. Jill grabbed Cedric's forearm and squealed jubilantly when she heard him say he bought his girlfriend an engagement ring, which left me pondering if her tone would be just as shrill if I'd done the same for Alonzo.

I wouldn't yet. It was far too soon in our relationship, while Cedric had dated Amira for a couple years. But *if* I bought a ring, would Jill be happy for me or would it incite more rude remarks? I didn't know, nor did I want to assume it would. This was a group apology as far as I was concerned, and I would have to let it go if I truly accepted their gesture.

I went back to my stack of hotdogs and ate another one, basking in the happiness and the ordinary conversations that surrounded me.

TUESDAY GAME time rolled around, and I was in the locker room lacing up my cleats. I hated breaking in new laces on a game day, but I had no choice when mine snapped at practice that morning. What I didn't like was how tight they felt when first laced up, but as they stretched during a game, my cleats always felt loose. I knew I'd have to step out during the game to retie my cleats, and that bothered me. I liked everything to flow in its normal pattern. I hated coming out of a game, period.

As I walked beside Doug along the sidewalk that led into the football stadium, I caught sight of Lance and Jason taking a seat two rows up and over to the left of the field. That would be our goal side for half the game, so they'd get a good view of some of my shots. More crowd searching and I spotted my folks, *both* of them, sitting in their usual spot.

I fisted Doug's jersey and pulled him around to my side as I pointed to my parents. "Look! My dad came."

He didn't even get mad that I crumpled the front of his shirt; he merely smoothed it down after I let go. "I see. I wonder why the change?"

I had no answer. I searched more and saw Cole and Rob, yet I couldn't find Alonzo. "Where's Lonnie? I thought he said he'd be here."

"Maybe he wasn't feeling well."

"He would have texted me." I took out my phone—no text messages.

"Hey," Doug said, bring my attention up from my phone to his face. "He'll be here. Let's play soccer, okay?"

I followed him over to the bench and dropped my stuff. It wasn't our last home game, but it was still a big deal. The cheerleaders were here tonight, as was the marching band, but my sudden funk was attached to Alonzo's absence. I sighed. I guessed I couldn't have everything. It wasn't like he promised to be at every game. He'd missed a few before. I needn't take it personally.

Doug kicked me a ball and I caught it on my toe, flipped it up, and tapped it back to him using the inner sole of my cleat. Doug bounced it on his knee three times and then passed it to Cullen. Coach Montgomery sent us onto the field to warm up, and I decided to leave my dour outlook on the bench. I could stew over it later. Now was the time to play soccer, and play it well. My dad was here—that was something.

THE WHISTLE blew and I wiped the sweat from my eyes. It was halftime, and the team needed to reenergize while Coach give us a pep talk. As we walked over to the corner of the field where we normally gathered, I glanced over at the cheerleaders, noticing they were lining up differently for some reason. Not that it mattered. They cheered equally well on every number I'd seen, only Kat was normally in the center of the formation and this time she was on the end. I noticed things like that. Their cheers, dances, or flip routines were all good, but Kat was their leader, and it was unlike her to be on the side.

I turned around and walked backward, confident I was walking somewhat straight and at a pace that would not ram me into anyone's back in the few seconds I chose not to look where I was going. I *had* to see what the cheerleaders were up to.

Their uniforms were different too. They had on green shorts instead of skirts, and half shirts that exposed their bellies, which I knew some of the guys would appreciate. This *was* one of the last home games of the regular season, but it was hardly the last time we'd play on this field. Our playoff position wasn't set, but we were definitely heading into postseason play.

I stopped for a second when the music started. This wasn't a normal cheer, either. This was set to a rock and roll beat. It sounded oddly familiar, and after a few seconds, I realized it was one of the songs by Green Day I'd listened to on YouTube. Green Day was Alonzo's favorite band; he should be here!

The girls cheered in unison and counted out the tempo: five, six, seven, eight. Lara, Jill, and Mindy held their pom-poms up and shook them as Kat and Candice did cartwheels. Then I spotted a different cheerleader on the end, one with short black hair and a flat chest. Not that it mattered much to me, but their outfits didn't complement her figure at all, and I could imagine how self-conscious she must be cheering with so many Barbie dolls. I felt bad for her until she turned around long enough for me to see her face, and I realized that she was not a she at all, but a *he*. That cheerleader was Alonzo!

What?

I stumbled over my own feet and landed on my butt. Josh came over and grabbed me under my arm to help me up. "Dude, what's wrong with you?"

"Chris? Are you paying attention to me or to the cheerleaders?" Ellis asked, none too politely. He was using his stern coach voice and it caused me to turn my attention to him if only briefly.

"Coach, I'm sorry. I was watching the cheerleaders because I'm dating one of them!"

Preet's eyes went wide. "What? I thought you were gay."

Doug pointed. "Holy crap! He's right. That cheerleader is Alonzo!"

The whole team at that point stopped paying attention to the coach and stared at the cheerleaders as they finished their last cheer. Two tumbled in front, Candice did a backflip, and then three of them got on the ground to form a pyramid. As I could have predicted, Alonzo joined in, although not on the very top as I assumed, probably because he was heavier than Mindy.

Another tune came on, and it was one I also recognized as Green Day.

As the cheerleaders lined up and shook their rears, Alonzo stepped around them, making eye contact with me as he lifted a microphone to his lips.

He sang an altered version of the song, I was sure, because one line said something about "family traditions" and I was fairly certain I hadn't heard that line in this song before. Alonzo strutted in front of the girls as they shook their pom-poms, singing his heart out. I couldn't believe it. Why was he doing that? He had always been so reserved. This blew me away.

When they were finished and the crowd cheered and clapped, I saw my father stand up. "Oh shit," I said, leaving the team behind as I rushed over to what might be a confrontation.

What if my dad yelled at him for ruining the cheerleading tradition? What if he cussed him out or something? My dad wasn't a mean guy, but Alonzo had messed with what he considered a sacred institution. First he dressed like a cheerleader, and then he sang instead of cheering. I couldn't imagine all the yelling my dad was going to do once he came down out of the stands.

I heard the whistle blow to start the second half as soon as I reached the sidelines where the cheerleaders normally lined up.

I stopped dead in my tracks as they squared off. My dad said something—I knew because I saw his lips moving—and I held my breath, staring at them staring at each other. In two beats of my racing heart, my dad grabbed Alonzo around his chest and crushed him. No... that wasn't quite right. My dad wasn't crushing him, he was... hugging him.

I moved closer and questioned shakily, "Dad?"

He clapped Alonzo heartily on the back and released him. "Son!" He turned his enthusiasm my way, hands held high, and grabbed me to him. He whispered in my ear, "You never mentioned he was a cheerleader." He released me and smiled at me with more pride in his eyes than I'd seen in months.

I glanced at Alonzo because I didn't have an answer for my dad.

Alonzo grinned and said coyly, "I told you I could be a cheerleader." Indeed he could be in his cute little shorts, half shirt, and his hair pinned to the side with a sparkly hair clip.

I beamed. I grabbed Alonzo, hugged him securely, lifted him off his feet, and winged him around in a circle, causing him to giggle. When I sat him back down on his feet, I caressed his jaw as I regarded him. "I don't understand how you did this, or why?"

His answer was simple. "Because I love you."

I had longed to hear those words for so long that hearing them in front of my dad helped keep my emotions from exploding all over the place. Instead of crying, I smiled and then kissed him, over and over until I heard my dad clear his throat.

"Sorry Dad, I got carried away."

He pointed to the field. "Don't you think you should be out there?"

I turned. My guys were scrambling to keep the ball away from John's Hopkins. We were ahead by one, but that wouldn't last if the highest scorer—me—was dilly-dallying around with his boyfriend, the cheerleader. "I gotta go," I told Alonzo.

"Go! I'll be fine."

My dad added, "I'll make sure your cheerleader is well taken care of. Don't worry."

I kissed Alonzo's lips quick and dashed back to the field. I was lucky that Coach understood all my issues from our many talks before practices and especially after Alonzo's episode.

"Everything all right?" he asked as we waited on the sideline for the ref to signal for a substitution.

"Yeah. Everything is awesome," I said, suddenly hearing *The Lego Movie* sound bite in my head. Everything certainly *was* awesome!

I stormed onto the field singing about how cool everything is when you're part of a team! I'd found my strength and energy in the final acceptance my father gave me in his words "your cheerleader." My father had accepted Alonzo, and all it took was a cheerleader's uniform, a couple of well-choreographed cheers, and a song. God, I loved Alonzo! He was so clever giving my father exactly what he wanted.

I charged down the field like an enraged bull running down the narrow streets of Spain, full of adrenaline and power. Nothing could stop me as I dribbled the ball and dodged all who came at me, faking left and tapping the ball right, zipping around the opponent's midfielder before he knew where the ball went. The next in line was a defensive player who stood like a wall, waiting for me to try to pass, yet I grabbed the ball with both feet and flipped it behind me, up over my shoulder, in a rainbow arc over the head of the player who thought he could stop my advance.

I laughed as I ran past him and caught sight of Doug by the corner goal post. I could pass to him, or make the shot myself. I charged. I lifted my right foot to shoot, but decided in that last second to stop the ball dead in the grass, turn, and use my left foot to kick it to Doug. He was closer, and in those few seconds, I had lured the goalkeeper into thinking I was going for the goal myself. Doug caught my pass on his knee and juggled it a second before dropping it to his foot and into the net.

The whistle blew. Goal!

Chapter 18
Game Winner

I ALWAYS knew my father would accept my choice of partner. I had no idea, however, how it would all come together. I'd never have guessed that my sexuality wouldn't come into play at all. I thought I'd have to hide it until I graduated, but it was never about being gay. My dad was stuck on cheerleaders, and if I'd have thought about asking Alonzo to join the cheerleading squad earlier, I might have avoided this whole disagreement with my dad.

Except I was glad I hadn't thought of it. By coming up with the solution himself, Alonzo showed me how far he was willing to go to make this relationship work. He'd set himself up for embarrassment and ridicule, for me! I think that was a huge step for him to feel confident about himself too, because no one said anything negative. People cheered. Fans clapped. My team swarmed the cheerleaders after we won and thanked them for their incredible support.

"HOW DID you pull it all together?" I asked Alonzo as we lay in my bed after the game, a shower, and, of course, sex because sex had become as necessary as breathing.

"I asked Steph for a favor. Since Katherine's her roommate, I thought she could ask about me being a cheerleader."

"Stephanie? I thought you weren't supposed to talk to her for a while because of the whole trigger thing?" I didn't want a phone conversation causing a blackout. I wanted to protect him and help him heal.

"I know. We promised each other not to call. She wants this to work just as much. I'll tell Dr. McKenna in therapy tomorrow."

I loved having him in my arms, especially when he played with my chest hair. That might sound funny, but I loved the feel of his fingers on my chest. "What time do you go?"

Alonzo answered, "Four. Do you want to come?"

His invitation threw me. It seemed so intimate to me. I mean, his therapy session? Wasn't that supposed to be private and stuff? "Um, sure. If you want me to."

Alonzo changed positions, propping himself up on his elbow to look at me. "You don't have to go if you don't want to."

He looked hurt. "I didn't mean to sound like I didn't want to go. I do. I was just thinking it's a big step. I'll hear all your private stuff."

"I know. I want you to. If we're to make this work between us, then I can't hide the things I struggle with. And if it seems like too much to handle, you can end it before we go on too long."

I sat up immediately. This doubt had to end or he might think I'd leave every time something tough came up. He sat up too, probably so it was easier to look me in the face as we talked.

"Alonzo, I'm not ending this," I said. "Get that through your stubborn head. I accept you as you are. If that means you come with baggage and a past that haunts you, well, so be it. I'll learn how to help you. But you need to get it through your thick, self-doubting skull that I am not in the habit of throwing my heart around lightly. I love you. I've never said those words to another person in my life." Then I thought about Doug, and I qualified, "In the romantic sense. I trust you not to break it. Even if your hands are shaking from night terrors, I know my heart is safe."

I saw his lip tremble one second before he dove into my arms. We sat there in my bed, legs awkwardly folded and overlapping as we held each other. I rubbed his back as he squeezed the breath out of me.

"I love you so much," Alonzo whispered.

I tightened my hold around him and held him closer.

Doug walked in. "Oh, sorry," he mumbled and turned around.

I stopped him from leaving. "Doug, wait." I released Alonzo and we both watched Doug tentatively turn around. "We're not naked. I promise. I'm in my underwear, but he's wearing sweatpants."

His face twitched. "It's weird seeing you in bed together. Even if you're clothed from the waist down, I can only see you from the waist up."

"What if I'm on top of the covers?" Alonzo asked, swiftly pulling his legs out from under the sheet.

Doug thought about it. "Maybe. I guess that isn't as awkward."

"Until he gets cold," I suggested. "Lonnie can't lie here on top of the covers all night."

"He's staying the night?"

Alonzo turned to me. "I'm spending the night?"

I caressed his chin and gazed deeply into the depths of his brown eyes. "If you want to."

"I want to, but only if Doug is fine with it."

I replied, "You know I hate saying good night. I just want to hold you forever."

Alonzo smiled sweetly, leaned in, and kissed me.

Doug cleared his throat. "So, um, yeah. I guess… I guess it's fine," he conceded, scratching his head. "I need to push past my discomfort anyway. You were right, Chris." We both turned our attention back to Doug out of respect. "If you were with a girl, I wouldn't have an issue with it. I've seen Cedric making out with his girl often, and it's never bothered me. I'll be okay with you guys once I get used to it."

"Thanks," I said.

Doug walked over to his bed and put his bag on the floor. He toed off his shoes and sat. "You left before Coach announced a change in practice tomorrow. We're skipping morning practice and moving it to six thirty in the evening. Coach said that new kid arrives on campus tomorrow. So the team thought we could get together anyway and kick around the ball. I know Alonzo likes soccer, so…." He left the suggestion hang there.

"You want me to play?" Alonzo asked.

"If you want to."

His face lit up. "I want to! I'll wear my ankle brace. Just don't laugh if I fall a lot."

Doug assured, "We won't. Unless Chris falls on another throw-in."

I chuckled and rolled my eyes. "Thanks."

"So tomorrow? Seven o'clock?" Doug asked.

"Sounds good," I said.

THE NEXT morning, I showed up on the practice field and waited for Alonzo. He wanted to change his clothes after spending the night with me. He didn't own proper running shoes and said he needed to borrow some. I wasn't sure from whom. The guys were warming up and goofing off with each other as I watched from the sideline. I took out my water bottle and squirted water into my mouth.

When Doug had given me this water bottle, he'd hugged me and said, "I hope we're friends forever. I love you like a brother, Chris." I glanced over at Doug, feeling sentimental. He was chasing after Cullen, laughing at something I hadn't witnessed. It was good to see him acting normal, given his trauma over the weekend. Cedric and Marshall were kicking the ball back and forth. Marshall glanced over and gave me a chin-lift as he grinned. Our friendship had settled nicely after the team spent all day Monday, two weeks ago, looking for Alonzo. Marshall now accepted me and my relationship with Alonzo.

I turned my head toward the school, hoping to see him walking over. My eyes locked on a guy all dressed in black, sauntering toward me. Sporting black sweatpants, a black T-shirt, black leather jacket, black eyeliner, black hair that seemed a tad too stylish for a soccer player, this guy had a swagger to his hips I could not tear my gaze from. And—*oh, fuck me*—he was wearing that damn black leather collar.

I swallowed hard.

"H-hey," I stuttered as he stepped up to me.

Alonzo grinned. I think he knew exactly where my mind was as I looked him up and down. "Hey, yourself."

I took a deep, ragged breath. "Why'd you wear that collar? You know what it does to me."

"Yup." His eyes glinted devilishly. "Doug said I could be on *his* team if I could think of ways to distract you from scoring."

I groaned and turned to find Doug on the field. I yelled across to him, "Thanks a lot, Doug! Glad to see how much my friendship means to you!"

Doug responded only with maniacal laughter.

Alonzo removed his jacket and laid it on the bench with my stuff. I hadn't seen that one before, so I asked, "Where'd ya get the jacket? I thought you liked that trench coat."

He glanced down briefly, but looked back up before I touched his chin. "The trench coat was Kyle's. I thought it was time I put it away."

I could see how pained he was to admit that to me, but I was proud he was processing his issues and brought his eyes back up to mine without my insistence. I ran my knuckles down the side of his face. "Good. So where did you get the new one?"

"Jason gave it to me. I asked him if I could borrow his shoes today, since we wear the same size, so when he dropped them off this morning, he brought the jacket too."

He was so nonchalant, but I was not. "Jason? He gave you his jacket."

"Yup. He's really nice."

I didn't like the smile on his perfectly supple lips. "I've been jealous of Lance for weeks, and just when I'm starting to get over it, you start wearing Jason's jacket? How am I supposed to contain my desire to punch the guy?" I didn't want Alonzo's sweet scent anywhere near Jason.

"He gave it to me," he insisted. "It was too small. It's mine, so I'm wearing *my* jacket, not Jason's."

"Too small? Likely story. I don't like the idea of him wrapped around you."

"Chris! What? He's not. You have to get over the jealousy thing. I told you, it was too small. His arms were too fat to fit in the sleeves comfortably and his shoulders were too wide."

I held my tongue before exploding all over my boyfriend. I'd seen Jason's arms. They were hardly fat. I knew it was most likely his biceps that were too big around to fit in the sleeves. "Lonnie," I broached quietly, fencing in my jealousy behind my teeth. "Using Jason's muscles and broad back as an argument of why I shouldn't be jealous about the jacket was not a wise choice." I tried not to breathe fire, but I couldn't intimidate Jason as I could Lance. Jason was also my equal in build, so I questioned my ability to outmuscle him. "I don't want you hanging out with Jason, or Lance."

Alonzo took a step back, crossed his arms over his chest, and shot up his eyebrow. "Seriously? You're going to go all domineering and possessive on me? Do you know how many friends I've had since I came out?"

"I don't know." I wasn't sure how that was connected to the conversation we were having.

"Six. Kyle makes one, and he's dead. You, Ellis, and Cole equal four. Do you have any idea who the other two friends I've had—*in my life*—are?" He paused and waited, tapping his foot.

I felt a chill down my back. I was an asshole. I answered humbly, "Lance and Jason?"

He uncrossed his arms and placed his hands on his hips, which was even more menacing as he challenged me. "Good guess. Do you think for a second I'm going to turn off all the emotions I feel for you and jump into Jason's arms because he gave me a jacket that was too small? Do you?" He cocked his head.

"No." I felt so stupid. Of course he was right. I was being stupid, again, and Alonzo had never given me a reason to be jealous in the short time I'd known him. He'd always gushed over me. So why couldn't I let it go? I took a step toward him. "I'm sorry. I was out of line."

He locked eyes with me and then gave me a half grin. "You were." Before I could say anything, Alonzo closed the gap between us and kissed me. His hands held my face as he tilted his head from one side to the other, kissing me repeatedly. No tongue, thank God, when I expected the guys to get weird seeing us kiss. Their response, however, was catcalls instead of protests.

I heard "Whoot, whoot, whoot," from one guy, maybe Steve by the sound of his voice.

Also, "It's about time!" came from Cedric.

After a couple other comments, Alonzo started giggling and pulled back. "I'm sorry. It's hard for me to be serious."

"It's fine. I don't think I could kiss you much longer if they kept shouting at us."

Alonzo explained, "Not just that. Lance knew you'd say something about the jacket. He encouraged me to stand my ground and put down my foot. That was really the best I could come up with. I'm not that assertive. I *do* think you were being dumb, and I was truthful about the six friends, but I think I have more than that now. I like Kelsey, Lance's friend, and Doug seems really nice. I am going to make more friends, Chris, and you have to realize that. You can't be jealous of every relationship I have. You have to trust that I love you."

I was going to say something else, but Cullen shoved in between us and pointed at me. "*And* you have to trust that I'm going to kick your ass if you make the rest of us wait any longer. Are we playing soccer, or what?"

"Lon?" I asked.

He answered, "We're playing soccer."

ALONZO WAS not lying when he said he couldn't pivot. Each time he got the ball and broke right, he fell. After the third time, he didn't even bother getting upset with himself. He got up and play continued. I was proud of him. Alonzo was playing soccer probably for the first time since he was fourteen. He would never be a star. Heck, he would never play on a real team, but with my guys he was able to run, pass, and score until he was too tired to play.

After two hours, Alonzo bent at the waist, hands on his knees, trying to catch his breath. "I'm… done," he panted.

"Me too," said Josh. "That was harder than I normally play."

"You're not kidding," Marshall added. "It's harder when you have to control your speed to play with someone who's…."

He let his sentence hang and Alonzo finished it. "Slow?"

Marshall said, "I was going to say crippled, but that wasn't really correct."

"No. And it would probably insult those who *are* physically challenged, but I know what you mean. I appreciate you guys playing at my speed and passing the ball to me so much. I had a blast."

Cullen clapped Alonzo on the back. "Sure. Any time. You're a lot of fun. Chris, you need to hang out at my house sometime with your guy. Too bad you missed the pool party."

"Yeah," I said. "Another time for sure. Right, Lon?" I reached for him and he came over to my side, slipping his arms around my waist. I held him around his back and kissed his temple.

"I'M PROUD of you," I told Alonzo when we were finally back from the field, showered, and in bed together. We skipped class, again, and opted to hang before Alonzo's therapy session. I knew I needed to stop skipping class, but I couldn't help myself. At least we were doing homework this time.

"For what?" he asked, glancing up from his chemistry book.

"For standing up for yourself, for working through your issues with the therapist, for playing soccer with the team even though you can't play as well as everyone else. I think you're amazing." I touched his hair and trailed my fingers down his neck and back.

"I'm just following the advice you have tattooed on your body."

I gave him an inquisitive look.

He explained, "'This above all: to thine own self be true.' *Hamlet*, act one, scene three. I've been trying to live by those very words since I was fourteen years old."

I gaped. "You *do* read Latin. Oh my gosh! Your sister told me you did, but I wasn't sure since you never said anything about my tattoo. You like it?"

Alonzo grinned impishly seconds before dropping his book in lieu of pinning me to the mattress. He winked as he descended, latching his mouth to mine, fervent and demanding. I sighed. *Fantasmical*.... Sex was so much better than studying.

I GUESS I unleashed a monster when I threw those gummy bears in the dining hall. I couldn't have predicted that this shy guy I met at the beginning of the semester would turn out to be an unpredictable conglomeration of wicked passion and unequivocal love, whose courage to overcome his pain was deeper than the depths of his mysterious, dark eyes. Alonzo was the embodiment of everything I needed and loved; and if gummy bears and cheerleaders had brought us together, then I was the happiest soccer player who ever lived.

MY ROOMMATE'S A JOCK? Well, Crap!

Wade Kelly

The JOCK Series: Book One

It's easy to become cynical when life never goes your way.

Cole Reid has been a social recluse since he was fifteen, when he was outed by his high school baseball team. Since then, his obsessive-compulsive behavior and sarcastic nature have driven away most of the population, and everyone else hates him because he's gay. As he sees it, he's bound to repulse any prospective friends, let alone boyfriends, so why bother?

By the time Cole enters college, he's become an anal-retentive loner—but it's not a problem until his roommate graduates and the housing department assigns Ellis Montgomery to move in with Cole. Ellis is messy, gorgeous, straight, and worst of all, a *jock*!

During a school year filled with frat buddies, camping expeditions, and meddling parents, Cole and Ellis develop a friendship that turns Cole's glass-half-empty outlook on its head. There must be more to Ellis than a fun-loving jock—and maybe Cole's reawakening libido has rekindled his hope for more than camaraderie.

www.dreamspinnerpress.com

WADE KELLY lives and writes in conservative, small-town America on the East Coast where it's not easy to live free and open in one's beliefs. Wade writes passionately about controversial issues and strives to make a difference by making people think. Wade does not have a background in writing or philosophy, but still draws from personal experience to ponder contentious subjects on paper. There is a lot of pain in the world and people need hope. When not writing, she is thinking about writing, and more than likely scribbling ideas on sticky notes in the car while playing taxi driver for her three children. She likes snakes, can't spell, and has a tendency to make people cry.

Website: www.writerwadekelly.com
Blog: writerwadekelly.blogspot.com
Twitter: @WriterWadeKelly
E-mail: writerwadekelly@gmail.com

Unconditional Love: Book One

A six-year downward spiral into a world of lies and deception leads to the end of one man's life when self-discovery crosses the line between being the perfect son or following his heart.

Jimmy Miller never intended to lead a double life starting the day he fell in love with Darian, but his parents' divorce, fighting in school, and constantly keeping secrets for his closeted best friend and protector, Matt, force his hand. Jimmy finds the demands too great to withstand and ends it all prematurely, leaving behind an angry best friend and a shattered lover.

Matt and Darian cling to one another in the aftermath of their loss, forging a new friendship immediately tested by the truths of their relationships with Jimmy that are hidden in the pages of Jimmy's journals. Will Matt and Darian discover what truly happened to their friend? And will this tragedy birth something beautiful between them as they learn the balance between life, family, and friendship when love is simply not enough?

www.dreamspinnerpress.com

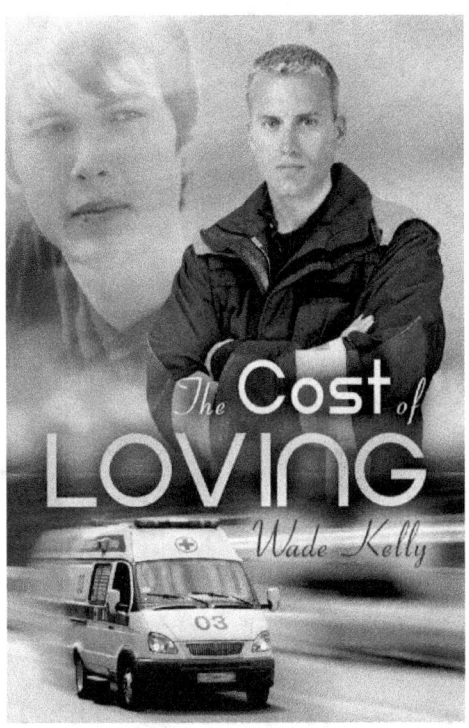

Unconditional Love: Book Two

Matt Dixon, a young firefighter, is the golden child of his family, and he never dreamed that coming out would challenge more than the way his church sees him.

For years, Matt has led a double life hoping to avoid ridicule. When a self-righteous pastor's statements provoke him to defend his recently deceased best friend's honor and subsequently out himself, he suffers the brutal aftermath of his revelation. Everyone in his life, including his family and his new lover, Darian, must deal with the ramifications as Matt struggles to come to terms with guilt, shame, and his very belief in God.

Darian Weston lost his fiancé when Jamie took his life, and his feelings for Matt added guilt to his burden of grief. Confused and lonely, Darian clings to Matt despite his inner strife. But small-town realities keep intruding, and if Matt and Darian hope to make a life together, they must first take a stand for what they believe in, even if they fear the cost.

www.dreamspinnerpress.com

What if sexuality wasn't a definable thing and labels merely got in the way?

Nick Jones can't remember a time when he wasn't part of the in crowd. Everywhere he goes, he stands out as the best looking guy in the room, and women practically fall into bed with him. Then, after kissing Corey on a dare led to much more and on many occasions, Nick's "screw anything" reputation escalated, but he didn't care.

When Nick meets RC at the restaurant where he works, it throws his whole life out of whack. RC lives up to his dubbed nickname "Scruffy Dude." He seems Nick's complete opposite, but Nick can't get him out of his head.

Because of peer-pressure and his fears about defining his sexuality, Nick struggles with stepping out of his comfort zone and caring about someone different than himself. If he's lucky, somewhere between arrogance and ignorance, Nick might find out what it means to be an adult, but if he's wrong, he could lose everything.

www.dreamspinnerpress.com

Also from Dreamspinner Press

Louise Lyons

BEAUTIFUL
THUNDER

www.dreamspinnerpress.com

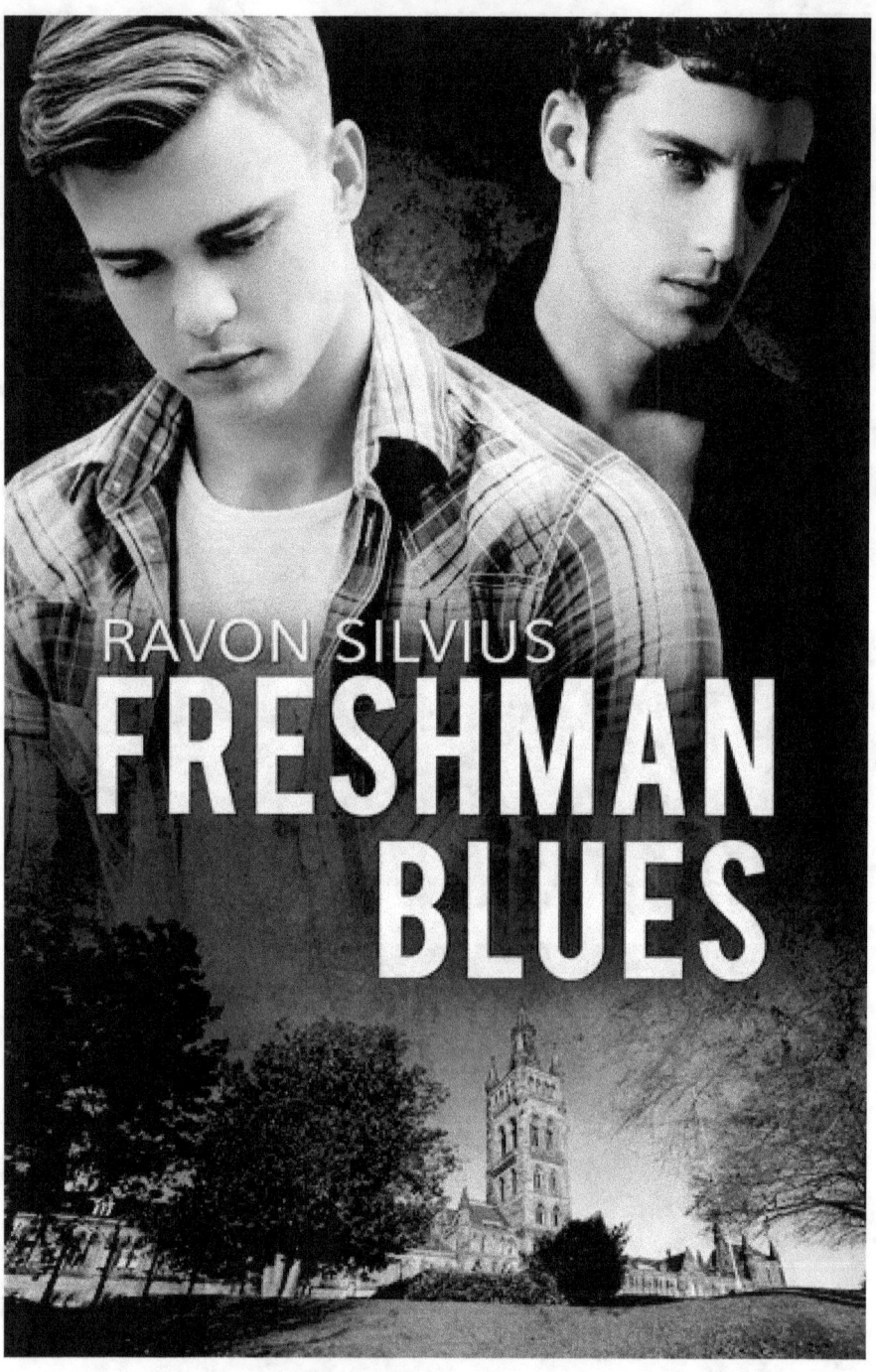

RAVON SILVIUS
FRESHMAN BLUES

Also from Dreamspinner Press

Hiding Things

S.C. Wynne

www.dreamspinnerpress.com

My Aim Is True

LEE PATTON

A STEEL CITY STORY
A COMPANION TO BROKEN GAIT

SIRE

KATE PAVELLE